"Where do I take Nina?" asked Kiley.

"Nowhere. She can identify every stop you made on your journey. Get rid of her."

"Kill her?" Kiley asked. His face was tense.

"What else?" Theo stared at him unbelievingly. "Do I need to tell you how to make it look natural? Use your cyanide pistol. Or an overdose. She isn't one of your addicts, but who is to know that?"

Abruptly, Kiley turned to leave.

"It is possible," Theo said, "she had duped you completely. She may be one of Renwick's agents. As you said—he has good taste in women."

Fawcett Crest Books
by Helen MacInnes:

The
HIDDEN
TARGET

Helen MacInnes

FAWCETT CREST • NEW YORK

To

Sir William Stephenson

—a man well named Intrepid—
with admiration and affection

CHAPTER

1

The church lay in the heart of the city. It was old, a thousand years old, his fellow workers at the bookstore had told him. And kept telling him, as if to impress the newcomer that Essen wasn't merely a West German town surrounded by coal mines: no more blast furnaces or steelworks since the war; modern factories, fine shops, a handsome art gallery, pleasant suburbs. Yes, they had assured him, he would find life agreeable here. In turn, he had assured them it would be most agreeable. How easy it was to be accepted, he thought as he approached the main entrance of the church, if you smiled and nodded. Criticism jarred, rousing animosities, even curiosity about any offbeat character who didn't fit in. If there was one success in the eight months he had spent in this industrial town, it was that he had fitted in. To his acquaintances, he was simply Kurt Leitner, a quiet, unassuming, undemanding young man, totally unremarkable. Dull? He hoped so. It had spared him from parties and overfriendly interest.

Leitner stepped into the church, cold gray dimness towering around him, glitter from the far-off altar to lighten the gloom, stillness broken by the slow shuffle of tourists' feet now entering the Gothic hall that formed the nave. Their guide's hushed voice droned on: that part tenth century, this part thirteenth, this built by so-and-so, that added by whoosis; notice the pulpit, the chancel, the narthex; all tributes of centuries past. The monotone faded into a murmur; the shuffles merged into silence. Leitner's eyes, accustomed now to the shadows, were fixed on the third massive pillar to the right of the nave. Slowly, with total unconcern, he moved into the aisle and approached the carved stone column. Theo wasn't visible from this angle, but Theo would be there. As usual, Theo would have arrived early and given himself time for a leisurely stroll around the church, studying the people in prayer or contemplation before the altar, checking the group gathered at a side chapel for some remembrance. Theo was thorough. Caution and care were his professional mark.

And Theo was there, a prosperous bourgeois in his dark suit blending with the pillar against which one shoulder rested. A man in his fifties perhaps, of medium height, with brindled hair cut short and a smooth white face. He glanced at Leitner, and gave an almost imperceptible nod of approval, not only for Leitner's casual approach, but also for his somber gray jacket and dark shirt. Then the two men, vague shadows in this unlit area of the church, faced the pillar ahead of them: two strangers lost in quiet reverence.

Leitner waited. Theo would set the pace. This was an emergency. No doubt about that. The signal for it had been simple, planned long in advance. "If ever I call you—before you leave for work—about your family in Munich," Theo had said when Leitner was being installed in Essen, "that will be the sign. We'll meet in the Minster seven minutes after the bookstore shuts down for lunch. When is that?" Leitner had answered, "Twelve-thirty. But I could be delayed. I'm the junior clerk." There could be a dilatory customer to ease out of the shop before he closed it. "Then," Theo had replied, "we'll make it twelve-forty-five—the third pillar to your right as you enter. One early-morning phone call and you'll be there." The call had come this morning. A brief, innocent talk with "Uncle Ernst" about Leitner's mythical father in Munich, who had slipped and broken his thigh. Simple. That was the way Theo liked it. Ultraclever voice codes or notes that had to be deciphered were something that could arouse suspicion if they were overheard or intercepted. Keep it natural, was his dictum.

Now, he stayed silent for a full minute: two strangers didn't start talking as soon as they had met. And then, as if making a remark about the church, even gesturing briefly toward a distant sculpture on which his eyes were fixed, he said in his low voice, "You do not travel to Frankfurt next week. You do not fly to London as planned. Instead, you leave tonight. Nine o'clock. By truck. From Leopold's."

Leitner nodded. He knew the place. It was one of the smaller machine shops on the outskirts of town. There was worry in his eyes. What had gone wrong? He did not pose the question. Theo would tell him—if he needed to know.

"You'll travel light. The night dispatcher at Leopold's is reliable. Leave your motorcycle and extra baggage with him.

We'll have them picked up within the hour. The driver of the truck will give us no trouble. It will be a safe journey. And short. You will be dropped off the truck at Duisburg."

Shock stiffened Leitner's spine, but his brief stare at the placid face beside him was its only evidence. Duisburg, on the Rhine, the largest inland port in Europe, with its twenty basins, vast stretches of silos and warehouses, oil storage tanks; Duisburg, the target his people had been aiming at for more than a year, long before they drifted quietly into Essen. It was a convenient half hour away by car or motorbike. Careful infiltration, well-directed sabotage, and the storage tanks, with their one hundred and seventy-eight million gallons of oil, could add considerable color to the background of red smoke from the Ruhr's blazing blast furnaces. "Tonight in Duisburg," he reminded Theo, his voice equally low, "we had planned some fireworks."

"We've postponed them."

This time Leitner's stare was long-lasting, challenging. All those preparations, all that work we put into the plan, the risks, the dangers... "I've got Section Two all set up in Duisburg. Section One in Essen is ready. They cooperate well. They—"

"We have an informer among us." Theo's face was expressionless.

"In Section Two?"

"No."

"Section One?" The section I organized and led for the last five years... Leitner's disbelief turned to alarm, even into a moment of panic. Quickly, with an effort, he repressed all emotion. "It's definite?"

"Quite definite. The police raided the Friederikenstrasse apartment at midnight and arrested Ferdi and Willy, your radio experts. They also found weapons. Amalie wasn't there, or Berthe."

"They had dates last night, picking up some information from a couple of army sergeants. Who is the—"

Theo signaled for silence, moved aside.

Leitner waited, head bowed. The disaster wasn't complete: the communications unit was destroyed, but they could be replaced. Not like Marco, with his assistant, Karl, installed in the Rüttenscheid area: Marco was the specialist, the expert in demolition. The other three members of Section One, with part-time jobs as hairdresser, drugstore clerk, bus driver, shared quarters in Töpferstrasse. He, himself, had his own place, a rented room within walking distance of the bookstore. None of the others, not even Marco, had visited it, or even knew where it was or where he worked. To them, old comrade Marco excepted, he was Erik, possibly a courier, a trusted go-between. His instructions were conveyed by public phone; meetings, only when necessary, took the form of a beer party in the apartment on Töpferstrasse. And there he had guarded himself by staying in the background, appearing to be a minor cog in this well-designed machine, listening to Marco giving out the orders Leitner had passed to him on the previous evening when they had met in the anonymity of Gruga Park.

As for Theo, their bankroll, their supplier of forged papers—passports, identity cards, licenses—their arranger of reservations on planes, their adviser and controller, none of the others, not even Marco, had ever seen him; and only Marco knew the code name Theo. But even with Marco, Kurt Leitner had kept silent about his secret encounters with Theo. He didn't allow himself too much speculation, either, about Theo. Yet some things were fairly obvious if you thought hard about them. Theo must run a tourist agency, hence his expertise in travel arrangements. His office could be in neighboring Düsseldorf. (He had, quite abruptly, refused Leitner's plan for an operation in that city, tempting as it was as the financial and administrative center of the major Ruhr industries.) But where Theo's supply of money came from, or what vast intelligence source supported him with world-wide information and contacts, these were matters best left unquestioned. They existed. That was enough.

Theo was still a few paces away, seemingly studying the nave of the church. He had been quick to notice the three wandering visitors who were exploring this aisle. But they had found nothing of interest in its unlighted alcoves and walked on, paying little attention to the young man in the shadows, his head bowed, his eyes covered by his hand as if in prayer. Theo returned to stand close again, and Leitner could drop both his hand and his far-ranging thoughts. He asked the question that had been bottled up for those last three interminable minutes. "Who is the informer?"

"Amalie."

"Amalie?" Recruited by Willy in Milan where she had headed out of West Berlin when the remnants of the Baader-Meinhof group were scattering. She had been one of its minor members, but dedicated and intense. At first, she had been doubtful about returning to West Germany, but Willy had persuaded her. Checked and double-checked, her credentials were good. And Willy kept her close to him. "That little whore—" began Leitner, and was silenced by a restraining hand on his arm. Checked and double-checked. By Theo, too. Nothing escaped his oversight. Except this bitch.

"We'll take care of her. And of Willy," Theo said grimly.

Leitner nodded. He had liked Willy, trustworthy, indefatigable, always willing. Too willing, as it had turned out, with a pretty little blonde called Amalie. "Who is she working for? The CIA?"

Theo was smiling as he shook his head. "Forget the CIA. Its throat is cut. Bleeding and paralyzed." He liked that picture. "She isn't with the British or French, either. But we'll find out. She had no direct contact with the Essen police; her information was usually passed to them through some Western intelligence unit. Just as well for us that she never was familiar with police headquarters, or she might have stumbled on my informant there." Theo paused, his eyes watching the nave. "Yes," he went on, "that's how I learned this early morning about the midnight arrests."

"Then you had time to warn Töpferstrasse," Leitner said with relief. "But Marco and Karl are already in Duisburg."

"Marco is on his way to Hamburg. Karl is in hiding. Time enough to warn the others when you and Marco are safely out of Germany."

"Time enough? The police could be moving in on them right now."

"No, no. The police are keeping the arrests quiet—no publicity for thirty-six hours. That way, they hope you will all be unsuspecting and gather as arranged for tomorrow night's meeting in the Töpferstrasse apartment. Then a mass arrest."

Yes, tomorrow night was to have been the celebration party for the Duisburg blowup. A surprise party for most of them—only Marco and Erik and Section Two had known the exact timing of that project. So that was one defeat for Amalie. At the last general meeting in Töpferstrasse, Marco had mentioned the end of next week as zero hour. Leitner's idea: security, security...And it had paid off. Partly, at least; for the police must be watching those oil and propane gas storage areas even if they expected the attack to come ten days away.

Theo seemed to guess Leitner's worry. "The police won't

cover the entire waterfront. They'll be nowhere near the Haf-entreppen."

Duisburg's quays stretched almost thirty miles along the Rhine. The Hafentreppen, a seamen's bar, was close to the docks but far from the target area. "I contact Sophie?" She worked there regularly; a raddled, blowzy blonde with a quick ear and sharp eyes, one of Theo's prized undercover agents.

Theo nodded. "She'll have one of her clients take you to his ship. It's loading right now. A coastal freighter. Sailing at midnight."

Half an hour to Duisburg, a ten-minute walk to the Haf-entreppen, another half hour making careful contact with Sophie, ten minutes or so before he could follow her seaman out of the bar; and how much distance to the freighter? He hoped it was short. "Do I stow away or stay topside?"

"You'll stay in the hold. Quite safely. The first mate needs money. It was easy to arrange that—easier than getting you seaman's papers at such little notice. Besides, your hands would have given you away."

"Sailing at midnight...down the Rhine to where?"

"Rotterdam should suit you."

"And there—the usual place?" A safe house, all necessities provided, from money and clothes to the American passport for his new identity. There would be a careful life history worked out for him, too.

Theo answered with a nod, drew a thick envelope from an inner pocket, slipped it into Leitner's hand. "For the journey as far as Rotterdam. Pay the seaman. The mate has had his in advance, but he could need a sweetener. There may be others, too, who'll look aside—with their hands out. That covers everything, I think." Theo glanced at his watch. He didn't need to ask if Leitner had memorized the details of the long journey in the months ahead of him. They had been over all that in their lengthy meetings in the woods beside the onetime estate of the Krupp dynasty. An excellent place for quiet conversations: visitors to the Krupp museum were constantly arriving and departing, so access was safely covered. And the visitors spent their time in the mansion or its vast gardens, had little energy left to explore the wild woods. "You'll arrive in London by next week. Good luck, Erik."

The code name had slipped out. Or a mark of confidence? Leitner wished he were as sure of the London assignment.

It was unnecessary, an addition to the original mission. "The girl worries me. Do we really need her?"

"Yes—an opportunity in a million."

"I know little about her. I'll need information, background—"

"You'll get everything from Greta. She's been in London for almost a year, scouting for talent. It was Greta who discovered the girl."

And added several headaches, possibly serious complications. Leitner shook his head. "Frankly, I'm wary about this. Didn't you tell me that Greta decided against recruiting her?"

"But not," Theo said sharply, "against using her. She's important to your mission, ultimately important. Once we heard who her father was—well, the decision was made at the highest levels. Not by Greta." He paused, added softly, "And certainly not by you." His white round face was set, all its usual amiable softness banished.

It's still a crazy idea, thought Leitner. "How do you know she'll even like me?" He tightened his lips, again shook his head. "Without that, there is no trust. Without trust—I'll never get her beyond Amsterdam."

"If you sense danger, then back away—drop her—continue your assignment as originally planned. But I insist you meet her—make your own assessment. Keep remembering that we consider her to be of the utmost importance to our future plans. Never forget that." The hidden command ended. Theo's voice lightened. "There's one small change in your itinerary. After Bombay, fly direct to Indonesia. Omit Malaysia, Singapore. You will reach Bali by early November. You and the girl leave Bali on the seventh of that month—by the cruise ship *Princess Royal*. You will have space reserved for part of that world trip—not unusual—I am taking a segment of the cruise myself. We shall have a very safe opportunity to meet for your last briefing before America." Theo's smile became almost angelic. "I'll join the ship one stage ahead of you—at Singapore—and leave it one stage later than you do. You and the girl disembark at Hong Kong."

"Why the diversion to Bali?"

"It will be a suitable place to leave your travel companions behind."

"Except the girl. If she is still with us."

"Except the girl. And she will be with you. I've never known you to fail with women, Erik. This time, no personal involvement for you, remember! The girl is an assignment, more important than you can guess. Blowing up oil tanks will seem a child's game compared to what I plan for America."

I plan? Not we plan? But it made a good exit line, thought Leitner as Theo pulled out a pair of heavy-rimmed glasses and walked into the nave. A good moment, too, to choose: Theo would have excellent cover all the way into the street. A straggling party of tourists was passing Leitner now, heading for the church door. Theo merged with them, wasn't even noticed.

Leitner waited for five minutes before he started up the aisle. Just what is planned for America? he couldn't help wondering. He and Marco would be working with local talent there. Perhaps they were being selected right now and sent to South Yemen, or to North Korea where he had been given specialized training almost ten years ago. But would they be as efficient as Section One? Marco, of course, would still be with him. The others—where? Regrouped or assigned to Section Two in Duisburg? Perhaps scattered, sent underground? Lying low for how long? Six months? A year? How would they feel tomorrow when Theo gave them the warning signal to clear out? As I am feeling, Leitner knew: enraged to the point of blowing up all of Duisburg, not just setting off a chain reaction of explosions in an oil-storage area. Section One was not dead—after America, he'd be back to give it life again—but it was badly mangled. Last week, it had been the most effective operational unit of the People's Revolutionary Force for Direct Action.

He came into the busy street, the June sunlight strong after the gloom of the church. For a brief moment he paused, lighting a cigarette. Anyone loitering around, waiting to follow him? Just a normal crowd, he decided, and stepped into the stream of people. Intense anger was controlled. Now he was planning his exit from Essen.

First, the bookstore and his pay collected. (What good German boy would disappear without the money he had earned?) Second, Frau Zimmermann, his elderly and inquisitive landlady. (What good German boy would leave by night without rent fully rendered until the end of the week?) In both cases, he would rely on the same story: a father in traction, hospitalized for months; mother ailing; Uncle Ernst needing urgent help with the family's butcher shop in Munich. Bloch, his boss at the bookstore, would let him leave early (half a day's pay, of course). Zimmermann would shake her head over the crisis that forced a young man back to a business he had never wanted—and would he be able to finish the book he was writing? So much work, so much reading he had done for it...He could guess the phrases, have brief replies ready, back away gracefully. But he had at least silenced the questions of eight months ago, by giving her just enough in the way of answers so that she, in turn, could answer the questions of her friends. It was a neighborhood of small gossip. Dangerous? Not if you kept your story straight, leaving Zimmermann's romantic imagination to supply an unhappy love affair. Besides, what police spy would think that anyone hiding somthing important would choose to live in the Zimmermann house?

Everything went according to expectations—except for one surprise punch delivered by Bloch. As he busied himself with Leitner's work papers, he looked up from his desk, cluttered with catalogues. "Have you returned all the books you took out?" Then he went on signing.

Leitner's face tightened. Briefly. "Yes, sir," he said, his eyes fixed on Bloch's bald head, as smooth and gleaming as an ostrich egg. "I brought back the last two books this morning. They were all from the secondhand shelves. I was careful with them, didn't harm them."

"Interested in travel, I see. You'd have found a wider selection in the public library."

And have my name noted along with the subject matter? Leitner looked apologetic and said, "I did try that, but it is difficult to get there when it's open. I'm sorry if I—"

Bloch waved a large expressive hand. "It's over. Forget it. No damage done to the books, but you should have asked permission. So you've got to go back to Munich and give up your travel plans."

"Plans? Oh, no. Nothing immediate. Not for some years yet. First, I read and gather background material. Next, I write. And if my book is successful—then I can start traveling."

"A writer, eh?" Bloch pushed his heavy glasses up over his domed head and studied this young optimist—a handsome fellow with steady blue-gray eyes, a beard and mustache and a thatch of brown hair that Bloch could envy. "Better stick to selling books. You'd eat regularly, at least." He dismissed Leitner with "I hope your father recovers" and a clap on the shoulders.

No bad feeling there, Leitner thought with relief as he hurried back to his room. But that was a surprise punch right to my jaw. Who'd have thought the old boy could notice so much through those thick lenses? Did he also notice the pattern of travel that interested me? Western to Eastern Europe, Asia Minor to India, the Far East...But I was careful not to take the books in order, and I added several old chestnuts— early journeys of the eighteenth and nineteenth centuries— just to keep my interest looking general. I underestimated Bloch: a sharp reminder to take nothing for granted, to remember that the smallest mistake might be the big one. Like Willy falling for Amalie's shy smile. Damn them both to everlasting hell.

There was no problem at all with Frau Zimmermann. In her best flowered print, she was preparing to leave for early supper and a game of bingo. That should hold her until nine o'clock, at least. He could pack without interruptions.

He did not need to burn any documents; anything important was well disguised. Such as his cryptic descriptions, no definite place names, of the camping grounds outside the towns and cities he was scheduled to visit in the coming months—all part of the folder boldly headed "Notes for a novel." There was also a page of scrawled first names, some scored out for the sake of realism, above which he had written "Suggested characters." And on another sheet of paper he had made out a list of ages for his proposed characters, giving date and place of birth. The places were entirely a random choice, meaningless. So were the years. But the days and the months were to be remembered. On them, precisely, he would make the arranged contact with the small terrorist factions of the various countries he would visit.

As he placed the folder carefully in his duffel bag, he reassured himself again that these dates appeared quite innocent. He needed that list. He had easily memorized the names of the localities where meetings would be held, but the dates were tricky. Theo had given him a quantity of them, and he couldn't risk any mistiming. Could there be so many groups of would-be guerrillas? Well, he would soon judge, once he met with them, listened to them, studied their leaders, decided whether they were worth taking seriously or not. His reports would go back to Theo, harmlessly phrased about the state of the weather—good, promising, disappointing—and on them the future of the local terrorists depended. Either they'd be found wanting and left to continue their holdups and wild shoot-outs like a lot of cheap gangsters, or they'd be accepted as potentially valuable. In which case they'd become, once their natural leaders had been given specialized training, members of the New International—Direct Action United. They would be ready and waiting for their assignments by the time Leitner was established in America.

Once more he found himself wondering at the cost of all this, at the months of preparation. But no important project came off the drawing board in a week or went into full production within a year. Revolutionary patience, he thought, and smiled. The marriage of opposites. Yet natural complements. Like love and hate. Like destruction and creation...

He finished clearing the room of all traces of his existence. Good-bye to Essen; and in Rotterdam, farewell to Kurt Leitner. And to Erik? No. He would always keep Erik, his one constant identity.

CHAPTER

2

Erik arrived at London's Heathrow Airport, his American passport (new to him; well used in appearance) stating he was James Kiley, born in Oakland, California, on October 10, 1952. This made him two years younger than he actually was, but he looked it with his beard and mustache shaved off, his mid-brown hair shorter and more controlled. It was, he had to admit, quite a transformation. American nationality was no problem: his accent was good, his vocabulary excellent; after all, he had spent a year in Berkeley after his return from North Korea. And one thing he could rely on: his future activities in the United States would certainly not be in the San Francisco area, where he might—a long chance, but still an added worry—be recognized.

As for his real identity—Ramón Olivar, born in Caracas, Venezuela, in 1950—that was past history. Like his parents. Father, a Spanish lawyer from Barcelona, with intense Anarcho-Syndicalist opinions that made him a professional exile; mother, a medical student from Sweden, with Marxist-Leninist views that were in constant argument with her husband's politics, each trying to convert the other. Ludicrous people. But they had taken him to Mexico when they escaped there. Ramón Olivar's name had last been used at the university in Mexico City (1967–69) and in 1970 for his trip along with forty-nine other socialist-minded students to Lumumba University in Moscow. A new name and passport for the concealed journey to North Korea. For the journey back to Mexico, another passport. Yet another, Dutch this time, for the flight into California once the Mexican police had started questioning the 1970 crop of Lumumba graduates (two of them, idiots, had been caught with dynamite all set and ready to explode). And still another passport when he was ordered to proceed to West Germany.

The only constant in all these travels had been the cover name Erik, his own invention. Chosen, unconsciously perhaps, because of his mother? Just as, like her, his hair was light, his eyes blue-gray? He certainly did not look Spanish. There his mother had won out over his dark-haired, dark-eyed father. But not in politics. (He was now far to the left of his father, much farther to the left than his mother.) He hadn't seen either of them since 1970. His father had escaped from Mexico and ended—literally—in Chile. His mother was still alive, and suitably in Cuba.

Other times, other places...All distant, all shut away in tight mental compartments. Now he was James Kiley, a foot-loose American. He had his history at tongue tip: California born, moved from Oakland with his parents to Illinois; and when they were killed in an automobile crash, became a ward of his well-to-do uncle in Illinois who owned a wire and sheet company—gold and silver, in other words, necessary for jewelry manufacture. No brothers, no sisters, no other relatives, no marriages, no complications...He looked the part he was playing: a young man traveling, with some ambitions to be a roving correspondent, looking for wider horizons than his uncle's factory in Chicago.

He passed through Heathrow's arrival formalities, no trouble at all, and walked briskly to the main entrance. Greta, Theo's devoted talent scout, would be waiting for him. And she was. A red-and-white-checked suit, a red purse over her left arm, as prescribed, so that his eye could pick her out even before he saw the familiar face. She gave no hint of recognition, either. As he drew near, she left. At a leisurely pace, he followed the red-and-white-checked suit until she had stepped into her dark-red car. Then, with his one bag heaved into its small back seat, he slipped in beside her and they were on their way. For the next hour, Greta would be responsible for his safety.

They hadn't met since Berlin, almost five years ago, but Greta, close up, hadn't changed much: the same slight figure, rusty-brown hair, eyes so light in color that their blue was almost colorless, a white skin that never tanned, pale lips, a furrow between her eyebrows that made her look helpless and anxious, and a smile that was deceptively sweet. He knew neither her real name nor anything about her origins, although his guess was that she came from the Berlin area itself—the accent was there when she spoke German in her brusque voice, and she had shown an intimate knowledge of its streets and shops that one didn't find in a guidebook. She had been well educated, obviously; a medical research scientist, registered for a course on tropical diseases at London's University College. She had entered England almost a year ago and was now established there as Dr. Ilsa Schlott from Stockholm.

"We are taking the quickest way into London," she told him. "Route A4. Then the Great West Road." Having announced that, she seemed to be concentrating on driving, but two brief side glances showed she was studying his new appearance. "If Theo hadn't told me to look for a light-green jacket and dark-red tie, I'd have taken longer to spot you. The beard always did make you look older than you were."

"That was the idea."

"You'd pass for twenty-six or -seven now."

That was also the idea. He said, "How are our prospects?"

"Fairly good. I've got them thinking about traveling."

Them? More than one girl? "How did you meet them?"

"They live where I live—at the Women's Residence for University College. It houses a lot of foreign students."

"How well do you know them?"

"Enough. I never force the pace. I sit near them at breakfast—long tables shared with other students. I have a weekly game of tennis with Nina O'Connell. In fact, that's how I managed to become her friend."

"Who wins?" Greta had been an excellent tennis player.

A smile parted the pale tight lips. "Somehow, she always manages to beat me in the third set."

"Nina O'Connell. Main target?"

Greta nodded. "The other is Madge Westerman. Two Americans meeting at college in London, bolstering each other in a strange new world. A peculiar thing about Americans: once the novelty of a different life wears off, they get homesick. Won't admit it, of course. But you'll find them grouping together, lusting after hamburgers."

"Attend the same classes?"

"No. O'Connell persuaded her father to let her come to study at the Slade School of Fine Art. She is just completing her first year there—still as unsettled as when she arrived. In America, Vassar and then Berkeley—one term only at each. Her father remarried two years ago, and that could be the key to her behavior. Westerman is the overseas scholarship girl, every penny budgeted. She's in escape from a middle-class home in Scranton. Her year is almost over—English literature, the history of the English novel, that's her field. At present, she's in a state of gloom. But so is the poor little rich girl. She doesn't like facing a year alone at the Women's Residence. She only landed there, in the first place, because it was either a room in that safe location or staying with friends of her father. That was his stipulation."

"Then he supervises her carefully?" And that could be a major difficulty.

"Actually, he's lax. And indulgent. He's like all busy and famous men. Every now and again they remember their fatherly duties and lay down a rule, and feel they've done a good job by insisting it be followed. Then they feel they might have been too strict and relax the reins again. Besides, Francis O'Connell is also learning to be married once more after being widowed for so many years. He was stationed in India when his first wife fell ill—some infection that never did get cured. She was sent back to Washington with Nina, aged four; she was in and out of hospitals for three years, and then died. Nina lived with her aunt and uncle while her father was stationed in various places abroad. Eight years ago he returned permanently to Washington, and Nina joined him there. Any trips abroad, after that, were always high-level conferences in Europe, where his daughter wouldn't catch a wasting disease like her mother in India. So from 1972 until 1977, Nina went with him, acted as hostess."

"Heady stuff for a teen-ager."

"She wasn't a gawky child, always seemed older than she was. From what I could find out, she was bright and self-possessed. Quite sophisticated, even between the ages of fourteen and nineteen. And then"—Greta was smiling again—"her father married. Nina was packed off to college; and I've told you the rest. Reach over into the back seat, Erik, and you'll find an old *Time* with the story of Francis O'Connell. He is being groomed for something important. The new Secretary of State? Or foreign affairs adviser to the President? And pick up that day-old *International Herald Tribune*, too; it's interesting. Or perhaps you've read it?"

"I've been busy," he said curtly. Four days in Rotterdam, holed up in a room with cassettes of American voices for company to get his ear tuned back in, with recent editions of New York and Washington papers to let him see what were America's current problems. He had read the columns, political as well as personal, and even studied the sports pages. From his set of new clothes, with Chicago labels sewn into place, to his accent and vocabulary and grasp of current events, he could face most real Americans.

"This," Greta said, her annoyance showing, "has all been a very great nuisance. I have other work to do." And she was not referring to a cram course in tropical diseases.

"A nuisance for all of us." He was studying the *Time* article on O'Connell. New wife given a nice play, too: a most successful Washington hostess. No reference to Nina—possibly the new wife had seen to that.

"What *is* Theo's idea behind this?" Greta asked suddenly, showing her own importance by dropping his name.

"He didn't say."

"Could it be to apply pressure—threat of scandal, important government official's daughter consorting with hippies and drug addicts? Possibly with Communists, too?"

"Would Theo risk blowing Marco's cover and mine?"

"If he comes to believe you are still anarchists, he will ditch you and Marco when he pleases," Greta said with a small laugh. But there was a jab of truth in her half-joking words.

Not as long as we are useful to him. And we'll put up with his Marxism-Leninism as long as Theo is useful to us. He said, "What gave you the idea that we were anarchists?" He pretended considerable amusement. Careful, he warned himself: Greta's ideas are cut from Theo's cloth, and everything I say will be reported back to him. "Because we use plastic and dynamite? When did Lenin ever ban them?"

"Marco talks too much about the absolute freedom of the individual. That means no obedience except to himself, doesn't it?"

"He was probably testing you to see if you had anarchist sympathies."

"I?" She was indignant enough to drop her sweet smile. She almost missed a traffic signal.

"If I remember you, five years ago, it was as the wildest bomb-thrower in Berlin. I had to straighten you out."

"And had me removed from your group?" It still rankled.

"That was Theo. He needed you elsewhere—for more important work than aiming a machine pistol. Any nitwit can do that. By the way, when did you see Marco?"

"He was here five days ago."

"Here?" Then Marco had been quick out of Hamburg.

"He's on his way to Amsterdam now. With a handsome caravan—"

"Caravan? Oh, you mean camper."

"Just right, he says, but too new looking. He hopes it will develop some scars on the car ferry across the Channel."

"British registration and plate?"

"All set, along with Tony Shawfield's British driving license and passport."

"Tony Shawfield? What part of Britain does he come from? Manchester?" Marco had lived there when Erik had been in the States, before they joined up again in Berlin.

"What does it matter? His papers are good, so is his accent. You've been together a long time, haven't you?"

Ever since we trained in North Korea. "Off and on." He unfolded the *Tribune*. "What page?"

"Three. But leave that until later—you can read it in your room. Where do I drop you?"

"Regent Street."

"Which end?"

"Wherever I can find a taxi."

"Cautious as ever, Erik."

And fishing as always, dear Greta. "Just following Theo's instructions." To mollify her, he added, "I'll let him know what an excellent job you did on O'Connell—you really got her talking."

"No, no. Too obvious. Westerman was useful," she said abruptly. She became absorbed in the problem of traffic, now increasingly complicated by pedestrians and buses and unexpected side streets.

London's maze always baffled him. He knew they had approached it from the west, but he had paid little attention to the initial stretches of suburbia, followed by warehouses, apartment houses, offices, pubs—he wasn't using this route for his exit; no use cluttering up his mind with unneeded details. Now he was beginning to recognize street names from the map he had studied. Soon they would be reaching streets that were recognizable by appearance as well as by name. A large green park on his left gave him a clue. Kensington— or Knightsbridge? Greta was heading in the right direction, anyway. Thoughtfully, he said, "Westerman...has she any final lectures to attend this week?"

"A couple I hear."

He might be able to audit one of these. A visit to

O'Connell's art class would be hard to explain: not within his competence. So he had better concentrate on Westerman first, although ten minutes ago he had almost decided to separate her from O'Connell, leave her out of this project as unnecessary baggage. "How close are they?"

"Like sisters. That's one of their jokes. Might pass, too. Except for O'Connell's blue eyes. Westerman has brown."

Then Westerman wasn't so unnecessary after all. One probably would help persuade the other.... "Does Marco know I'm bringing two girls to join us in Amsterdam?"

"I told him. He didn't like it. He's the recruiter for your trip."

James Kiley thought back to Amalie and Willy. "He'd better make sure we take no informants along with us," he said grimly.

Greta nodded. "That's the reason he didn't stay here any longer than it took to pick up the caravan—everyone he recruits in Amsterdam will be checked."

"Triple-checked. Theo's friends can start using their computers."

Greta dropped all her defenses, became the ingenuous girl who had enlisted in Berlin. "Do you actually know who Theo's friends are?"

"No. But we can guess. Who else had us trained?"

"They certainly have the power."

"And the money." In the last couple of years, there had been plenty of that.

"Changed days from the time you and Marco founded the People's Revolutionary Force for Direct Action. When I first joined—"

"I remember."

"That manifesto you and Marco wrote—do you still believe all you declared in it? Destroy to build. The insurrectionary act is the best propaganda."

Suddenly, he was alert. Was this how she had edged Marco into his talk about absolute freedom? And get the quotations right, he told her silently. He curbed his irritation, laughed, made his own small attack. "Don't knock that manifesto. It brought you running to join us." He looked around him with interest. "Piccadilly, I see. Now I'm beginning to know where I am."

"You always do, Erik," she said quietly. She drew an envelope from her pocket. "Here's a ticket for the concert at

Wigmore Hall tonight. I was supposed to be going there—
with O'Connell and Westerman. I'll let them know I can't
manage it, that I'm turning in the ticket at the box office. It
won't be a good seat—students' rates—but you'll be sitting
beside them. And then it's up to you. By the way, if you want
to attend that lecture on the English novel, it's tomorrow
morning. University College. Eleven o'clock." She was eyeing
the traffic ahead of them. "I'll drop you near Fortnum &
Mason's—that's close enough to Regent Street," she decided.
She selected a vacant slot near the curb and drew up. He was
as quick as she was: he had the door open as he reached for
his bag. "If you need help," she said, "you know the telephone
service that will take your message. I check with them each
morning. But where can I reach you?"

"At that number. Same procedure. And thanks, Greta.
Many thanks."

A nod for good-bye and she was driving off. He went searching for a taxi, resisted hailing one that was just passing.
Greta might have seen him enter it, and followed out of sheer
curiosity. She had plenty of that. Which made her a damned
good undercover agent. Certainly she had done a superlative
job on O'Connell and Westerman.

Five minutes of loitering and he found a taxi, directed it
to a small hotel off Russell Square. It had been carefully
chosen: the Women's Residence was nearby; University College, in Gower Street, was not much farther away. As for this
evening, with the concert ticket in his pocket and English
pounds in his wallet, he was equally well prepared. Wigmore
Street was easily reached. No problem at all. But what would
he have to sit through in Wigmore Hall? He had no interest
in music whatsoever. Just grin and bear it, he told himself,
and opened the *International Herald Tribune* at page three.

It contained a news item from Essen, headed CAPTURE OF
FOUR TERRORISTS. Two men arrested in an apartment on
Friederikenstrasse; two women taken into custody on their
return to the building. Arms and sophisticated radio equipment discovered, along with maps and documents. One of the
women, known only as "Amalie," had collapsed with severe
chest pains and was taken to the prison hospital. The real
names of all four terrorists were yet uncertain, but Berlin
police were hopeful of identifying them. They were thought
to belong to a terrorist organization known as the People's
Revolutionary Force for Direct Action, which had been re-

sponsible for at least four major bomb explosions (five dead, thirty-seven injured) and three assassinations in the last two years. Their activities had centered around West Berlin and Frankfurt. Their main objective in the Essen area seemed to be the storage tanks in Duisburg. Thanks to the vigilance of the police..."Et cetera, et cetera," said James Kiley. So Amalie had chosen a hospital room for her means of escape. All very neatly arranged.

But not so neatly, he discovered as he saw a small paragraph, a later report. Amalie's body had been found in her heavily guarded hospital room. Death seemed from natural causes.

Seemed...Theo's ways and means were highly efficient. And just as Kiley was relaxing, scanning the rest of the page, he found a stop-press item. Three more Essen terrorists belonging to Direct Action, residing at Töpferstrasse, had been identified in Duisburg. Arrests were imminent.

Fools, thought Kiley, making their way to join Section Two in Duisburg, endangering its members and sympathizers. What was Theo's idea? Keep the police concentrating on that area? Keep them from tracing Marco to Hamburg, or me to Rotterdam? It could be. He could find no mention of either Marco or Erik—and Amalie had known these two names. No mention at all. Somehow, that worried him.

He was in a grim mood when the taxi deposited him at the sedate entrance to the Russell Arms. Carefully, he counted out the strange money—but he would soon get used to Britain's present system, changed from the £.s.d. he had once known—and calculated a ten percent tip. The driver gave him a hard look, refrained from saying what he thought, but his face spoke adequately. Kiley added three more pence, coldly received, but he couldn't stand here adding coins to an outstretched palm like some yokel from a hick town. He strode into the hotel, grim mood replaced by annoyance. In Rotterdam he had studied guidebooks, maps, but not one item on tipping. Small things can trip you up, he warned himself; that cabbie is going to remember your face and where you are staying. And then, as he looked at the paneled lobby and saw the mixture of ordinary tourists and small businessmen, annoyance with his own stupidity changed to a strange uncertainty.

It was a long time since he had walked into a reputable hotel and openly claimed his reservation; or crossed a lobby without pausing behind that large flower vase, for instance, just to note if anyone seemed interested. A long long time since he had shared a lift to his floor without getting out at the one above and walking down to his room by the back stairs; or entered a room such as this, where he'd come and go for two weeks (three weeks, if things moved slowly), curtains wide open and only to be closed when the lights were turned on, a window at the front of the hotel and not facing a blank wall in a back alley. Yes, it had been years since he had lived as an ordinary civilian. He had forgotten how this kind of life felt. Disturbing, somehow.

He tipped the boy who had insisted on carrying his bag and opening the room door, on showing him closet space and bathroom and the bedside radio. This time he must have calculated correctly, perhaps even too generously. But that was more in keeping with his American clothes and voice. The boy left, a happy grin added to his thanks, blissfully unaware of Kiley's opinion of him: a human being debased by gratuities, living on perpetual handouts; a typical example of the serfdom that capitalism had imposed. When the people had established a true social order, there would be no need for tips that lowered the worth of a man, turned him into a leech sucking other men's blood.

Kiley looked around his room, at an untapped telephone, at walls that hid no microphones or concealed cameras. Pure luxury, he thought, and began unpacking his bag: three weeks ahead of him, three weeks of leading the ordinary life of an ordinary man. For a moment, he felt a surge of elation. And then crushed it down, replaced it with a touch of guilt for that brief, inexplicable betrayal. The ordinary man, he reminded himself, was enslaved by a system that was long overdue for destruction.

As he stripped and showered in bourgeois comfort, he was quoting Anarchist Bakunin to a steam-fogged mirror: "There will be a qualitative transformation, a new living life-giving revelation, a new heaven and a new earth, a young and mighty world in which all our present dissonances will be resolved into a harmonious whole." Yes, you had to destroy to build. Bakunin had said that, too: "The passion for destruction is also a creative passion."

If he felt any exhilaration now, as he dressed and left for the concert, it was only from the challenge ahead of him. No

time for dinner, but that was of little account—the assignment was all that mattered. I'll begin carefully, he decided,
take things slowly, coolly. Yes, that was the angle needed for
a first encounter.

CHAPTER

3

The encounter went as planned. Except for the first five minutes after Kiley had arrived at Wigmore Hall. In the lobby, like most of the crowd who had gathered there, he walked slowly around, putting in time before he went searching for his seat. His eyes, traveling over the small groups, the couples with pink and glassy faces, the standers and the strollers, were in quest of two blonde girls. They'd be easy to find—look-alikes who probably thought it amusing to carry the effect still further by matching clothes. He couldn't see them, had a sharp attack of worry over a no-show possibility, tried to reassure himself: either they were already seated in the concert hall or they were late.

There were a few blondes, mostly faded, but all attached to intellectual types with long gray hair and glasses. Was this what Bach did to you? (He was well out of luck in the music tonight: a chamber concert, of all damn things; not one trumpet or drum to keep him awake.) There was a drift of people, a thinning of the crowd near the staircase. Standing to one side of it, keeping out of the traffic's way, was a solitary blonde, not at all flustered by waiting alone. Her light-gold hair was shoulder length, brushed smooth, falling free. Medium height. Excellent figure. That he could see from this distance, and a perfect profile. He continued his stroll, passed in front of her.

She turned her head to look at him, observed his glance. Their eyes met. And held. Dazzling blue eyes, brilliant against the honey tan of her skin, edged by curves of dark lashes. Involuntarily he caught his breath, his pace slowed, hesitated, almost halted. Then he came to his senses and walked on. He was still stunned by that moment when everything had seemed to stop, a strange weird moment that now angered him. What the hell had come over him?

It was then he saw the second girl with shoulder-length fair hair, hurrying from the cloakroom, busy fumbling with the low shoulder line of her blouse. "It would happen,

29

wouldn't it?" she was asking as she joined her blue-eyed friend. "These darned shoulder straps..." He halted this time, watched them ascend the stairs, deep in talk. He didn't need the sound of their American voices to know who they were. He followed slowly.

His seat was on the aisle. He slipped into it, paying the two girls little attention. Nina O'Connell was next to him. He read the program, then kept his eyes directly ahead. She was sitting as still as he was, each sensing the nearness of the other, each ignoring it. He was actually grateful when the music began.

At the intermission, he let the girls out first, as if he were undecided whether to stay or to leave. His foot edged out just enough as Madge Westerman passed him so that her heel came down on his toe.

"Oh, I'm sorry! Please—"

"That's okay," he told her. "I'll live." Brown eyes looked contrite as he gave a reassuring smile. Enough for now, he told himself, and waited until they were well ahead of him before he followed. He didn't join them in the foyer, just studied the crowd in his role as tourist, looking (he hoped) both remote and lonely. He succeeded.

"Don't you think we should take pity on him?" Madge Westerman asked.

"Why should we?"

"Well—he's an American, and alone in London."

"So are a hundred other men."

"I must have hurt him. My heel came down—"

"Not your night, it seems."

"I ought to make a proper apology." I really don't go around tramping on other people's feet, Madge thought.

"Don't worry. He will be over any time now to collect it. I know that type." Handsome and self-contained, although I did shake him for one brief moment, Nina decided. And I was shaken, too, she admitted. It was that look he gave me, the same look when I first met— Oh, ridiculous, stupid. Geneva was six years ago—how do you remember the way a man looked at you six years ago?

"Something wrong, Nina?"

"Nothing."

Annoyed about nothing? Madge wondered. "All right, I'll omit the apology and leave him alone and loitering."

"I'm just tired of strange men trying to pick us up."

"But he didn't—"

"He has looked twice this way." Nina began to study her program notes. A tantalizing man. Should she cut him or talk with him?

Madge said with a laugh, "Forget it. He has no designs on us. He's leaving."

Nina, to her credit, said, "I guess I was wrong. Oh, well ... Is the intermission over? But let's move in slowly. I'll step on his foot this time." If he can lip-read, she thought, I'll be really embarrassed sitting beside him.

She needn't have worried. When they arrived at their seats, his was vacant. "What discouraged him? The music or us?" And now they were both laughing.

Satisfactory, James Kiley was thinking as he left Wigmore Hall: one small, ludicrous move—a high heel coming smartly down on his foot—and the scene was set for tomorrow. They wouldn't forget him, these two. Just as well to teach Miss O'Connell that a man could gawk at her like an idiot when she caught him for a split second off balance, but that didn't mean she had made another little conquest. She had had too many, too easily. As for Madge Westerman—less sure of herself, a simpler character. She would be no problem.

No problem at all. Next morning, at eleven o'clock, he was seated at the back of a somber lecture hall with rows of dutiful heads in front of him. Madge Westerman was among them. She hadn't noticed him, too busy with frantic note-taking. Conscientious type, worried about failure in the coming exams. Inclined to be a loser, just as O'Connell clearly considered herself a winner. Attraction of opposites?

The lecture ended five minutes short of noon. So much useless knowledge, he thought, a meaningless parade of names who had never made any impact on the world except as producers of imaginary plots and characters. Reality would have scared them witless. Slowly, he made his exit in a stream of a hundred or more students, some young, some aging, with few thoughts now in their heads but a midday meal. I could have given them a lecture, he thought, that would have stiffened their spines, sent them into the streets without those grins on their faces. He was watching Westerman's blonde hair, and marked time until she was near the door. He was there just as she reached it and stared at her in surprise. Would she, or wouldn't she? But of course she did.

"Hi!" she exclaimed, brown eyes staring back at him.

"And hi to you!" He looked equally astonished, and then grinned. "How was the rest of the concert?"

"You were wise to miss it. They substituted a—" They were bumped aside by someone trying to meet someone else. He steadied her, caught the slipping books that had been cradled in her arm.

"Let me carry these until we get rid of this mob scene."

She laughed then. Really a very pretty girl, he decided, if not quite as spectacular as her blue-eyed friend. "No one has carried my books since school."

"What's happening to higher education?"

She laughed again, lost most of her nervousness. "About last night—I'm really sorry—I hope I didn't hurt you too badly."

"Oh, that! Forget it."

"But I don't make a habit of—"

"Of course you don't. Are you enrolled in this class? What's it like? I mean, what did you get out of the course? I was auditing it, trying to see whether I should think of taking it next year."

"What courses have you been taking?"

"None so far. I only reached London two days ago. I'm just in the process of trying to decide."

"Decide what?" She was definitely interested.

They had come into the open, a square patch of ground with a broad walk leading into Gower Street. A batch of white-coated medical students, two with stethoscopes proudly displayed from bulging breast pockets, swept past. "Everyone seems to know where he's going—except me," he said with a rueful smile. "That's my problem. Do I hang around London, take a summer course? Or wait for the fall? Come on, I need your advice. Say—why don't you have lunch with me?"

She looked regretful. "Sorry—I'm meeting a friend."

"I'm sorry, too. Perhaps another time?" He paused at the entrance to Gower Street. "Tell me one thing: where's a good place to eat?" Nothing here but gray houses and college buildings.

"Good in food, or good in price?"

"I can't get both? Okay, okay. Someplace cheap, but clean. Is it too much to hope for a real hamburger?"

"Would spaghetti do? Or a BLT?"

What the hell's that? he wondered. "Either," he told her.

She considered for a fraction of a second. He's really alone, she thought as she remembered her first week, when she had been overwhelmed by the strangeness of everything. "Don't you know London at all?" He looked so self-possessed; it was a relief to find he was as naïve as she had been.

He shook his head. "But I have a good map in my pocket."

"Why don't you join us for lunch?" she asked impulsively.

"No. I don't want to impose—"

"You wouldn't. My friend and I see each other every day. Come on." She began walking down Gower Street.

"He'd object perhaps to—"

"Not a he. It's a she. Oh, there will be men around. There always are. But it's no big deal—just a café near Charlotte Street, half Italian, half American, and filled with students. The hamburgers are awful—the beef is ground into paste. But the bacon, lettuce, and tomato sandwich is for real. By the way, I'm Madge Westerman."

"And I'm James Kiley."

"From where?"

"Chicago four weeks ago, arrived in London from Paris, Brussels, Amsterdam."

"Paris?" She was impressed. "I'm envious."

"It isn't too far off, nowadays," he reminded her.

"I know, I know. But..." She sighed. "It's maddening. Here I am, about to end a year in London. And just across that little bit of water there's the rest of Europe—Paris and Rome and Venice. Maddening because *when* will I ever get so near to them again?"

"Surely you could—"

"No," she said abruptly, "I can't." She pushed aside a heavy strand of hair from her brow. "I'm here on a scholarship. It ends next month." Then she pretended to laugh. "Back to the coal mines. Scranton—that's where my people live."

"Why don't you get a job in England, save up, fly over for a week in Paris? It's worth it. Expensive, though, as I found out. It was a relief, in a way, to get to Holland and stop figuring what the dollar had sunk to."

"Holland—what's in Holland except tulips and dikes and windmills?"

"More than you think. I had a pretty good time there."

"Well, I'll even have to pass up Holland. Because I'm a

foreign student in London, can't take a job here unless it contributes to my studies. That's the law. I can't see myself applying for a job to teach a British family how to speak English, can you?" She was laughing again. Then she turned serious, remembering his first approach to her. "If you are thinking of taking a course on the history of the English novel because you'd like to be a writer, forget it. It will only depress you: hundreds and hundreds of novelists in the last three centuries, and only half a dozen remembered." She corrected herself. "Well, only half a dozen are read. All the rest—just names to be memorized for examinations."

"Did you ever think of writing a novel?"

"Who doesn't? How about you?"

"Oh, I'd settle for some articles being published."

"So you *are* a writer?"

"Not yet." He hesitated, then sounded as if the admission was dragged out of him. "Actually, I'd like to be a free-lance journalist who writes about international incidents. That's one way of traveling and seeing the world, isn't it?"

"Yes," she said, and sighed again. "What kind of incidents—" But they had come to the door of Matteoti's Café; yellow curtains over its windows rippled by an electric fan, warning of a small interior packed with people. At one table near a wall he saw Nina O'Connell. Her eyes looked at him in disbelief, and then she recovered herself.

What's it to be? he wondered. Freezing temperature or mildly sunny? Easy does it, he warned himself. So far, all goes well. Keep it going, Kiley.

He shook hands—slightly freezing temperature, he noted, as she merely nodded a how d'you do—and pulled out a cane chair and looked around the room. "I'm overdressed," he said with a grin. Flannels and tweed jacket, clean shirt and tie, were definitely out of style this season. "Ought to have remembered myself as a student."

"Where?" asked Nina, curiosity beginning to melt the ice.

"Berkeley."

"Oh! I was there, too. In 1977."

"After my time," he said regretfully. And smiled. It was a warm, generous smile that had won him approval before now. It had its usual effect.

The ice melted rapidly. There was an answering smile, small but friendly. "Let's order. I'm starved," said Nina.

I have been accepted, he thought. Tentatively, at least.

Keep conversation light and general. Let Madge tell her all about me later. She will.

The two girls walked slowly down Gower Street. "You liked him, didn't you?" Madge asked, eager for reassurance. James Kiley had been fun to meet. She wished he had arrived nine months earlier.

"As far as we got to know him," Nina conceded, and then relented. "Yes—he's better than I thought." Not the usual pattern of young men who had been hanging around her this year. "At least he didn't dog our footsteps for the rest of the afternoon." It had been a long lunch, with extra coffees and *tortelloni* being ordered just to keep the table.

"Well, he did want to get to the Admissions Office and find out about courses and costs. If he does decide to enroll, you'll be seeing him next term, Nina."

"If I'm here."

"Why shouldn't you be?"

"I've just about had it with the Women's Residence."

"You'll feel differently after the summer."

"What summer? Three weeks at a time with four of father's old friends? Oh—I just hate feeling I'm all packaged and delivered."

"And I'll be looking for a job in Scranton," Madge reminded her.

"Why not cut out for California?"

"I don't know anyone there."

"You soon will."

But there were always those three, four, five weeks when you wondered if you'd stay lost and lonely forever.

Nina was laughing. "Just look at the way you picked up a strange man today."

"I didn't!"

"He picked you up?" Nina's laughter had faded.

"No, no. It was just accidental." And Madge plunged into a full description of what had happened.

Nina relaxed. She was two months younger than Madge, but somehow she always had to do the protecting. "He's almost as unsettled as we are," she said, and felt sympathy for a fellow sufferer. "But I think he'll do something about it. Not like us, who talk and talk and stay undecided."

"Well," Madge said, tactfully avoiding any mention of Nina's adequate allowance, "he does have the means to travel.

I wonder if I inherited money when I was twenty-seven, would I have the courage to blow it all in one year?" Just a small inheritance, James Kiley had said, nicely embarrassed when the subject of cash flow and life style had somehow risen: enough to let him do what he wanted to do for twelve months.

"You know what? I don't think he will be here next year. I think he's deciding right now to take off like a bird. And why not?" Nina ended gloomily. "He's free. Free to do what he likes."

"That mad friend of his—Tony Something or other—"

"Shawfield."

"Well, if I were James I'd take Shawfield up on his offer. Imagine—around the world in eighty days in a camper. Isn't that something?" Madge's eyes were filled with dreams.

"Yes," said Nina, "it's wild."

"So why isn't he jumping at the chance?"

"Because he has more sense than we have. You heard him: he'd have to find out what kind of camper, what kind of route, what kind of arrangements, what kind of people his friend was corralling for a trip like that."

"You take the fun out of traveling."

"Well," Nina said, the expert on foreign countries, "you just don't step on a flying carpet and away you go. There are visas and inoculations and officials at frontiers."

"But you loved every moment of it, didn't you?"

Yes, thought Nina, I loved every moment of it. Geneva, Paris, Rome, Venice…But you can't go traveling alone. What's the fun in that? "Look—don't get angry—you always do, you know, but not this time, Madge. I've got some spare cash, so let me lend you—"

"No." Madge's voice was sharp.

"But I can't go traveling by myself. The two of us would have a wonderful time. You know we always laugh at the same things. And it's only a loan."

"No." Madge's voice was less on edge. "I get my bank statement tomorrow. I hope. Or the next day. Then I'll know how I stand." Probably cut off at the knees, she thought. Still, I might juggle something around. I could sell my books; and my winter coat—that would save me packing it home. "Tomorrow, he said he'd meet us for lunch if we didn't mind. Do you?"

"No."

"But will you be there?"

"Perhaps. Will you?"

"Yes," Madge said. "I like him. He's different." Then, as they turned the corner away from the busy street and headed toward a quiet green square, she remembered to ask, "Are you keeping that date with Barry and Jack tonight?" Nina had been undecided at breakfast.

"I think I will. You're included, you know."

"Can't possibly." Madge hefted the books in her arms. "I'll be cramming all the rest of this day—and every day for the rest of this week."

"Except for lunch, of course," Nina suggested. She might smile, but she was feeling that elder-sister attitude worrying her again. She didn't like the role yet someone had to look after Madge, the perpetual innocent. Not that James Kiley was any real danger: he'd take one look at student life, recall his Berkeley days, and be off to wider horizons. Wider horizons...She looked around her, everything neat and quiet, buildings solid and asleep, iron railings. An attack of summer fever, she thought as she repressed a sigh.

In silence, the two girls climbed the steps into the hall of the Women's Residence. "Irish stew," Nina said as the smell of cooking hit them. "If it boils for so many hours, why is there always so much water in the gravy?"

They fell into silence again and climbed to the second floor. Nina halted at her door. "I'm going to start packing."

"A bit early, aren't you?" Madge called over her shoulder.

Nina shrugged, went into her room, four walls which she had tried to brighten with her posters, a back-view window blocked from sunlight by the opposite houses. "Couldn't be too soon," she answered both Madge and herself. But of course it wasn't possible to start packing: trunk and suitcases would have to be hauled up from some lower depths. Even gestures were thwarted, she thought as she stared at herself in the small looking glass. Could be worse: her eyes could squint, her front teeth could be broken, her hair could be thin and falling out in patches.

Then she looked down at the letter from home that had come this morning and lay unopened on the dressing table. It was addressed in Beryl's writing—a stepmother just nine years older than she was. ("That's the good thing," Francis O'Connell had said cheerfully. "You two can be really close friends.") Slowly, Nina opened the envelope. Beryl and Francis were leaving for a summer at the Maryland shore. Time to get out of hot Washington. All well. Much love. Hoped to see Nina in September when Francis and Beryl would be in London for a few days. Ever, Beryl. And a postscript from Daddy: See you in September, kitten. Have a splendid summer. Keep us posted. All love always.

The Maryland shore, easy commuting distance for Francis O'Connell, pleasant house parties for Beryl to arrange. And, thought Nina, not even the smallest hint of an invitation for her. She could hear Beryl saying, "Francis, darling, you know it would be useless. Nina is having much too good a time. We really can't drag her home just to please us." At least she hoped her father had to be persuaded about that. She wasn't sure any more. She tore the letter into small pieces. Would she have gone to Maryland? Perhaps not, to be absolutely honest. But it would have been nice to have been asked.

Oh, well—tonight could be amusing. She'd better call Barry and warn him to find another girl, unless the prospect of a threesome didn't bore him and Jack. It wouldn't. She never had any trouble with two beaux to her string. Safer that way, actually. Less satisfactory for them perhaps, but a respite for her.

At the small bar in the Russell Arms, James Kiley sat over a beer and thought about today's encounter. It had gone well. Tomorrow, a third meeting. And after that, a stepped-up schedule concentrating on Nina O'Connell who had no examinations to keep her occupied: dinners as well as lunches, a movie, a theater, sightseeing (he was the stranger, wasn't he?) at Hampton Court or the Tower or what have you; and of course an exchange of life stories, of future hopes as well as of past disappointments. All of it laying a strong foundation for friendship and trust. That's what she wanted now, he was sure of it: she had too many men chasing after her, too many macho types obsessed by sex. So he'd play the opposite, keep her interested, let her think she made the decisions. It wouldn't be too difficult. The opportunities were there for him to take; all he was doing was to make the most of them. She liked him. He was sure of that. There was an attraction between them that was hard to explain. But it was there.

He left the bar, paying scant attention to the clutter of strangers around him. Foolhardy? Scarcely. German Intelligence, far less the Essen police, didn't know he was in London. His escape had been clean. Amalie had certainly given them the name Erik as well as his description, but now he was unrecognizable: no need to look over his shoulder as he reached the street, no need to avoid brightly lit thoroughfares or crowded restaurants. Even so, he warned himself, don't let your guard be too far lowered. It's enough to stay alert, without acting the conspirator. This whole assignment was turning out to be easier, more enjoyable, than he had foreseen. He had even stopped brooding about the Duisburg fiasco. If it ever could be resurrected, that was Theo's responsibility. His responsibility, too, to have his lawyers win the release of those who had been arrested.

Theo... Was Theo having him watched right now? Probably, he admitted, and felt a slight chill. It passed. Theo would receive only reports that James Kiley had merged nicely into the London scene. A beginning had been made, no suspicions aroused, progress favorable. Just give me three weeks, perhaps less, he told Theo, and I'll have these two girls in Amsterdam.

CHAPTER

4

It was a cheerful morning, bright and sparkling, spreading its smile over the waterways of Amsterdam. Robert Renwick had allowed himself an extra hour in his early-morning drive from Brussels—in July there were thousands of tourists and hundreds of sightseeing buses as well as the usual trucks to cope with, not to mention some unexpected delay at the frontier. Today, there had been no complications at all. He had an hour and a half on his hands before he met Crefeld. Purposely, he chose a garage near Central Station: it lay on the far side of the old town from Crefeld's discreet office. Not his official office; that was in The Hague with the rest of the government buildings. Because Crefeld, in his scrambled call to Renwick yesterday, had suggested Amsterdam for their meeting, there must be a piece of highly important business to discuss. Crefeld, of Dutch Intelligence, attached to the North Atlantic Treaty Organization until two years ago, was not inclined to suggest a face-to-face meeting unless the information he had was both urgent and vital. Renwick's response had been quick. He had dropped the work that had piled up on his desk during his absence in Germany last week, and headed in a nicely anonymous rented car for Amsterdam.

An hour and a half...Well, a walk would stretch his legs. He set out at a leisurely pace, in keeping with his civilian clothes—tweed jacket and flannels, nothing flamboyant, just old favorites that made him feel comfortable. The man-made island on which Central Station lay was well behind him. He headed south, then slightly to the west to escape the main thoroughfares and their jam of traffic. Here, in the close huddle of streets, medieval houses edging ancient canals, pointed gables, brick, and sandstone decorated with elaborately trimmed cornices, walking was almost pleasant: still too much traffic, torrents of flying Dutchmen on their bicycles. So he changed direction again, traveling a little to the east to reach the long narrow stretch of Kalverstraat, where traffic was banned and pedestrians could walk without any nervous glances over their shoulders. Too many shops here, for his taste, but you couldn't have everything. And most of Amsterdam, the tourists, too, seemed to be window gazing.

It was the usual problem, he was thinking, of an old city trying to cope with the twentieth century. From a bird's-eye view, central Amsterdam would seem to be a completely geometric layout, a concentric sweep of straight-running canals and parallel streets suddenly twisting, but neatly, carefully, in true Dutch fashion, to let canals and streets run as straight and parallel as ever until the next sharp turn. On a map, the pattern would be logical and easy; on foot, especially a stranger's foot, it could be mystifying. It had taken him several visits to Amsterdam to master short cuts.

Ahead of him were two of the mystified, pausing in the stream of pedestrians, hesitating about their direction. Two newly arrived lemmings—Renwick's word for the trek of backpackers swarming off the trains for a week or two of reclining on grass, cozily squashed together, unperturbed by the mixtures of music from a hundred radios or by the polite policemen trying to separate heroin users from the dreamers on hashish. But these two girls weren't bent under backpacks: their shoulder bags were large but smart. Striped shirts were tucked into tight blue jeans that didn't have a quarter inch to spare over neat buttocks. Their blonde hair, shoulder length and no doubt parted in the center to swing free, was gleaming clean. Two most attractive lemmings, he thought as he noted the slender waists and thighs, the well-proportioned legs poured into skin-tight trousers. From this rear view at least, he added to that. Then one of them obliged his curiosity by turning to face him. Good God, he was now thinking, it can't be, it couldn't be—but it was.

Nina O'Connell's casual glance turned to wide-eyed astonishment. "Robert Renwick—Bob!" She came running toward him, arms outstretched. He had been about to shake hands. Instead, he was caught in a tight hug. Laughing, he hugged right back. She hadn't changed much in six years. She had been fifteen then, against his thirty-three. Hopeless from the start, he reminded himself as he felt the soft touch of her cheek against his. Then just as quickly, she released him, suddenly remembering she wasn't fifteen years old any more. But she was still beautiful, a glowing girl, with the same direct glance he remembered only too well. "Madge," she told her friend, "this is Bob Renwick. Bob—Madge Westerman. Oh, Lord—I got that all the wrong way round, didn't I?" She was slightly flustered, perhaps embarrassed by that spontaneous hug.

"Let's forget protocol," Renwick said with a grin. No, she hadn't changed much. He shook hands with Madge; gentle brown eyes, he noted, with warmth and a lurking smile. "And I don't need to ask what you are doing here. On your way to Paris or points south?"

"Much farther," Nina told him. She glanced at Madge and laughed.

Madge said, the smile spreading to her lips, "It's a chance we couldn't refuse."

"It isn't a joke, Bob." Nina had been watching his face. "We really *are* traveling. We decided this morning."

"Just like that?"

"The same annoying man as ever! You never take me seriously. But why are you here? Or shouldn't I ask?"

She remembers too damn much, Renwick thought. Better get it over with, quickly, and hear more about this far journey. They're in earnest, both of them. Two innocents abroad. "I'm considering a change in jobs." Which was true enough.

"What? Are you leaving NATO?" Nina was astounded. She turned to Madge. "He's a disarmament expert—"

"Oh, come on, Nina," he interjected.

"Well, you were at that disarmament conference in Geneva—"

"A minor flunky," he informed Madge. "I opened doors for the generals and saw that the pencils on the conference table were properly sharpened. What about getting out of this foot traffic? An early lunch?" And a fast one. He had only an hour to spare.

"Can't possibly," Nina said with real regret. "We're meeting our friends in"—she glanced at her watch—"forty minutes. How far is the university from here?"

"Which one?"

"The one near the palace."

"Ten minutes away, perhaps less. What about some coffee? There's a café in that alley." He pointed to its sign.

"Indonesian?"

"Why not? Java, after all."

Madge laughed. "A cup of Java—but of course!"

"All right," Nina said, starting toward the alley. She was

a little annoyed she had been slow to catch his small joke. "And afterward, will you point us in the right direction?"

"I'll deliver you there in five minutes—if you can walk as quickly as you once could."

They entered the café, barely ten feet wide, with minia-ture, closely packed tables along one wall. "Cozy," Renwick said, "but the coffee smells just right." One good thing: they had friends; they weren't traveling alone. Stupid of him to worry. They were two competent young women. He noted the unobtrusive way they placed the large handbags between their feet, their ankles guarding against any expert snatch from a quick-fingered thief. "The floor is clean," he reassured them.

"You notice *everything*." Nina shook her head.

"All your valuables?" he teased.

"Well, it's the safest way to carry them. We're traveling light, you know. A duffel bag for our clothes; they roll up easily, don't crush, drip dry."

So this was no usual tour, he thought. "Where are you staying now?"

"In a small hotel near the waterfront. The Alba. Perfectly respectable and clean, although it isn't much to look at."

"You're lucky to find a room at this time of year."

"A friend in London—she's a Swedish doctor, knows all about tropical diseases—she recommended it. And we were lucky. There were two cancellations on the day we arrived."

"You see," Madge said, "we delayed leaving London until the last minute. So many things to be done. And I—well, I really had to be sure I had enough money for a week here." He looked a little puzzled, so she rushed on. "I'm cashing in my return ticket to New York, so that helps me get around the world." And I'll pay back the Scholarship Foundation later. They were accustomed to that, James Kiley had said.

"Around the world?" Renwick asked. On a shoestring? "How are you traveling?" On a freighter, possibly. Even so . . .

"In a camper," Nina said. "And it's a beauty. It's really a minibus. Plenty of room. All the comforts of home. Air con-ditioning. A refrigerator—"

"Four-wheel drive," broke in Madge, "and an eight-cyl-inder engine. Tony has even got an extra gas tank installed, and there's storage for canned food and space to sleep at least three. The men will be outside in sleeping bags, of course, and—"

"Hold on," Renwick said with a wide smile. "You're traveling way ahead of me. How many are going?"

"Eight. Three girls and five boys, with two guitars, one cassette player, and of course there's a very special radio. James and Tony were getting that installed this morning, making sure it really will keep us in touch with the world."

He kept his voice casual, amused. "And where are you going?"

"Across Europe first of all, but we are still deciding about Asia. Tony will have the last say, of course. It's his camper, and he does know the best routes."

"Oh?" He didn't need to do more prompting. Now that the world tour had come into the open, the two girls were explaining how this magic opportunity had come about. Tony Shawfield was English, a car buff who knew all about engines; this trip he was planning was a test run for a firm that had supplied all the special equipment—a kind of promotion job. James Kiley was an American they had met at college in London; he was hoping to get some stories that could give him a short cut into free-lance journalism. The others who were going—well, Tony had to choose from fifty students clamoring to join him. Once the news was out about the trip, he had been besieged. James hadn't made up *his* mind about going until a few days ago: he wanted to be sure about the camper, about travel companions.

"He sounds sensible," Renwick conceded. He kept trying to think back to himself aged twenty-one. Would he have jumped at the chance of such a trip? Yes, he damned well would have. "How old are James and Tony?"

"Twenty-seven, I think," Nina said. "Much more practical than we are. It's really all right, Bob." She sensed some reservation on his part. "James is a good friend. I trust him. He really is reliable."

"And the others?"

"Near our age, I'd guess. There's a French girl, Marie-Louise, married to a nice Dane. And a Dutch law student—at least, he's going into law after he gets back from this trip. And a friend of his from Italy. But we won't have much trouble with languages. Tony insisted that anyone traveling with him had to speak English."

"That figures."

"He *isn't* your typical Englishman," Nina protested. "It's just that he's the captain of the bus, as it were."

"He will have to know more languages than English to let him pilot it through all these foreign countries—"

"But he does speak three languages. James knows even more—not well, but enough. And Marie-Louise knows some Syrian—she was born there. And Sven Dissen, her husband, who is in medicine, has been working with Pakistani students in Paris. Guido Lambrese was in Greece and Turkey last summer—he's an archaeologist. And Henryk Tromp—he's Dutch, from Leyden—can speak Spanish. They all know English, of course. Madge knows French. So do I—and a little German, too. We'll manage."

It was certainly a well-arranged travel group. "What's your route?"

"Oh, we're still arguing about that," Madge said. "We've all got ideas, but Tony says we've got to be sure they are possible."

"And James says he wants to avoid Communist countries," Nina added.

That, thought Renwick, with the way things are going might not be so easy nowadays. "Just keep out of the trouble spots."

Nina laughed. "You sound like Father."

I suppose I do, Renwick thought. It wasn't a role he fancied. Damn it all, I'm thirty-nine, he told himself, not Francis O'Connell approaching sixty. "What does he think about all this? No, don't tell me—I can imagine." He expected Nina to join in his amusement. She didn't. "He doesn't know?"

"Not yet. I'm writing him tonight."

"And when do you leave? Tomorrow?" he asked jokingly.

"Tomorrow."

"You know, I'll be seeing your father when I'm in New York next week. Any messages?"

"You do get around, Bob."

"Just visiting my friends before I settle back in Europe."

"You're taking a job in Europe? I think it's sad that you're leaving NATO. Why, really?"

"I'm still making up my mind about a change. Advancing years, you know." His smile was infectious.

Madge thought, he isn't old. But of course NATO never made any man rich.

"What will you do?" Nina asked.

"At the moment, if I don't hurry you out, we'll have to run all the way." He was counting the money for the coffee, adding a lavish tip with some guidance from the smooth-faced waiter in his Indonesian turban. "I like their headgear. Natty. That twist of cloth sticking out in front—" But he wasn't to be let off so easily.

"What *will* you do, Bob?" Nina insisted, reaching for her bag, leading quickly to the door. There, she turned in the wrong direction.

He caught her arm, steered her to the left. She winced sharply. Behind them, Madge said, "We don't need to go all the way to the university—just toward it. We're meeting the others near there, where Rokin Street meets something called Spui."

"That saves us three minutes." He slackened his pace slightly, caught Madge's hand and pulled her alongside. She winced, too.

"Can't you talk about your new job?" Nina asked.

"Well, I'm undecided. Which would you choose—an oil company in Amsterdam or an import-export firm in London?"

"Oil would bring money," Madge said reflectively.

"But the other job offers more travel. I think I'll settle for London."

"I'll be back in London by Christmas," Nina said. "I'll miss the first term of the year at the Slade, but they don't seem to mind. Actually, I'll learn more about decorative art on our travels than I'd get from any old lectures."

"And where will Madge be at Christmas? In London, too?"

Madge shook her head. "Scranton, probably. I'll be dropped off in America. The first to leave," she added slowly.

"What if you want to leave before then? Either of you."

The two girls looked at each other, then laughed.

"I'm serious. You could get bored—a camper is a pretty confined space for that length of travel. Or fall ill."

"We won't get bored," Nina said. "We'll be lapping up enough memories to last us a lifetime. And we won't catch smallpox, typhoid, paratyphoid, cholera, or anything. We've come prepared. We've even had booster tetanus shots."

Shots? So that was why they had winced. "You've had a busy morning. I hope the doctor was—"

"No, no," Nina said. "We didn't get them here. We had the inoculations in London before we left."

Something didn't quite match. They had only decided to go on this trip around the world yesterday. "And you thought you needed a cholera shot for Amsterdam," he said. He looked around at the healthy Dutch faces filing past and shook his head.

"Ilsa advised it. So many refugees and foreign laborers from faraway places. They are a time bomb, she says, medically speaking."

"Ilsa?" That helpful Swedish friend again.

"Ilsa Schlott. She's a doctor, you know. Tropical diseases. She's taking a course on them at University College."

"She could be useful on your world tour."

"She doesn't know about that," Madge said. She turned to Nina. "Won't she be astounded when we send her a postcard of the Blue Mosque?"

"She'll start worrying that you didn't get yellow fever shots, too," Renwick predicted.

"Oh, she did tell us to get them. But I don't think it's necessary," Nina said. "Or is it?"

"If I knew what places you were visiting—"

"Don't worry. James will make sure we get these shots if we must have them. I hope we don't need them, though. They sound ghastly."

"Is he in charge of you?" Then I hope he is as sensible as Nina said.

"He's taking care of the details. Visas and that kind of stuff. That's why we're meeting him—to have a lot of pictures taken, regulation size. Isn't it an awful fuss? James knows a photographer who is guaranteed *not* to make us look like scared rabbits."

"Then after that," Madge said, "we'll pack into the camper—it's in the garage, right next door to the camera place—and we'll have a little test drive out to Haarlem for lunch." She giggled. "Or, as Tony says, he will take us for a spin."

Nina had a small fit of amusement, too. "One good laugh a day," she agreed. Then her smile was directed at Renwick. "And you thought we might get bored," she chided him gently.

He took it with good grace, just wished that with all this merriment and general jollity he wasn't nagged by his own private doubts. Am I really getting old? he wondered. "Well, in case you break a leg or get run over by a camel, just remember there's always an American embassy or consulate. They'll cable your father, and he'll have you whisked back to Washington in no time. By the way, when I see him, shall I drop a tactful hint where he can send your next allowance?"

Nina considered. "Why not? We'll be in Istanbul by the beginning of September. Ask him to send it to American Express."

"It's called Türk Express in that part of the world." And if they were reaching Turkey only in September, they'd never be back in London by Christmas; not at that rate of travel.

They had come to the end of the long narrow street, but not long enough for the questions he'd like to ask. Although, Renwick reminded himself, this was really none of his business. The girls were healthy and happy, confident and determined, foot loose and ready to go. He knew that feeling well. "Here is where I turn you over to your friends. Are they visible?" One helluva place to choose for a rendezvous, he thought, looking at Spui, broad and busy with traffic as it met crowded Rokin.

Nina's eyes searched the other side of Rokin. "They should be near the bridge, just across the street. Yes, there's James." She raised an arm to wave, let it drop. "He's too busy listening to Tony."

Renwick glanced over at the two men. The one who seemed to be doing all the talking was tall and thin, dark-haired. The listener was of medium height, medium build, brown-haired. Blue jeans, checked shirts. From this distance, that was all that could be seen. Tony finished his speech. James clapped him on the shoulder. Good friends, Renwick judged by the way they laughed. Then they consulted their watches, looked across the street, caught sight of Nina and Madge. They started over, misjudged the traffic, were halted by its sudden swoop.

"Good-bye," Nina was saying. "This was wonderful, Bob." She reached up and kissed his cheek. "See you in London?" And then, as if surprised by her question, her cheeks colored and she averted her eyes.

"I'll see you," he promised. He shook hands with Madge, and turned away. Somehow, he didn't feel like meeting the young men now plowing through a stream of pedestrians.

Nina said softly, "He was the first man I ever loved."

Most of the old Geneva story had been told to Madge, but this was something new. "And how did he feel about that?"

"If I had been three years older, I might have learned."

"He still likes you a lot. At least, he was worried about you."

"Why should he? I was surprised he even remembered me." But he had.

"He must be your type. Didn't you notice that James looks something like him?" Except for the smile and the thoughtful eyes.

Nina was startled for a moment, and then recovered enough to say, "Nonsense." She became absorbed in the decorated barrel organ now being wheeled past them. It halted and blocked James and Tony as they were about to reach the sidewalk. Now why is Tony so mad? she wondered. It can't be us: we weren't late. "He's cursing out the barrel organ," she told Madge, and they both laughed.

CHAPTER

5

Yes, Shawfield had cursed the barrel organ, something to vent his anger on as they had to change course and found they were now blocked by a car. Kiley said, "Ease off, Tony. Hold it down." (The names Erik and Marco had been laid aside; so was their knowledge of German, even when they spoke in private: a precaution against a slip in security.) For the last five minutes, as they waited near the bridge, Tony's worry had spilled out in a stream of angry advice: ditch the two girls now, and to hell with Theo: tell him they're unpredictable, dangerous—no discipline at all. Our first and only concern is to make contacts with revolutionary elements, judge their possibilities. "I know, I know," Kiley had said, "but O'Connell is of more importance than you think." Then he had added, "It could be worse than having them along. We could have had someone like Ilsa Schlott." That had raised a reluctant laugh, and he had clapped Tony's shoulder.

But as they started to cross Rokin, Tony's mood sharpened again. He stared at the stranger on the opposite sidewalk. "Who's that? She kissed him. Did you see?" A sudden rush of bicycles forced them back to wait some more. Yes, Kiley had seen.

"Well, well," he said as they reached the girls at last, "you collect friends everywhere, Nina."

"Oh—just a friend of Father's."

"Does he live here?"

"No." She seemed more interested in the barrel organ with a string of paper flowers draped around it. "Hideous colors. But should he be parking it right up on the sidewalk?" For the organ-grinder, small and lithe but obviously well muscled, had eased its wheels over the curb and then brought it to rest in front of a store's busy entrance.

"He knows where he can draw a crowd," Madge observed.

"Let's move," Tony said impatiently. "We haven't all day to hang around barrel organs." They were part of Amsterdam's street music, like the carillons from the churches. For a city that had been run by socialists and Communists for so many years, it had too many bloody churches, he thought; a fine bunch of Marxists, they were.

Kiley said, "Why didn't you ask your friend to spend the rest of the day with us? He probably was counting on having lunch with you when he arranged to meet you."

"We met by accident—just ran into him on Kalverstraat. Is that enough information for you?" Nina noticed the sudden flush on his cheeks, and relented. "I knew him years ago. He taught me how to volley and play a good net game. That's all."

The four of them began to walk toward the corner, but slowly in spite of Tony's urging. Madge looked back at the barrel organ. "No music? He won't make much money that way. And I think he did choose the wrong place." Two policemen, young and tall, long hair jutting out from the back of their caps, were making a leisurely approach, half curious, half amused. "He probably doesn't know the regulations. He certainly isn't Dutch by the look of him."

"Come on!" Tony said, catching Madge by the wrist. He glared back at the policemen, saw the little man dart off, one officer starting to give chase, the other still standing at the barrel organ. Tony's spine stiffened. As the explosion burst out, he was already dropping flat on his face with Madge pulled down beside him. In the same split second, Kiley acted, shoving Nina onto the ground, falling partly over her with a protecting arm around the back of her head.

There were screams, shouts, traffic screeching to a halt, children crying, a woman moaning near them. The two men picked themselves up, helped Nina and Madge to their feet. "Okay?" Kiley asked.

Nina nodded. Apart from the sudden fall, jarring every bone in her body, and street dust clinging to her shirt and jeans, she was all right. Breathless and dazed, but all right. So was Madge.

But it had been close. Near her, two women were bleeding, a man was covering his wounded eye, children had been knocked to the ground; and over by the twisted remains of the barrel organ, the policeman lay still.

"Let's get out of here," Kiley said. Soon there would be more police, and ambulances, and possibly a TV news camera.

"I agree." Tony was shaking his head. "To think," he added in a low voice, "you and I might have been put in a hospital for six months by some home-grown terrorists. Imbeciles! What did they accomplish?"

A splinter group working on a small scale, thought Kiley: a half-baked operation, ludicrous. "Not German, at any rate," he said thankfully. That would have brought West German Intelligence onto the Amsterdam scene. *The sooner we get out of here, the better.*

"Indonesians?" Tony suggested. He couldn't repress a laugh. South Moluccans putting him and Kiley out of business, the bloody fools.

"Don't think so." So far the Moluccans' protest against Indonesia had limited itself to occupying a train and holding its passengers as hostages, or secreting arms in their housing developments, or talking, talking, talking.

Madge was still staring around her in horror. But Nina had recovered a little. She had heard that last interchange. "Indonesians?" she repeated. "Why should they do this?"

"Let's move," Kiley said. He slipped an arm through Nina's, steadying her. He set a slow pace. Both girls were obviously shaken.

"They've been independent for thirty years," Nina said. Shock was giving way to indignation and anger.

"Some Indonesians want to be free from Indonesia," Tony snapped.

"Then why don't they bomb Indonesia?"

"Because," said Kiley patiently, "they now live in Holland."

"Refugees? And so they take it out on the Dutch?" She shook off Kiley's guiding arm. Her voice was more decisive than it had ever been. "Terrorist logic," she said scathingly. "Cowards, too. All of them! They leave a bomb and run. Oh, no, they don't get killed or mutilated. They'll telephone the newspapers later, claiming they were responsible. How very brave—how noble!" She laughed unsteadily. Tears were approaching. "Don't terrorists ever think of people?"

"They are fighting for the people," Kiley suggested, his tone mild.

"So they kill them?"

"We can get a drink in here," Kiley said, and led the way.

Nina said, "We ought to have stayed and helped," but she followed him inside the restaurant. She suddenly noticed his arm had been bleeding.

"Nothing," he told her. It wasn't much, actually—a glancing blow from a splinter of wood: it could have been a shard of glass from the store's window. But the small wound was effective. Both girls became silent.

Then, "Thank you," Nina said to James Kiley; and Madge looked at Tony Shawfield, smiled shyly, and thanked him, too.

"You were so *quick*," Madge told him. "If I had been alone, I would have been caught standing up. Like that woman with the blood pouring over her face...Oh, God!" She saw Tony frown. In sympathy, she guessed.

But what worried him was the thought that some trained eye might have seen the way he and Kiley had dropped to the ground just as the bomb was about to explode.

Kiley ordered Scotch for everyone. No expense spared: it was the quickest restorer, raising them all back to normal again. "We'll lunch here before we get the photographs taken. We'll cut out the jaunt to Haarlem. Instead, we'll leave this afternoon. How's that? You don't want to stay much longer in Amsterdam, do you?"

After what had happened? Nina shook her head. "Just one thing, though. It has been bothering me for some time."

He waited, suddenly tense. Tony was sitting very still.

Nina said, "I just can't go on calling you James. It's too— too—" She laughed. "It doesn't sound natural. Too formal for a real American. What shall it be? Jim or Jimmy?"

"Jim will do." So I made a small mistake, he thought: I insisted on James. *Too formal for a real American*...Real? He looked at her sharply, but she was quite oblivious of the scare she had given him. "So we leave today," he said. "You are ready, Tony?"

"Any time you say."

Nina was looking at the stains on her shirt. Madge needed a change, too. "Let's not bother about the photographs. We can have them taken later. We don't need visas right away, do we?"

"We'll keep to the arrangements," Kiley said. The photographer could be trusted: a loyal comrade, knowing what was needed, following instructions and keeping his mouth shut. "Besides, the others are having their pictures taken at this very moment."

Tony rose. "I'd better get over there and tell them about the change in plans. They have gear to collect and stow on board." He was already halfway to the door.

"What about his drink?" Madge asked.

"I guess he didn't need it," Kiley said. Tony's blood pres-

sure must already be high enough. He'll have to remember
to tolerate all the damn silly thoughts about clothes that
women find natural. The more they chatter about nitwit top-
ics, the less they'll discuss anything serious. As for Nina's
outburst against terrorists, that couldn't be better cover for
Tony and me. Who'd expect Nina's friends to be anything
except political dolts like her?

"We have our own gear to pick up," Nina remembered.
"The bags are at the Alba. That's nowhere near the garage.
So what do we do? Take a taxi?"

A taxi? With some sharp-eyed driver linking two blondes,
the Alba, and the garage? In spite of his own advice to Tony,
Kiley drew a long breath to steady his voice. "No. We can stop
and pick up your bags on our way out of Amsterdam. Or have
you got to pack?" That wouldn't do at all. The camper waiting,
waiting; Tony's fury unleashed in some savage though apt
phrases.

"A couple of minutes," Nina assured him. "Just tooth-
brushes and soap. That's all."

"There's the bill—" began Madge.

"I'll settle it," Kiley said.

"We paid six days in advance. So they owe us for two."

God give me strength, he thought, and then realized he
had called on the name of a deity in whom he didn't believe.
For Christ's sake... He took a deep draught of the Scotch,
newly arrived, and choked with sudden laughter. Very
American: God and Christ, and two pretty blondes trying to
understand and failing. Real enough, Miss Nina?

"Let's eat," he said. "We haven't time to waste." And we'll
be out of Amsterdam before the police search reaches garages
and courtyards and workshops near the university area. For
that barrel organ couldn't have been pushed for any great
distance—too cumbersome. And that little man hadn't been
running blindly. He was headed for his escape route, must
have had a car parked safely out of sight. In our garage?
Kiley wondered. Always a possibility, considering it's owner's
sympathies. Not that a camper, all prepared for a long trip,
couldn't be satisfactorily explained. Even so, police made
notes in little books. "What will you have?" he asked Nina.
Whatever she'd choose, Madge would choose.

"I'm not really hungry."

"Then we'll order the *Koffietafel*. It's always ready to
serve." He finished his drink and signaled to their waitress.

"I don't think—"

"You'll eat," he told her. "Your next meal will be in Belgium." He lifted Tony's glass. "To our travels."

"To our travels," Nina echoed.

"Far and wide," Madge ended, and smiled happily.

CHAPTER

6

BRUNA IMPORTS, read the restrained legend above the doorway of one of the restored houses on the Prinsengracht. There were other commercial establishments, too, on this Old Amsterdam street, including expensive restaurants and a luxury hotel, so that the firm of Bruna was not remarkable, tucked away as it was in the middle of a row of ancient gables. Crefeld's office was on the top floor, reached by a very small private elevator installed years ago for someone's heart ailment: it could hold two people if they were thin enough and pressed in a tight embrace. Renwick touched an ivory button to signal Crefeld. The elevator door was released, and he could ride up in solitary state, avoiding the staircase that would have taken him through the busy second and third floors, where imports of coffee and pepper were actually marketed. Bruna was authentic, not a false front for mysterious activities. But how Jake Crefeld—Jacobus van Crefeld, to give him his full name; Brigadier-General to give him his equivalent rank—had ever managed to secure an office in this building was something that aroused Renwick's admiration. Knowing Jake's diplomacy, he wasn't astounded.

The corridor was short and narrow. Crefeld's door, as old and heavy as all the other carved woodwork in this building, had a faded sign, small and difficult to read: J. SCHLEE / RARE BOOKS / BY APPOINTMENT ONLY. The door swung open as Renwick was about to knock, and Crefeld was there with his broad smile and firm handshake to welcome him inside. "Had a peephole installed, Jake?" Renwick asked, studying the carved upper panel of the door as it was closed and bolted behind him. The small cutout was centered in a wooden rosette, part of the door's decoration both outside and in, not noticeable except by close scrutiny.

"And necessary," Crefeld said. "Such are these times, Bob." His large round face tried to look sad and failed. He was a big man in every way, in voice and laugh as well as in body and heart. The surprising thing was his light footstep, his quick movement. Nothing heavy or lumbering. Now he was at his desk, pulling a chair in place for Renwick. "I am sorry to bring you all the way from Brussels, but I thought it wise if we weren't seen together there. Den Haag was also out of the question for the same reason."

"I guessed that. No trouble at all. I enjoyed getting away from the office." This one was still the same as when Renwick had last visited it: dark paneled walls enclosing a square room, with a large desk, two comfortable chairs, a filing cabinet, and three telephones. There was one powerful lamp for evening work; by day, light beamed through the diamond panes of two windows, narrow and tall, which stood close to the desk. Everything was well in reach of Crefeld's long arm. Now, he was lifting a large attaché case onto his lap. Renwick waited, wondering if the business that had brought him here necessitated so many documents. Then he smiled: he had forgotten that Jake never let business interfere with regular mealtimes.

"We'll lunch first," Crefeld was saying as he opened the attaché case, "and talk of this and that. I heard a rumor that you were resigning. Are you?" He swept blotting pad and letters aside, and in the cleared space spread out a checked napkin which had covered the food. Next came a plastic box containing cold cuts and cheese, a smaller box with cherries, a sliced loaf, two mugs, two plastic glasses, two paper plates, a Thermos of coffee, and a flask of gin.

"Negative. Only a rumor." In fascination, Renwick watched the deft way in which Crefeld's massive hands arranged the items in logical order. "Just a nice little piece of camouflage."

"Because of your new project?" Crefeld poured gin into the two glasses. "That's wise. No useful purpose in spilling the— What *do* you Americans spill?" He frowned at the glass he held out to Renwick. He prided himself on his command of colloquial English, acquired over his years of service with NATO.

"Beans." Renwick smothered his gin. It was years since he had heard that phrase.

Crefeld inclined his head in acknowledgment. As usual, a strand of fair hair—now graying and thinning, Renwick noted—fell over his high forehead. He pushed it aside, a temporary victory, and studied his glass. "Glad it was only a rumor. You've still got twenty years ahead of you before you reach my age."

If any of us are still functioning by that time, thought Renwick. Or alive. He raised his glass. "To survival."

"To the project," Crefeld said. They both drank to that. "Have you got a name for it yet?"

"The choice seems to lie between Counter-Terrorism Intelligence and International Intelligence against Terrorism. Pretty heavy. Any suggestions?"

"Well, your idea is based on something after the style of Interpol. Find something short and snappy like that."

"Interintell?" Renwick's grin was broad.

"Why not?"

"Sounds like a cable address."

"So does Interpol. Few people know it as the International Criminal Police Organization that began in Vienna."

Renwick added tactfully, "Nineteen-twenty-three," and ended a short discourse on the history of the international crime-chasers before Crefeld could deliver it.

"Interintell," Crefeld said reflectively. "I like it."

"So you really have decided to join us?" Renwick kept his tone light, but he waited anxiously. Crefeld would be excellent as the head of Interintell's main office. Larsen, in Oslo, and Lademan, in Copenhagen, were his close friends. Add to that trio Richard Diehl, in West Germany, who was already co-operating: his country, after all, had more than its share of terrorists who sought refuge abroad when the heat became too great. (Only a few months ago, one of the Baader-Meinhof gang had been arrested as she tried to cross into the United States from Canada.) Then there was Ronald Gilman, in London—also definite. So was Tim MacEwan, in Ottawa. And Pierre Claudel, in Paris, had been enthusiastic from the start. All were old friends, had worked together in NATO, and now were back with their own intelligence services. A real blockbuster, reflected Renwick: brains and guts, and clout to match.

Crefeld was watching the younger man with a smile. "Of course. Did you ever doubt it? Who else has been rounded up?"

Renwick, with relief undisguised, gave him the names. "Next week, I'll be in Washington and talk with Frank Cooper."

"He has retired out of everything, hasn't he? He's on the old side, I'd say."

Not as old as you, Jake, thought Renwick. "He's still a good man."

"What is he doing now?"

"International law. New York firm with a branch in Washington."

"Ah—that could be useful. Well, you've made an excellent start. And I must say it is a first-rate idea."

"But borrowed, as you said, from Interpol," Renwick added.

"With considerable differences. They go after international crime. We go after international terrorists. But we face one difficulty."

Only one? thought Renwick.

"Police forces of a hundred countries co-operate with Interpol. Will intelligence agencies do the same for us?" Crefeld shook his head. "They keep their records to themselves."

"We aren't asking them to open their files. All we ask is any information they have collected on terrorists, and in return we'll give them all the evidence we've developed. We'll act as a kind of clearinghouse for them. It's much needed. Terrorism is international."

"Terrorism . . . And that is a second difficulty. Whom do we call terrorists? We shall have to be quite clear about that, or else we'll be in trouble. Some more gin?"

"No thanks. Breakfast is a long time away. I think I'll make myself a sandwich." Renwick selected a slice of ham, a slice of cheese and cushioned them between two thick slices of bread. "We'll make the definition as clear as we can. Easiest done, perhaps, by stating what terrorism is not. It is not, for instance, resistance to alien forces that have invaded a country—against the will of the majority of its people: resistance fighters are not terrorists. Again, revolutionaries are not terrorists when they represent the will of the majority of their people."

"The will of the majority," Crefeld said. "That's your measure?"

"That's the way votes are counted, Jake."

"In a free country," Crefeld reminded him.

Renwick nodded agreement.

"But what if resistance fighters or revolutionaries find they don't have a majority of the people behind them? Are they then terrorists?"

"If they use bullets and bombs to gain power over a majority that wants none of their ideas—yes, that's what they have become: terrorists. Amateurs, of course, compared to the hardcore activists who think of power in terms of world revolution.

Poor old world—whether it wants it or not, it's to have anarchy thrust down its throat, for its own eventual good."

Crefeld was helping himself to two of everything for a hefty sandwich. "When I was a boy, an anarchist was something left over from the nineteenth century. Bakunin—"

"'The passion for destruction,'" quoted Renwick, "'is also a creative passion.' Or Malatesta declaring that 'the insurrectionary deed is the most efficacious means for propaganda.' Or Kropotkin cloaking the total overthrow of the state as it exists—and all the chaos that would bring—by preaching that anarchism is a moral and social doctrine before it is a political one. That has its appeal, you know. Freedom from the tyranny of national and corporate giantism. Everyone equalized and co-operating; under anarchist control of course. But where is freedom then? Somehow, no anarchist seems to face that problem. Or is their control good, and all other control bad?" Renwick shook his head, his lips tight.

"The simplifiers," Crefeld said. "Terrible and terrifying. Not too many of them around, though."

"Not as yet. Wait until the neo-Nazis start using them as shock troops."

"But they belong to the left—the far left at that."

"If the Communists can use them to create a revolutionary situation, so can other totalitarians. It's the old delusion: you use me but I'm really using you; I'll deal with you when the revolution is won. Where else do you think the anarchists get their money and training right now? Their ordinary sympathizers don't carry that kind of clout. So they use their future enemy, and intend to get the final jump on them. The old delusion," Renwick repeated, "and a mountain of trouble for the rest of the world."

Crefeld studied his friend. "Why this interest in the anarchists? Have you found some evidence that they are actually in alliance with the Communists? You know their opinion of Soviet Russia—a betrayer of the revolution, curtailer of freedom."

"But the Soviets are still socialists who could be set on the correct track again. And if there's a choice between socialism and nonsocialism, the anarchists will make it on the side of the far left. Or the far right. The Nazis called themselves socialists, remember? As for actual evidence of an alliance with hard-line Communists—yes, I think we've found something."

"Was that why you visited Essen two weeks ago?"

The quiet question jolted Renwick. Then he laughed. "You've got ears and eyes everywhere, Jake. Yes, I was in Essen. Following another lead, and found something else, too."

"What kind of lead?" There was more than curiosity in Crefeld's question, a definite interest. He had finished his outsize sandwich and was now onto dessert.

Renwick poured himself some coffee, lit a cigarette, measured his thoughts. Keep them crisp and clear, he warned himself, for it was a long story, beginning two years ago. "Remember my report on Vienna? Uncovering one source of the money that was subsidizing terrorists?"

Crefeld nodded. "Deposited in a numbered bank account in Geneva."

"With a million and a half dollars already paid out before we tracked down that account. So we started tracing the people who had been sent that money. Three names, in three separate cities—in France, Italy, Denmark. But before we caught up with their bank accounts, transfers had been made to three more names: customers of three banks in different cities, but all in Germany this time."

"Half a million dollars in each account?"

"Yes. That was careless of the man who was laundering the money—made a difficult search a little easier for us. But I guess he was in a hurry, or had a mania for keeping things as simple as possible."

"Did you trace him?"

"We had to wait until all the money was eventually transferred to the firm where he works. Ostensibly, he's only second-in-command there—it's a travel agency in Düsseldorf—but his boss delegates a lot of responsibility to Otto Remp."

"Remp, Otto Remp," Crefeld searched his memory, then shook his head.

"It baffled us, too. Nothing on Remp. A stalwart citizen, quiet in manner, pleasant, popular in the firm. With some trouble we managed to get one decent photograph after fifty failures, and a set of his fingerprints."

"Surely he couldn't explain a windfall of one and a half million dollars. Wouldn't that have been enough to uncover him?"

"But if the money disappeared into the many financial transactions of Western Travel Incorporated? Soon to develop as West-East Travel? They are expanding beyond Europe.

They have begun arrangements for branch offices in Istanbul, Bombay, Singapore, Hong Kong, Honolulu, Los Angeles."

"And you say the head of this agency, Western Travel, is mostly a figurehead?"

"He enjoys his leisure. And his income. No complaints."

"A fool."

"All of that."

"And this Otto Remp—" Crefeld paused, then smiled. "What did you find from his photograph and fingerprints?"

"Your old friend Herman Kroll. Remember him? You did a pretty good report on him ten years ago when he was head of Special Operations in East Germany. Our photograph doesn't quite match the one your agents took: basically, it's similar, but he has altered his appearance enough to deceive most people. The fingerprints, however, are identical with your sample. That was quite a file you kept on East German Intelligence."

"And their KGB advisers," Crefeld said softly. Then, "Good God—Herman Kroll! So Theo is alive and well."

"Theo?"

"A code name he used in earlier days when he was an agent in the field. He dropped it when he was promoted to an office and two secretaries. The last I heard of him was five years ago, when he was reported killed in a helicopter crash." There was a pause, and then a sudden question. "How long has he been in Düsseldorf?"

"Five years."

Crefeld laughed. "Theo wastes no time. You're keeping him under surveillance?"

"Yes. We watch and wait. The old routine."

"No results?"

"Three visits to Essen in the last eight months. He's elusive. Remembers his past as an agent in the field."

"You mean you lost him in Essen?"

"Twice. On his last visit he was less alert—perhaps deeply worried. He had cause to be. Three terrorists had been arrested that morning, along with the girl Amalie. Who was she working for, Jake?" Renwick ended blandly. His own guess had been based on deduction. Now he waited, hoping for a confirmation. He got it.

"For us. But I didn't send her in. That happened a few years ago when I was still in Brussels. West German terrorists had been using Holland—they were responsible for two murders and a brutal kidnapping, so Amalie went into West

Berlin, attending its Free University, and started from there. She had an independent hand, no direction except to act through the local police in an extreme emergency, and to send brief reports of progress back to The Hague—to me, in fact, since my return there. She was a good agent—just a slip of a girl." Crefeld's eyebrows knitted. "Why the hell do we have to employ women, Bob?" he burst out.

"Because they are often better than a lot of men." Renwick thought of his own loss, back in Austria. Almost two years now. Avril Hoffman . . . No, he couldn't forget her. But I never sent her to infiltrate, he told himself, as if to help remove the burden of guilt, the sense of responsibility, an emotion Jake obviously shared. Avril was liaison between me and— He cut off his memories. Avril was dead. "Also," he went on, "they volunteer. They want a mission that will mean something. Just try keeping women out of intelligence work, Jake, and you'll be picketed from here to Greenland." That eased the tension, but Crefeld had backed away from the subject of Amalie. Renwick let it drop. For now. Amalie's reports on the Essen terrorists could be vital.

"So on the day of the arrests in Essen," Crefeld continued, "you managed to follow Theo."

"Not all the way. As far as the center of the city, near the Minster. Just over half an hour later we picked up his trail again—as he was coming out of the church. Alone. We didn't see whom he met there. Another failure," he admitted wearily. Then Renwick brightened. "He went to a suburban bank, withdrew his account—it was under a false name, of course. A considerable sum, almost twelve thousand dollars. No doubt it was there for the expenses of Amalie's terrorist friends in Direct Action. Isn't that what they call themselves now?"

Crefeld nodded. "Section One of Direct Action, to be exact. But go on!"

"With Richard Diehl's help we found out who had been cashing checks drawn on that account, which orginally had amounted to forty thousand dollars. Always a man, young and bearded, of medium height, brown hair, grayish eyes, pleasant manner. Name of Kurt Leitner. We traced him to his rented room. But he had left on the previous night—right after Theo's visit to Essen. Then we traced his motor bicycle—it had been left at a warehouse. But all we could learn was a vague story about a bearded young man whose motorbike had broken down and who asked for a lift in a truck. He was dropped, the driver said when the police started questioning, near the Duisburg docks. Anyway, Kurt Leitner has vanished. We have a composite drawing of him, with his employer—a bookstore owner—and his landlady obliging. But we needed Amalie to identify him. It wasn't heart failure that killed her, was it?"

"No. Possibly cyanide. A gas pistol disguised as a fountain pen. Theo would know her hospital room number—from the same informer at police headquarters who gave him the warning about the police raid. Amalie hadn't, of course, submitted any full report to the police on Direct Action—just identified herself, as instructed, and told them of the addresses and names she knew, and of the imminent attack on Duisburg. It would have been a disaster. Not just the oil destroyed, but fire sweeping part of the town. Untold deaths."

"Who was the leader of Section One? Kurt Leitner?"

"She never reported that name. She did emphasize that two of that gang were known only as Erik and Marco, definitely the leaders."

"Any descriptions?"

"Both had beards at that time. Both dressed in the same style—wool hats pulled well down on their brows. Hair hidden, even indoors. Erik wore dark glasses. She couldn't risk any photographs. Marco seemed to be in charge. But they were both important, she felt."

"She was right. They were the ones who got away. An early warning by Theo? The others he left to take their chances. As if—" Renwick was now thinking aloud—"as if he wanted them safely out of Essen before the others started scattering. Yes. They're important, all right." It was an ominous thought. He rose. "Well, if that's all the business on hand, I'll start Richard Diehl on a search for Marco and Erik. They could be named in the Berlin police records of five years ago when Direct Action was robbing banks to finance its operations. A rash of bank robberies, in fact: a warning signal of trouble to come." And then, he thought, Direct Action stopped its robberies and holdups. But not its operations. Five years ago...Just when Theo came on the West German scene.

Crefeld waved him back to his chair. "Sit down, Bob. We haven't finished all the business. Here's an item I thought might interest you. It ties in, perhaps, with your findings in Essen." Crefeld pushed aside the remains of their picnic, lifted a thin briefcase onto the desk. He took out a slim folder, extracted three typed pages, glancing at them as he talked.

'A coastal freighter sailed from Duisburg on the night Kurt Leitner disappeared. It docked at Rotterdam to discharge a cargo of cereal. Fifteen minutes after its arrival, a roughly dressed man, bearded, appeared at a house close to the docks. He was immediately admitted and taken upstairs to a room. The woman who owns that house is Cuban, pro-Castro Cuban. She spoke sharply to the newcomer in Spanish, telling him he should have waited until it was dark. He asked her in rapid Spanish whether she wanted him to hang around the docks until it was dark enough to please her.

"Our informant is a police undercover man. He works at that house, sweeping and cleaning and emptying the garbage. He was assigned there because the Rotterdam police suspected drug smuggling. But, from his reports, visitors who arrive and depart are not dealing in drugs. They arrive on some freighter, stay inside the house for a few days, get a change of clothes, leave."

"A safe house?"

"Exactly."

"The man spoke Spanish?"

"Fluently. Too quick for our informant to catch everything."

"Then if this was Kurt Leitner—" Renwick broke off. Fluent Spanish?

"Whoever he is, he's a linguist. Our informant was given a heavy bundle to take up to the stranger's room. Before this parcel was left outside the door as instructed, our man had a look inside its brown paper cover. American newspapers. A mass of them. Another time, he left a tray outside the door and knocked. As the door opened, he was waved away, couldn't look inside. But he heard an American voice, on a radio or from a cassette player."

"An English lesson? Or was he learning an American accent?"

"And the newspapers?" Crefeld asked. "Studying present-day problems?" He paused. "I don't like it, Bob."

"Nor I."

"There is not much more to add. Except that the man had arrived with a dark beard and mustache."

"That could be Leitner. His hair was lighter—mid-brown?"

"Couldn't be seen. He was wearing a close-fitting knitted cap. Also an old leather jacket and heavy glasses. Four days later, he left—June 14, 8:15 exactly. Our informant caught only a glimpse of him. No face description possible except that there was no beard. Black hair, heavy and thick. Good shoes, gray flannel trousers, jacket hidden under a raincoat. He was unrecognizable. In fact, it was only when our informant was sent upstairs to sweep out the emptied room that he could confirm his suspicion."

Renwick said slowly, "There must have been a car waiting for him. And there had to be a tailor involved—or someone who could make expert alterations on store-bought clothes."

Crefeld laughed. "The Rotterdam police are attending to those problems. They had the house under outside surveillance."

"No luggage?"

"One large but lightweight bag."

"Air travel?"

"Perhaps. Perhaps not. Again, we've asked the police to—" He was cut short by the ringing of one of the telephones. Unerringly, he picked up the right one.

Possibly identified by its bell tone. All different? Jake, thought Renwick, is a well-organized man. A pleasure to work with him.

"Excuse me," Crefeld said hurriedly. "This may be a fuller report on that bombing today in Rokin Street." He was listening now, speaking in his turn in Dutch, listening, speaking, listening. With his hand over the receiver, he made a quick aside in English for Renwick's enlightenment. "From my office at The Hague. Johan Vroom."

Vroom was Crefeld's assistant, reliable and competent and a little long-winded. Renwick waited patiently, his thoughts on the Rokin bombing. He had been only a short distance away when the explosion had swallowed up all street noises. He had halted, turned, started to run back. Nina, he was thinking, Nina....But she was all right he could see as he reached the fringe of a gathering crowd; so was Madge. Judging from the way they lay on the ground, their two friends had shoved or pushed them down, then fallen on their faces, too. And saved the four of them from flying debris. Near and around them, other people hadn't reacted in time. They had paid for it. The policeman had had no chance whatsoever.

Renwick, once he saw the girls being helped to their feet and dusted off, backed away. They weren't hurt, except for bruised egos. As for the men—attractive-looking types, he had to admit—they seemed fit and healthy, and they were certainly capable. Must have had military training, he decided as he looked at his watch, remembered Crefeld, and began a brisk walk to the Prinsengracht: they had certainly shown a proper respect for explosives. Sensible types, too. So that was a relief. He could stop worrying about Nina.

Or can I? Renwick asked himself now, waiting for Vroom's long call to end. She's so damned independent, thinks she can take on the world and come out winning. But you don't win all the time, Nina. Not all the time. You're the same vulnerable, romantic girl I met six years ago; in spite of your grown-up airs, you're still just that. Why the hell did I have to meet you today, start remembering—

"What?" yelled Crefeld into the phone, and Renwick's memories ended abruptly. "What?" Crefeld repeated in a quieter voice. "You are sure? I'll be back this evening. Call me if you hear more." He clamped down the receiver, swung around to face Renwick, and broke into English again. "You know who the man was? The one who wheeled the bomb into position? A Japanese. A Japanese, for God's sake."

There was a brief silence. Crefeld went on, "A member of some terrorist group called the Red Banner. Came here from Tokyo to arouse the conscience of the workers against the fascist government that is persecuting their Moluccan comrades. Persecuting, for God's sake? We took them in when they left Indonesia. And a Japanese, of all things..." He was outraged. Then, "If there weren't people wounded and one man killed, I would laugh." Another pause. "Ironic note: he was caught by three workers on bicycles. They ran him down, breaking his leg, and held him firmly until the police arrived."

Lucky about that leg, thought Renwick, or else he would have karate-chopped their necks and high-kicked their jaws and left three more injured Dutchmen on the pavement. "There must have been a backup man in a car, an escape route planned."

Crefeld agreed. "The police have begun checking all cars parked in that area."

"What about garages? Or the small warehouses? The barrel organ must have been prepared some place nearby."

"Everything will be checked. But first, there are questions to be put to the people who live in that district. Information. A lead. That could save a lot of searching. You agree?"

"I'm not sure," Renwick admitted frankly.

"But you are sure about a barrel organ? How did you learn that, my friend?"

"I was there."

"You just happened to be there?" Crefeld was now highly amused. Did Renwick attract trouble or did trouble attract Renwick? Crefeld had often wondered about that.

"Not exactly." Renwick gave a three-sentence explanation of meeting Nina O'Connell and her friend, escorting them to Rokin, leaving them there for Kiley and Shawfield to take over. "They're planning a trip around the world. No, I mean it, Jake. In a camper. With some other students."

"I thought you looked worried when you arrived here. In a camper?"

"It sounds as if it were a custom-built job. So that's possibly safe. And Kiley and Shawfield are not college students: older. In their late twenties, I'd guess."

"Couldn't you persuade your young friend—"

"Nina? She has reached the point of no argument. Besides, I'm not her father. He is Francis O'Connell, by the way."

Crefeld was impressed. "I can see why you might be worried."

About Francis O'Connell? That self-centered career-artist? "What is nagging away at me is this: the girls arrive in an Amsterdam packed with tourists, no reservations of course, go to a recommended hotel called the Alba, find that two cancellations have just occurred. Lucky girls, Jake. Too lucky?"

Crefeld's lips were pursed. "The Alba? Don't know it. Who recommended it?"

"A friend in London, a Swedish doctor, name of Ilsa Schlott. She also recommended inoculations for an Amsterdam visit. The works—cholera included. Nina balked at the yellow fever shots, though. Schlott knows something about tropical diseases. She knows Amsterdam, too, obviously. So why suggest these inoculations for a visit here?"

"She possibly heard of this world tour."

"She knows nothing about it—according to Madge Westerman. That's Nina's friend."

"Cholera and yellow fever?" Crefeld was bemused. "For Amsterdam?" He repressed a laugh. In a desk drawer, he found a sheet of paper and began noting: "Alba—Dr. Ilsa Schlott—Madge Westerman—Nina O'Connell." He looked up to ask, "Any other names you can give me?"

Suddenly embarrassed, Renwick said, "Look, Jake, perhaps I've been exaggerating the problem." Personal interest could distort judgment. "No need for any—"

"You've aroused my curiosity," Crefeld said. "Cholera and yellow fever in Amsterdam?" He laughed openly this time and then tapped his pencil on his notes. "I just like things complete. You know that, Bob. Who owns this camper?"

"Tony Shawfield, English. His friend is James Kiley, American. Then there's a Sven Dissen and his wife—Marie-Louise. Two others: Lambrese, and Henryk Tromp from Leyden."

"Tromp? There's a Henryk Tromp at The Hague. A lawyer. Friend of mine. He has a son, Henryk too, who was a student at Leyden. He hopes young Henryk will join the firm someday."

"Possibly a father-son relationship. Young Tromp is going to law school when he gets back from this trip."

"Well," Crefeld said, "if the others on this trip are like Henryk, you needn't worry about your friends. Doesn't that reassure you?" He didn't destroy his notes, though, but slipped them into the desk drawer. "I'll get word to you about any more reports from Rotterdam. Quite a useful exchange of information we've had. A successful launching of Interintell, wouldn't you say? Let me know further developments. You'll be arranging for others to join us—Italy, Greece, Turkey?"

"I'll keep you informed," Renwick said as they shook hands at the door.

"The sooner the better," Crefeld suggested.

Another handshake on that, and the door closed behind Renwick. Almost four o'clock, he noted with surprise, as he reached the street and began walking along the canal side. Yes, quite a useful exchange of information, and possibly more to come from Rotterdam. Just where was Kurt Leitner bound for, with his nice new clothes and his traveling bag? One thing we do know for a certainty, Renwick decided: he left the name Kurt Leitner along with his leather jacket in that house by the docks.

Renwick chose the Breda road for his return to Belgium. Traffic was mixed in the late afternoon, fewer trucks but more sightseeing buses and small cars loaded to the gunwales with holiday baggage. Outrageous gas prices were having little effect on vacationers southward bound. At the border, there was a general slow-up, unusual in the Benelux countries, where goods and people flowed easily across frontiers.

But the bombing in Amsterdam was having its effect: closer scrutiny than usual of all vehicles leaving Holland.

Renwick eased his Citroën's speed and joined the line of cars that edged their way forward, stopped, moved forward again. A Europa bus was released and sent on. One more car behind it, then a minibus, two more cars, and Renwick's turn would come. That wouldn't take too long. He would make good speed on the road bypassing Antwerp, be able to wash up at his apartment before he went out to dinner at his favorite restaurant, where he could meet a couple of his friends.

Then as he looked along the road ahead of him, he noticed there was a small group, a half-dozen people or so, gathered close to the minibus. Or camper, he decided. Green, well-built body, tarpaulin strapped securely over the baggage on its roof. Would they have to open that up? he wondered in dismay, glancing at his watch. Just in case a Japanese terrorist was hidden topside? Kids, he thought now, as he heard the small group break into laughter, saw some light-hearted horseplay between two of the young men. A couple, affectionate, holding on to each other. Two girls; shoulder-length golden hair, slender, medium height, outsize shoulder bags. He looked again, amazed. Nina. And friend Madge.

He recovered from his surprise. Where were the remaining two, Shawfield and Kiley? Still inside the camper talking with the Dutch officials? But all was in order, for the group was called together, climbed back into the camper. It moved off, quickly gathering speed. The two cars ahead of him, now getting into position for identification, blocked Renwick's view of the plate above the camper's rear bumper. When he could see the camper again, it was too distant to note its number. An automatic reflex, he thought, excusing his curiosity. Anyway they were off, with a clean bill of health: no Japanese stowaway—that hadn't worried him—and no evidence of drugs being smuggled or used, and thank God for that. He could smile and shake his head at that brief touch of suspicion. They were safely off, a day ahead of schedule. There would be no Dear Daddy letter written to Francis O'Connell tonight: he'd be lucky if he got a postcard from Brussels.

CHAPTER

7

Crefeld had allowed fifteen minutes, after Renwick's departure from his office, before he left. The remnants of their luncheon, gathered up inside the checked napkin, had been thrust back into the attaché case. The letters on his desk—addressed to J. Schlee, Rare Books—could be locked away in his cabinet. He'd attend to them on his next visit, nothing urgent, nothing important. But the slim briefcase was. With it tucked securely under one arm, his hand holding the attaché case—a nuisance, but useful, letting him avoid restaurants and crowds whenever a special meeting had to be arranged, and where else but in this office could secret reports be handled securely?—he doubled-locked the door behind him.

He had already summoned the elevator, so it was waiting for him. Its stately descent always reminded him of his maternal grandfather, the last Bruna to use that top-floor room when he wanted to stay overnight in the city. Crefeld had often wondered about the elevator: no heart weaknesses in the Bruna clan; possibly a lady visiting who found stairs hard to climb in her tight-corseted waist. The days of whalebone, he thought, and was smiling broadly as he stepped into the dimly lit hall. Apart from a telephone operator at her switchboard, kept neatly out of sight, built under the curved flight of staircase, the hall was empty. From the floor overhead came the sound of a typewriter clacking away, making good time before closing hours.

The hall wasn't empty. A man was standing in one corner near the front door, leaning on his rolled umbrella, his neat dark suit blending into the mahogany wood paneling of the walls. His hair, cut short, was gray—prematurely gray, for his thin face was unlined. He smiled shyly. "No receptionist here?" he asked. "How do I get in touch with the accountant's office?"

So he had just entered, wasn't waiting as I first thought, Crefeld decided. His suspicion leveled off, but he still kept a

71

distance from the stranger. "Try the telephone girl—you'll find her just around that curve of staircase."

"Thank you." The stranger came forward, but he was giving Crefeld ample room to pass him.

"Not at all," said Crefeld as he averted his face and made for the front door.

Suddenly, the stranger raised his umbrella, its ferrule pointed at Crefeld's thigh.

Crefeld felt a sting, hot and sharp. He stared at the man, then at the umbrella. He raised his voice to shout and gave a strangled croak. He had no strength in his body at all. His legs were beginning to buckle. The man hit him sharply over his hand that held the briefcase. Crefeld's grip was loosened; the briefcase was pulled away from his arm. He saw only a blur as the dark suit turned and hurried to the front entrance; he heard only a faint noise as the heavy door was closed.

Crefeld fell backward to the ground, the attaché case clattering beside him on the wooden floor. He tried to shout again, knew it was useless. Only his brain seemed to be working. He made an effort to reach into his jacket pocket, take hold of the card he always kept there in case of emergency. He could feel it, even gripped it, but he couldn't pull it out.

"What's wrong? What's wrong?" It was the telephone girl, kneeling beside him, looking in horror at the man who lay staring up at her. She screamed and kept screaming until heels came running down the staircase.

"He's alive," a man's voice said. "Get an ambulance."

"I thought I heard the door close. Then I heard a crash." The telephone girl pointed to the attaché case. "And another crash. Together almost. He's trying to speak." She lowered her ear to his lips.

"He's Schlee, the book collector. Saw him one day—"

"Get an ambulance!" The telephone operator was yanked to her feet. "Call now!"

"What's in his pocket?"

"His hand!"

"But why?"

Crefeld's hand was pulled out gently.

"A card. Emergency, it says. A telephone number. A name: Jake. Here," the man's voice said, "call this number, too. First, the ambulance; then the card. Quick, quick!"

High heels retreated. "She's always so damn slow," said

the man's voice. "Hurry!" he yelled after her. Then, as an afterthought, "What did he say? Could he speak?"

"Didn't make sense," the girl called back. "Sounded like umbrella."

"Stupid as well as slow," the man told the rest of the small crowd. Umbrella. Schlee wasn't carrying any umbrella. "Heart attack. Don't move him. Keep back. Give him air."

Somberly, helplessly, they watched the man whose eyes stared up at the vaulted ceiling. His lips no longer moved.

CHAPTER

8

By the time Renwick had crossed the Dutch frontier into Belgium, the green camper was well ahead of him, mostly out of sight except as a distant blob when the road ran straight. Here, the long flat stretches of well-tilled fields and windmills had given way to a gentle rise and fall of land. Blue canals, reflecting the color of the summer sky, were replaced by streams edged by woods. By the outskirts of Antwerp, the camper had disappeared from view completely, probably taken some turnoff to a picnic ground or park on the perimeter of the city. Good luck to you, Nina of the sparkling blue eyes and golden hair and warm, ready smile. Good luck to you. But why Antwerp? Why not Brussels?

He kept his speed steady, like the other travelers on the road, fore and aft, all dutiful citizens. It made for pleasant driving: no zigzagging in and out like a demented hornet, no one tailgating and forcing the pace. He could relax, thinking now only of Essen and Rotterdam, of Theo and the monies paid out to Kurt Leitner; but mostly of Theo.

Should he try to suggest that the West German authorities pick Theo up? Or should he still go along with their decision—standard practice, he had to admit—to keep watch on Theo's movements and contacts? He hadn't much choice: his pet project, International Intelligence against Terrorism, would have no powers to detain or arrest. Like Interpol, it could only track down, gather the evidence, and ask the participating countries to make the arrest. Or get them to demand extradition if that was necessary. But, he reflected, have we sufficient proof to set things in motion? The answer was a definite no. The evidence was circumstantial. As yet, he promised Otto Remp presently of Düsseldorf, Herman Kroll late of Leipzig, Theo. As yet...

When he entered the busy streets of Brussels he noted a small white Fiat, which had chosen the same route as he had, following him still more closely. He hadn't noticed it until he was just south of the frontier, and from there it had kept its place in line, like all the others on the road, staying four cars behind him. Someone tailing him? Had someone picked him up as he left Crefeld's office on the Prinsengracht? Kept him in sight all the way to the garage near Central Station? All the way to the Breda road? Damn me, he thought, for an idiot, too occupied with Nina and her friends, with Crefeld and his information about Rotterdam, with Theo, to notice anyone following. If surveillance had occurred, it was pretty skillful. Expert job, involving two or three men passing him one to the other. He would have noticed one man dogging his heels through the streets of Amsterdam. Yes, an expert job. If it had occurred.

He tested that, now, by heading for the crowded center of the city, without too many twists and turns to betray the fact that he had been alerted. In spite of the heavy traffic, the white Fiat hung on, at a safe but definite distance. So he didn't drive to his office or his apartment, or make for the garage where his rented car had been delivered that morning, but left it in the parking area of the Dove, a thriving and expensive restaurant. The Fiat decided to park there, too. No one got out. Perhaps the prices had scared him off, or—more seriously—the man at the Fiat's wheel was alone and now debating whether to follow or wait. Always a mistake, thought Renwick, to put one man alone on a tail. He could have radio contact, though, and be calling for a backup at this very moment. So be quick, Renwick, quick but casual.

He made a leisurely entry into the Dove. Once inside its fashionable gloom, he headed for the bar. He ordered a short drink, paid for it, gave himself just enough time to make sure that the man he had briefly glimpsed wasn't following him after all, and then left for the men's room. If his memory of this place was accurate, there was an adjacent service door. His departure was speedy. Into a passageway dodging a waiter with a loaded tray, passing the clatter and heat of a busy kitchen, taking a back entrance into a small courtyard, another exit from there that led into a short stretch of cobbled alley. No one in sight. No one waiting at the other end of the alley, either, or in the narrow street that brought him into the Grand' Place. There, in the huge square dominated by seventeenth-century façades, he could ease his pace, blend into the constant movement of people, pass the outdoor cafés, flower stalls, elegant restaurants, and reach a street where taxis could be found.

Within a minute, he was being driven to the air terminal, a short haul, where he had left his own car that morning. Five more minutes—he was counting each one—and he was in his Volkswagen of nondescript gray, joining the stream of cars leaving the city. Twenty minutes at most, and he would be in his office. No one was following.

First, he must call Jake Crefeld, who would be back in The Hague by this time, warn him that the House of Bruna on the Prinsengracht must be under observation. Because of Jake or because of me? he wondered. Who had led to whom? Always a baffling question, but one that needed answering.

Renwick, in his private office mostly occupied by a wall of filing cabinets, a desk with two telephones (one line to the general switchboard downstairs, another for direct outside calls), and a couple of hard chairs that kept visitors alert and attentive, wasted no time. He dialed Crefeld's own special number. If Jake wasn't in his office, he'd have to try Crefeld's home, something he disliked doing: no scrambler available there.

His call was answered promptly on its first ring. But it wasn't Jake at his desk. Nor Johan Vroom, Jake's assistant. The voice was recognizable: Luisa, Jake's faithful secretary, who, like Vroom, had gone back to The Hague from Brussels along with her boss.

"Working late, Luisa?" Renwick asked, his voice light, his manner easy. When she hesitated, he added, "Renwick speaking."

"Oh, Major Renwick—I mean Colonel—"

"Half colonel," he corrected her.

"I was putting my desk in order; so much to clear up at the end of the day." She sounded flustered. But then, he had caught her at Jake's desk, not at her own in the outer office. That didn't surprise Renwick, though. Luisa was not only efficient but also officious, the perfect factotum who would drive him crazy. Her command of English was perfect, thank heaven. That saved Renwick from floundering around in his meager Dutch. "Is the Brigadier available?"

"No."

"Do you expect him soon? Or has he gone home?"

"He said he would come here first, on his return from Amsterdam."

"Is Major Vroom there?"

"No. He hasn't returned."

"Oh?"

"He left about half past four. It was—some kind of emergency, he said."

There were always emergencies, thought Renwick. "Leave word for the boss, will you? Ask him to telephone me."

"Your number?"

"He knows it," Renwick said. "Good night, Luisa. Don't work too hard."

He went scouting in the small refrigerator next door, where there was also a cot, a closet with his tennis and running gear and change of clothes, an adjacent bathroom. He found some cheese and hard-crusted rolls, apples, a bottle of white wine, and drinkable milk—the remains of yesterday's lunch. He chose the milk rather than the wine: it would settle the tension building up in his stomach. The cheese was a mild Edam, the rolls still fresh. It was all the supper he needed at this moment. He ate it slowly, worrying about Jake: what had delayed him? Then he went over today's mail and the morning newspapers. And waited.

At nine-fifty, the call came on his private line. It wasn't Jake. It was Johan Vroom, his voice easily identified by the American accent he had brought back, along with a Virginian wife, from two years at Georgetown University, but his initial words were too quick, too emotional to be fully understood.

"Take it easy," Renwick advised, his own tension rising. He could see Vroom's face, thin and sharp, with its dark brows knitted.

Vroom sounded hoarse. "I've just got back from Amsterdam. Crefeld is dead." His voice was unsteady, then he mastered himself, went on. "I got the word at sixteen hours twenty-five. I—"

"Dead?" Renwick repeated blankly. "Dead?"

"Heart attack, they say." Vroom was bitter, almost savage. "But I think—"

"Hold on, hold on. Get the scrambler working." Renwick reached for his own, adjusted it to receive. He drew a deep, long breath, steadied his own emotions.

"Okay," Vroom said. "Can you hear clearly?"

"Clear enough. So you got the word at twenty-five past four?" Just over half an hour after I said good-bye to Jake, fit and strong, vitality bursting out all over him.

"Yes. From the Bruna building—that's where he was found. In the hall, halfway to the front door."

"Was he already dead?"

"Not then. Paralyzed. He was taken to the hospital, and I went directly there. But too late. Then I went to his office—just to make sure that nothing else had been stolen. You see—in the hall—all that had been found was an attaché case lying beside him. But he had had a briefcase, too. I saw it this morning as he left for Amsterdam. Valuable papers inside it, Bob. A police report—highly confidential. Sorry I can't say more. He said he would be seeing someone who would be interested in it."

Renwick hesitated. Then, as a precaution, he asked, "Only one person?"

"Must have been. Luisa was told to pack lunch for two—have it ready early this morning."

"When was she told?"

Vroom was mystified. "Yesterday, of course. She always prepares the attaché case for his Amsterdam meetings."

"When did Jake receive that highly confidential report?"

"Yesterday. It came by special messenger. He read it, then showed it to me. We have been working together on—well, on a problem connected with—well, the report was a possible addition to the solution of that problem. About one of our undercover agents."

About Amalie possibly, thought Renwick. Not about Theo, thank God. Vroom knew only a tenth of the problem, perhaps not even that. "And after Jake showed the report to you?"

"He put it in his briefcase."

"Not in his safe?" Renwick was surprised.

"That was later. First, Luisa brought us our coffee, and he made a special call to someone—don't know who."

To me, thought Renwick. "Then he told Luisa to pack lunch for two people—for the following day?"

"Right. And he put the briefcase in the safe once Luisa had left the room."

"Who knew of his visit to Amsterdam?"

"No one except Luisa and me."

"Don't forget the man who had lunch with him."

"He worries me. He's in danger, too—he knows the contents of that report."

"What if he was followed from the Bruna building but managed to shake the tail?"

"He's still in danger—if he talks about that visit."

"You're in danger also. Jake discussed that report with you."

"With the door closed and no one in the outer office."

"Not even Luisa?"

"She was in the pantry at the end of the hall, making us that cup of coffee."

"Who, besides Jake, had access to the safe?"

"Only I had access." Vroom's anxiety sharpened. "Security is tight. Day and night guards in the corridor, alarm signals—"

"Take it easy, Johan. Access to the safe may have been unnecessary. All that was needed was someone in your antiterrorist section to be alerted to watch for any special delivery from—a certain quarter." From Rotterdam.

"Someone here? Alerted?"

"And saw the document arrive; then made an outside call to his contact, who'd pass on the word to someone who could arrange the theft."

"And Crefeld's death."

"And had me followed from the Prinsengracht." But at least I know now, thought Renwick, I didn't lead the killers to Jake. It was the Rotterdam report that focused interest on the Bruna building. Whoever planned all this was well informed. Recent information, too: the Bruna building was secure until today.

Vroom said sharply, "You took your time telling me."

"Just like you. We've both been circling around each other." Renwick's voice hardened. "So give me the details. Who found Jake? Was he able to speak? Who telephoned you?"

"The telephone girl—from the Bruna switchboard. There was a card in Jake's pocket marked *Emergency: Call at once*—with my number on it."

"Who found him?" Renwick insisted.

Vroom plunged into the telephone girl's description of the scene in the hall. "She swears it's true, she didn't invent it. He tried to speak, could only say one word. He said it twice. Umbrella." There was a pause. "Everyone else in the hall thought she was crazy."

Renwick said softly, "Not so crazy. Tell me, Johan—there's an autopsy going on right now?"

"Yes. I've sent one of our medical men to attend it."

"Call him. Tell him to look for a small, a very small puncture of the skin—not a needle mark, not a hypodermic. Not a deep puncture, either; that wouldn't be necessary. And it's probably some place that could be overlooked, some place seemingly protected by clothing. So have Jake's suit examined for a neat little hole that would overlie the puncture—shoulder, back, thigh, wherever the point of an umbrella could have been easily aimed as the trigger in its handle was pulled."

Vroom was silent. Then he burst out, "The Bulgarian refugees—the writers who were working for Radio Free Europe!"

"That's right." There had been one, perhaps two mystery deaths of Bulgarian intellectuals in London, from a raging fever that ended, after four days, in heart failure. Then another intended victim, in Paris, had dodged a full attack and lived to tell about the incredible weapon: an umbrella. It had been a sensation in the newspapers for almost two days. *Vive détente,* Renwick thought. "Let me know what your doctor discovers. Whatever poison was used in Jake's case, it was something damned speedy. Not the usual four-day fever."

Vroom was hesitant. "But the umbrella was always used logically—in a crowded street or subway. Why now, in an empty hall?"

"In Jake's case, a briefcase had to be snatched. He would have hung on to it if a delayed poison had been used."

"I get it. Instant paralysis, and no one around to notice the briefcase being stolen? Yes—" Vroom's deep breath was noticeable—"that's possible. But why not a cyanide pen? Much simpler."

"Jake would be watching for that, wouldn't he?" I bet he was keeping as much distance as possible from the man in the hall, averting his face, holding his breath, ready to raise the heavy attaché case as a shield. Jake, thought Renwick, had known of too many cyanide attacks. "One thing is certain: the report from the Rotterdam police must have been dynamite. It wasn't complete, though. They were still checking on the possible destination of that man who came off the Duisburg freighter. So hurry them up, if you can, and let me know—"

"Oh, God," said Vroom, "how do you tell them you've lost their confidential file? It was a special favor from the inspector to Crefeld."

"Do you know the inspector?" More important, does he

know you well enough to grant *you* a favor? Renwick wondered. For that matter, do I really know Vroom well enough to ask him to replace Jake on the Interintell Committee? One thing is definite: I had better contact all its members, tell them to recruit replacements. Jake's death has proven that necessary. Jake...I'm going to miss him, I'm going to miss that man.

Vroom was talking about his knowledge of the Rotterdam police inspector who had recognized a safe house when he saw it in an undercover report about suspected drug smuggling. "Bright lad," Vroom finished.

"Young?" Renwick liked that idea.

"Yes. About our age."

In spite of the weight of depression in Renwick's heart, he almost smiled. Vroom was thirty-seven, two years junior to Renwick. "Only people over forty call that young."

"I feel eighty tonight."

"You'll be taking Jake's place, of course?"

"I'll fill in. Until they find someone..." Vroom sighed.

"Who is eighty?"

"Oh, well, I've had no experience in the field. I'm a desk man. Analysis and—"

"Stick to that." You've a pretty little wife, Renwick told him silently. "Leave the action to unmarried types."

"No guarantee that I'll live. Look at what happened to Crefeld."

"It happens. Listen, Johan, when you are finding out about Jake's office—who had access, who drifted in and out—just remember one thing."

"To trust no one?"

"Play it safe. No open phone calls to Rotterdam, or to me."

"You think we have a mole in our department?"

"All the best people have that nowadays," Renwick said bitterly. "But perhaps not a fully trained mole—just a small mouse picking up crumbs of information."

"We must meet—"

"Carefully, carefully."

"Carefully," Vroom agreed. "I'll keep you informed. About the umbrella. About Rotterdam. About my search for the mouse."

"I'll be here around six every evening. Until next Friday. Then I leave for ten days' vacation." A visit to his own country would be a vacation, Renwick hoped, even if it was coupled with a little business. Suddenly, he felt tired and sad and drained of words. "Good night, Johan. A bad day for all of us." He switched off, went into the small room next door, flung himself down on the cot, stared up at the ceiling.

Half an hour later, Renwick rose and went back to his desk. Not to work. No more work tonight. He picked up his telephone and called Thérèse. She was long in answering, and his hopes faded. Then he heard her voice clear and light, *"Ici* Madame Colbert." His heart rose.

"Hello, Tessa," he answered. "What about seeing—"

"Bob—I've been trying to reach you all day. The party is off tomorrow night."

"Forget tomorrow. I want to see you tonight."

"Tonight? It's eleven o'clock. I'm just getting ready for bed. Oh, really, Bob, why didn't you call me earlier?"

"I'll be with you in twenty minutes."

"But you can't come here. Not tonight. Mother has just arrived from Bruges—she's staying with me for a few days."

He broke into English. "Tessa, I need you."

Thérèse hesitated. "She's asleep in the spare room. At least I think she's asleep."

"Lock her in," he suggested, and heard a ripple of laughter.

"I believe you would," Thérèse said. "But no, Bob, we can't risk it."

"Then what about my place? I'll be outside your door in twenty minutes in my little Volkswagen. Just pull a coat on. No need to dress."

"And how would I look tomorrow morning, leaving your apartment in nothing but some black lace with a coat pulled over it?"

"In twenty minutes," he said.

Luck held. At this time of night, traffic through the approaches to the city had eased. Renwick reached Tessa's apartment with three minutes to spare. She was waiting, and watching: he saw the light in her living room flick off. He found he was smiling. Tessa, never forgetting her upbringing by that old battle-ax from Bruges, switched off lamps, went marketing in the mornings and counted her change, turned down the heat when she wasn't indoors, didn't leave the radio or television playing, and yet looked like a girl on the front cover of *Elle*. She dressed like it, too: a combination of much taste and some money. That came from her interior decorating business, certainly not from her late husband, who had provided her only with eight years of miserable marriage. Now she was free, and staying free by choice; a convert, through sad experience, to complete independence. Which suited Renwick's own life style. He'd marry someday, once he was content to stay with a desk job and concentrate on analysis and evaluation. But now—well, you served where you felt you were useful. In his line of business, that could mean unexpected absences, indefinite hours, friendships and secrets that couldn't be shared even with a wife. Nor could danger be shared, ever-present danger making her vulnerable, a hostage to fortune. Perhaps some men could carry that load of worry around in their minds; he couldn't.

And there was Tessa at last, her smooth dark hair highlighted by the bright door lamps, a white coat covering what she was or wasn't wearing, coming decorously forward. Then her pace quickened as she neared the car's opened door, and she was beside him, eyes smiling, lips soft and inviting.

CHAPTER
9

In the week that followed, the work piled up on Renwick's desk, and he was on the point of deciding to postpone his visit to New York. Another four days, what did it matter? But suddenly it did matter. A report came in from Richard Diehl, of West German Intelligence: Herr Otto Remp, of Western Travel Incorporated, had left Düsseldorf and was now said to be in the United States. Diehl had contacted both the CIA and the FBI, but no confirmation of Remp's movements was available.

Diehl's inquiries at Western Travel Incorporated had been discreet, but produced no further information. Remp's sudden departure was considered normal: he was now making a world-wide tour in connection with the firm's expansion into West-East Travel. He would set up financial arrangements and oversee the selection of qualified staff to begin operations early next year. Such things took time, various employees of Western Travel had stated. They were more interested in the promised increase in their pay, once West-East Travel was established. As for Remp's itinerary, the same list of place names was supplied; but when he would visit these countries, or how long he would stay, depended on any difficulties he might encounter. He would overcome them, an assistant manager had said emphatically: Herr Remp was a seasoned and successful negotiator.

Indeed he was, Renwick thought as he read the report. A very successful con man might be closer to the truth. Shipped out, had he? Yet Renwick couldn't blame the West Germans for that. This was no sudden exit by Theo: it was long planned, carefully arranged. Once out of Germany, he was free: no extradition possible unless there was evidence of a crime. If the Germans had even one piece of real evidence against him, they would have arrested him four weeks ago.

So all we can do, Renwick decided, is to watch him. Where? *Now said to be in the United States* . . . If this was accurate, then it seemed as if Theo had started his travels in the opposite direction from his listed itinerary. It had begun with Istanbul, gone on to Bombay, Singapore, Hong Kong, Honolulu, and ended in Los Angeles. Or can we even be sure he will take that list in order? Why not Los Angeles, then jump to Bombay, just to keep us guessing? Difficult to follow him in any strength: two of the countries concerned were outside of NATO, while Hong Kong and Honolulu thought more of the Pacific than they did of either Atlantic or Mediterranean problems.

If only, Renwick's mind raced on, if only we had Interintell all set up and ready to go. With luck, it would be in good working order in another two months. Two months...And where will Theo be then? What will he have already accomplished? The places listed were possibly accurate. Possibly? More than possible. Theo as Otto Remp, big wheel in an expanding travel agency, would have to give his company a true list, for the simple reason that he would indeed be expected to open branch offices in these cities; and if he didn't— if he switched to other locations—he'd rouse so many questions back in Düsseldorf that his entire job would be at stake. Which meant he would have blown, all by himself, a most useful cover. No, no, Theo wasn't stupid. Remember, too, that Theo had no way of knowing that he had been traced to Essen, far less to East Germany. If he had known, he wouldn't be setting out on this long business trip; he'd be in East Berlin, heading for Leipzig at this moment.

Thank God, thought Renwick, that no one did try to stop him leaving Düsseldorf. He'd have got away, in any case, either by a sudden maneuver or by the help of his lawyers. And he'd have known we were onto him. End of the trail for us. Reappearance of Theo a year, two years later: just a slight deferment in plans. His agents, gone to ground, would be there to carry them out. They never give up, these bastards, thought Renwick; they'll take one big step backward if that lets them jump two forward.

He rose and went into the bathroom. He pulled wide the open neck of his shirt, splashed the cold water over his face. Then he stared at himself in the small mirror. He looked normal, not like a man under the worst attack of anxiety he had experienced in a long time. He smoothed down his rumpled hair. If you were Theo, he asked himself, in what country would you begin? Wherever you had most to do, to arrange.

You'd make sure of all that before you moved on to less important places on your list.

So, Renwick decided, no postponement of New York. He'd leave tomorrow. There was a full afternoon and part of the evening ahead of him before he packed and saw Thérèse.

He began reading a folder that dealt with three thousand fully equipped Soviet troops now in Cuba. When does Washington admit this? one report ended bitterly. (Six weeks later, to keep the record straight, Washington admitted it.) Renwick just shook his head, and moved on to a bulkier file dealing with a Soviet breakthrough in thermonuclear fusion. Renwick was no armaments expert, but he knew enough to be able to maintain a credible cover. Three hours, four reports, and one final staff meeting later, he could consider he was actually ahead of schedule. Except for one thing: news from Vroom at The Hague. He had heard nothing at all, either about the confirmation of the use of an umbrella in Jake's death or about Rotterdam's additional information on the travels of a man once known as Kurt Leitner. Or about the mole in Crefeld's section. Which could mean nothing at all had been discovered. There must be something, Renwick thought irritably. Vroom knows I'm off on my own travels tomorrow. So what's delaying him? It's five o'clock now. Do I just hang around here hoping for a call from The Hague?

Ten minutes later, as he was packing his tennis gear (part of the vacation myth), his telephone did ring, a call from the lobby downstairs. A special messenger had arrived from The Hague with a sealed envelope to be delivered to Renwick. "We've checked it," the sergeant on duty was saying. "No booby trap. The messenger's credentials are in order, too."

"Then have it sent up."

"That's the trouble, sir. The messenger has instructions not to hand over the envelope to anyone except you. Shall I have him escorted up to your office?"

Vroom is really taking no chances, Renwick thought. But I don't have any messenger, however reliable, coming up into this department. "Tell him the house rules."

"I've tried that, sir. He insists he must see you. He has a verbal message to deliver."

"I'll come down," Renwick said. He reached for his tie, pulled his shirt sleeves into place and buttoned the cuffs, found his jacket, and left.

The lobby was crowded and bustling at this time of day.

Between forty and fifty people, some in uniform, some in civilian clothes, were in constant movement in and out of the building. The sergeant and two guards were at the desk near the entrance. No sign of any messenger. "Where is he?" Renwick asked.

"Over there, sir, standing by the bulletin board. Gray hair, dark-blue suit, and a cane."

"I see him." The man was holding the large envelope tightly against his breast. "Doesn't trust anyone, does he?" Renwick asked as he started toward the somber-faced messenger: a man who took his duties seriously, Renwick thought as the stranger caught sight of him and, after a moment's hesitation, came to meet him. The man moved slowly; his left leg limped heavily. And then Renwick noticed that the cane was held in the wrong hand—the left hand. No proper balance for any injured left leg. He's faking it, Renwick thought, suddenly alert. A crowded lobby, a press of people, a walking stick instead of an umbrella? He halted abruptly, let the man approach. What now?

The maneuver was subtle. The envelope slipped from the messenger's free arm, fell to the floor. The man tried to pick it up, but his left hip appeared to make that painful. "Sorry," he said. "Could you?"

So I bend down for the envelope, and the tip of the cane just happens to strike me? Renwick said with a smile, "Sorry, too. I've a slipped disc." He kept his eyes on the walking stick, took a step backward. "We'll call the guard, shall we?"

The man's face froze; he made an attempt to reach down, stumbled slightly. The cane seemed to skid on the waxed floor, came pointing up toward Renwick's thigh in a sharp angle. Renwick caught it midway on its shaft, held fast. He could feel the full strength of the man's arm trying to direct the cane at its target. "Easy, easy," Renwick said, twisting the cane suddenly to slacken the man's grip. "Or do you want to lose an eye?" The man stared at him, let go, ran for the entrance.

"Stop him!" Renwick shouted, and the two guards came to life. The man never reached the front steps. "Detain him for questioning," Renwick told a startled sergeant. "Make sure he doesn't escape," he added grimly. "Get highest security onto this."

The envelope contained only two sheets of typed paper giving this week's weather reports for western Europe. Renwick left it in the sergeant's charge as evidence of an attempt at false entry. The walking stick he trusted to no one but carried it carefully upstairs, not even risking the elevator with its jostle of people. He'd let the laboratory boys experiment with it. Pressure on the handle at a certain spot that ejected a miniature pellet coated with poison? And then a raging fever that would begin to work on him halfway across the Atlantic?

Down in the lobby, the brief sensation had subsided. Few had even been aware of it. "Another kook?" someone asked, and got a shrug for an answer as the man, now subdued and under heavy guard, was led away.

Renwick reached his office, placed the cane carefully along the center of his desk, its tip turned well away from him. He telephoned Security, just to make sure they'd fully understand the possible importance of this prisoner, and then called Evans in the lab. He explained, quietly and succinctly, what was needed. "Is this one of your jokes, Bob?" he was asked. So he lost his temper and let a few curses burn up the wire. Within ten minutes, Evans and an assistant were carrying away the cane, handling it with the proper respect.

Strange, thought Renwick, that it takes a string of oaths and a voice raised like a drill sergeant's to make people listen. As for the fact that he would look like a bloody fool if the cane turned out to be harmless—well, he'd just have to sweat that one out.

He poured himself a Scotch and settled down to wait for Evans's report. The grip of his right hand was still painful, a sharp reminder of that short desperate struggle in the lobby. The man had recognized him, had come forward to meet him without waiting for a signal from Renwick. The man had known in which building he'd find Renwick's office—and in the huge complex of NATO's sprawl, that was quite an achievement. Especially when Renwick's office was in no official listing, and when his name was in no directory. But what really perturbed Renwick now was the feeling that he had seen that man before. Just once. Fleetingly. Yet in circumstances that had stamped the solemn face—gray hair, tight lips, pointed jaw line, high-bridged nose—on Renwick's memory.

*   *   *

His phone rang. It wasn't Evans. It was Millbank, whose office lay at the other end of the hall. "I've got Vroom here," Millbank said. "He's down from The Hague arranging a memorial service for Crefeld. You knew Crefeld didn't you?"

"Yes."

"Then I'll bring Vroom along to meet you. Okay?"

"Okay."

"We'll be with you in three minutes flat."

"Okay."

But nothing was okay at this moment. Delayed shock, Renwick told himself. The attack had shaken him more than he had been willing to admit: a near thing. Much too near. Much too quickly arranged. Someone—and who the hell was someone?—had wanted to deal with him before he left for America, make sure he'd never return. One moment more and he might have lost that battle if the assailant's will power hadn't suddenly weakened and let his grip loosen. That was all it would have taken, one moment, in a crowded lobby with only two or three bystanders even noticing—and not understanding a damned thing.

The door opened and closed. "Are you all right?" Vroom was asking as he waited for Renwick's greeting. It wasn't given. Vroom noted the untouched drink, the half-packed bag, and drew up a free chair to face Renwick. He might have congratulated me, Vroom was thinking, on the way I managed to see him—no attention drawn to this particular visit, buried as it was among all the other interviews I've been conducting in the last two hours. "Sorry I couldn't contact you before this. But I do have some results to give you. First, about Crefeld's death."

That captured Renwick's attention.

"It was murder. A close examination of Crefeld's body and clothing showed a matching puncture on both. A miniature pellet no bigger than a pinhead was found under his skin."

"What poison, this time?"

"No definite opinion, as yet. Does that matter so much?"

It didn't. Dead was dead.

"Secondly," Vroom went on, "about the Rotterdam report. It was easier to approach the police inspector than I had thought: their files on the safe house near the docks are missing, too. The Narcotics Squad is blaming the antiterrorist section, and they in turn are blaming Narcotics. But what isn't missing is the final report on the escape route of that man who came off the freighter from Duisburg. For the simple reason that no report has yet been drawn up. There are just pieces of information from the detectives who were trying to follow his trail from the house in Rotterdam."

"Trying to? They didn't succeed?"

"Not altogether. Again we had the conflict between two different departments: the antiterrorist section taking over midway—almost at the end of the trail, in fact. Which was at Schiphol Airport, in Amsterdam."

"An international flight? To the United States?"

"No. At the time he disappeared, there was only one flight scheduled to leave—for London. En route to New York, possibly. That could be.... Why else did he study so much about the United States in that safe house in Rotterdam?"

Renwick nodded a tentative agreement. "But how the hell did he manage to dodge the cops at Schiphol?"

"By the way of the men's room. It had only one entrance, no window. He was only one minute there. Walked out with a couple of strangers. No longer wearing a raincoat or his black wig. They were found later, stuffed into a cistern. And he had help. Someone ran interference for him—collapsed against the cop just as he was about to enter. A gray-haired man who seemed to have lost his balance." Vroom paused, frowned. He was getting ahead of himself. Further information about the gray-haired man belonged in the next segment of his story. He liked things in their proper order, neat and clear. He was saved from his indecision by the telephone.

Renwick reached for it at once. "This should be Evans— I hope. Pour yourself a drink, Johan," he said quickly, and gave his full attention to the message. "Better contact Security," he told Evans. "Make sure that they don't release that man, and they don't spread the word around about assault with a deadly weapon. Once you've tracked down that substance, the charge could be attempted murder. Meanwhile, tell them to keep it quiet, will you? Also, you'd better get in touch with New Scotland Yard's antiterrorist squad. The poison their scientists found in a similar pellet was ricin." Renwick replaced the receiver, looked at Vroom's startled face. "So I wasn't a damned fool, just damned lucky." He picked up his glass and drank deeply. "Go on. He took a flight to London?"

Vroom recovered from his bewilderment. Murder? Whose

murder had been attempted? He said, "That was the deduction, once he couldn't be found anywhere in the airport."

"Any attempt to check the passenger list of that flight?"

"Not until later. Much later," Vroom conceded unhappily. "I made my own inquiries, but remember that all this happened five—almost six weeks ago. And the carrier was British Airways. We should have any further checking done in London."

"What about immigration?"

"I checked with them, too. They have a record of eleven American citizens traveling to London that day from Amsterdam. No names."

"They had no warning to keep a watch for any American?"

"The man wasn't *known* to be an American. And the policeman who was watching the passengers loading had a different description in mind. Not just clothes and hair, but also the wrong age. When he was wearing a raincoat, the man had seemed middle-aged—hunched shoulders, slow movements, heavy around the waistline."

Renwick nodded. "An adept performance." More than police routine had been necessary. If only Crefeld's department had been alerted five weeks earlier...Well, it hadn't been. "I'll see what help Gilman can give us in London," he said, but without much hope. The trail was cold by this time. And yet—Renwick's thoughtful gray eyes studied Vroom's unhappy face. He said, "There may be one link, one connection. Someone tried to eliminate me today. He was using a cane, not an umbrella."

"The gray-haired man in the lobby?" Vroom burst out. "Attempted murder? Was that the one? My God, I never realized....Just saw him being taken away by the guards. I was coming in with Millbank, stopped at the desk for identification—" Vroom broke off, shook his head. "I thought—we all thought—it was someone trying to gain unauthorized entry. Kept it quiet, didn't you?" Then Vroom's thin dark face broke into a wide grin. "I think we've got that link. Two, in fact."

"Two?" The obvious one was quite enough, thought Renwick: the identity of the man who had been followed from Rotterdam to Schiphol Airport had to be protected at all costs. Crefeld had known of his importance; I could know; so, get rid of us both along with any existing copies of that police report.

"Two," Vroom insisted, now enjoying himself. "And that gray-haired man is both of them. Attempted murder today; running interference at Schiphol five weeks ago. It's the same man, Bob. What do you think I was doing at the Rotterdam police station a couple of days ago? Studying a composite drawing of the man's face, reading his description. Gray hair, sharp jaw line, narrow lips, thin, high-bridged nose."

That could be the man, all right. Renwick stared at Vroom. "Why didn't you tell me—"

"I was just coming to that. He is part of our investigation on the informer in our department." There was no disguising the triumph in Vroom's voice.

"So you've traced him."

"Her."

"Luisa?" Jake's devoted secretary? It was hard to believe.

"Not too difficult to uncover, once I started thinking the unthinkable and delved into Luisa's private life. Her first reaction to Crefeld's death was embarrassing—that was the night I returned from Amsterdam with the news and told her I was convinced it was murder." Vroom was thinking of that scene. Luisa waiting in Crefeld's office, hours later than her usual routine allowed, her face contorted with the shock, her abnormal protest, a voice rising into hysteria: "But why— why? They didn't have to kill him, they didn't have to kill him!" Vroom shook his head. "She went to pieces. Excessive anguish. Yet the news about the stolen briefcase had left her quite unmoved."

"You told her a lot." Renwick's quiet voice held a touch of reprimand.

"I trusted her," Vroom said simply. "But after that hysterical reaction—well, we started investigating. Hard. Intensively. She's been living secretly with a man called Maartens. Younger than she is. Handsome. Ardent. Most flattering for a woman over forty who isn't particularly attractive."

"Was she aware she was being investigated?"

"We made sure she was aware. And we got results. She asked for sick leave, pleaded doctor's orders, a visit to a clinic in Switzerland. But we caught her yesterday at the German border, on a train for Berlin."

"You've had a busy week," Renwick observed wryly.

"Unpleasant," Vroom admitted. "Most unpleasant. Except that Maartens is an important discovery. We had his telephone tapped. He has been very busy in these last eight days since Crefeld was murdered. He has connections here in Brussels as well as his little love nest in The Hague. He works on women, and through them." Vroom drew a snapshot from his pocket, handed it over to Renwick. "Ever come across him?"

The photograph was poor—hazy background of café tables—but the fair-haired man, face turned for a quick moment toward the hidden camera, was clear enough. I've seen him, Renwick thought: I've seen that face. Once. Briefly. With the gray-haired man? Renwick kept his voice normal. "Works on women, does he?"

Careful now, Vroom warned himself. He said, "That's his specialty. Some through sex. Some—" he hesitated slightly, avoided Renwick's eyes—"through money. Subsidizes a failing business, brings it new clients and success."

Renwick's face was unreadable. "Any connection with the gray-haired man?"

"Luisa admitted she had seen him once, when he paid a late-night visit to Maartens. She never learned his name, but her identification of him—we showed her a copy of the composite drawing made by the Rotterdam police artist—was definite."

"So that's how he got directions to this building? From Maartens, by way of Luisa?"

Vroom shook his head. "Not through Luisa. She didn't know where you worked. That information must have come from—from someone in Brussels." His voice was hesitant. He almost spoke again, and then cut himself off.

Renwick looked at him sharply. Vroom was the voluble man, quick-witted, with phrases to match that often covered his nervousness. Tonight he had been showing a new assurance—perhaps the prospect of promotion, a sense of accomplishment, had added to his confidence. So why all this backing and filling now? "Did Maartens telephone Brussels?"

Vroom nodded. "He wanted information about you. His call—" again there was that agonizing hesitation—"was to an interior decorator here. To a business he subsidized eighteen months ago."

And suddenly the long-buried memory of those two men rose to the surface. A cold bitter evening in November just after he had met Thérèse Colbert—a visit to her apartment an hour earlier than intended—two strangers stepping out of Thérèse's door into the elevator, brushing past Renwick as they pulled on their overcoats. Gray hair, blond hair; one with a sharp beak of a nose, a pointed chin; the other, smooth-skinned, even-featured. Clients, Thérèse had told him without any prompting, two men who were in the hotel business giving her a contract as their decorator.

Vroom was saying, "The name of that firm is..." Again the tactful hesitation.

"Colbert et Cie," Renwick said.

"Of course, Madame Colbert would have no idea what his real purpose was. He'd ask information about your office, your movements, in a roundabout way."

"Of course." Renwick rose abruptly. And there, in Thérèse's apartment, Maartens would have made sure of a photograph for his files. Together with a photograph taken as Renwick left Crefeld's building, his identification had been easy. Small wonder the gray-haired man could recognize him on sight. Renwick drew a deep breath, slowly poured out two more drinks. "One for the road," he said as he handed Vroom his glass.

Vroom took the hint, got to his feet, spoke hurriedly. "Yes, we've spent too much time together. But I'd like to question the gray-haired man. Can that be arranged?" He finished his drink quickly. "I'll see you on your return from America. There is still a lot to clear up."

"A lot," Renwick agreed. "Can I keep this photograph of Maartens? You've other copies?"

"Of course. And one thing more—" Vroom remembered as he reached the door—"did you ever come across the name Herman Kroll? This man Maartens was one of his young men. That was some time ago—in East Germany—before Kroll was killed in a helicopter crash." With that, Vroom was out of the door, leaving Renwick to stare after him.

Kroll—Otto Remp—Theo; and the man Maartens. Renwick set aside his glass. In that last second, Vroom had given the most important piece of information of all. Unwittingly. Didn't he know Kroll's death had been faked? That Theo was alive and functioning? Of course he couldn't have known: talk of Kroll had been only between Crefeld and Renwick, and Crefeld had never lived to take Vroom into his confidence. I was too slow, too damned stupefied, Renwick thought, too shocked by Vroom's information on Thérèse....I ought to have told him about Theo. I ought to have warned him. And why didn't I even get around to telling him about Interintell?

Or asking him to take Jake Crefeld's place? I was just too damned stupefied.

He still was. The agony of betrayal was hitting him hard. His fist clenched and struck his desk a heavy blow, as if physical pain could be a substitute for what he felt.

Then he thought, I can either sit here and get soaking drunk. Or I can take a good look at myself and start reshaping my life. Too much desk work in these last eighteen months. Apart from my visits to Essen and Amsterdam, I have been Brussels-bound, tied by responsibilities. That came from my promotion, of course: paperwork and conferences, committees and decisions. Too much of that by day. And by night? Smooth white arms, blue eyes wide with sympathy, and wild embraces...

Forget her, he told himself. You can't even allow your vanity the luxury of doubting Vroom's word. Vroom had been too sure of his facts. A man intent on becoming Crefeld's replacement was not going to jeopardize his promotion by wild statements or half-cocked deductions. Vroom had more information than he had divulged. Out of friendship—or at least a desire for friendship? Or perhaps give him credit for believing this could happen to any of us. As it had done to Crefeld, with his complete trust in an invaluable secretary. Except in your case, you goddamned fool Renwick, you weren't deceived by a woman's efficiency. You fell for the oldest game in this sorry world.

All right, he told himself now. Make out your report of today's events, deliver it along with your resignation. This was as good a time as any to turn the rumors—a nice little piece of camouflage, he had told Jake—into something that could be believed by the opposition. But he would have to make two things clear in that report: he had no interest in Kurt Leitner or Maartens. As for Thérèse Colbert—no connection with Maartens, just a woman on the make.

Quickly, he uncovered his small typewriter, began batting out the reasons for his tendered resignation. There were two of them, compressed into one page—the Big Man upstairs liked all urgent business condensed to a quickly readable statement. First, the assassination attempt in this building (briefly described) proved Renwick was under close scrutiny: all future work, based here, was now rendered difficult and ineffective. Second, Thérèse and his stupidity (no punches pulled there) made this resignation obligatory.

Yes, he decided as he read his brief report: this would be believed by men like Theo. The acceptance of his resignation would also be believed. (And, he reminded himself, any more mistakes like Thérèse and his resignation would indeed be accepted. How could he have been so easily gulled—as if he were a naïve twenty-one-year-old, filled with trust in sincere blue eyes?)

The office upstairs would still be open. The Big Man worked late, never left his desk until eight o'clock at the earliest. It was now almost seven. Renwick reached for the telephone and made a request for an emergency meeting. His luck, grim today, had turned: his request was granted.

What if, he wondered wryly as he took the elevator upstairs, I lose this gambit? What if I have my resignation actually accepted? Then no backing for any future work—no base for operations, no files to be called on, no computers to help, no pool of information, no agents working under my control. Without all that, a project like Interintell would be dead, and Theo's man, so carefully groomed for future stardom in America, could slip away from us as adeptly as he had left Essen, Rotterdam, Schiphol Airport.

His luck held. He won his gambit: Theo, and the file Renwick had collected on Mr. Otto Remp of Düsseldorf, won it for him.

By nine o'clock he was back in his office, finishing his last job of clearing up. He made one final telephone call. To Thérèse.

She sounded slightly rushed, a little flustered. "Oh, darling—I'm so glad you called. I've been trying to reach you for the last hour. Tonight's impossible. I'm just leaving. Mother isn't well—I've got to go to her."

"At this hour?"

"It isn't so late—a short drive to Bruges."

"How long will you be there?"

"Overnight. We'll leave tomorrow for Switzerland. Mother's doctor says she ought to visit a clinic."

"Sounds dull for you. Where is it?"

"Near Lausanne. It depends on Mother's health how long we'll stay. August is soon here, the shop will be closed for the vacation, so I'm free to be with her. You do understand?"

"Of course."

"What about you? When do you get back here?"

"I don't. I'm looking for a job."

There was a marked silence. "Where? What kind of job?"

"I'm still deciding. I've had two offers—London or Paris."

"You are really resigning? No more Brussels?"

"I handed in my resignation tonight."

"Oh, Bob!... There's the doorbell. It must be my driver to tell me the car is waiting. Good-bye darling." And the line went dead.

Good-bye, darling. Just like that? He replaced the receiver, shaking his head. He had heard no doorbell ringing, although her telephone was on the table in the small hall only six feet away from its entrance. And that long silence—a hand covering the mouth of the receiver? There had been no sound whatsoever—a complete clamp-down. Who had been with her? he wondered. Who had shared the call, prompted her to ask what kind of job and where?

Or perhaps he was overreacting. What had he wanted to hear from her, anyway? Words that would reassure him she hadn't known what she had done. A voice that recalled memories of nights past. Goddamned fool, he told himself. The verdict is in but you want it miraculously reversed. Quickly, cutting off all sentiment, he seized his bag, locked the door of his office suite, dropped the keys with Millbank's office.

Millbank, the complete diplomat, had been waiting to make a formal good-bye. He was still a little stunned, but secretly delighted, with his sudden promotion. "I'll take care of your office," he reassured Renwick as they walked together to the elevator.

He would, thought Renwick: he was a capable man. "Couldn't be in better hands."

Millbank dropped his voice. "How long?"

"Indefinitely."

"Oh?"

"But I'll keep in touch."

"Yes. Any time we can help—"

"I'll lean on you," Renwick said. "See about renting my apartment, will you?"

"I've got a secretary who's already putting in her bid."

"News does get around."

"We'll have your things stored for you."

"There isn't much that's valuable. But have the place gone

over thoroughly, will you? We don't want your secretary having her love life bugged."

That startled Millbank. "You think someone had your
place wired for sound?"

"Shouldn't be surprised. But don't let that bother you. I
never talked business there."

"Careful fellow," Millbank said.

"Not careful enough." There was no smile now in Ren-
wick's voice or eyes. But his final handshake was warm.
"Take care of the shop." He will, thought Renwick; otherwise
I couldn't be leaving with this feeling of freedom.

"Good luck, Bob."

"And to you." With committees and conferences and files
upon files. Poor old Millbank, he didn't know what he was
getting into. But it was possible Millbank was the type to
enjoy it all.

"One thing—" Millbank had suddenly remembered—"I
had your travel arrangements changed as you asked. You'll
have a—"

"Yes. Thanks for that," Renwick cut in. He would have a
stopover in London to have a quiet session with Ronald Gilman. Agenda, in order of importance: Theo; the "American"
from Rotterdam, traveling to London on June 14; the tropical-
disease expert, Dr. Ilsa Schlott. The last two items were difficult, might be impossible to trace. But Ronald Gilman had
the resources, and the brains and the tenacity. Interintell
was no longer an idea; it was now being put to work. "Thanks
again," Renwick said, as the elevator arrived at last.

"Just watch out for men carrying walking sticks," was
Millbank's parting advice to the elevator's closing door.

Yes, Renwick thought, news does get around. But in this
instance he had no objections. He couldn't help wondering
what kind of reputation would be left him, once speculation
had done its work: an attempt on his life, so he picked up and
ran. Just part of the picture, Theo. You haven't much of an
adversary, have you? You can forget about me. You've more
important enemies to worry about.

CHAPTER
10

"So," Nina O'Connell said, "this is Greece." She shook her head. In the dusk, the empty sands and the curve of gray-dark waters looked desolate. More desolate still were the half-dozen blacked-out houses edging the shore. Even the lights in the adjoining café, the one sign of possible life on the beach, were dismal. Madge came stumbling out of the camper, stiff from the long jolting ride, over the Yugoslav border and down through the mountains to this stretch of flat land. She halted abruptly. "Where are we?" she asked in dismay.

Guido Lambrese said, "It isn't Athens, certainly. Or Sounion. Or Delphi." Then he added a quick phrase in Italian that sounded far from complimentary. His friend Henryk came to stand beside him. "Perhaps it will look better by daylight," Henryk suggested.

Nina glanced at the Dutchman, the perpetual optimist, but tonight his constant smile had vanished. Nothing will look better in the morning, she thought; this place can never look better at any time. She eased her tired shoulders, tossed her long fall of hair back from her brow, said nothing.

Marie-Louise and Sven Dissen joined the silent group. The French girl, small and plump, dark eyes flashing indignantly, said, "But this isn't a campsite! Where do we get water, where do we—"

"At the café," James Kiley said as he reached them. Tony Shawfield was still in the camper. Fussing as usual, Nina thought, checking all his equipment before he locked everything tight. "We can get food there, too. We won't need to do any cooking for the next few days. Come on, let's get moving." His arm went around Nina's waist, and he drew her toward the café. The others straggled behind them.

Sven looked back at the far-stretching sea, halted briefly as he pointed over the darkening waters. "Isn't that the Gulf of Salonika?" He was the avid studier of maps and guide-books. Not, thought Nina, that all his information has done any of us much good except to remind us of the capital cities

99

we've bypassed. Europe had become a series of campsites, she decided angrily, with long stretches of scenery in between. Jim had always, of course, his day in the nearest town—collecting the cash that he had waiting for him at Basel, Innsbruck, Zagreb. And Tony, guarding the camper and fiddling with his radio while Jim was absent, would have his day in town as soon as Jim had returned—there always seemed to be some piece of equipment he needed to have checked or replaced. Of course, she had to admit, all of the campsites had been adequate; some of them attractive. And there were the necessary chores to take up time: laundry—my God, she thought, at the end of this trip I'll never want to drip-dry a shirt again—the buying of food, the cooking of meals, the cleanup jobs to keep litter from gathering; details that no one had thought about back in the comforts of Amsterdam.

"Or," Sven was saying, forever the purist, "should we say Thessalonica?"

Guido, the expert on Greece and archaeological remains, set him right. "It's the Thermaic Gulf. At the head of it—to the north"—he waved a hand up the coastline—"we have Thessalonica. Or Salonika. What does it matter? It is still only a northeast corner of Greece."

Madge ventured, "How far away is Salonika, Jim?"

"About twenty miles. Thirty-two kilometers, or thereabouts." Kiley sounded vague.

"And to the south of us?"

"Katerini."

Sven said, pleased with his memory, "And across the gulf, there are three peninsulas with hotels, bathing beaches, rich Greeks—"

"Too crowded, too expensive," Kiley said and forestalled any questions about why hadn't they headed in that direction. He went on easily, "The beach here is just the same kind of sand. We can catch up on our sun tans without bankrupting our budget." And that silenced them completely: compared to Shawfield's expenses with gas and oil and camping-site fees, and Kiley's expenditures on basic foods, they hadn't spent much. It was practically a free ride. Who could grumble at that?

Kiley's arm tightened around Nina's waist. Her silence worried him. "Are you all right?"

She nodded, her eyes studying the six miserable cottages

they were now passing. They were deserted. No sign of life at all.

Kiley spoke hurriedly. "This is a fishing village, but in summer the fishermen move down the coast, nearer Katerini. There's a better market for their fish. In winter, they come back here—this part of the bay is more sheltered."

Nina looked at the thin trees sparsely scattered, the bushes that bunched in clusters where the sand ended and the rough road began. To think that only a hundred yards away there was the main highway, down which they had speeded this evening, down which they could have traveled all the way to Athens. "What made you choose this place?"

"Tony phoned ahead from the frontier and found that the camping sites near Salonika were all full. It's August, the European vacation month. A campsite manager told him about this beach." He didn't need to invent any more excuses. Nina's attention was now on the Café Thermaica, which they were entering. Simple but clean, he noted with relief: scrubbed wooden floor, oilcloth covers on the long tables carefully washed, a charcoal fire against the back wall glowing and ready to broil the fresh fish piled on a small serving counter. He ignored the two men, roughly dressed, who sat in the darkest corner of the room, just as they were ignoring him and the group of hot and crumpled people who came straggling behind him.

The woman who owned the place ("Can be trusted," Kiley had been told; "widow of a faithful party member who died fighting the fascists") switched on an extra light bulb along with a brief smile of welcome that softened her usually intense, haggard face. Beside her, a very young girl and an even younger boy ("niece and nephew, orphaned, negligible" had been the report on them) hesitated nervously, dark eyes fixed in wonder as they stared at the foreigners. Then at a string of sharp commands from their aunt, they hurried forward to serve.

They were so anxious, so willing, so pathetic, that Nina's resistance eroded. To please them, she even drank the *ret-sinata* wine that tasted of turpentine, tried a mouthful of cold rice wrapped in cooked vine leaves, ate—with enjoyment—the crusted black bread. And the fish, when it came to the table at long last, was excellent.

Kiley relaxed. Exhaustion and hunger had been the trouble. Now, everyone around the long table was in a more docile mood. But we nearly had a mutiny on our hands, he told himself. He rose, saying, "I'd better find Tony before we eat his dinner." And then to Nina, "Okay now? Hardly the Ritz, I know." He left, glancing briefly at the two men in the corner, who were making a glass of wine last all through their evening. I'll be with you, he told them silently, once I get this crowd bedded down for the night.

Shawfield had finished receiving the latest instructions and was locking the thin metal doors that protected his special equipment. "Coming, coming," he called to Kiley as he slid into place a screen of medical supplies and canned foods—all tightly secure on narrow, deep-lipped shelves backed by a wooden panel—that covered the metal doors exactly. A neat job, he thought—as he always did each time he used his radio transmitter—a pleasure to work with: so carefully set into the side of the camper that no customs official yet had noticed the depth of the shelves was less than the total depth of the supply cupboard. He closed its wooden doors and locked them, too. All complete.

He let Kiley enter. "No Istanbul," he reported. "It's canceled."

"Why?"

"Turkish Intelligence is snooping around Istanbul. Something has stirred them up."

"So we go directly to Bursa," Kiley reflected.

"That's where our meetings are scheduled, anyway. So no problem."

"But that could cause us more trouble. We nearly had a mutiny tonight," Kiley said as they left the camper.

Shawfield locked its door, turned to stare at Kiley. "Now what reason could they—"

"This beach is the reason. No Salonika. Before that, no Dalmatian coast, no Belgrade, no Venice, no Vienna."

"This beach suits you and me. You gave them a good explanation about why we had to come here. They accepted it."

"And what about my absence tomorrow—for three days and nights? And your three to follow?" A long stretch, thought Kiley worriedly. Usually, his one-day disappearances had a standard explanation: someone to be interviewed, a place visited for a future story, a finished article to be mailed to a Paris agency that handled free-lance material. All that, and the collection of money waiting for him at prearranged banks or travel agencies, took care of a busy day with no time for ordinary sightseeing. Marco's standard excuse had also worked: the firm subsidizing his trip had sent various spare parts ahead to be picked up in certain places; wanted tests to be made and radio reports on the results. "It's a long absence this time. They're just in the mood to start questioning—"

"Bloody hell, we can't arrange our schedules to suit their whims. You've heard them: six different ideas on what they want to see at every discussion session."

That was true enough: everyone with his own demands, his own interests to satisfy. "Democracy, it's called," Kiley said with a laugh, and turned Shawfield's anger into a smile.

Shawfield said, "You'll find an additional excuse to shut them up. Tell them you've got an old college friend who married a Greek girl, and they're living on her father's farm not far from here. Can't refuse their invitation, can you?"

"It might work. If Nina were persuaded, Madge would listen. Possibly the others, too." Nina, surprisingly, had more will power than all the rest added together. "A strong-headed girl."

"A spoiled little bitch."

"No. I thought that at first. She's just too damned independent, that's all."

"You know how to handle her."

"Look, you told me to ease up." Kiley's lips tightened. "In Innsbruck—"

"Only as far as you were concerned. Keep her tied to you, but no real involvement on your part. Wasn't that your plan?"

Kiley was silent.

"You aren't in love with her?" Shawfield asked sharply.

In love? Perhaps I've been in love since I first caught sight of her standing at the foot of a staircase in Wigmore Hall. Kiley drew a long breath, said, "Don't be a damn fool, Tony. I have other things on my mind. Being in love is no part of them." He pretended some amusement, changed the subject back to the six days ahead of them. "What excuse will you give for your absence?"

"I'll find one. The engine needs extra special attention after all these mountain passes, don't you think? I can take the camper to Katerini and have it checked there—a three-day job." Then Shawfield glanced at his friend. "Or perhaps

I should start giving them pills for malaria?" He slapped Kiley's shoulder, led the way into the café.

The air was bland, still warm from the intense heat of the day. There was no sound except the gentle lapping of the sea. A night with little moon, but the sky was free of clouds and the stars were brilliant. Nina sat alone near the water's edge, her arms folded around her knees, her head tilted sideways with her blonde hair falling unchecked over her brow. *Hardly the Ritz*...Jim's parting shot had rankled. I don't and never did expect the Ritz, she told the ripple of dark water; dammit, I've only been in the Ritz once in my life, when Father took me to that reception in Paris. For a moment, she had an attack of nostalgia: life had seemed so much simpler then. Now, she was completely and thoroughly confused. About Jim Kiley. And because of Jim Kiley.

What had she done to change him? He had been in love with her—she knew that. Then something had happened—but what? Her fault? He was still friendly, still affectionate, but different, too. Ever since Innsbruck, all through Austria and that mad dash through Yugoslavia, he was changed. It was her vanity, she tried to tell herself: she had always been the one to push a man aside; no one had ever pushed her. Except—the long-past memory quickened—except Robert Renwick...But not this way; and now that she was no longer a girl of fifteen, she could understand what Bob must have felt. A silly romantic, she chided herself, embarrassing the hell out of a man who liked you. Liked you a lot. More than liked you. If only you had been—well, you weren't.... God, how you cried your eyes out after he left Geneva so suddenly, went back to Brussels....And then she realized that this was the first time she had ever thought about Renwick's feelings instead of remembering her own. Perhaps, she thought in surprise, perhaps I'm growing up at last. Perhaps—

She heard the light footsteps only as they reached her. One hand caught her shoulder, another laid its fingers across her lips as they opened to cry out. "Let's not wake the others," Jim Kiley said as he knelt beside her. "All asleep." Except Shawfield, who was again back at the café, deep in quiet talk with two hard-bitten characters. Kiley's fingers moved from her mouth to caress her cheek, trace the line of her neck down into her loosely buttoned blouse. He dropped back on the sand, pulling her with him. She tried to speak, make one small protest, but his arms were tightly around her and his lips silenced hers with a kiss that was as vehement and hard as his body.

She tried to free herself, but he caught a long strand of hair and pulled her back. Nina cried out in pain. He eased his grip but still held her captive. Now his kisses were soft, smothering. At last he released her. "Is that what you want? You just want to play at love. Is that it, Nina?"

She sat up slowly, tried to fasten her blouse. "I just want to be sure of love," she said. She was close to tears.

He noticed her trembling. Wrong tactics, he told himself. "Did I scare you?" he asked gently, his hand caressing her hair, fondling her cheek.

Three times, she thought. First, the silent approach. Then the sudden attack—as if I had no say at all, just a puppet that danced when he pulled the strings. And now—this sudden change to tenderness, all passion turned off in one short moment. It was this change that upset her most of all. Yes, he scared her.

"Nina..." He sat up beside her, slipping an arm around her waist. "You've got to understand. These last weeks have been pure hell for me—close to you, watching you. I'm sorry if I scared you."

Her smile was nervous, uncertain. "You shouldn't slip up behind me in the dark. I didn't know who it was."

He relaxed a little. "Stupid of me. But you looked so tempting, sitting there, lost in dreams."

"If I had been an enemy sentry," she said, confidence returning as her voice steadied, "you could have slit my throat. Where on earth did you learn that trick, Jim? In the army?"

He turned that aside with a laugh. There had been no army listed in James Kiley's history. "In the Boy Scouts." That was safe enough; untraceable. He had got her laughing, too. So he kissed her again. "A pity to waste the starlight." Then he said, "You are right, you know. We can't let emotions run away with us, not when we're crowded into a camper, and six other people are noticing every look we exchange. And at the campsites, there are just too many strangers around, children everywhere, no privacy. Not like this beach. It's the first time we could get away from everyone. Do you realize that, Nina?"

She nodded, staring out at the quiet sea.

"So you forgive me?"

She nodded again.

"Once we get rid of the others—"

She turned to look at him.

He cursed himself for that slip. Nina had scattered his wits. "Perhaps in America," he said, "we'll get away from them."

"Aren't we going back to London?"

"First, we have to travel through America, don't we? I'd like you to meet my uncle. He'd certainly want to see me. And you."

This really startled her. She had been thinking so much about Asia and the Far East that she had forgotten about America. "No doubt my father will expect to see me, too. He'd be hurt if I didn't make an effort to get in touch."

"Then I can meet him?" Would Theo approve of this suggestion? he wondered. It could do no harm at the moment; later, if Theo had other plans, it could be canceled. Excuses came in the hundreds. It was only necessary to choose the most acceptable and make it believable.

Her amazement grew. "Jim—do you really want to meet him?"

"I'd like his approval."

Nina waited. But nothing was added. What was he trying to say? That he wanted to marry her? "You're the strangest man, Jim Kiley."

"Then we make a very good pair." He drew her close again and kissed her. She's so damned beautiful, he thought.

And Nina, looking at the handsome face, the tender eyes, felt a surge of emotion. "Jim—what do you really want?" she asked. He made no reply to that except to kiss her and pull her—gently, he warned himself—down onto the sand beside him.

"Almost midnight," Kiley announced, so suddenly that Nina, still under the spell of bright stars, could only look at him in surprise. "I've an early start tomorrow." She sat up slowly, staring at him. He gave her three kisses, lightly, one on each eye, one on her lips. "That's for the days I'll be away."

"Three days?"

A visit to an old college friend, Kiley explained: he had married a Greek girl, was now helping her father run his tobacco plantation just west of Salonika. A couple of days with him, and a day in Salonika for a visit to the bank, and he would be back here to join her on the beach.

"And then Tony has his three days?" she asked bitterly. "What about us?" Six days in this place...

"You'll all catch up on your sun tans, swim, relax. The next stage of this journey won't take you near any seashore. It will be a long haul until we reach Bombay." As for Tony, he went on explaining, he'd need three full days to get the camper thoroughly overhauled. He was worried about the front axle; had to make sure everything was in good condition for some of the mountain passes through Iran, Afghanistan. Sure, there were trouble spots there, but she wasn't to worry. In Salonika, Kiley would arrange for local guides to meet them and ease their way, help steer them clear of the fighting. There was a definite highway all the way into India—didn't she remember the two campers they had met at the site where they had stopped after crossing the Yugoslav frontier at Ljubljana? A German teacher, wife, and two young children in one, an Englishman with wife and three children in the other? They were taking the same route; it was practically becoming a main thoroughfare nowadays. "I'll make sure it's safe," he ended, watching her reactions warily.

"Of course you will." He always did. "So we are here until Saturday." She frowned.

"For rest and recreation," he said, smiling.

"Then we'll reach Istanbul by next Tuesday at latest?" That would be the fourth of September, she calculated, and time enough to collect the money that would be waiting for her at Türk Express. She had written her father about that from Basel, weeks ago—just in case Robert Renwick had forgotten her message.

"We'll cross the Bosporus into Asia by ferry from Istanbul, and make our main stop at Bursa. It's the old Turkish capital; you'll find it interesting. You could even make a visit to Troy from there. You'd like that, wouldn't you?"

"No stop at Istanbul?" she asked in dismay. "What about Topkapi, Saint Sophia, the Blue Mosque, the Bazaar? Oh, Jim—we *can't* miss them!"

"The good campsites are already booked full. August, you know—the holiday month in Europe. We'll be better off in Asia. Bursa is old Turkey, authentic. No hordes of tourists from France and Germany and—"

"Jim! We must have two days at least in Istanbul."

"Come on," he said, raising her to her feet, "my bus leaves for Salonika at six in the morning."

"Leaves from where?"

"On the main highway, just as the road to the café branches off."

That was only a short distance away. She remembered the sudden cutoff they had taken that evening, and the large modern hotel that stood well back from the highway at that point. Its gay blue and yellow wall decorations had caught her eye: Mondrian design, Matisse colors. "Why didn't we park at the hotel?" she asked suddenly. "We might have had hot baths there." I'd give anything for a long hot tub, she thought, brushing her shoulders and hips free of sand. Her hair, too, was filled with fine grains. She'd never sleep tonight, even if she combed her hair for an hour.

"It's a motel, government-run," he said curtly. "Doesn't allow stray campers. Come on, Nina, come on." He was already starting over the beach.

She gave one last look at the quiet, dark waters. The salt wouldn't help her hair, she decided, even if the sand was washed out. She caught up with him, saying, "I'm going to the café." It hadn't closed as yet: meager lights still showed.

"Why?" he asked, worrying now about Shawfield. He must still be there.

"To get a bath. They have a tub, surely."

"Zinc, no doubt. And three inches of cold water."

Remembering her horrified retreat from the café's one toilet, the size of a telephone booth, stone floor with a hole in the center, overpowering smell of chloride of lime, no window, a hundred flies, she admitted that Jim could be right. "Okay," she said in resignation. "I'll have a swim even if it leaves my hair sticky and dull." She halted, began lossening her blouse, unfastening her jeans.

"Nina!" He pointed to the four sleeping bodies sprawled near the caravan.

"Dead to the world," she told him. "Coming?"

He turned away, began walking toward the road.

Where was he headed? The café? Okay, damn you, she told him, stripping completely, and ran into the tepid waters. She had almost a hundred yards to wade before her waist was covered. No swimming possible but she could float, letting her hair spread around her head like a silver halo under the stars.

* * *

Quietly, Nina slipped into the camper, decided against switching on its light and wakening Madge, fumbled her way toward her narrow bed. This must be the way you lived on a submarine, she thought as she reached into her overhead locker and groped for a towel: every foot of space accounted for, and not one inch wasted. Comfortable enough, once you remembered what to avoid and spared yourself some sharp bumps. All these windows would be useful now that the camper was heading into hot weather, although their thin curtains, even if they gave privacy, weren't any protection from being awakened by early-morning light. A long sleep, a real bath, that was all she asked for. So far, she had taken everything as it came—except for six days stuck on this beach with all the rest of Greece beckoning. And Istanbul? We'll see about that, she decided as she finished drying her hair. Jim could be persuaded. If he loved her, he could be persuaded.

"Nina?" Madge's voice was half asleep. "Turn on the light. Where were you?"

"Having a swim."

"Alone?"

"Yes. Jim balked."

"Why on earth?" Madge wakened enough to raise herself on one elbow. "Too romantic for him?" She was speaking slowly, softly.

"He's a mystery to me." There was a long silence. "What about going into Salonika tomorrow? There's a six o'clock bus."

"In the *morning?*" Madge shook her head. Her weak laugh turned into a yawn.

"We'll all be awake by then with that damned sun."

"Not me. I'll be sleeping until noon." Madge sank back on the pillow. "Another time, Nina," she said dreamily, totally at peace with the world.

"Are you all right?" She's been on edge all day, thought Nina. Why this sudden bliss? The bunk wasn't as comfortable as all that.

Madge's answer was another small laugh, another yawn.

"We'll be here six days, Madge."

That roused no response.

Nina said, "We may not even stay in Istanbul—just a quick ride to the ferry."

There was a brief response. "No Istanbul?" But there was no indignation, no outburst. Instead, Madge was suddenly asleep.

Nina laid out a fresh shirt for tomorrow. She'd ride with Jim into Salonika, borrow some drachmas from him until she could change dollars in a bank. Then she'd leave Jim, wander around, see the Byzantine churches and their decorations, and then—oh, well, when she felt good and ready, she'd find her way to the bus stop. Or even take a taxi back here. She checked her wallet and counted her traveler's checks, packed sketchbook and pencils into her large shoulder bag. All set.

Her rising spirits declined sharply when she discovered Madge had drunk most of the water in the carafe beside the collapsible basin, leaving her a couple of sips. No washing of her face, no brushing of her teeth tonight. She'd have to rise at five tomorrow and get to the café and scrounge some water from the Dragon Lady. Those poor kids, she thought as she slipped under the sheet: that awful woman with the harsh voice that sent the two children scurrying. Remembering their thin faces, their large eyes watching the foreigners leave so much on their overheaped plates, she wondered what she had to grumble about.

It was going to be a restless and brief night. She threw off the sheet, let the gentle breath of air from the wide-opened windows glance over her body. It was easy to rise when her watch told her it was almost five o'clock.

She left Madge deeply asleep. Outside, in the pale light of a new day, the others were asleep, too. Tony Shawfield was among the scattering of living corpses. No Jim. Was he having breakfast at the café? But he wasn't there, either. The small boy was already up and around, sweeping out the earth floor. Her English was beyond him, so she unwrapped her facecloth and showed him her toothbrush and soap and did some sign language which amused them both. With teeth cleaned and face washed at the kitchen sink, and a quick visit to the obnoxious toilet—the bushes might be better in future, she decided; oh, the joys of carefree travel—she waved a cheerful good-bye and took a short cut over the rough grass to the highway. She'd have breakfast in Salonika while she studied her guidebook.

As she reached an outcrop of rock just above a short line of trees along the highway, she saw the bus approaching. It was headed north—the right direction, but its timing was wrong. Barely half past five, her watch told her. Either it was slow or the Greek buses ran ahead of schedule. She saw Jim rising from his seat on the grass, but he didn't move forward, didn't signal. The bus trundled past, its top covered with string-tied suitcases, baskets, cartons. She halted in astonishment, hesitated, and then—as a car approached from the south and Jim stepped out—she retreated behind a meager bush, as if it could hide her confusion. So he's hitchhiking to Salonika, she reassured herself; probably the bus is too crowded with local people market-bound.

She was about to call out, wave, start toward the highway. Jim was too quick for her. The car was too quick. It barely stopped, a door wide open to let him step inside before it sped on. She dropped onto the grass beside the bush, her shoulders sagging along with all her plans. Then she heard the car again. It had made a turn at the driveway to the Mondrian-Matisse motel and was coming back. For a brief moment she felt a surge of hope. Jim had seen her in spite of all the scraggy bushes around her. He was coming back to get her.

But he didn't. The car was traveling at high speed toward the south.

For many forlorn minutes, she sat watching the empty highway, the lonely stretches of dry grass and gray-green scrub. Then she raised her eyes to the background of hills, of far-off mountain ranges etched against a sky that was turning a clear light blue. She rose, her plans still vague but beginning to have shape like those distant peaks on the horizon, and started toward the motel. I'll damned well show him, she told herself.

The motel was a recent addition to the landscape. New, its bright colors and bleak design proclaimed: give me another twelve months, add some condominiums and cafés, a shopping center, a pool and tennis courts—then my three stories jutting high over this empty plain won't seem so lonely. Certainly, thought Nina, the large parking space set to one side of the building showed that expectations were high for the future, although now there were only a dozen cars or so waiting for their owners to awaken and have breakfast. There was also a solitary bus, a large glossy model, the type that toured Europe and supplied package deals. Apart from a gardener watering the young trees and plots of geraniums, and a man hosing down the bus while he chatted with a girl perkily dressed like an airline stewardess, the motel seemed deserted.

Better and better, thought Nina: anyone in charge would have leisure to talk, give advice, even help. How would she begin? Transportation, first: there must be a taxi or a car for hire. Or—she studied the bus: traveling where? And after transportation had been arranged—she'd even settle for any nearby railway station and a slow train to Athens—she'd get help with a phone call all the way to the Maryland shore. It would still be Sunday there; midnight, possibly; perhaps later, if the call to her father took a little time to go through. But, once he got over his annoyance about being hauled out of bed, he'd listen. And then, finally, information about inexpensive hotels in Athens. Elated by her three-point program, hoping for the best, she called a cheerful good morning to the bus driver and the girl, answered their surprised stare with a friendly wave, and entered the lobby.

Empty; except for a boy mopping the floor, a middle-aged woman absorbed with passports behind a cluttered desk, and a tall young man, impeccable in a neat black suit, with carefully brushed hair and a melancholy Greek face. Its normally impassive expression gave way to a look of astonishment as he stared at the newcomer. She had a moment of nervousness; then she smiled. "Good morning. I need your advice. Would you be so kind as to help me?"

The young man's dark eyes scanned her expertly. Clean and crisp blouse, neat-fitting jeans—and who would quibble with them since the Jacqueline Onassis era?—expensive shoulder bag and shoes, a charming voice, quiet manners, and, above all—he ceased staring—a figure and face that were remarkable. "Yes," he told her in excellent English, "how may I help you?" He left the desk, came forward to welcome her.

This may just work, thought Nina, her blue eyes sparkling.

By half past seven, she was back at the camper pulling a dazed Madge out of bed. "Rise and shine! Come on, come on! Pack and get ready to move out. The bus starts loading within the hour."

"Bus?"

"For Athens."

That wakened Madge completely. "But how—"

"Tell you later when we're squashed into two back seats."

Traveler's checks, obligingly cashed by the motel manager, had helped to secure that space. Impossible, the bus attendant had said in halting English, impossible to sell any seats: this was a private tour. Yes, there were four vacancies in the back row, the girl admitted sadly, but impossible to sell. The emphasis was slight but definite—a timid hint? Nina had taken it. "Then don't *sell* them," Nina had suggested. "Just let two be occupied? This is what I intended to pay for a car to take us to Athens," and quickly she slipped fifty dollars into the driver's unrefusing hand. (He had been shaking his head all along, over wasted space and agency regulations.) She then had clinched the arrangement by assuring them that she and her American friend, a girl just like herself, wouldn't bring much luggage, would find their own lunch, keep to themselves, be practically invisible, cause no trouble at all. The little conference broke up in smiles and handshakes. Nina's budget was sorely dented, but it was a long journey to Athens, and a hired car—if one had been available—would have cost twice fifty dollars and bankrupted her completely. She eased her attack of conscience by noting the clean but fraying cuffs on the driver's shirt; both he and the thin-faced, harried attendant were obviously overworked and underpaid. Tips from a busload of package-deal tourists being steered through the wonders of Greece couldn't be overly generous.

"But how—" repeated Madge.

"Wear your best shirt," Nina advised. "If we hurry, you'll have time to brush your teeth in a real bathroom."

"What about breakfast?"

"We'll get coffee and a croissant at the motel, too."

"Motel?"

"Shut up, darling. I'm thinking." Nina had drawn out her sketchbook, torn off a page, and was writing. "A message for Jim," she explained. "I didn't see Tony around, so I'll leave it with Guido. He seems the only one who's half awake." Nothing but comatose bodies outside. The dead and the dying. What was wrong with them? "How much wine did you drink last night?"

"Two sips for politeness."

"You slept as if you had been hit on the head."

"Exhausted." Or, thought Madge, it might have been that malaria pill handed out by Tony. Perhaps that was the way it acted. Pleasant, anyway: relaxing. "Didn't you take your pill?"

"What pill?"

"For malaria. Tony left one on the washbasin for you. You were down on the beach and—"

"Didn't see it. Malaria? But there are no mosquitoes around here?" There wasn't a pool or a stream or a stagnant puddle in this bone-dry piece of real estate.

"We should start taking them in advance, Tony says." Madge knotted the cord of her canvas bag. "Ready to leave."

Nina handed her the note to Jim. "Will that do?"

It was brief. *Taking our R and R in Athens and points east. Meet us in Istanbul, four o'clock, September 4th, Hilton Hotel. See you then, Nina.*

"He won't like it," Madge said.

"Why not? It says all that needs to be said." Nina took the note, folded it—no envelope, but let them all read it—and picked up her tightly packed bag.

"He will be worried sick."

"Good."

"Points east?" Madge asked, puzzled.

"The Aegean. We may not have much time to land on any of the islands, but we can see them, can't we?"

"We're crazy."

"Yes, aren't we?"

With light hearts, they stepped down into the strong sunlight. There wasn't one cloud in that bright-blue sky.

CHAPTER

11

Renwick's exit from Brussels by way of London paid major dividends. They didn't mature, of course, until a full month later but—even without foresight of information to come—the brief meeting with Ronald Gilman was encouraging.

Renwick was then at the stage of taking extreme precautions: if a man called Maartens, linked to Theo and East German Intelligence, had been given instructions to eliminate him, there could be a second attempt on his life. It was only when he was considered to be out of the game, showed no interest in anyone or anything connected with Theo, that he might be regarded as possibly negligible and left in uneasy peace.

He would now be under surveillance, of course. That would last until the reports on his movements became dull, repetitious, boring, and he would make them all of that. So his first twenty-four hours as a man who had quit his job at NATO—even Theo's agents would have little suspicion that his intelligence-gathering wasn't strictly on Soviet military maneuvers—were a very tricky period indeed. Yet he had to meet with Gilman, that quiet self-effacing man who had dodged suspicion for his fifteen years of highly classified work. This was not the time for Renwick to draw Gilman to anyone's attention, far less Theo's.

So there had been precautions for his visit to London. First, he changed his flight and hoped he had complicated others' arrangements. Next, he made a brief call to London from the Brussels airport, a couple of unremarkable sentences that let Gilman know he was on his way. Then it was a matter of following their previously set plans: baggage left at Heathrow until the early-evening flight to New York, a long stretch of empty hours ahead of him; why not visit the city, drop into a movie house near the Strand? The place was less than half filled, ill-lighted, and noisy with the bangs and booms from a World War II film. Gilman was already seated in the empty back row, a thin tall figure slouching in his unobtrusive way;

no one within listening distance even with any hearing device—the noise of the sound track would take care of that. Renwick slipped into an adjacent seat. He sat in silence for several minutes, making sure he hadn't been followed. But no one entered the cinema, and they could talk.

There was a succinct briefing of Gilman on Theo; Essen—Kurt Leitner and Section One of the Direct Action terrorists, his tie-up with Theo, his well-arranged escape, his transformation in Rotterdam into an American, his departure for London. "Any possibility about tracing him at this date? Through the airline record of reserved seats, handled by a travel agency that buys them en bloc and pays for them months later? An airline is bound to keep records of what is owed them. Certainly, Leitner wouldn't risk any delay in buying space at the airport. He must have been booked in advance."

"June fourteenth, afternoon flight from Schiphol to Heathrow." Gilman's face was imperturbable, as usual, but his voice was far from optimistic.

"Then there is another puzzle, smaller, less important perhaps. Ilsa Schlott." Renwick told what he knew.

"That's simpler—if she is a student at University College. Anything else?"

"Yes. Now that Crefeld is dead, I'd like you to head Interintell. Any problems about getting an office, a place for files and communications?"

"Not if I can suggest to my boss that the French would like to have the Interintell headquarters in Paris."

"They're trying hard. But they already have Interpol in Paris, so they can hardly argue against London having its fair share."

"Why not in Washington? Why not Frank Cooper in charge?"

"Frank would be the first to agree with me: no security possible with this right-to-know kick they're on." What foreign intelligence agencies would trust their secret files on terrorism, their classified information on the doubtful activities of American citizens, to Washington? "That really would dry up our sources of information." He paused. "How quickly can you set up headquarters? It's urgent."

"We'll make it most urgent. Give us a month." Gilman already had an office selected, a skeleton staff in mind. "I'll be on a quick visit to New York at the end of August."

"See you then. Meanwhile, get the word about Theo to Oslo and Copenhagen. I've already briefed Claudel, in Paris, and Diehl, in Germany. And what about Vlakos, in Athens? And we need someone in Ankara."

"I have a good friend there." Gilman's quiet smile lightened his calm face. "It seems that Interintell is really on its way."

With a file on Theo as its first case. Most fitting, thought Renwick: Crefeld's death would not be meaningless. "Would you meet with Vroom? Brief him on Interintell, get him to replace Crefeld—if you think he fits in."

"Don't you?"

"I'm not sure." Or, wondered Renwick, is my bruised ego still smarting? "He's making himself too visible for my taste. Could be a danger—to himself, to us."

"Justifying his promotion? That may wear off. What other choice do we have?"

"Not much. I was betting everything on Crefeld." He could sense Ron Gilman's empathy. It was a good moment to leave. Renwick rose, walking unhurriedly to the nearest fire exit for a quick but safe route back to Heathrow.

Precautions, precautions...They seemed comic, an unnecessary waste of time and energy. Until you remembered a man approaching you in a crowded lobby with a highly sophisticated weapon disguised as a simple walking stick.

Arrival in New York was the usual confusion when several major flights descended on Kennedy. It was natural, perhaps, that the attractive young woman who was traveling alone should look so helpless and harried as she waited for her luggage to appear on the roundabout. She had stuck close to Renwick on most of the long journey from the landing area. They had gone through immigration together, so she was American—or at least traveling on an American passport. Customs had separated them temporarily, but here she was beside him again in the main hall with the late-evening sun streaming in from the street outside. The odd thing was that, in all this time, she hadn't given him one small glance: most of the transatlantic passengers had noticed each other, exchanging the usual cursory look as they angled for the best position to grab their suitcases or compete for the attention of a porter if one did deign to arrive. For someone who was now standing at his elbow, it was strange that she seemed totally unaware of his existence. Their luggage should be arriving any moment now. Would she ask his help, delay him enough to let them leave together? And would she take a taxi to follow his?

Renwick lit a cigarette as she faced his direction briefly. His lighter missed twice, flamed on his third try. He had just time for a couple of drags before he saw his bag near two dark-blue suitcases, a matched set varying only in size, come circling slowly toward them.

"Oh!" she said, pointing to the larger of these cases, which lay far up on the conveyor and needed a long arm to be reached.

Renwick extracted his bag and her smaller case, a nice excuse to let the larger one go majestically on its way. He placed it at her feet. "Don't worry," he told her. "The other will come around again." In four or five minutes. And with an encouraging smile that was met by a look of complete frustration, he left for the door. No porters available, either, he thought with some satisfaction.

Outside was turmoil complete, taxis and buses and a row of limousines with drivers at their wheels. People on the sidewalk, people darting into the roadway to get hold of a cab. It took him several minutes to secure one, and as he threw his baggage inside to stake his claim, he noticed one limousine in particular. Its driver, impatient, stood by its opened door, scanning the crowded sidewalk. As he caught sight of Renwick about to enter a taxi, he slipped back into his seat. But his way out into the turgid stream of traffic was blocked by a tourist bus that halted, no apologies, in the middle of the road to load a group of Japanese businessmen. Renwick's last glance at the sidewalk showed him the young woman emerging, her large suitcase abandoned in her desperate haste. So was her diffidence as she saw Renwick's taxi ease through a narrow space and then speed off. Now there were two frustrated people left behind him. How nice for them if she could have emerged on his heels, stepped into the limousine with no bus to complicate the easy following of his taxi. Renwick's smile was broad. He made sure his lighter was safe in his pocket. He could take photographs, too.

He might have judged the woman on a hunch, but there had been no guesswork on the man. Fair hair, thick and waved; smooth handsome face, the type that some women, such as poor middle-aging Luisa, found irresistible. Maartens, definitely, but no longer pretending to be an embassy employee in The Hague, no longer the big hotel man throwing business in the way of an interior decorator in Brussels. Had Thérèse found him irresistible, too?

Renwick's smile was wiped from his face. "Grand Central," he told his driver, "by way of the Queensboro Bridge and down Lexington to Forty-second Street." And having established the fact that he knew his way around this town, he relaxed and didn't have to worry about the meter.

He would find another cab at Grand Central Station and drive to the Stafford, a busy hotel in the East Fifties where he could get his thoughts in order before Frank Cooper paid him a quiet visit for intensive briefing on both sides, and a discussion of tactics. (Strategy would come later, when Frank Cooper had gathered information and put the search for Theo into motion.) And that would be all Renwick would see of Frank, for the time being. Discretion was the better part of safety.

Tomorrow, he was heading for Vermont and a visit to his parents' summer cottage on Caspian Lake. (Scattered farms, groves of sugar maples burgeoning for tapping at winter's end; browsing deer by day, bobcats screaming over the hills by night, skunks dodging under the woodpiles, an occasional bear wandering down from the Canadian border.) Two weeks later, he would jaunt to San Diego for an eight-day stay in nearby La Jolla with his young sister and her husband. (Tennis and scuba diving, flowers for all seasons, people from everywhere.) After that, the mountains of Wyoming for a week with his older brother, wife, seven children, five horses, three dogs. Then a return to the East. August would be almost over. Ron Gilman would be arriving from London with full reports. Frank Cooper's news-gathering should be producing results. And Maartens, with his interest fixed on Renwick, might even be discouraged: what intelligence officer could be taken as a threat when he spent four crucial weeks in holiday pleasures with no communication, no contacts that were in any way connected with his work?

The end of August... It couldn't come too soon. Suddenly, his mind was jolted out of all those neatly planned prospects as he remembered his promise to Nina O'Connell for the beginning of September: a message to Daddy for money money money, ready and waiting at Türk Express in Istanbul. Hell and damnation, he thought, how do I put in a call to

Francis O'Connell at the Bureau of Political-Economic Affairs in Washington when I'm practicing nonexistence in New York? It's the last thing I need, making a call to a State Department number, identifying myself by name to O'Connell's secretary, being questioned by him about Amsterdam, of all goddamn places.

Then, as the taxi drew up at Grand Central Station and he was hauling his luggage onto the sidewalk, he knew one solution: he'd unload Nina's message onto Frank Cooper's broad shoulders. Frank knew O'Connell well. No problem there. Nina, Nina, Renwick was thinking, you do complicate people's lives in your own sweet little way. In a moment, he had a spasm of sympathy for Francis O'Connell, quickly dissipated as he began wrestling with more practical matters such as counting out the dollars and calculating a sizable tip. No audible thanks, either. I'm home, he thought as he hefted his luggage out of the pedestrians' way, and waited for another taxi.

A month might not seem adequate enough for a view of America, but on Renwick it had acted like a tonic. No need to judge his country by the headlines any more; now he had a wider frame of reference—people in all their variety, with all their opinions and beliefs and pride in their jobs. Sure there were some weaknesses here and there, even some rents and tears, worrying self-indulgences, but the main fabric was still strong. A good place to live, and worth a good fight. Renwick's return to New York was definitely upbeat.

"Raring to go," he told Frank Cooper over the phone. "I'll be leaving by the end of this week. What about having a drink with me? Or lunch? I know you're a busy lawyer, but..." He left the suggestion hanging. If anyone were listening in to this call, its vacuity might make it seem negligible.

"Just let me have a look at my calendar. Let me see..." Cooper's deep, rumbling voice hesitated, as if he were really consulting his engagement book. "Washington tomorrow, dammit. A prospective client. That could take until Thursday. Then Friday is the start of the Labor Day weekend. Why not join us in East Hampton? The kids and their friends will be there before they go back to school. A full house. But we'll always find room for you."

—— Renwick had to smile. Frank's summer cottage had only

three bedrooms, a giant living room where stereo played well into the night, and Frank's sacrosanct den with everything from trophies to gun rack struggling for space among bookshelves. He took the concealed hint. "I'd like that, but my new job in London begins with September. They don't allow for Labor Day over there, you know."

"What about tonight? There's a cocktail party at my place. We've just won a major decision, so I thought I'd have a celebration for my staff and our happy clients."

"Tonight is pretty well planned—dinner and theater."

"Drop in, if you can manage it. It will be a madhouse; you know how these things multiply. Too bad you didn't let me know when you were planning to pass through New York."

"I really wasn't sure myself. Next time, I'll—"

"The party begins at six. But no one will be there before six-thirty, I hope. I've got an emergency meeting midtown at four-thirty—a couple of important clients."

"Then you'd better hang up. It's almost four now."

"So it is, dammit. Hope to see you at my place—it's the old stand on Sixty-first Street. Remember? Good to hear from you."

Renwick replaced the telephone on his side table and stretched out on his bed. An emergency meeting at four-thirty... Cooper would just make it from his Wall Street office to his suite at the Stafford, kept for the benefit of out-of-town clients and his own private meetings. Renwick's room (booked by one of Cooper's friends) was on the floor below, but the fire staircase near Cooper's suite had its uses. And Ronald Gilman, who must have arrived from London by this time, would have had similar arrangements made for him. Frank Cooper was a believer in easy access: friends all together under one roof, no visible coming and going.

Four-thirty exactly. The door to Frank Cooper's suite had its lock released, ready for Renwick's arrival.

"You look well," Cooper told him, studying the younger man, lean and trim, sun-tanned, as he reactivated the lock and closed the door. There was a warm handshake, and then a quick embrace with two hefty pats on Renwick's shoulders. "Good to see you, Bob. Pick a chair. Sorry about the decor. I take what the hotel offers, but the wives of my South American clients seem to like it."

"You still make a good telephone call," Renwick told him

as he chose one corner of a spindle-legged sofa, glanced around the green-and-gold room, and took his turn at studying Cooper, now pouring a couple of Scotches at an elaborate serving tray. Cooper was a large bear of a man, big and deliberate; he had lost weight in recent years, and his face—large and craggy—showed permanent furrows. His hair, thick and heavy, was now almost white. His fine dark eyes were more serious, almost sad in expression. His clothes hadn't changed, though they hung more loosely on his big frame: thin dark-gray suit worn carelessly, and slightly crumpled—enough to drive his custom tailor into a nervous breakdown.

"Well," Cooper was saying, "you know what's expected of the typical New Yorker. He has the best intentions but he's always too damned busy to spend much time with his friends."

"Your phone is tapped?"

"Let's say that someone likes to listen to my conversations. A recent development."

"Because of me?"

"Perhaps. Or perhaps it is just someone trying to get inside information on one of our legal battles." Cooper's face relaxed as he handed Renwick his drink and then lowered himself into an opposite chair. He stretched out his long legs, raised his glass in salute. "Don't worry, Bob. We'll find him. Or her. But it's wiser, at the moment, to play along with them, give them no hint of suspicion aroused." He glanced at his watch. "Quickly, any new ideas on Theo? What's his plan, do you think?"

"It isn't clear yet. Could be aimed at America. That's my hunch. Just a gut feeling, mostly. Didn't Gilman have any more details on Theo?"

"He passed on all he knew when I saw him in London two weeks ago. Including something you didn't mention in our last meeting: the attack on you. That wasn't pretty, not pretty at all, Bob."

"It only proves that Theo's plan must be damned big."

"Any signs of interest in you recently?"

"Not in the last four weeks."

"Then any interest in me must be the result of the inquiries I was making in Los Angeles about Herr Otto Remp and his new West-East Travel bureau." Cooper pursed his lips, shook his head. "And I thought I was being careful."

"What did you find out?"

"That Theo is one smart operator. He slipped into Los Angeles, made the necessary appearance, with his lawyer and real-estate agent and his new manager in charge of the West-East office, to sign all the papers at a local bank. Also a hefty check for his newly acquired property. He had to use his Otto Remp identity, of course, to keep everything legal for that brief interlude. Then he departed as quietly as he had arrived, the office left in charge of his manager. Impossible to trace, so far—we've no idea of the name he used to enter the country or travel around in it."

"When did he make that visit to Los Angeles?"

"Damn quick. It must have been within a couple of days after he arrived here from Germany."

Before any of us knew he had disappeared from Düsseldorf. "So all arrangements for the purchase of an L.A. office must have been made while he was still in Germany. Who handled them? The manager?"

"No. The manager is a stalwart citizen. So are the real-estate agent and the bankers and the lawyer. It's the assistant manager who is not quite what he seems to be. He's the real boss of the Los Angeles branch of West-East Travel, affiliate of Western Travel in Düsseldorf. Theo's contact man, in fact. Handles the finances."

"You found out a lot," Renwick said, recovering from his initial disappointment. Of course Theo would act as quickly as possible, before any alert about his movements could be given.

"Not enough. We don't know if he is still somewhere in America; or has he left us? We've quietly circulated his description, of course, but there are a hundred ways of leaving this country without presenting a passport—even a false one."

Circulated his description . . . "You've put yourself in some danger, Frank."

"Well—like you—the more I studied Theo's case, the greater my gut feeling that this man is worth stopping. Whatever it costs us." Cooper laughed off his touch of drama, but his eyes held something of the old zest. He glanced at his watch, pulled himself out of his chair, lumbered toward the door and unlocked it.

Gilman, guessed Renwick: arrivals spaced twenty minutes apart? Frank and his experience—OSS agent dropping into unfriendly territory, CIA analyst in its early years, National

Security adviser, and now a corporation lawyer on the international scale—might just discourage Theo's recent interest in him. Renwick couldn't be sure, though: the inquiries around Los Angeles must have been extensive even if discreet. And the innocent civilian was often an ignorant one, too: he never knew when to keep his trap shut, not indulge in a little gossip to enlarge his self-esteem. Some people just couldn't resist confiding.

"He's late," Cooper said, glancing once more at his watch. "Is he staying in the hotel?"

"Sure. He has brought Gemma with him."

Gemma was Gilman's wife. "Cozy," said Renwick.

"Nice and normal. Probably they've gone shopping."

Or something, thought Renwick.

"Maggie used to try to drag me around the stores when we were abroad." Cooper's voice had softened at the mention of his wife. Even if she had been dead for eight years, her memory was still alive.

Quickly, Renwick drew him away from the past by saying, "About Theo—isn't it possible he would have invested in a furnished house somewhere in Southern California? A safe house, where his agents could stay and be subsidized by payments through his travel bureau in Los Angeles? I mean, why else would he have chosen L.A. if it weren't convenient for the payment of his people's expenses? That was the pattern he set up in Essen."

"Somewhere in Southern California," Cooper said thoughtfully. "That covers a lot of territory."

"Somewhere within easy driving distance of L.A.—two or three hours away." A hundred miles, as Renwick had discovered on his visit to La Jolla, was considered an acceptable distance to drive out for dinner. "He'd have negotiated that deal, of course, well in advance—like finding the premises for his West-East Travel branch."

"Using the assistant manager?" Cooper's interest had quickened. "Who would, perhaps, employ the same real-estate agent? But the house wouldn't be bought under Herr Otto Remp's name."

"Nor under the assistant manager's name. He'd choose something mythical: his cousin or a good friend from the East needs a winter home in sunny California."

"Could be. We'll start some checking."

And be careful, thought Renwick. Tactfully, he didn't offer

Cooper that advice. Instead, he took out two snapshots. "You should look out for these, Frank. The man is definitely one of Theo's. Maartens by name. The girl? Possibly working with Maartens. They were both in New York on the day I arrived from London."

Cooper studied the photographs: the blond man sat at a café table; the girl's picture was clearer, taken close up. "I've seen—" he began. But at that moment the door opened quietly and Gilman slipped inside. "Put that lock to work, Ron. And welcome!"

"Four minutes late. Unforgivable." Gilman was definitely annoyed with himself. "But Gemma went shopping and brought back two dresses. She had to try them on for my approval. You know how it is."

"Don't look at me," Renwick said with a grin. I like Ron's style, he thought: no false excuses about waiting on a back staircase until the corridor cleared of people. Gilman's equanimity returned. He was, as usual, immaculate; tall, thin, his pleasant face made solemn by horn-rimmed glasses, and not one blond hair out of place. The perfect picture of a quiet civil servant in one of Her Majesty's less glamorous departments. Renwick rose and joined in the general handshaking.

"Hope I didn't hold up the proceedings," Gilman said, noting the snapshots in Cooper's hand, ignoring them politely.

"Just discussing Theo and Los Angeles," Cooper said. He had briefed Gilman in London about them.

"And as you were saying, Frank"—Renwick pointed to the snapshots—"you've seen one of them? Which?"

"I've seen both. Last weekend." Cooper handed over the photographs to Gilman. "Of all the damned impudence! They came visiting my house. At East Hampton. I had gone down to the beach for my daily walk. But the rain came—it's been one hell of an August for weather—and so I jogged back. They were at my front door, trying to talk their way past Libby— that's my oldest girl. Their story? The woman said she was a real-estate agent, heard our house was for sale; there has been a lot of selling and buying around us. The man with her, exceptionally polite, handsome, almost convinced Libby I had put our house on the market. I've talked about that, vaguely, in these last few months. Once the kids are off on their own—and that's coming; I can see it—why the hell do I need a place in the country?" He took possession of the photographs once more. "Do you need these?" he asked Renwick. "I'd like to have copies made. Two more for your rogues' gallery," he promised Gilman.

Trying to get inside Frank's cottage, a polite look-around? Brief enough not to be annoying, but sufficient time to plant a bugging device? Renwick looked at Cooper worriedly and dropped all tact. "Be careful, Frank."

"I was in the business of being careful before those two were born. Or you, either. Okay, Ron—what news from London?"

"Promising, I think. The office is ready—a nice old house, narrow, four stories high—in a small side street. Top floor has my cubbyhole; and communications to keep us all in touch. Below that, two rooms of maps, reference items, filing cabinets waiting to be filled. Then there's a floor for our borrowed computer, deciphering machine, and other miracle devices. Staff selected. Some foreign contacts already established. The first floor, above the main hall, is for genuine business, with a couple of expert surveyors dealing with any actual requests for our services. The entrance hall is for reception—and security."

"Surveyors?"

"Just part of our firm," Gilman continued smoothly. "Actually, here's the full scope." He drew out two small cards from his waistcoat pocket and handed one each to Renwick and Cooper. "For the benefit of our representatives who travel in foreign parts."

In restrained type, the card's legend read:

J. P. Merriman & Co.
Consultant Engineers
Advisers on Construction Abroad. Surveys Made.

"Not bad," Cooper said. "In fact, damned good. There's a hell of a lot of construction going on all around the world. Your first-floor experts, Ron, may even make some money for you. You'll end up as a successful businessman yet."

"Not my line."

"But who's paying for all the initial expenses?"

Gilman looked bland. "Oh, there's always a little extra money available when a state sees a threat to its security. As the free countries are linked now, like it or not, danger to one is danger to all. I think they'll find that Interintell is the best investment they can make." Then he studied Ren-

wick. "Any objections to being one of our traveling representatives, Bob?"

Renwick shook his head. "I was just going over their backgrounds in my mind." He, himself, had earned an MIT engineering degree before he went into the army. Claudel? Yes,
the Frenchman had worked in aerospace dynamics before his
stint with NATO. MacEwan, the Canadian, had worked in
mining. Larsen and Diehl had been sappers. "Engineers? I
suppose so. But we're stretching it a bit, aren't we?"

"It's the one common denominator you had in civilian life.
Not much, but enough. What else would seem feasible for all
you ex-NATO types? Certainly not interior decoration or tex-
tiles and ceramics." Gilman was ruffled. "I thought you'd be
comfortable with—"

"I am, I am," Renwick cut in. "We'll have ample cover."
If no one starts questioning us too closely. But then, that's
part of our job: avoid the questions. Certainly, I'll be able to
move around a foreign country, meet officials more interested
in terrorists than in bridges, dams, or new hotels. "It gives
me enough traveling room, anyway." And Gilman had
planned well. For that all-important cover, export-import was
now suspect; so were tea or wine merchants, wandering reporters, news photographers, moviemakers, lecturers—you
name it, they've tried it. "Original," he conceded, and brought
relief to Gilman's watchful eyes. "Do I have some backup?"

"You can choose your team. Two or three. Don't you
think?"

I do think, old boy. That's the way I like to work. The lone
eagle looks damned foolish when one of his pinions is torn
off. Renwick said, "Okay. That's that."

"You'll be in London soon? You'll find Merriman & Co. at
7 Grace Street—between the Strand and the Embankment."

Cooper had a question. "And what about some aids and
comforts for your agents? Or do they just rely on karate and
smoke signals?"

"Gadgets will be provided. But from another building in
another location. That should baffle any of the opposition who
might come prowling around. All the technology we have on
the premises could be used by any modern-minded business
firm. Okay with you, Bob?"

"You're the right man for the job, Ron."

"I agree," said Cooper, and he meant it. "I couldn't have
handled it, not with legal cases piling up." He hesitated, and

then added, "And not with the climate of opinion that's fogged everything over here—I don't know if we're coming or going. Am I depressed? You bet I am." Then he tried to laugh that off. "There's one man more depressed than I am. Francis O'Connell. Telephoned me this morning, a long spiel about his daughter, Nina." He began pouring another round of drinks. "Have to watch my time. That damned cocktail party. Never could stand them. A hundred guests milling around; and that allows you one minute per person. How's that for hospitality?"

Renwick said, "What's this about Nina?" Frank, he was thinking, is not only overworked and depressed, he's also beginning to digress. He ought to take a vacation, travel across his own country for a change, lose some of his pessimism, come back to New York and Washington with his old sense of purpose restored. "Nina," he repeated firmly. "What has she done now?"

"Got her father out of bed last night with a call from some place in northern Greece. She needed her money to be delivered at the American Express office in Athens instead of Istanbul. Seemingly she decided to leave the camper."

"Good," said Renwick.

"Not permanently," Cooper corrected him. "She and her friend Madge wanted to see Athens and the islands. The camper is parked on a beach on the Salonika gulf—it's staying there for six days."

"Six days?" Gilman asked. He knew that part of the world. "Why six whole days?"

"Poor old O'Connell," said Cooper. "Never got a postcard or letter from her all across Europe." Thank God for my girls, he was thinking. "Her aunt Eunice—she looked after Nina for years, you know—never got a postcard, either. But here's the strange part: Nina told him she had written him from Basel and postcarded Aunt Eunice from Dijon and Innsbruck. Of course, she might have been trying to pacify him. He's had friends at the various embassies keeping a watchful eye for any blonde American girls traveling in a camper, but with no luck."

"But have they been passing through any capital cities?" Renwick asked. Neither Dijon nor Basel nor Innsbruck qualified for embassies.

"It seems not. He couldn't find out too much. Her call was

brief—not enough cash to spare, she told him. She had spent a lot on a bus ride to Athens."

"And after the Greek islands?"

"Istanbul. She's rejoining her camping friends there by September fourth." Cooper glanced at his watch. "My God, look at the time!" He picked up a heavy briefcase on his way to the door. "Sorry about the party, Bob. Next visit, we'll spend a couple of evenings together."

"Watch out for the uninvited guest."

"A gate-crasher? Expecting you to be there?"

"And perhaps wondering if we are using the mob scene to retreat to your study for a little talk."

Cooper was suddenly smiling. "Could be an interesting party after all." Then to Gilman, "See you in London on the tenth." With that, and a wave of his hand, he left.

Twenty minutes' clearance before one of us starts leaving, Renwick reminded himself as he rose and made sure the door had locked automatically. He checked his watch. Gilman was doing the same thing.

Gilman said, "Why did Francis O'Connell phone him? Not just looking for sympathy, surely."

"Probably he wanted Frank to get in touch with any friends in Istanbul, find out what they can about this damned camper. I suppose O'Connell is trying to handle everything quietly: no publicity. Everything done on the discreet old-boy level."

"Afraid of drugs?" That wouldn't make a pretty story if it started spreading around Washington. And what about the inevitable leaks to the press? Francis O'Connell's daughter, no less: *the* Francis O'Connell.

"Nina isn't the type." But Renwick was worried. He changed the unpleasant subject. "What about those two people I asked you to check on—any luck?"

"A lot of luck with Ilsa Schlott—but it came sideways, not through our efforts. We did verify that she is a foreign medical student, postgraduate research in tropical diseases at University College. She lives at the Women's Residence, where she met Nina and her friend Madge Westerman. Schlott attended a lot of rallies and demonstrations, seemed to be merely an interested observer studying the London scene. That was all we found out until I had a meeting with a friend in New Scotland Yard's antiterrorist squad. The subject of the meeting was actually those bloody umbrellas and their high-velocity pellets. After we talked about Crefeld—and you, too, old boy—I branched onto the subject of terrorists. Had my friend seen signs in London of anything being plotted on a wide international scale? Nothing so far, he assured me. Unless recruitment of terrorists could be the beginning of an international plot. And after I promised an exchange of future information between his department and Interintell— You've no objection?" Gilman asked, interrupting himself.

"It makes sense. Go on—recruitment, you were saying. In London?"

"Yes. Last April, four young men had been quietly selected as suitable material and, after six weeks of indoctrination and testing, were about to travel abroad—to a hard-training camp for terrorists in South Yemen. One of them—a Trotskyite—had a change of mind. He managed to break his ankle on his motorbike just in time to evade the trip. His recruiter didn't altogether believe his story, and he became scared. Scared enough to make contact with my friend of the antiterrorist squad and ask for protection. In exchange, he told all he knew. Including the name of the person who first approached him. It was a code name, of course: Greta. He described her, gave details about their meeting places. And with some hard-working detectives on the trail of Greta, they uncovered her identity: Ilsa Schlott. How does that grab you, my friend?"

Renwick recovered, said, "It grabs all right. Good God, Ron—"

"That's not the end of the Ilsa Schlott story. She was put— still is—under tight surveillance. And so she was observed meeting a flight from Amsterdam on June fourteenth. She made eye contact only: she knew the man, and he knew her. Then she walked some distance to her car. He followed, got in. She drove skillfully, used every bus and truck to blot her car from sight. She managed that, too, when she skirted a bad holdup in traffic just before it became a complete snarl."

"So they lost him," Renwick said, curbing his bitter annoyance. Schlott didn't matter: the police knew where to find her. But the new arrival—that was something else.

"He is recorded as being five feet ten or eleven, medium weight, good-looking sort—brown hair, clean-shaven—wearing a green tweed jacket and flannels. He was photographed, too. Here!" Gilman reached into a pocket, produced an envelope. "And the detective who took the photograph made immediate inquiries about the passenger list of that plane. You'll find a copy of it along with the snapshot. I've marked the Americans—eleven of them; but canceling out three children, four women, two elderly men, we have only two names really to consider."

Renwick opened the envelope. The snapshot was that of a half-turned face, as if its owner had sensed danger. The shape of the head, the cheekbone, chin, were vaguely familiar. Not familiar, exactly: just glimpsed once... Renwick's lips tightened. Quickly he glanced at the listed names, two of them underscored in red: Wilbur Jones; James Kiley. "Kiley," he said, his eyes once more on the photograph. "Yes. James Kiley."

Gilman was startled. "You know him?"

"He's conducting that camper tour."

"Nina O'Connell?"

"Her good friend."

"My God..."

They looked at each other. "I agree," said Renwick. My God—James Kiley. "Which is he—Erik or Marco? Theo made sure they both got safely out of Essen."

"There was another man," Gilman said, recovering himself. "He was in England just a week before Kiley arrived. Met Ilsa Schlott briefly, and then disappeared. He was six feet, dark-haired, thin. No photograph of him, I'm afraid. Could he be connected with Kiley?"

Tall, dark, thin... Again Renwick's mind went back to the bombing in Amsterdam, to two men helping Nina and Madge to rise to their feet. Tall, dark, thin. "Is he a car buff, by any chance?"

"He vanished too quickly for anyone to notice his hobbies."

"Check out the name Tony Shawfield, will you? Says he is English."

"Shawfield." Gilman spelled it out, memorizing it carefully.

"Right. Could have taken possession of a green camper, custom-built probably, British registration definitely, and then had it ferried over to Holland. It might have been ordered well in advance from Ilsa Schlott's favorite garage."

"We'll check," Gilman said tersely. He rose. "Have to go, Bob. Gemma will be ready and waiting. We're taking in a show tonight."

"I'll give you ten minutes and then leave, too."

"What are your plans?"

"First flight I can get for London, so let Merriman & Co. know I'll soon be on their doorstep. I'll need some help, a lot of help. Including a trace put on two young blondes, who look almost like sisters, arriving on some crummy ship—a freighter, possibly—in Istanbul. Around the beginning of September."

"Why a freighter?"

"You don't find many Greek interisland boats sailing into Istanbul, do you? Besides, Nina will be watching expenses. So flying is out. Also cruise ships."

Gilman said reflectively, "But what small cargo vessels sail from any Greek island to Turkey? Coastal steamers from the Levant or Egypt?"

"Lesbos," said Renwick. "They used to call in there, didn't they?" As far as he could remember, it was the only island that did have that link with Istanbul.

Gilman nodded. Lesbos, in the northeast Aegean, a few miles from the Turkish shore, was on the trade route from the Levant to Istanbul. "Could be that your blondes will head for Lesbos—if they have any sense. Or else they'll find themselves retracing their journey to Athens."

"Why not call Vlakos in Athens and get him to steer Nina in the right direction? She's collecting her allowance at the American Express office tomorrow," Renwick suggested.

"You want her in Lesbos?"

"I want her in Istanbul before her friends arrive. Can't go chasing through the Aegean after her. Nina wouldn't appreciate that."

"Kahraman is in Istanbul. He can help—"

"I'll get in touch with him from Merriman's."

"Will you be able to persuade her to leave her friends?"

"I can try."

"And if she won't listen?"

Renwick said nothing.

"If she were dependable enough," Gilman said, "she might travel along, co-operate—"

"No." Renwick was definite. He quieted his voice. "Too dangerous." He thought of Amalie in Essen, of Avril in Austria two years ago. "No. Not that," he ended.

"A pity. She could be useful."

"You're going to be late for dinner," Renwick said.

"We can have supper after the theater. I'll call Vlakos right away."

"And perhaps see if he could send someone over to Lesbos?"

"Just to make sure the coastal steamer isn't in the white-slave traffic?"

"Can Vlakos send someone?" Renwick persisted.

"With luck and good friends in the right places."

They shook hands quickly, firmly. Yes, thought Renwick as the door closed behind Ronald Gilman, that's what it took: good friends in the right places. And a large dose of luck.

CHAPTER

12

There had been a fresh breeze turning into a cool wind when the sun came up, light still weak, the Turkish coastline as yet a vague white line edging a flat stretch of land. It can't be Gallipoli, that was before we reached the Dardanelles, thought Nina as she stood by the rail and watched the struggle of waves and current; we must now be in the Sea of Marmara. Twenty-four hours on this decrepit little freighter, but we are lucky to be here, and with no strain or stress. Yesterday, on the Lesbos quay, the crew had looked like Hollywood's idea for a pirate movie. All they had needed was a knife held between their broken teeth to complete the picture. They might have stared but they had kept to themselves. The captain, equally in need of a bath and a dentist, had seen to that. And possibly that most amiable Greek, Mr. Christopoulos, who had befriended the girls in their little waterfront hotel in Lesbos—he was a teacher from Athens on holiday and spoke perfect English, thank heaven—and even came down to the wharf to see them safely off, might just have smoothed the way in his talk with the captain in some incomprehensible language. Certainly, Mr. Christopoulos had bargained for the small price of their trip, paid from Nina's dwindling store of Greek drachmas, and advised them to keep dollar bills out of sight. Not much in the way of food, he had warned them—but the coffee would be good. He was right about that. A very nice man indeed, Nina thought, and in the last excitement of boarding he forgot to give us his address. Now I can't send him a postcard to thank him.

The light was strengthening. Nina turned away from the rail, looked at the deck behind her where Madge was still trying to sleep, head pillowed on her duffel bag, a windbreak formed by the loosely roped sacks and olive oil drums that had been dumped on board at Lesbos. Forward, at the ship's prow, two goats were tethered. The rest of the passengers— three shabbily dressed men and two women swathed in black cotton, from head scarf down to shapeless trousers partly covered by equally shapeless tunics—were below in the cabins. Dirty gray blankets on thin straw mattresses hadn't deterred them from a good night's rest.

At last, Madge gave up her pretense and rose stiffly, drawing her cardigan more closely around her shoulders. "You didn't sleep much."

"Trying to think things out."

"Still mad at Jim?"

"Just puzzled. That's all." Keep off the subject of Jim Kiley, Nina's tone of voice said.

Madge took the hint. "Where's Istanbul?"

"Somewhere toward the sun."

She doesn't have to get cross with me, thought Madge. What on earth is worrying her about Jim? He's a perfectly normal guy; in fact, I like him. I like him a lot. "So you are going on with the trip?" In Athens, Nina had talked of spending a week there, a week in the Aegean, and the hell with Jim Kiley.

"Yes," Nina said.

"I'm glad." Even if I'm feeling miserable now, I'm glad. She shivered, looked wanly over the rail at the strong current battling the small waves. The boat was steady enough. It was she who was definitely shaky.

Nina said, "What about some hot coffee? That should warm us up."

"Coffee..." Madge shuddered at the word.

"Are you all right?"

"Just a little upset. That last meal in Lesbos..." Madge didn't finish, shuddered again.

"You shouldn't have eaten that camel stew. Mr. Christopoulos did try to steer you away from it." But Madge had been stubborn. Poor Madge, thought Nina, the world-wide traveler who wanted to be part of the local scene.

At the mention of camel stew, Madge said, "Don't!" And as one of the crew, the least prepossessing in that motley bunch, appeared with two mugs of coffee, she averted her head.

Nina took the mug with no cracks apparent around its rim. "Wonderful," she told the man. He didn't understand her, but he caught her meaning. His sudden toothless smile changed hard brown eyes into a friendly beam. "For you," Nina said, pointing to the torn undershirt exposing a hairy chest, waving the second mug away from Madge. He understood after some more pantomime gestures, and with nods and a spreading grin, he drank the coffee as he stalked off. "Just an upstanding citizen," Nina said. "He's got a wife and ten children back in Alexandria."

"And another ten in Tyre," Madge said, almost coming to life.

"You'll be all right." But Nina was worried. This could really complicate things. "You only need a decent bed and some sleep."

"Where will we stay?"

Not so easy to choose now. "We'll find something. We've done pretty well so far, haven't we?" But this time I'd like a bathroom of our own. What wouldn't I give to soak in a hot tub without the door handle being rattled every three minutes by some stranger in the corridor!

"How long will we have in Istanbul—only a day and a half?"

"Just about that." Tomorrow was Tuesday, the fourth. "Perhaps the others will be delayed and give us an extra night."

"Will I see anything of Istanbul at all?" Madge asked, misery increasing.

"You can have a look at it, anyway." Nina pointed ahead. On a promontory that jutted out from Europe's last stretch of land rose the domes and minarets of mosques and palaces, close-packed on a sloping hill. Walls encircled the Sultan's old domain, a city within a city, to reach the water's edge. There, a low white mist drifted upward, thinned, disappeared, setting stone columns and rounded roofs afloat on a gossamer veil.

They had passed the Golden Horn, crowded even at this hour with small craft, and entered the Bosporus. "Thank heaven we're on the European side," Nina said as they gathered their belongings and headed for a shaky gangway. Docking on the Asiatic shore of Istanbul might have been more than she could have handled. Madge was pale under that rosy tan they had both collected on Mykonos. And the sun was coming up, hot and strong, with all mist vanquished. "This shouldn't take too long," she reassured Madge as they crossed the quay toward a wooden shed. Not many passengers disembarked at this section of the Galata quays, just goats and black-swathed women with stocky husbands wearing old tweed caps.

Nina hesitated at the wide doors of the shed. It was small, low-roofed, and bare: two long tables, two serious-faced men in uniform gray jackets, an opposite door firmly closed, a host of notices around its wooden walls. And nothing I can understand, thought Nina. She heard Madge gasp as she, too, stared at the notices. Nina held out her passport, waited for further directions. "Do you speak English?" she asked in her politest voice, adding a friendly smile to sweeten the atmosphere. Two pairs of dark eyes stared at her, then at Madge. Solemnly, the passports were studied. Solemnly, the expressionless eyes looked at the girls, looked back at the passports. Trouble? Nina wondered. Yet the officials must understand English, for they could decipher the passports. Or couldn't they? They were talking together now, in a burst of vowels and consonants that left Nina more depressed. Culture shock, she was thinking. How do we, a couple of idiots who can't understand a word, manage to cope with this place? Then one of the men, Nina's passport still in his hand, moved to a telephone. Definitely trouble, Nina decided. She looked at Madge, resting her weight against a table, white-faced and mournful, and said nothing.

There was a long wait, their small baggage examined briefly, most of the time spent watching their five fellow travelers being thoroughly questioned while innumerable parcels and baskets spilled out on the tables. Hotter by the minute, Nina thought, and wished that the opposite door could be opened for a through draft of air.

It did open. From the street, a man entered briskly, well dressed in silver-gray, carefully groomed, dark-haired, dark-eyed, dark mustache, middle-aged, authoritative. A sharp glance at the wilting girls, a brief look at their passports, a voluble exchange of words with the official who had telephoned. Then the stranger came forward, spoke in excellent English, his smile friendly. "Everything is solved now," he reassured Nina. "Your friend is ill?"

"Not really." No communicable diseases being smuggled into Turkey. "Just the heat—and exhaustion, I think. She'll be all right once we get to our hotel and she can rest for a few hours."

"What hotel?"

"I thought we could get advice from a tourist bureau. Is there one near this dock?"

"Not here. Do you speak any Turkish?"

Nina shook her head. "Perhaps the tourist police could direct us—"

The man brushed that aside. "You should have a guide and interpreter. Not expensive," he added quickly. "How long do you stay here?"

"Until tomorrow."

"One night? Then you should consider one of the large hotels where English is spoken. For one night, not too expensive."

He knows who we are, Nina was thinking. What is he? Someone high up in the tourist police? Or what? I bet, I bet this is Father's doing: somehow he has arranged all this. "Not the Hilton," she said firmly: that would be her father's choice. She drew from her shoulder bag the small secondhand guide to Istanbul she had bought in Athens. Ten years out of date, but streets stayed the same although hotels might change. She consulted the list she had marked. "I thought this hotel might be suitable."

The man shook his head, shrugged, signaled to the door, which he had left open. A much younger man entered. Turkish, Nina decided—these same dark brows and solemn eyes; but in dress and manner he could have passed for an American student. He stood still, smiling and pleasant, while his long name was rattled off in a quick introduction. Nina could only catch part of it: Suleyman, she thought. "Most reliable," the man in the silver-gray suit told her, and turned away for a brief word with the immigration official who saluted. Actually saluted, Nina thought in amazement. Then as quickly as he had appeared, he departed.

Suleyman said, "It is all right now. You can leave. I shall bring a taxi. Wait there!" He pointed to the doorway to the street. A street of low buildings and a maze of traffic; movement and noise and complete chaos.

Madge roused herself. "We'll wait. Thank you." And to Nina, as he hurried away, she said, "We need him."

I guess we do, thought Nina. They left the shed, the officials too busy shaking out every tightly rolled piece of clothing even to notice their departure.

Suleyman was polite, efficient, and at three dollars a day—his frankly stated price—not expensive. He even directed the taxi, without comment, to the hotel Nina had selected. Built of wood, one bathroom to a floor, lethargic ceiling fans, no dining room, no English spoken in spite of its advertisement: otherwise possible enough for a grade-B establishment, although the floors needed scrubbing and the lopsided curtains had a year's dust ingrained in them. Nina, guidebook opened at "Accommodations," had another hotel to suggest. Outlying district, Suleyman said, very nice but sixteen kilometers away. Ten miles? I give up, thought Nina. "What do you advise?"

"A hotel near Taksim Square. It is the center. Taxis, buses—"

"What hotel?" And I know his answer.

"Perhaps the Hilton?"

"Too expensive."

"Not all rooms are so expensive. I can arrange something. I am guide and interpreter for many guests."

Madge said, "We're wasting more money on this taxi ride than we'll spend in one night at the Hilton."

Hardly, thought Nina. But she still had much of her allowance money intact, and she was too hot and damp and tired and bewildered to argue. "All right. We'll try it. At least I can get my traveler's checks cashed there. Will the taxi driver take dollar bills?" She had hoped, naïvely it now appeared, that there would have been a money exchange at the pier.

"I can change your dollars now." Suleyman took a wad of large Turkish notes from an inner pocket. "Very good rates."

"I'm sure. Are you a student, Suleyman?"

"Some of the time," he said, with his bright smile.

"And what are you going to be?" Surely not just a guide forever, Nina thought, as she watched him deftly counting out the right monies.

"A poet," he said.

Completely bemused, Nina asked no more questions for the rest of the journey.

Suleyman made his call from the Hilton lobby. His voice was cheerful. "All is settled. I directed them to the place you wished. This afternoon early, we sightsee. One only. The other is not well."

"Which one?"

"The brown eyes."

"Serious? Does she need a doctor?"

"No, no. A little rest, that is all."

Sightseeing, thought Renwick. It would have to be Top-kapi; tomorrow, as on all Tuesdays, the palace would be closed. And if he knew Nina, the Sultans' seraglio would be at the top of her visiting list. "There will be a lot of walking, many courtyards," he suggested, to give Suleyman a clue to the place he had in mind for a meeting.

Suleyman caught it. "In the third courtyard? Ladies like to see the—"

Quickly, Renwick cut off the identifying word: "harem." "The second is better. Near its entrance gate. About four o'clock?"

"Later, perhaps."

If Nina began her sightseeing early (the seraglio opened at one), she'd be collapsing by five o'clock closing time. "Not much later," Renwick said firmly, and hung up.

He turned to Pierre Claudel, seated in the bedroom's one lopsided armchair, which he had angled as much as possible under the ceiling's fan. "You heard most of it. Topkapi Palace around four. The Divan courtyard."

"Who's ill?"

"Madge. Nothing serious. I hope."

"Then you won't need me to take her off your hands?"

"I'd like you to stick around, just see if Nina is all right."

"Trail after her and Suleyman? Deliver her safely to you?"

"Might be an idea." Claudel wouldn't be noticeable: dark-haired, dark-eyed, dark-mustached, he could be taken easily for one of the young Turks who sat around the cafés talking politics and poetry. In addition, his Turkish was excellent, thanks to eighteen months in Ankara a few years ago. Renwick grinned. "I may need you as a guide and interpreter once Suleyman bows out."

"You're doing not so badly by yourself."

"Don't kid me, Pierre." His previous visit to Turkey, when Greeks and Turks had been forgetting their NATO alliance in the heat of the battle over Cyprus, had lasted only five weeks: enough time to get him interested in the language, but to give him only a minimal grasp. It was this feeling of inadequacy, the struggle to understand and be understood (he managed better than he imagined) that had prompted him to steer Nina and Madge toward an English-speaking hotel. Not that Nina would thank him for it, if she knew.

"How the hell do I persuade the girls to leave that goddamned camper?"

Claudel's bright eyes looked at him in astonishment. "I thought you had that worked out. Dangerous terrain ahead. And that's the bloody truth. Haven't they been listening to the radio? Nothing but revolts and armed attacks all the way down through Iran into Afghanistan. Or perhaps the Soviet advisers there will give Mr. Kiley and his party a safe-conduct guarantee."

Renwick said nothing. Once into India the camper would be safe. But after that? Bangladesh again in turmoil, Burma, Malaysia and brigands, Indochina with all its vicious politics and millions of helpless victims. Surely Kiley must be planning to have the camper ferried from India to Hong Kong—the land route was now a death trap. "I wonder if anyone, except Kiley and Shawfield, has been paying much attention to the news."

"Then you might have to let Nina know, that—well, that Kiley is not exactly what he seems."

"And how do I do that without blowing the whistle for all to hear?" Including Theo. Particularly Theo. His new branch office of West-East Travel was now open and flourishing in Istanbul. "Kiley..." Renwick paused, shook his head. "If we only had the whole picture."

"We've got enough evidence on him."

"There's still a gap. Two, in fact. No one actually witnessed him boarding the coastal freighter in Duisburg. The captain and crew swear they saw nothing. And we haven't heard yet from the Rotterdam police about that blocking of the men's-room doorway at Schiphol Airport. Three men came out, the cop noted. Later, he discovered the suspect must have been one of them. He must have made a report on what he could remember about them: rough details, certainly."

"Such as a green tweed jacket? Yes, that would tie Kiley to Heathrow and Amsterdam's Schiphol Airport. One gap closed, at least. But Duisburg? We know all we'll ever know about that: a man called Kurt Leitner, from Essen, definitely important in Section One of the People's Revolutionary Force for Direct Action, traveled by truck to the Duisburg docks and vanished completely just before a coastal freighter, called the *Maritza*, sailed. What more do you need, Bob?"

"Something that one of Theo's clever lawyers won't twist

around in court. Give them three inches of a loophole and they'll stretch it to twelve feet."

"So that's why you aren't asking the Turkish police to detain Kiley here, and have the Germans request his extradition to Essen. It's tempting, I must say: it could end Theo's plan before it achieved anything."

"It would end only Kiley's part in his plan. Theo would lose one man, but he'd wait, do some reorganizing, and try again for another angle. The ground is too well prepared; there's been too big an effort, too much thought and money invested, for everything to be discarded along with Kiley. Whatever that plan is, it's a shocker, Pierre."

Claudel nodded. "Then our best chance of uncovering it is to let Kiley go on his way, stirring up trouble wherever the camper stops—possibly organizing or recruiting terrorists. And, of course, get Nina O'Connell safely out—without breaking our security. Will you manage it, Bob?"

"I'll make a damned good try. And we'll find out Kiley's stops, tip off the governments involved—if they'll listen."

"But if Nina won't listen?"

"God knows," Renwick said wearily. He looked at his watch. Ten past eleven. "Time to separate. I'll see you in the distance around four o'clock. Okay?"

"In the second courtyard, the place of the Divan. A good choice." It was spacious, filled with numerous trees, pleasant cover on a hot afternoon. Cooler than this chair, thought Claudel as he rose and pulled his shirt free from his back.

"It's the closest to the seraglio's entrance gate—making sure I don't get lost," Renwick said with a smile.

"Meanwhile, I'll take a little drive with my friend Fahri around the outskirts and visit another camping site, see if any advance reservations have been made. Do you know how many camping grounds Turkey has? Hundreds. Incredible."

"The old caravanserai spirit, perhaps."

Claudel cocked his head to one side. "Now why didn't I think of that?"

"You will, Pierre. You will."

With a laugh and a nod, Claudel closed the door behind him.

Renwick sat on the edge of the bed, reached for the telephone. With some care, and the help of his little book *Useful Phrases*, he asked for Kahraman's number. Extraordinary language, he thought as he waited for the call to go through. Where else would one two three be *Bir Iki Üç*?

Kahraman came on the line, as crisp and confident as ever. His impeccable silver-gray suit wouldn't dare sport a crush even in this weather. He rushed into conversation in his usual way, answered everything before it was asked. All had gone well at the quay this morning. Fortunate that he was there. Renwick's delightful friends might have had just a little trouble. Because of the companions they had on their journey. Three men, two women. Smuggling. Definitely. Sticks of dynamite inside tightly rolled bits and pieces of clothing. Could not be too careful nowadays, could one? And what about lunch? And a long talk between old friends?

"A short lunch, I'm afraid," said Renwick. "Only two and a half hours." But time enough to get Kahraman's help to communicate with London. Claudel's remark about "recruiting terrorists for training" had sparked another train of thought about Dr. Ilsa Schlott.

"No time for a little drive?" Kahraman was audibly disappointed.

"Some place central," Renwick insisted, remembering Kahraman's favorite haunt up the Bosporus for four hours of good food and good talk. "I remember an excellent meal we enjoyed on my last visit. At the Grand Bazaar?" It was a small place near the pepper market, and easy to reach.

Kahraman was delighted he had remembered it, and pleased enough to forgive his American friend for being the first to suggest it. "At the same time as on your last visit?"

"Perfect," said Renwick. Twelve-thirty would be just right.

He prepared to leave, now thinking about Ilsa Schlott and his message to Merriman's. Gilman must contact Diehl in Berlin, immediately. Some hard probing might uncover Schlott's connection there—if she had had one—with the People's Revolutionary Force for Direct Action, founded by Erik and Marco. Then any story she was concocting would fall to pieces.

What would it be? She had been meeting James Kiley at Heathrow simply because he was someone she had known, and liked, on a visit last year to Chicago? Or in New York? Or wherever? Theo would make the fabrication seem plausible. But a direct connection with Erik and Marco—well, that was something to baffle even Theo's ingenuity. Let his well-paid lawyers wrestle with that evidence.

Still not enough to pin down Erik or Marco. Schlott wouldn't identify them; she'd go to jail with a smirk of triumph on her face. There could be another way, though. Get Diehl to explore that item recorded by a Dutch undercover agent about the man who had arrived on a coastal freighter from Duisburg: extraordinary expertise in Spanish. Which of them—Marco or Erik—had any Spanish-language background? And then we would know which of these men was the one that left the safe house in Rotterdam as James Kiley. That's vital if he comes to trial. How would it sound to a jury if we could only testify, "He may be Erik, he may be Marco"?

He dropped all thought of terrorists as he reached the street and concentrated on finding a taxi. A walk would have been enjoyable, down the broad avenue, over the bridge at the Golden Horn, into the old town, but he hadn't the time. The taxi would allow him half an hour of wandering inside the Grand Bazaar before he met Kahraman.

He chose one small area of the walled and covered market, four thousand little shops jam-packed along narrow, twisting, bewildering streets. Noise and confusion everywhere, the usual bedlam of bargaining; Turks and foreigners as crowded together and as varied as the objects on display. Easy to lose anyone who might be interested in his movements; too easy to get himself lost as well. So he limited his choice of routes and paid attention to the direction he followed rather than let his mind be sidetracked by antiques, clothes, carpets, amethysts, lamps, furniture, gold bracelets, slippers, everything and anything imaginable. He came safely out of the gate near the pepper-market area just as Kahraman entered the restaurant ahead of him.

Renwick loitered among the crowd, made reasonably sure that Kahraman hadn't been tailed, either, and then followed him inside. The room hadn't changed: blue-and-yellow patterned tiles over the walls, overhead fans, a display of cold dishes, the smell of well-seasoned food; and alcoves. Discreet and comfortable alcoves.

"A good morning?" Kahraman inquired politely.

"A very good morning," Renwick said as they bowed and shook hands. He could only hope that the afternoon would be as successful.

CHAPTER
13

They were almost on time, a mere ten minutes late, which was probably a record in punctuality for Suleyman. Renwick, who had been exploring the seraglio's second courtyard, always keeping a watchful eye on the area around its giant gate, suddenly saw the two figures coming his way through the plane trees. Suleyman he recognized immediately. The girl needed a second look. Today, Nina had abandoned blue jeans for a wide-skirted dress. Fair hair was swept up from her neck, pinned high on her head, a few tendrils escaping. Dark glasses and earrings added to the change. She was tired, tripping once on the cobblestones in spite of her sandals' low heels. Suleyman, as enthusiastic as ever, was doing all the talking. He was so engrossed that he had never noticed the quiet, compact man, dark-mustached, who had followed them at a comfortable distance. Claudel looked the part of the tourist, a guidebook opened in his hand, stopping to consult its map whenever he needed to slow down, merging with other visitors when that was prudent. He noticed Renwick before the engrossed Suleyman did, began closing his map. Renwick judged the right distance between Nina and himself, went forward to meet her with a wave of his hand to attract her attention.

She stopped abruptly. Disbelief spread over her face.

"Hello, Nina," he said, taking both her hands. "I thought it was you—couldn't be sure at first. Is this a permanent change?" He stood back to look at her, smiling wholeheartedly, not even trying to conceal his pleasure.

"It's cooler." She laughed delightedly as she recovered from her surprise. "But, Bob—what on earth are you doing here?"

"The same as you. Dipping into a spot of history."

"If you are just arriving, you won't have time to see everything. I didn't. And I've been here for three hours. Oh, this is Suleyman." She turned to the boy, who had backed off a little and was now waiting for a signal from Renwick.

"Perhaps Suleyman could scout around for a taxi?" Renwick suggested. "Where will we find you?"

"By the Bab-i-Hümayan Gate. At the esplanade. You know where to go? Shall I show you?" Suleyman asked hopefully.

"We won't get lost." Once they left here, there was only a stretch of the first courtyard's almost empty space to cover before they reached the entrance gate at the street.

Suleyman left regretfully. It had been a splendid afternoon, and now it was over. Judging by the way the American had caught her hands, held them, looked at her, there would be no evening ahead for Suleyman, either.

"But I need him to get me back to the hotel," Nina said. "He's my guide."

"I'll get you back. Perhaps not as efficiently as Suleyman, but we'll manage. I know a café where the seats are comfortable."

"That's tempting. But I don't want to drag you away from here."

"I've seen enough for one day. I believe in taking museums in small slices. Remember?" He was thinking back to Geneva, six years ago.

She remembered. She looked quickly away, but barely noticed the trail of tourists now passing by. Claudel, walking leisurely, didn't even exchange a glance with Renwick. "Today," Nina was saying as she and Renwick began following the slow exodus, "I hadn't the time for small slices. I only had one afternoon. Poor Madge couldn't even have that. She's in bed. She ate some camel stew."

"Adventuresome. And where are your other friends? Or did they also eat some camel stew?"

And that led, naturally, into explanations—vague about the reason for her sudden rebellion at the Thermaic Gulf, more expansive about her travels through Greece—which lasted well into the wasteland of the first courtyard. In its center, she halted, looked around: "Whatever happened here?"

"A lot of churches were razed when the Sultans started building their seraglio. Then the Janissaries were stationed in this courtyard, outside the main palaces, of course—a fierce bunch of fighting men. Originally, for a couple of hundred years, they were tribute children. Fair-haired boys from Greece in great demand."

"Tribute children?"

"Recruited by force. Taught to be savages. They terrorized Europe, including their homeland."

"Didn't they remember anything about Greece?" Nina asked in horror. "How old were they when they were taken as tribute?"

"Practically kindergarten age. By the time they were fourteen and trained to fight, the whole world outside these walls had become their enemy." Renwick turned bitter. "Complete and thorough indoctrination."

"Was it really possible?" Nina's voice faltered.

"It was." And still is. How else could today's hard-core terrorists be willing killers of their own people?

"It's so empty, so peaceful now. No sign of any buildings."

"Blown to pieces by the Sultan's artillery when the Janissaries become too much of a threat to their masters. Those who survived the bombardment were executed." A hundred thousand dead. A quick end to a brutalized force, to four hundred years of complete terror. "Come on, Nina. Suleyman will think we've really lost our way." He took her arm, urged her toward the street gateway ahead of them. He hoped she wouldn't notice the large nails on either side where decapitated heads had once been hung as a reminder of the Sultan's displeasure.

But she was more interested in him. "What *are* you doing in Istanbul, Bob?"

So he talked, briefly, about Merriman & Co. His explanation, much to his relief, seemed to be acceptable.

"Of course," she said thoughtfully, "you did get an engineering degree at MIT. And then the army. Artillery, wasn't it? Then you went into NATO and attended disarmament conferences. And now you are a consultant. Very impressive, Bob."

"You remember a lot." He was both surprised and pleased. "But I'm not a consultant—just one of the firm's representatives abroad. There's a lot of building being planned around the world."

"Exciting. How long will you be here?"

"Well, I arrived three days ago. Another four days might be necessary."

"And then?"

"Wherever a client needs some practical advice."

"Well, I hope your travel expenses let you stay in the best hotels. You know, Madge and I landed in the Hilton. All

Father's arrangement, I am sure," she said ruefully, and then laughed. "But I did have the most wonderful bath. We're really pampered, aren't we? Americans always have a longing for good plumbing. Tony calls me a complete bourgeoise, but he wouldn't have thought so if he had seen us arriving this morning. The dock was kept for grade-C traffic, I think. We got out fairly easily—thanks to Father again. That disguised colonel or general didn't arrive by accident. Father probably phoned someone in Ankara to watch out for his helpless little daughter at the Galata quays."

"How would he know?" Nina was quick, thought Renwick: what had prompted her idea that Kahraman, in his silver-gray suit, was a man of authority? He could only hope that she had been as quick to notice strange details in her journey across Europe.

"Because I called him from Greece, told him we'd be here around the beginning of September. Actually, the Hilton couldn't be more suitable. That's where we're meeting Jim tomorrow. At four o'clock. Unless, of course, he's so mad at me he won't turn up."

"He will."

Something amused her. "Now Tony will just *have* to find a space for his camper near Istanbul and let the others have at least a little time here. You see, we weren't going to stop in Istanbul at all. Jim said the campsite was all booked up— he always likes to arrange everything in advance, you know."

"Only one campsite near here?" Renwick was smiling.

Sharply, she looked at him. "Are there more?"

"So I've heard."

She frowned, halted at the gate, turned to stare back at the far walls of the seraglio.

What the hell did I say? he wondered. He said, "If not Istanbul, where were you going to stop?"

"Bursa."

"Bursa?"

She nodded, fell silent, became engrossed by her last view of Topkapi: towers and cupolas, palaces and gardens, court-yards and terraces, all guarded by the vast encircling wall. "Riches and treasures..." Then her eyes traveled over the courtyard of the Janissaries. Her voice stifled. "Poor children." She turned toward the gate.

He had taken her arm. Suddenly, he kissed her cheek.

"For what?" she asked, a smile coming back to her lips.

For hearing the cries of pain. Not many did. They'd marvel at history as it was laid out before them, wonder how much money it had taken to build this or furnish that. Eyes were bewildered by incredible treasures. Ears were deaf. He said, leading her through Bab-i-Hümayan into the esplanade, "I wanted to. That's all."

"Bob, did you see those huge nails? In that black-and-white marble gate?"

"More history, I guess. Where's Suleyman the Magnificent?"

He was there, gesticulating from the other side of the street, urging them to hurry. So they did. Either the taxi driver was impatient or there were rules and regulations to be obeyed. Their departure was equally speedy, Suleyman looking after them with regret but partially consoled by Renwick's tip, tactfully concealed in a warm handshake.

"I have to pay him," Nina said, rousing herself, looking back in dismay.

"Taken care of."

"And I'll need him tomorrow morning. Madge and I will be visiting—"

"He'll be at the hotel tomorrow, waiting for you."

"You arranged that? I didn't hear."

"You told him your plans, didn't you?"

"Well, I did mention the Bazaar and the Blue Mosque."

"Then he'll be at the hotel tomorrow. Now, let's see..." Renwick fished a map from his pocket, and began reinforcing his directions to the Café Alhamra.

The café delighted Nina. It was small, set down in a public garden on a twisting hill road, with a terrace and flowerpots to mark its allotted space. From here, she could see the Bosporus and the coast of Asia. "How far?" she asked, eyeing the stretch of water and its busy traffic.

Renwick studied it. "More than a mile, perhaps a mile and a half. The port for the car ferry is just below this hill. That's where you'll be crossing over on Wednesday morning. I don't imagine you'll start out for Asia late tomorrow and risk traveling in darkness to Bursa. The roads over there can be tricky."

She studied her glass. "This tea is marvelous." As in all cafés in Islamic territory, only coffee or tea or fruit juice was served. "The best I've ever tasted. Where do the Turks get it?"

So we're slipping away from the topic of Bursa, he thought. "It's home-grown. Once they had orange groves. Then there was a stretch of bad frosts. So they planted tea instead. But over on the Asiatic side, winters must be warmer. That's where the fruit orchards are. You'll pass through miles of them on your way to Bursa."

"Have you been there? What's it like?"

"I've never seen it. But I hear it has a lot of charm—purely Turkish, of course. Not many foreigners around. You'll like it." He studied her eyes. Thank God she had taken off the dark sunglasses. Now he could really see the Nina he knew. "Don't you want to go to Bursa?"

"I'd like more time in Istanbul."

"Well, can't you manage that? Don't any of you have a say in the selection of major stops? The ones where you spend several nights?"

"Oh, we talk and plan and talk. But everyone has his own idea of where he wants to go. Someone just has to take charge and decide."

"Who does?"

"Tony and Jim, usually. It makes sense. Tony has certain routes to follow—he is making a sort of test run, you know, for the manufacturers in England who want to know how their camper behaves. And Jim—well, he's paying more than his share of the expenses as well as coping with all the documents and details."

"What about sightseeing when you have several days to kill? Do you scatter, or does Jim shepherd you around?"

"Heavens, no. Jim—he's writing some pieces for a newspaper, you know—goes off to meet people who can give him details for a story. And there's money to be collected at a bank, and our mail to be weighed and sent off at a post office. Things like that," she ended lamely. She was frowning.

"Don't," Renwick said, and reached out his hand, gently smoothed her brow. He could guess what had troubled her: a letter and two postcards that never had reached America.

She tried to smile, rushed on with talk about Tony, who guarded the camper while Jim was away, and, once Jim returned to take charge of it, took a day off himself to have something replaced or checked or repaired. "He ought to have been a mechanic. He's always tinkering around his machine, always fussing over his radio equipment."

"You don't like him too much, do you?"

"How did you guess?"

By the tightness in your voice, he said silently. By the cloud that's still hanging over those beautiful eyes. "I just feel something is troubling you. What's wrong?"

"Nothing."

"Oh, Nina —come on."

She was silent, stared unhappily at the view which had so delighted her fifteen minutes ago. "I really ought to phone Madge. She may be worrying—"

"She's probably asleep. In any case, the Hilton is near—just at the top of this hill—and I'll have you back there by half past six." That is, if our taxi driver returns here at six-twenty, as he promised. "Then you can have another wonderful bath, and rest, and I'll be waiting in the lobby at eight-thirty. We'll drive up the Bosporus—not too far—and have a leisurely dinner. How's that?"

"I'd love it. But Madge—"

"If she feels up to it, bring her along," he suggested without much enthusiasm. He didn't want to wish Madge ill but he hoped she couldn't face a Turkish dinner, not tonight. If she could? Then there would be no quiet meeting for two, no possible chance to persuade. Perhaps he'd better start the persuading now. My God, he thought as he looked at Nina, she can't go with Kiley; she's got to be eased out of his grasp. But how do I begin?

"Now you're the one who's looking worried," Nina challenged him.

"I am. I'm thinking about that journey ahead of you. It's the wrong time for it, Nina. Haven't you been reading the news? Listening to the radio? There is trouble all along the line; if not war, then armed revolts and—"

"Jim says we can bypass the danger points."

"I suppose he's arranged in advance for the fighting to stop as you approach?"

"Now, Bob! The main routes must still be safe. We've met other campers, with wives and children on board, who are traveling to India."

Wrong tactics. Swallow your bitterness. "All right. But that doesn't mean they'll be safe from a raiding party or a bunch of guerrillas who mistake them for the enemy." That had happened last week: a German schoolteacher, wife, two children, shot dead in Afghanistan, mistaken by the rebels for one of its hated government's equally hated Soviet advisers. "I just don't want to see you running these risks."

Nina's eyes softened. "You really *are* worried. Oh, Bob—we won't be near the danger spots. Do you think Tony is going to have his precious bus shot up?" she asked lightly.

"Nina—how well do you know these two men?"

She glanced away at the other tables. So many foreigners, even in this small space, so many different kinds of people.

"Nina," Renwick pleaded, and brought her back to him.

"How well do we know anyone?" she asked. "How well do I even know myself?" She shook her head, tried to smile, said sadly, "Perhaps I'm the one who is at fault. Perhaps I fall in love with a man and then—just as suddenly—start falling out for no reason at all. At least, no real reason that makes any sense."

"In love with Kiley?" Renwick's lips were tight, his voice almost inaudible.

"I thought I was. Why not?" She was on the defensive now. "He's attractive, very attractive. And he's in love with me." Suddenly, she was miserable. "He has never actually said it. But—but—"

"But what?"

"Oh, this is all so difficult, so stupid. You don't want to listen to my—" She broke off, then said, "It's just that I have no one to talk to. Madge—no, that's difficult—she was ready to fall in love with Jim herself. But you, Bob—you know how men feel. If you *were* in love, would you never even say 'I love you,' never even mention marriage, and yet tell her that you want her to meet your uncle and that you want to meet her father?"

"To meet your father?" Renwick was startled. "When?"

"Around Thanksgiving—we'll be passing through America then. But what does that mean, Bob? Marriage?" She shook her head, sighed. "He isn't shy. He isn't one of those awkward, tongue-tied men. What does it mean?"

He could guess what it meant: instructions. Get the girl to fall for you; it will make sure she'll go along with you on this trip. But don't let your emotions run away with you; keep your mind in control.

"Bob?" She was watching him anxiously, almost regretting her confidences.

"If you were in love with me, Nina, I'd be telling all the world. Kiley's either a goddamned fool or a trickster."

"Trickster?" She was indignant. "He couldn't be more honest." And then she frowned. "Not altogether," she admitted. "Oh, how I hate lies! They make you feel used—as if you were some idiot who'd believe any story. Am I an idiot, Bob?"

He shook his head. "Only if you insist on going around the world with Kiley."

"But I want to go."

"Why? You aren't in love with him now."

His words had been sharp, almost angry. Surprised, she let his eyes hold hers, felt uncertainty, bewilderment.

"He isn't the man for you, Nina."

And who is? "How do you know so much about him?" she demanded. Annoyance increased the color in her cheeks, brightened her eyes. "You just don't want me to make this trip. Why? Did Father send you here, ask you to—"

"I never saw your father. I wasn't near Washington."

"No?"

"No." He eased his voice, added, "And that's not a lie, either." He glanced at his watch, signaled to the waiter. In a brisk five minutes, with silence complete from Nina, they were out of the café, into the taxi.

Her silence still held for another long minute. And then, contritely, she said, "Bob—I'm sorry."

"I'm sorry, too."

"About what?" I was the one to blame, she thought.

"That you won't listen to me."

"Perhaps I did. In my own way." She paused. "If I don't rejoin the camper, where do I go? Maryland, for Beryl's dinners and parties? Or England again, to make my apologies for being late in arriving at Lower Wallop?"

"What about Paris? I have a friend there with an apartment on the Left Bank. He would lend it to me for September, and I'd lend it to you. That's better than Lower Wallop or Upper Twistleton."

"Pronounced Twitton?"

But in spite of the lightened mood, Renwick's worry deepened. Was she or wasn't she leaving with Kiley? If that guy could make love as well as he talked, Nina was lost.

"You look so serious," she told him as they entered the hotel. "Am I such a responsibility?" Not yours, surely.

"Think about Paris. And let me know this evening. Will you?"

"But I must go on this trip, Bob. Because I'm curious."

He didn't quite understand, looked at her questioningly as they waited at the desk for her key.

"Exactly half past six," she said delightedly. "Bob, you're wonderful. No, don't come any farther. Look at the crowd around us, all speaking English. I won't get lost." Suddenly, she reached up and kissed him gently. "Just wanted to. That's all," she quoted.

He caught her hand. "Nina—because you're curious? About what?"

"About Jim. If he isn't in love with me, why does he pretend? Why so eager to have me along on this trip? I didn't force myself on him, you know."

"I know," Renwick said, releasing her hand. He watched her enter the elevator. Then he turned toward the bar, where Western rules prevailed and he could have a non-Islamic drink. Pierre Claudel had already found a table and ordered two tall glasses of Scotch and soda.

"How did it go?" Claudel asked.

"She's a hard girl to convince." Apart from that, it had been a good afternoon—one of the best in a long time. She was easy to be with. Too damn easy, thought Renwick. And too unsettling.

"No large green camper with British registration and plate has yet crossed the frontier from Greece. And at the camp-sites, no inquiries have been made in Shawfield's name or in Kiley's."

"Then they are late." Nina might have her extra day in Istanbul after all. "That will give them something to worry about. They'll have to juggle their timetable in Bursa."

"Bursa?"

"That's their main stopover. Not Istanbul."

"What scared them away? The police arrests?"

"Could be." In the last three weeks the Turkish authorities had been exceedingly active: the large political demonstration scheduled for this Sunday near the stadium was not, if the police could help it, going to have terrorists inciting a riot. This summer, politics were at boiling point, and both parties—the Republican socialists and the Justice conservatives—had their bands of wild extremists eager for bloody action. Renwick glanced around the placid bar, well filled with well-dressed people—some businessmen still worrying over contracts; some tourists relaxing after a hard day's pleasure. "Drink up," he told Claudel. "We'd better get Kahraman to switch his attention from Istanbul to Bursa."

"Damned annoying. He had it all nicely planned here."

Renwick nodded. Kahraman might also have a more recent report from the Greek frontier.

Claudel drained his glass. "Meet you back at our hotel. Kahraman will be there at seven-fifteen."

"I'll have to leave before eight-thirty." Their hotel, Kahraman's choice, was a bare five minutes' walk along Cumhurijet Avenue from the Hilton. "Help me disentangle by a quarter past eight." Kahraman, brisk when he dealt with something that was already decided upon, could become painstaking and explorative when new tactics were being discussed. Bursa would mean an entire reshaping of his plans.

Claudel, quick in thought, quick in action, could sympathize. "I'll do my best." He was master of the sudden but polite departure. He nodded as he rose, and left.

Five minutes more and Renwick could leave, too. *Why does he pretend? Why so eager to have me along?* Nina's questions lingered in his mind. They were only the first of more to follow: they were bound to arise, Nina being Nina. And questions demanded answers: she'd search for them, too. Bright, intelligent Nina was something Kiley hadn't bargained for. Nor Theo... She was placing herself in extreme jeopardy: one question too many, one sign that she had found an answer, and she became a danger to Theo's plans. She would be dumped out, abandoned in the wilds of Afghanistan—if she lasted that long.

Grim-faced, Renwick passed through the huge lobby, with its swirling currents of voice and movement. Outside, the light was golden, the glow of sunset spreading warmly over the wide avenue that lay beyond the hotel's driveway. But the first hint of coolness was in the air, a first touch of night lay in the far horizons. Goddamn it, he told Nina, you just don't *know* what could happen to you; you just don't know, goddamn it.

CHAPTER
14

Everything was normal. The DO NOT DISTURB notice still dangled; the door to their bedroom was locked, as it should be. After a small struggle with the cumbersome key—an ideal shape to prevent forgetful tourists from walking away with it—Nina could enter. She went in, smiles and cheerful words ready for Madge. The invalid was recovering. She was sitting on her bed, dressed in shirt and jeans.

"Feeling better?" Nina asked. "Better enough to go out for dinner? But change into your dress. We're driving up the Bosporus to one of those restaurants that—"

"Going out for dinner?" a man's voice asked, and James Kiley stepped out of the bathroom.

Madge said quickly, "When we heard your key in the lock, Jim wanted to surprise you."

And when, Nina wondered, did he get here? How did he find us? She stared at him unbelievingly.

"I hope it was a nice surprise," Kiley said, coming forward to remove her bag from her shoulder and throw it on her bed. He looked into her eyes. "Not the kind you gave me. Oh, Nina, Nina!" His arms slid around her and drew her close. "Don't do that ever again! Don't do that to me, Nina." He kissed her hard; then suddenly letting go, he turned to glance at Madge.

"Don't let me stop you," Madge told him, but he walked over to the window, stood looking out, his back to the room. Madge shrugged her shoulders, said to Nina, "How was it?"

From silence, Nina broke into a rush of words. "Fabulous. I wish you could have made it, Madge. And tomorrow, Topkapi is closed. But Suleyman will take us to the Bazaar and the Blue Mosque. He's an excellent guide. And I think he really is a poet. Flights of phrases." She eyed Jim's back. Am I suppose to go over to him and say I'm sorry? Or is he really so upset that he doesn't want to face us? "As we were leaving the second courtyard, the one where the kitchens have miles of shelving with all the Ming dinnerware displayed..." She didn't end the sentence, cutting off any reference to Bob Renwick. She could hear Madge saying, but how wonderful, how is he, was that why you were late in getting back here, what did you talk about? And if she replied that Bob had been persuading her to leave? No thank you, she decided: Jim was in a bad enough mood right now. Her fault, too, she had to admit. So she rushed on, "I was so tired and hot that I decided I wanted a seat at a café and something to drink. Tea was all I got. But it was marvelous."

"So that's where you and Suleyman were," Madge said. She spoke to Jim's back. "See, I told you Nina was perfectly safe. There was nothing to worry about."

Kiley swung around to face Nina. "Wasn't there?" he asked quietly. "First, you scare the daylights out of me when you took off in Greece. Next, you spend hours with some little tout who picked you up at the docks."

Madge cut in. "I told you all about that, and he isn't a tout. I told you all about our travel in Greece, too, so you don't have to keep worrying about Nina. You might think a little about me. I'm the one who fell ill." Then she tried to laugh, said to Nina, "He's been here for the last hour—almost—and nearly drove me back to bed with all his questions."

Kiley said, "I had every right to be anxious. Nina can't go wandering off by herself like that in a strange city."

Let's end this, Nina thought. "I'm sorry, Jim. But I really didn't expect you here until tomorrow afternoon. Did you cut your visit short in Greece?"

"Oh, they drove like mad all yesterday," Madge said, "and crossed the frontier last night. No wonder he's in a bad mood."

Nina was surprised. "Why all the rush, Jim?"

He said, "No rush, actually. Just trying to get back on schedule."

"And where is everyone now?"

"We found an inn on the outskirts of the city, nice little place with a courtyard. There are some gypsies around—local color, you know—so Tony's keeping an eye on the camper."

"And how is our Jolly Green Giant?"

Kiley stared at her.

Don't tell me he has to have that little joke explained, thought Nina.

Madge was smiling. "Don't you ever watch TV commercials, Jim?"

"Rarely."

"Our Jolly Green Giant is now dark brown," Madge told Nina. "It had an accident and the paint got scarred. Nothing serious, otherwise. But *you* know Tony. He had to have it looking perfect."

"But why not keep it green? I rather liked it."

Kiley said, "There was only a light green available. It would have taken three coats of spraying to cover the damage."

Nina dropped down on her bed. "I really am tired. We must have covered miles and miles. All I want now is a hot bath and then—"

Madge said, "You'll have to hurry. Jim has a car waiting for us."

"The innkeeper's son drove me in," Jim explained. "He'll drive us back."

"We're leaving, Nina," Madge said. "No dinner on the Bosporus. But there's one at the inn—all arranged—gypsies and music and dancing."

"Leaving?"

"Yes," said Jim, "and we are late as it is."

Nina sat bolt upright. "Look, Jim, I'm not leaving tonight. I'm going to have—" She halted abruptly.

"Have dinner with a guide? A young kid who just happened to appear at the docks this morning. Who sent him?"

"Jim—"

"Some story he laid on you! What's his name—his full name?"

"Jim—I wasn't going to have dinner with Suleyman. Madge and I were going to—"

"What's his name?"

"I didn't catch all of it. Did you, Madge?"

Madge shook her head. "He *is* a guide and interpreter, Jim. And we needed one. Without him, we wouldn't even have found a hotel where I could be sick in comfort."

"So he steered you here? I think I'll get the police onto this."

"And get him into trouble for doing nothing wrong?" Nina demanded. "You ought to thank him for making your job easy."

He looked at her sharply.

"For helping you to track us down," Nina said patiently. "There are a lot of hotels in Istanbul."

"And I must have phoned half of them."

"Come on, Jim. How many, really?" She was thinking, he really was worried about me.

"Three," he admitted and laughed and took her hands to draw her to her feet. "All those where Americans are sure to be found. Now, have a quick bath if you must—five minutes? Madge can pack for you." His arms were around her. "My God, anything could have happened to you today. I'm sorry if I was uptight. But—"

"Pack?"

"We're leaving. Madge told you."

Nina struggled free from his embrace. "Look," she said angrily, "I'll go to the inn for dinner. But I'm coming back here to sleep in that bed. It's mine and I haven't—"

"There's a bed at the inn, if that's what you want. Now hurry, or you won't even have time for that bath."

"But we have this room. Why waste the money?"

"Counting your dollars?" he teased her.

"Why can't we stay here tonight?"

"Because we leave at the crack of dawn for Bursa."

"What? We don't even have one more morning in Istanbul?"

"We've got to be in Bursa by tomorrow. That is, if you want the others to have time on the following day for that side trip to Troy. Or have you forgotten about them, Nina?"

I'll scream, she thought, if he reminds me that Troy is one place I've always wanted to see. But he didn't. He gave her a gentle push toward the bathroom. "Five minutes," he said.

She reached for her bag.

"Going to wash that, too?"

"My make-up," she told him and left for the quickest of showers. "Madge," she called back, "hand me my shirt and jeans, will you?"

And what about Bob? she was thinking as she slipped out of her Greek dress. I just can't leave without an apology, some explanation why I cut his date. I can't do that, not to Bob....From her bag she took out her small sketchbook and pen. She tore off a page, carefully leaving intact the ones already filled with her copies of decorations and designs. Her message had to be brief: the shower, now running, was ready; minutes were vanishing. She finished writing, folded her note, slipped it into her wallet.

"Seven minutes," Jim told her when she came back into

the room carrying her folded dress to pack into her duffel bag. He was at ease, tension and worry banished. "Changed your hair back to normal? I prefer it. But I liked that dress. You looked good in it. When will you wear it for me?"

"Whenever we can get dressed up for dinner. Not much chance of that for a long time. I've been looking at a map, Jim. We're really going to be traveling through some wild places. I think you should buy three black bed sheets. Then Marie-Louis, Madge, and I could wrap ourselves up like cocoons, and no one would give us a second look."

"You'll be safe. All the way into India. I'll buy you a sari there. How's that?"

"In New Delhi?" She had been trying to persuade him toward there for a major stop—after all, he knew she had spent two years in New Delhi with her parents. "I wonder how much I remember of it. I was four years old when I was sent home with Mother."

"You were too young to remember anything. It's always a disappointment to go back."

"Then where do we make a major stop? Calcutta—oh, no!"

"What about Bombay?"

"And before that?"

"Curious, aren't you?"

She concentrated on repacking the top items of her duffel bag, said, "We just like to know what we are going to see. Don't we, Madge?"

Madge nodded. "Something to look forward to. No more dead ends, Jim—like that awful café on that empty beach in Greece. Six days there? I ask you."

"We'll stop at plenty of interesting towns and villages," he assured them. "Even the wildest places will be safe." He was amused. He began walking around the room, making sure nothing had been left.

"What about languages, road signs?" Nina asked. After today's experiences, her confidence was shaken. "Tony may be good at following maps, but what about food and shelter?"

"We'll manage," Jim said. "We've got an interpreter for each country where language is a difficulty. We have one for Turkey right now. He met us at the frontier last night."

"But how?" She was knotting the duffel bag's cord, securely but slowly, wondering now about her note to Bob: would Jim find an excuse to read it when she left it at the desk?

"Advance booking. Simple. There's a tourist agency that handles these things."

"Such efficiency!" Madge exclaimed. "But what extravagance."

"Not much. You pay a little and you get a lot."

"Oh, heavens!" Nina was horrified. "Three dollars a day. Madge, we forgot all about that!"

Kiley stared at them in turn.

"Suleyman's fee," Madge said.

Nina moved to the writing table. "I'll leave him a message canceling tomorrow."

"There's no paper left, just envelopes," Madge said. "I used it to write my mother and Beth Jenson and Herb Galway and—"

"Letters?" Kiley asked. "I'll mail them downstairs while you check out. The time you waste, you two! Come on, come on."

Nina found an envelope. "I'll put the money in this and leave it at the desk."

"Marked for Suleyman? Some hope that he'll ever get it."

"At least I tried." That would make a nice epitaph for her tombstone, she thought as she scrawled Suleyman's name on the envelope. She took out her wallet and removed three dollars from her American-money section. Her note to Bob was among them. She had a brief pang of guilt as Jim, with Madge's bag in his hand, came to pick up hers. "I'll leave Suleyman's envelope downstairs with our room key," she said, and wondered at her calm voice. Not really a lie, she told herself: I didn't tell the facts, but who asked me for them? A lie is the opposite of truth, and that's a different matter. I wasn't the one to say I was going by bus to Salonika and then took a car in quite another direction.

Still troubled by that memory—but now she knew somehow that she'd never challenge Jim on that story—she followed him into the corridor.

In the lobby, Madge said, "There's Suleyman!" He was standing by one of the decorative plants, talking amiably with a bellboy. But his eyes were alert. He had seen the girls and the stranger. No astonishment showed on his face. He looked completely unconcerned, and totally innocent of the stranger's sharp scrutiny.

A seventeen- or eighteen-year-old kid, thought Kiley;

nothing to worry about there. "I'll get the right stamps for your letters," he told Madge. "Shove them in my pocket. And you tell the desk you're checking out. I'll pay the bill when it's ready."

Nina said, "I'll do that, Jim. But first—Suleyman."

"Keep it short."

"I will," she called back, already on her way. "Suleyman—your fee," she told him, handing him the envelope. "With our thanks."

"You are leaving?"

"Yes. And inside the envelope you will find a note. Please give it to my friend—the man who met us today at Topkapi. He will be here at half past eight."

"I will give it to him."

"And tell him not to worry. We are having interpreters and guides all the way to India."

"To India?"

"Yes." She smiled. "They speak English there. We will have no need for an interpreter in Bombay."

"Bombay," he repeated.

"Yes."

"I will tell him all that," Suleyman assured her solemnly.

"Thank you, Suleyman."

He pocketed the envelope, bowing politely, thanking her with a flow of charming phrases. Suddenly, he was aware that the stranger now buying stamps at the porter's desk had a keen eye directed at him. So, with another small bow, he quickly turned away to resume his conversation with the bellboy.

Abrupt, thought Nina, as she joined Madge. But she was more puzzled by herself: why mention Bombay at all? The name had slipped out. Purposefully? Just a need for a little insurance—in case the letters she'd write in Bursa to her father and Aunt Eunice would go astray like the rest of her mail? Her suspicion distressed her, stabbed at her conscience. She glanced over at Jim, now posting Madge's envelopes. At least he was standing in front of the letter box going through the right motions, although her view of them was partially blocked. Really, she asked herself, why shouldn't our mail arrive home? You're ridiculous, she told herself. Just because two postcards and a letter, sent on three different dates from three different places, never arrived. They could have been delayed by a coincidence of strikes or a slowdown in services;

such things happened nowadays. She clung to that hope as she saw Jim coming to meet her. There was a warm smile on his lips, pleasure in his eyes, and admiration, too. He'd never hurt me, not Jim. And if he lied about Salonika? There could be an explanation for that. She hoped so.

"All set?" Jim was asking. "Then let's not keep the gypsies waiting."

Suleyman seemed unnoticing of their departure, but his chat with the bellboy was over. Slowly, he moved around the lobby. Then, reassured, he headed for a public telephone.

Robert Renwick glanced at his watch: fifteen more minutes and he would have to leave. Claudel and Kahraman had now finished with the problem of Bursa and were discussing the green camper. Kahraman's verdict was that it must cross the frontier by early tomorrow morning. Otherwise, their four o'clock appointment with Miss O'Connell would not be kept. "You are quite sure it will be kept?" he asked Renwick.

"I'm sure. If not tomorrow at four, then certainly as soon as they arrive."

"Then what puzzles you, my friend?"

"That six-day stay south of Salonika."

"Twice the length of any other major stopover," Claudel agreed. "According to Gilman, that is." Merriman & Co. had been making inquiries, with excellent results. The intermediate stops of the camper were unknown as yet, but Dijon, Basel, Innsbruck, Ljubljana had been verified: three nights in each place.

Kahraman said, "They perhaps had twice as much business in northern Greece." He smiled benevolently.

"Vlakos won't like that idea," Claudel said. Nor had Vlakos liked the report of two agents sent up to the gulf to scout around its quieter beaches. After a careful search—difficult, because they couldn't question too noticeably and arouse suspicion—they had found a neglected stretch of sand, with four young foreigners in a state of happy daze. Spaced out, obviously. But no camper. No Englishman who owned it. No American called Kiley. From the woman who ran the solitary café, there had been only a blank stare and a harsh curse for the four foreigners who had invaded her beach yesterday. As for the foreigners, they had lost all sense of time, could give no sensible reply, no verification or denial of the woman's date. The agents had left to continue their search, returned two days later. The foreigners had gone. Transportation? Probably a bus, the café owner had said, and good riddance to them and their pills. "Drugs..." Claudel shook his head. "Surely they can't be so stupid as to get into that scene?"

"At the border we will search the camper," Kahraman said. "That might be a quick solution to all our problems."

And the end of any lead to Theo's plan, thought Renwick. "Kiley isn't so stupid," he told Claudel. "There will be no drugs carried across frontiers. If they are being used—" he corrected that—"if they are being administered, it will be well inside a country."

"Administered?"

"To begin with. Once the habit is started, then there will be dependence."

"And control," Claudel said. "No rebellions, no defections. Kiley wants them to stay together. Why? Cover for his own trip?"

Kahraman nodded. "Excellent cover. All innocent young people, you tell me. None with any connections to terrorists or agitators or lawbreakers. A very excellent cover for—"

The telephone rang. Kahraman took the call. It was brief, his reply equally so. He looked grave as he faced the two men. "That was from my office. My nephew just phoned to leave a message for me. Very urgent. He is on his way there now to give us the details." Kahraman was, in a surprisingly quick movement, already at the door, beginning to open it.

Renwick said, "I've got an appointment to keep."

"She will not keep it, my friend." The door closed quietly.

Renwick and Claudel stared at each other. "Five minutes?" Claudel suggested.

"Three." That was long enough to wait. Even three were an agony.

Claudel said, "I'll take the short route to Kahraman's office."

A back alley from this hotel, two courtyards, a covered passage. "We'll go together, waste no more time," Renwick said. It was dark now, and there wouldn't be many lights strung along that short distance: little danger of being seen. He kept his eyes on his watch. "Okay," he said quietly and fell silent again, his sense of failure increasing with each passing moment.

They left the radio playing, the two meager lamps glowing feebly. Cautiously, they took the service stairs, reached the ill-lit hall that would lead to the alley. There, in its heavy shadows, their pace increased. "Identification?" Claudel asked worriedly as they came to the end of the covered passage. But Kahraman, sharp-minded as always, had guessed their route: the man stationed at the back door to his office was Claudel's old friend Fahri. Claudel relaxed into a small laugh, sheathed the knife he had been carrying since he had stepped into the alley.

The rear of this three-story building might seem decrepit, but its front put quite a new face on it. Its imposing entrance near a busy avenue had a number of firms identified at its doorway—all of them dealers in rugs, handwoven and expensive, Turkish, Persian, Afghan, Indian, Chinese. Kahraman's name was among them, nestling unobtrusively in the middle of the list, his business inherited from his family when he had retired from the army. His private office was the one both Renwick and Claudel knew. The rest of his suite—four rooms strung along a winding corridor on the top floor—was a mystery. At least one of them must be devoted to import and export; the others, to Kahraman's particular interests. They were extensive. It was impossible, thought Renwick, not to be impressed by Kahraman's ingenuity and energy.

The office was medium in size, furnished with only the necessities: a desk, four chairs, two tray-topped coffee tables, but their Turkish workmanship was both intricate and perfect. The carpet was a treasure of Persian design. A prayer rug was spread near one bare white wall; a copy of the Koran lay on an elaborately carved stool. In contrast to this, the overhead lighting was a glaring monstrosity. But Kahraman would see every expression on any visitor's face: no change in a smile, no drop of the eyes would be hidden by any silk-shaded lamps.

He was seated at the desk, impatient to begin. Suleyman, at one of the brass-topped tables, was pouring three small cups of coffee. With those safely delivered, he stood aside and waited while the coffee was sipped down to its halfway level. Then, at a wave of his uncle's hand, he began his report. It was concise and clear, ending with the delivery of the note to Renwick.

"Well?" demanded Claudel as Renwick read the slip of paper.

Renwick, for politeness' sake, passed the note to Kahraman as he quoted its contents to Claudel. "Jim is here. The camper crossed the frontier last night—waiting for us at an inn on the outskirts—leaving at dawn tomorrow for the early ferry. So tonight is impossible. Truly sorry. Always, Nina."

Kahraman's composure vanished. "Crossed the frontier last night?"

Some poor devil of a border guard will have to pay for that, thought Renwick. He said, "They've changed the color of the camper."

"That long stopover in Greece..." Claudel said. "But of course! What about the camper's registration? They must have had a faked copy all prepared, giving the new color."

"New plates, too, probably. Shawfield's name would be kept—because of his passport. His signature is possibly an illegible scrawl, anyway."

Kahraman controlled his anger. "We will watch the ferries tomorrow morning. Impossible to find that inn on the outskirts—a hundred or more. And in which direction from the city? Our best chance is with the car ferries. We do not know the new color of this camper, but we shall look for eight young people, two of them girls with fair hair. We will follow them into Asia and see if they indeed go to Bursa. I do not trust these men." He shook his head sadly.

"I'd like to—" Claudel began, fell silent as he noted Kahraman's small gesture: a hand raised delicately for one brief moment.

"You did well," Kahraman said to his nephew. "The young lady was definite when she spoke about interpreters and guides? Not just one interpreter and guide?"

"Interpreters and guides. All the way to India. In Bombay there would be no need for them. That is what she said."

"Thank you, Suleyman." Kahraman smiled a dismissal. As the door closed behind the boy, Kahraman could not resist saying in his most offhand manner, "Fortunate that I had him posted in the Hilton lobby."

"Most fortunate," Claudel said. Thank God, Renwick was thinking as he nodded his agreement.

"And what would you like?" Kahraman asked Claudel. "To go on that car ferry tomorrow morning? Follow the camper to Bursa?"

"With Fahri, if that doesn't inconvenience you."

"Go with Fahri, certainly. But not to Bursa. I shall arrange surveillance of the camper. It would be best if you and Fahri were not visible immediately. Later..." Kahraman paused and considered for almost a minute. "We have so many frontiers. Greece and Bulgaria we no longer need consider. But Russia, Iran, Iraq, Syria—which border will the camper cross on its way to Afghanistan?" This was developing into a wide-scale operation. Kahraman's eyes gleamed with pleasure at the difficulties facing him.

Renwick said, "In Amsterdam, Nina said that Kiley was avoiding Communist countries. There's no work for him there—no rebels to be encouraged and organized. Definitely not allowed."

Claudel laughed. "He traveled through Yugoslavia. That shows his opinion of its politics."

"Syria, Iraq, Iran." Kahraman was thoughtful. "There's unrest in Iran. Trouble will come in another month or two. But if Kiley makes haste, and if he has the right guide, he will pass through quite easily by following the main route east. Iran has a frontier with Afghanistan. Syria and Iraq do not. But we shall see, as we follow his direction from Turkey. And you," he said to Claudel, "will be informed in time to cross whatever frontier the camper uses. You will need Turkish papers—was that what you would also like? And Fahri will, of course, be with you. He speaks several dialects, he knows Parsee. He has traveled much through these regions— all the way to India. Carpets and rugs. They take many months, sometimes a year, to make. Naturally, Fahri, as my firm's representative, visits the makers of these rugs to place another order. Yes, I think it is a possible mission."

"A car big enough to let us sleep in it?" Claudel asked. There were stretches of desert and wastelands with no inns.

Kahraman nodded. "Changes of cars may be necessary. It will be arranged."

"Communications?" Renwick asked. I'm out of all this, he thought unhappily. My Turkish isn't adequate, I don't look like a Turk. And yet, and yet...

"Continual communication," Kahraman assured him, but gave no details. "It is customary practice. We are not only interested in buying extraordinary rugs. We also must try to learn what our neighbors are doing. Their political changes can affect us, too."

Renwick nodded. But his depression grew. "Will Pierre and Fahri be enough surveillance? Two cars, perhaps?"

"And you in the second one?" Claudel broke in. "No, Bob.

Fahri and I can handle this assignment. Neither of us will
be recognized by the O'Connell girl or her friend Westerman.
What explanation could you give them if you met in some
unlikely place? Your Nina might have enough sense to keep
quiet about such a meeting. But Westerman? Too much risk,
Bob. Better wait until Bombay. You can take over then."

As usual, Claudel made good sense. Renwick's lips tightened, but he said nothing.

Kahraman studied him. "No need for further discussion,
my friend. You are needed in America. A message from Gilman, in London, came here just as I returned to this office.
It is decoded." He opened an embossed leather folder on his
desk, drew out a sheet of paper. "For you," he said, handing
it to Renwick.

The message was brief. "Frank Cooper advises you see him
in Washington soonest. Interesting developments need immediate study." Renwick passed the sheet to Claudel.

"Developments?" Claudel speculated.

Renwick shrugged. "Could be anything." It was certainly
urgent. And important enough to be sent as a carefully coded
message. He rose. "I'll leave tomorrow. Early. Or," he asked
Kahraman, "is there a late flight tonight?"

"For Paris, perhaps, by way of Rome. I shall check and
telephone you at your hotel. Next visit"—Kahraman rose
from the nest of red silk cushions in his carved armchair—
"we shall see each other more often." There was an affectionate embrace and wishes for a safe and good journey.

Claudel was also on his feet, uncertain whether he should
go or stay.

Kahraman decided for him. "We have much to discuss.
Fahri will join us. Your strategy must be well planned."

"Then it's good-bye," Claudel said to Renwick, walking
with him to the door. "Until Bombay?"

"I wish you better luck than I had on this trip. Keep in
touch if you can."

"I'll keep you briefed, when possible."

"If you feel—sense—some crisis, some danger—"

"I'll make contact with Nina, show her she has friends."

"Get her out!" Renwick's voice was sharp.

"Kidnap her?" Claudel was smiling. "Fahri is just the man
for that." Then he turned serious. "Stop worrying about those
spaced-out kids on that beach. Kiley wouldn't risk drugs with
Nina. He wants to meet her father, doesn't he?"

"Tell Nina I gave you this." On impulse Renwick reached into his jacket for Merriman & Co.'s card. In pencil he wrote: *Courtyard of the Janissaries.*

Claudel read the message, raised an eyebrow. "Adequate introduction?"

"If you need more, remind her how she pitied the tribute children."

Claudel looked at his friend curiously, pocketed the card in silence. They shook hands in a tight grip. Then Renwick left, with a last salute and a word of warm thanks to Kahraman—an imposing figure standing erect beside his massive desk, not one crease in the silver-gray jacket, not one hair escaping from its brilliantine hold, not one furrow on that smooth benign face.

"Now," said Kahraman, "I arrange for transport to Paris. Then to business, Pierre." He seated himself on the red silk cushions, switched on intercommunications, began giving orders.

CHAPTER
15

At Dulles Airport, Frank Cooper was in the car that met Renwick. Cooper, large frame and long legs occupying most of the rear seat, white hair almost hidden by his battered felt hat, well-tailored suit worn uncaringly, had the look of repressed excitement in his broad grin of welcome. At the wheel, Salvatore Marini also showed pleasure, with a smile of white teeth all the brighter by contrast with his olive complexion. His thick hair was still dark although he was almost of Cooper's vintage—they had worked as a team in their OSS visits to occupied territory some thirty-five years ago: Cooper, the lieutenant in charge; Marini, his sergeant and radio expert.

Renwick dropped his bag into the front seat with a "Hi, Sal!" before he slid into a corner of space beside Cooper. Controls were pressed to lock the doors and raise the glass partition. Not even Sal, now guardian and general factotum to Cooper for the past thirty years, needed to hear all the details of his boss's business. Sal understood: the less he knew, the safer he—and the information—would stay.

Cooper was studying Renwick. "A bad journey?"

"Delays. At Rome. And at De Gaulle. Sorry if I'm behind schedule."

"Not at all. You're on time. How was Istanbul?"

"It's fine. But I wasn't. I missed. Badly."

"Not your fault. A matter of luck. Sometimes it's with us; other times, against."

"You've heard from Kahraman?"

"At six this morning. Nina and her friends are about to leave Bursa. The camper is brown, by the way."

"That was a short stay." Renwick tried to calculate it exactly, but the long flight and time changes had left his mind soggy.

"Two nights. But productive from Kahraman's point of view. No details, of course. I'll hear more when I visit Gilman in London on Monday."

That's where I'd like to be right now, thought Renwick, on top of all the reports coming in. Of course, they might not: there could be long gaps when I'd sit staring at a map.

"I've just bought you a house."

Renwick's exhaustion left him.

"Rather, I've leased you a house with a view to buying it. Your hunch about Mr. Otto Remp's interest in real estate near Los Angeles was on the right track."

"Theo has got himself a safe house in Southern California?"

"I thought that would revive you," Cooper said.

"And you've rented a place near him?"

"About five miles away by road. Half of that distance by a climb over rough terrain. Let me explain." Cooper took out a map of the area. "Theo, as well as purchasing an office for his West-East Travel bureau, used the same agent to find a house for his friend from New York, a Mr. Walter Gunter. Gunter took possession about a month ago. It's a large property, several buildings, many acres, called Rancho San Carlos. The house where you'll be staying for a couple of weeks is much smaller—just room for you and Sal and Tim MacEwan. Mac is flying to San Diego today from Montreal. Sal will leave tonight to join him. They'll pick up the keys and have the house opened and ready for your arrival. You'll go in by Los Angeles, reaching there by Friday."

Today was Thursday. Or wasn't it? Renwick asked himself. "And do I just waste today in Washington?"

"Catching up on your sleep and getting mealtimes back to normal," Cooper suggested. "Sorry to have brought you here on such short notice, but this is urgent business. Something is going on at Rancho San Carlos. All we could learn from our real-estate firm—don't worry, we didn't use Theo's agent: we got our little house through a San Diego outfit— is that Rancho San Carlos needs a lot of improvement and the new owner has brought in his own work crew to do the job. Who are these workers, Bob? Who is Walter Gunter? We had inquiries made in Los Angeles, where he seemingly put in an appearance at the real-estate office. From the description, he comes close to the photograph you gave me—taken at a café in The Hague.

"Maartens." Renwick caught his breath.

"Could be. We'd like to know, wouldn't we? And what's the purpose of Rancho San Carlos?"

"It might be a training camp, or a briefing station," Renwick suggested.

"Something's being cooked up. One hell of a brew." Cooper spread out the map and pointed. "There's Sawyer Springs—just over seventy miles southeast of Los Angeles, about fifty miles northeast of San Diego, and some forty miles from the Pacific. Your place is three miles east of the little town—fewer than eight hundred inhabitants, a gas station, agricultural implements, a general store, not much else. You'll find the house easily: its name, Buena Vista, is well marked. All clear?"

Renwick nodded. "I rent a car at Los Angeles?"

"One has been booked for you. Name of Roger Black."

"What's my line of work?"

"You're a writer—natural history."

"The open-air life?" A good excuse for wandering around rough terrain.

"That's it. Mac is your secretary. Sal is cook and bottle washer, chauffeur and buyer of supplies."

"At least we won't starve." Sal was a master at cooking as well as an expert in electronics. "But can you spare Sal?"

"He's all set to go with you. Like an old war-horse, he senses action ahead. Wish I could be there, too, but I'll have a couple of quiet days at East Hampton to get my thoughts ready for London on Monday. After that, it's Rome with a team of lawyers, and then over to Algiers. I'll be in New York by the time you get back. Well, here's your motel, Mr. Black. I hope your room is comfortable." Cooper pushed an envelope into Renwick's hand. "Driver's license and ticket for tomorrow morning's flight to Los Angeles. You board the plane at Dulles. I thought this place would be a handy location."

The car drew up; the glass partition was lowered. "Good hunting," Cooper said softly. "Sal will bring you some equipment and heavier clothes. Hope they fit." Then he remembered one last piece of news, small but amusing. "About that cocktail party I gave on your last evening in New York—just as well you didn't appear. We had gate-crashers. One came with a young man from the State Department: beautiful woman, brunette, an interior decorator from Brussels."

Renwick, reaching for his bag, looked back sharply at Cooper, who went on, "She's now living in Washington. She asked me how you were." Cooper laughed, shaking his head. "She was so sorry you weren't at the party."

"Still using her own name?"

"Thérèse Colbert? Of course. She thinks she is in the clear, that no one suspects. Cool customer. But damned attractive."

"She's all of that," Renwick said, tight-lipped. He opened the car door and stepped out. "Be seeing you," he told Sal. By the time Renwick reached the motel entrance, the car was already on its way to Cooper's branch office in Washington.

California's multiple-lane highways brought Renwick halfway to Sawyer Springs. The rest of the journey from Los Angeles was then on narrow roads, well surfaced against all weathers, nicely cambered for any twists or turns as the route began a long ascent. The fruit ranches, with their orange groves drinking in the hot September sun to nurture their fruit for next January, gave way to the avocado farms, acre after acre of neatly spaced trees, richly green against the red soil of the gentle slopes. Then, as the incline increased, there were rough fields with wild flowers of blue and bright yellow, with scattered boulders and outcrops of rock, with groupings of trees. To the east, farther than he would travel but near enough for the dark green of bristling pines to be marked, were the forest-covered reaches of Mount Palomar, with its observatory on the crest of six thousand-odd feet. But this was hardly the time for stargazing, Renwick thought regretfully. Bird-watching, and of some ugly specimens at that, would keep him well occupied for the next two weeks.

Sawyer Springs was like the rest of the isolated small towns—villages? settlements?—he had passed: a stretch of two-story houses along a lethargic main street. If there was a church, it was well disguised; probably hidden, spireless, in the background of eucalyptus trees. One small motel, no cars visible; a post office adjoining the general store; no police station; a volunteer fire truck near a repair shop for tractors, only one evident; a small café; a gas station, which seemed to be the one flourishing place of business—it, at least, had been given a recent coat of paint. There were few people visible at this time of day, and only two dogs asleep under the tractor. This was a town, thought Renwick, with its life ebbing.

Beyond Sawyer Springs were more fields and a gentle slope away of land on the right-hand side of the road. To his left, there were a few houses, well separated, each with considerable acreage. Buena Vista was the third one, shielded like the others by trees and its own spread of ground. The short driveway was of hard-packed earth, no longer red but grayish brown, a color matched by the weathered wood of the two-story building. There was an adjacent garage, a large chimney of rough-hacked stone, a garden that had been abandoned, window boxes unplanted. The door was wide open, and Sal was standing there: one encouraging note, thought Renwick as he got out of the car. He looked back at the road. Buena Vista lived up to its name: there was a clear view of the southern hills, rolling limitlessly to the east and west. Space and peace, a feeling that nothing had been touched by man.

Sal stood beside him, eyeing his clothes. "You'll need something warmer for this part of the world. We're three thousand feet high."

"Above snake level?" Renwick smiled. In Wyoming, that was the safety limit, he had been told. Only a month since he had been there? Scarcely two months since he had met Crefeld in Amsterdam? How much learned, how much planned since then, how much still to do. He turned to the house. "Where's MacEwan?"

"Mixing the drinks. Snakes—what kind of snakes?"

"Probably not here," Renwick reassured him. "Nearer the coast, you get rattlers in the canyons. Climb up into people's back yards."

Sal didn't believe him. "You notice the drop in temperature? Twenty degrees cooler, at least. And no humidity." Thinking of Washington and New York, his smile was back to normal.

They entered directly into the main room, medium-sized, furnished with odds and ends—a makeshift for renters, no polished surfaces to be marred or scarred, no carpets to be spotted by stains or burns. But there was a fireplace and logs at its side; three armchairs and a deep-cushioned couch; tables, one large and strong, two small and rickety; a shelf of paperbacks, a radio, and a TV set.

"They work," Mac said, bringing over a Scotch-and-soda. "Everything works. Miss Gladstone tested it all. Good to see you, Bob."

"Good to see you here, Mac." Renwick took a long drink. He pointed to the flowers in a vase on the mantelpiece, then at a basket of fruit centered on the large table. "Miss Gladstone?" The woman's touch, he thought. "Who the hell is Gladstone?"

"Works for the San Diego real-estate office. She was waiting for us there when we picked up the keys, led the way here to make sure we didn't get lost. Actually," MacEwan went on in his serious Canadian voice, tinged with Scots, "she was very helpful. Stopped at Escondido—that's a fair-sized town about twenty miles from here—and showed Sal the biggest supermarket. He bought enough food to feed us for the next week."

"And some light bulbs," Sal called from the kitchen, which was almost a part of the room. He came back with his can of beer. "Yes, she went around this place, switching on and off lights, turning on faucets, flushing the toilet, checking the refrigerator, stove—everything."

"Too helpful?" Renwick asked.

"Just a nice warm-hearted woman," Mac judged. Then his thoughtful face cracked into a smile. "When she left, Sal went around this place. With his useful little gadget. Found no bugs, no nasty surprises."

"Changed the light bulbs, too," Sal said cheerfully.

"Relax, Bob," Mac told Renwick. "Have a seat."

"I've been sitting for the better part of three days." Renwick paced around the room, looked out of its windows—two faced south, toward the road, three faced west toward a field bordered by a few old trees. Very few.

"Well, I'm resting my legs. Sal and I've been unpacking for the last two hours—got all his paraphernalia set up in his room. That's on the ground floor."

"Lets me keep an eye on the doors," Sal said. "There's a big TV aerial; we'll have no trouble disguising our own. You want to see upstairs?"

"Later, Sal."

Mac said, "Our rooms are up there. A lot of windows. View at the back of the house is mostly of hill, and of burned trees. There was a big fire in this region a few years back. So Miss Gladstone says. I tell you, Bob, she was very helpful. She was born near here, lives in Escondido, still keeps in touch with Sawyer Springs. That's why, I guess, she was miffed by the sale of Rancho San Carlos through a Los Angeles real-estate firm: she had it on her list, and L.A. shouldn't have horned in."

"You actually asked about San Carlos?" Renwick's step

had halted. He stared at MacEwan in astonishment. Mac was a careful man; definitely cautious. That was the reason, Renwick supposed, why Gilman had sent him here—to act as a brake on Renwick's hunches. That reason, as well as the fact that Mac and Renwick were solid friends, a good team dating back to five years ago.

Mac's blue eyes, strong in color against the contrast of his reddish fair hair and pink cheeks, were amused. "I just asked about our neighbors in the next house up the road. They are a retired couple, quiet, live there year-round. But that led to a complete tour of the district: the house after that one belongs to some Hollywood character who's seldom here. Then the road starts turning to the north, passes San Carlos. All that, and more, came out unsolicited."

"Talkative, isn't she?"

Sal said, "And big. Must be five feet ten, a hundred and fifty pounds, in a pink pants suit." Sal, who was close to five feet six, preferred smaller European types, nicely rounded, who wore black silk dresses.

Mac said, "She was just hoping we'd like it here—enough to buy this place. So she wanted to make us feel it was peaceful, just right for a naturalist. We are not to let the excavating at Rancho San Carlos bother us—a few bangs now and again, but soon it will be over. The workmen keep to themselves, sleep up there in the old stable—the horses left years ago."

Sal finished his beer. He had heard all this. "Time to get dinner on the stove," he said and headed for the kitchen, closing its wide double doors carefully behind him.

Quietly, Mac said, "The workmen don't come into Sawyer Springs, not even on a Saturday night. They are driven down to Escondido in a minibus. But some people in Sawyer Springs have sharp eyes: no beards went out last Saturday to Escondido; two beards traveled back on Sunday afternoon. Gladstone thought the workmen were coming in relays to speed up the work. She offered that little item as part of her not-to-worry theme: soon all the bustle would be over, and peace would be everywhere."

Renwick relaxed, poured himself another drink, sat down. "My belated apologies to Miss Gladstone," he said. "They're coming in relays, certainly. But what kind of work? How many at a time? Or did Sawyer Springs' sharp eyes miss on that?"

"I've the impression they miss very little. And why not?

They've been given no employment by Rancho San Carlos; no custom, either. They've told Miss Gladstone—she's one of them, went to school here when there was a school—that if Gunter had any sense, he'd have hired locally, got the work done just as well, instead of bringing in five or six at a time."

"And what does Sawyer Springs have to say about those big bangs?"

"There are cottages to be built. The workmen ran into rock, so they have to level the ground by some blasting."

"Gunter is expecting a lot of guests?"

"He's planning a Foundation for Ecological Studies—with seminars. Miss Gladstone thought you'd like to meet him, since your interests coincide." Mac was enjoying himself immensely. "But not this weekend. He left yesterday, told the post office to hold all mail until Monday."

If Gunter is Maartens, why would he leave for a weekend when a new group of workmen was due? Renwick wondered. "Frank Cooper thinks he may be Maartens. He was the one who directed Crefeld's assassin, you know."

Mac's smile had vanished. And almost had you murdered, too, he was thinking.

Renwick said, his voice flat and emotionless, "He also controls Thérèse Colbert. She's operating in Washington, I hear."

"Are you sure—that she's one of his agents? She could have been just another innocent caught up in—"

"I hoped for that. I kept hoping. But no innocent makes a calculated move. She turned up at one of Frank's parties, expecting me to be there—possibly thinking we might start where we left off. She could only have known I'd be at that party through a telephone call from Frank's office."

"Cooper's office phone was bugged?"

"Must have been."

Mac said angrily, "Where was Sal? Doesn't Cooper have him check all phones?"

"At home, yes. But bring Sal continuously into the office? Difficult."

"Cooper takes chances." Mac shook his head.

"Let's trust he didn't have anyone connected with his law firm rent this house."

"We're in the clear, I hope. Cooper had someone in San Diego do the renting."

"Thank heavens for that." Frank did take chances, though. He must have made a lot of inquiries in Los Angeles about

Mr. Otto Remp and his new branch of West-East Travel—how else had he found out so much in so short a time? Why else the tap on his phone? "You know, I think we ought to advise him to cancel his visit to Merriman & Co. Postpone it until Theo's interest in him fades a little." Suddenly, surprising Mac by his speed of movement, he was opening the kitchen doors. "Sal—can you contact the boss at East Hampton?"

Sal looked astonished. "At East Hampton? No. In his New York house, yes. But we can always reach him by phone at the cottage."

Not from this place. "It would have to be a call from Escondido." Even that was unsatisfactory, when you were trying to argue Frank out of a visit he was all set to make.

Mac echoed Renwick's thoughts. "You'll never persuade him unless you can give details. And that's impossible. What details, anyway, Bob? You're overworrying. Come on, let's get some fresh air before the sun starts setting. The view from the back porch will interest you. Once it's dark, we could take a stroll up the hill. Sal's brought you some rough clothes, and I've some thick-soled sneakers you can borrow. We take the same size in shoes, remember?"

Renwick nodded, repressed a smile. Mac wasn't a tall man, but he always—perhaps to make himself feel closer to five foot ten rather than three inches shorter—wore shoes that were too big, and filled up the extra space with heavy wool socks.

Mac led the way out of the back door onto the porch. A small terrace faced them (patio, it was called in this part of the world), ending in a stretch of grass bounded by a few trees that had survived the forest fire. A change in the wind perhaps? Fires played strange tricks. Beyond the trees the hill slope steepened, a place of sad reminders in the blackened trunks and leafless boughs, yet a place of new promises, too: man-size saplings, thick bushes, grass, even wild flowers, had replaced burned-out ashes.

"That," Mac said, looking at the hill, "is our quick route to the back of Rancho San Carlos. The distance, if my map is accurate, is less than two miles. By road, it's between four and five. That's because the road—once it's past the retired couple and the Hollywood guy—takes a sharp curve north, leaving our immediate neighbors in a kind of peninsula. We'll cut across its neck, won't even have to cross their land—get the idea?"

"I've got it." The saplings and undergrowth should afford sufficient cover. "Tomorrow, we'll spend the day bird-watching—see the general layout, note who is prowling around. By night, we could have a closer look."

"Enter the grounds? My God—you move fast."

The workmen, so-called, would be in Escondido; replacements not due until Sunday. There would be a caretaker and a couple of guards, but Gunter himself would be absent. "This Saturday might be the best chance we could have," said Renwick.

CHAPTER

16

That night, Renwick and MacEwan explored the hill behind Buena Vista, testing the terrain and the cover it afforded. The sky was clear; the moon in its last quarter was at half strength. Once they were over the crest, they could sit, catch their breath, and study whatever lights they could see at Rancho San Carlos. There were few of them. But at least, thought Renwick, we know the position of the place; we see the kind of ground over which we'll travel; we can even calculate the time it will take for a closer approach, much closer than this. In daylight, with field glasses and telescope, we'll try for a front-row view.

"Enough?" he asked. Mac nodded. Carefully, they worked their way back to the top of the hill. All was quiet; nothing stirred around them: a peaceful scene, and an eerie one. Moonlight turned grass to pewter gray, bushes and saplings into islands of dark shadow, burned trees into black telephone poles—scarce and scattered—that pointed to the stars.

In half an hour, they reached Buena Vista, welcoming them with lights and warmth. Sal had had his own job to do under cover of night: extending the long wire, which would act as the antenna for his transmitter, right up the outside wall from his bedroom window. Safely attached, he told them, to the base of the existing television mast. His transmitter was small but powerful; so was his short-wave radio. He could reach London with ease. Seven thousand miles were no difficulty at all. "Just encode the words and I'll send them." He smiled, his dark eyes amused. "I even had time for a little drive past the front of Rancho San Carlos. Nothing much to see. Just dark windows and a light over the door, a garden with a wall and a big iron gate, a driveway. How was its rear view?"

"Quiet. But that's where the buildings are. Tomorrow night we'll need you."

"So?" Sal's eyes beamed with pleasure. Then he went to

check locked doors and downstairs windows, and there was a general drift toward bed.

Next morning, Renwick and Mac took a normal stroll around Buena Vista's acres. By ten o'clock, with a sideways approach, they had started climbing the hill. Movements became cautious: they were no longer two nature lovers out on a bird-watching spree. In long-sleeved shirts and jeans, both dark blue like their heavy-soled sneakers, they were not obtrusive. Mac had covered his fair skin with an antisun lotion that gave him a banana tan—better, he stated, than a third-degree burn. By day, September could be blistering hot in this high country, even if night was shivering cool.

They reached the crest, went over it at a low crouch. Carefully, they selected their way downhill, headed for a spot that seemed promising, keeping shoulders bent and their heads well below the height of the bushes and saplings. They halted. But they could see only part of the buildings that were grouped around a wide field stretching almost to the base of this hillside. "Not close enough," Renwick murmured. Mac nodded. They would have to go much farther down, until the bushes began to thin out. At present, from this nice safe cover, a complete view was broken by clusters of shrubbery.

Progress was slow, and painful on the hips. The incline was not steep, but definite enough to make them descend half-sitting, half-slipping. Give me a belly crawl any day, thought Renwick. But he'd have that, too, on his way back. The bushes became scarcer, thinning into a broken line. Over to his left, some distance away, the hillside was bare except for boulders and crags. He rejected that direction, aimed for a large bush not far from one of the burned trees. It seemed perfect: its branches didn't hug the ground, giving Mac and himself about eighteen inches of clearance as they lay prone under its leaves.

"Careful," Renwick whispered, pointing upward.

Mac nodded. As he raised himself on his elbows for a clear view of the compound below them, he could sense the branches were only a few inches away from his raised head. One careless movement would send leaves swaying. Slowly he adjusted his minitelescope, took out his pad and pen from one breast pocket. The other one bulged with a flask of water. It was going to be a long morning.

Now let's see what we face tonight, Renwick thought, and
brought his field glasses into focus.

In the foreground was the field—short grass, but rough—
bounded by a tall chain-link fence, new-looking, no sign of
weathering. In the background there was a two-story house,
not as large as expected but still dominant: yellow stucco in
Spanish style with a ripple of red tiles on a low-pitched roof;
tall, narrow windows on the second floor with wrought-iron
balconies; on the first floor, fewer and smaller windows with
total protection in their elaborate screens; a door that led
onto a small paved terrace with a large wooden table and two
benches. No driveway around the house from the road, so all
deliveries must be carried into those back premises from some
service door at the front of the house. Cumbersome but effective as far as security went: no curious eyes would have
a chance to see the extent of the compound.

To the left of the main house, adjoining it at right angles,
was a one-story building, whitewashed, undecorated; windows small, one door. A mess hall perhaps? At the moment,
with no activity visible, it was impossible to judge.

The old stable was easier to identify. In Californian custom
it was situated some distance from the main house; a long
building, solid, that—like the possible mess hall which it
faced across the open ground—ran at right angles from the
line of the main building. Near it was the barn, with its huge
door closed and small windows boarded over. Abandoned? It
looked that way. Yet there were vents under its high roof
equally spaced. Air-conditioning units? One thing was definite: it was part of the compound, enclosed by the fence that
ran from the right-hand side of the main house to the stable
and barn, then swept in a wide semicircle around the grass
to reach the rear wall of the mess hall.

Garage? It must lie to the front of the house, near that
driveway Sal had noted last night, with easy access to the
road. He could check on that later. Now it was this rear view
that interested him. The fence in particular. Where was the
gate? Possibly close to the right-hand corner of the house.
Only one? His eyes searched the fence, section by section.
Right in the center of its long sweep around the field, situated
immediately below him, was a narrower section of fencing—
perhaps three feet wide. Definitely a gate, edged by heavier
supports. He tapped Mac's shoulder and borrowed the telescope.

Adjusting it carefully, Renwick could bring the gate right up to him, almost as if he were standing six feet away. It was secured by a lock, a solid-looking piece of metal, with a dark spot in its smooth surface. A keyhole? So that the gate could be unlocked from either side? Logical enough: anyone who came out onto the hill would need to get back into the compound, unless he wanted a long walk around the property to the front of the main house.

Renwick's eyes traveled up the height of the gate, about eight feet, he guessed. Well above the lock he saw something that blocked the edge of daylight between the gate and the fence. Small, neat, its color white. A circuit connector for an alarm system? Yes: two white-covered wires were attached, carefully strung through the heavy mesh, one running around the left of the fence, the other crossing the gate to pass its upper hinge and continue around the right side of the fence. A very complete alarm system, probably switched on from the main house. Renwick drew a long breath. But problems were to be expected.

He angled the telescope lower, studying the base of the fence. Then he noticed something resembling a path, a track made by footsteps, that led from the gate straight to the hillside. Anyone following it might pass near this spot. Too near, perhaps, for any comfort. Renwick tapped Mac's shoulder, returned the telescope, and gestured to a bush farther off to their right.

Mac wasn't enthusiastic about any change; he was nicely settled where he was. But Renwick was already on the move, flat on his belly, propelling himself by elbow power across the sloping hill. Mac pocketed pad and pencil and telescope, and followed. At least, he was thinking, he had made some preliminary sketches of the layout. His forebodings were correct: the new hiding place might be secure but it was hellishly uncomfortable. The large bush Renwick had chosen had low-sweeping branches so that they had practically to fight their way into the middle of its tangle. But the view, Mac had to admit, was good.

Renwick said, almost inaudibly, "Do you see lights around the fence?"

Mac shook his head. "Could be well hidden. Floods perhaps. Turned on by a master switch?"

Renwick nodded. No floods were visible, but they must be somewhere, ready to beam over every inch of ground at the first alarm. It seemed as if Gunter preferred to leave his place looking as natural as possible: a nightly blaze of lights would set the sky aglow and Sawyer Springs wondering.

Suddenly, peace ended. The house door was flung open, a voice commanded, two large Dobermans came bounding out. They made directly for the mess hall. A man—black-haired, early thirties possibly, broad-shouldered, dressed in jeans and sweat shirt—followed them as far as the terrace, stood watching them as they reached the end of the building and began a patrol of the entire fence. As they approached the barn, the man gave a whistle, fingers at his mouth. The dogs halted abruptly, raced back to their handler, stood on either side of him as the barn door opened. Six men trooped out, dressed in work clothes. Young men, Renwick saw; early twenties, he guessed. A heavy-built man, older, half-bald, was the last to leave the barn. He closed and padlocked the door, started after the others, shouting directions. There was a babble of replies, some laughter, and the troop of six jogged over to the mess hall and disappeared inside.

Eleven-thirty, Renwick noted. A bit early for a midday meal. If mess hall it was.

It wasn't. The six men came straggling out. Two carried automatic rifles; two were joking about the grenades they had strung over their shoulders; one carried a small box, carefully; his mate, with a canvas bag on his back, was horsing around with something he tossed in the air and caught (much laughter) before it reached the ground. A yell from their instructor, waiting near the fence, ended the fun and games. The group joined him, drawing together as the dog handler, with his two Dobermans now leashed, came slowly down center field to unlock the gate and swing it inward. The six armed men and the baldheaded supervisor passed through. The Dobermans, never a bark or a whine, walked back to the terrace with their master. There, he sat down on the corner of a bench, the dogs resting beside him. Peace returned.

Not for long, Renwick was thinking. It had been plastic that was tossed in the air. The small wooden box held blasting caps. No spool of wire had been visible, so the canvas bag carried the means for detonating the caps by remote control.

"God," said MacEwan as he heard footsteps on the path. "Plastic. Here?"

"Keep praying." Renwick rolled over on his side to watch for the armed men. Now he knew why he had seen no signs of any demolition down in the compound. The practice ground was on this hillside.

The voices drew nearer. Too near. American voices. They were a talkative bunch, but the phrases overlapped and Renwick could pick up nothing of importance. Except the names— that could be their supervisor who was calling them out as he posted the men to their positions on the hillside. First names or nicknames, not much help at all. Renwick exchanged a glance with Mac and received a look of equal frustration. There was a scramble of feet. (Receding, Renwick judged thankfully.) Then silence, a long silence, broken only by the heavy tread of someone approaching where they lay. The footsteps halted. Slowly, Renwick's hand parted a cluster of leaves. The baldheaded man was clearly in sight, barely five yards away, his face turned to the hillside, his arm upraised, waiting.

The arm dropped. There was an eruption of violent sounds. They came almost simultaneously: the swift blast of automatic fire, the explosion of plastic, the burst of a grenade. The bullets had been aimed at the blackened trunk of a burned-out tree, close enough to let Renwick see the wood splinter. The plastic had been used in a rock crevice farther along the hill, with only a few shreds of stone visible as they shot into the air. The grenades—and these men had taken a big chance; they must have held them alive in their hands while they waited for the signal—left a small cloud of dust farther uphill.

Renwick glanced again at Mac. He, too, had found a viewing space between the leaves and was staring at the settling dust. Then he looked at Renwick, shook his head partly in surprise, partly in admiration. It had been a neat maneuver, three separate operations to sound as one. Sawyer Springs would hear only a distant bang and say, "There goes more demolition."

Instructions were shouted. The maneuver was repeated. And again. That seemed to be the allotment, possibly for the town's sake: not enough to arouse curiosity, just enough to give the men practice. They were good, too damned good, thought Renwick. They weren't beginners. This morning's exercise was a matter of keeping their hand in. Or of learning teamwork? That idea depressed him still more.

The instructor was slow to leave the hill. First, he inspected the blasted tree, its trunk now split in two. He moved out of Renwick's sight, but his heavy boots could be heard as he scrambled along the slope toward the small boulders where the plastic had been detonated. Then he returned nearer to the path and had a look where the grenades had landed, presumably checking how close they had come to some marked target. At last he was satisfied, and hurried down to the fence where his men were waiting for him. They weren't a silent crew: talk, jokes, laughter rose up the hillside. A merry romp, Renwick thought bitterly: is that all it is to them? No sense of responsibility, no thought about the deadliness of the weapons entrusted to them? Nothing but the feeling of power—exciting, exhilarating? He nodded to Mac, and once more they were lying prone, raised on their elbows, field glasses and telescope trained on the compound.

"Close," said Mac.

"Too damned close."

The group eased back through the fence gate, kept well apart from the handler with his two Dobermans as he came toward them, then hurried to deposit their equipment in the armory.

"Careless," was Renwick's comment. "He left that gate unlocked while they were on the hill."

"Or too confident." The man was taking his own good time in securing the gate. Perhaps his movements would be brisker if Gunter was around to watch him from an upstairs window.

"Comes to the same thing." Renwick was watching a middle-aged man coming out of the main house, carrying onto the terrace a heavily loaded tray. He dumped it on the table, returned to the house for a second load. No one else in the kitchen to help him? He was the cook, apparently: a large white apron was tied around his bulging waistline. Again he lumbered back into the house, brought out a third tray. Once it was set on the table, he left without a glance at the seven men who were reaching the terrace. The handler paid no attention to them, either. With the leashed Dobermans closely at heel, he followed the cook into the house.

Two things probable, thought Renwick: the kitchen—judging from the speed of the tray deliveries—was close to the door; and there was no socializing between staff and terrorists. Security reasons? The less the exchange between the two groups, the greater the anonymity of identities and backgrounds. There was a third thing to be noted, and this was definite: not even terrorists trusted those Dobermans. That was marked: the group had kept silent, even motionless, as the dogs had been led across the terrace.

Now, with the door closed, food was set out and talk began. Voices were low. The instructor began a monologue, perhaps a post-mortem on this morning's exercises. The others ate, listened intently. It was a long meal. Mac drew out his flask of water and handed it to Renwick with a smile.

The meal was over. The talk went on. And then it ended. Renwick gave a sigh of relief, stretched his back and rubbed his neck and shoulders. Mac finished his last sketches, jotted down the scant names he had heard—Joe, Bill, Shorty, Tiny, Hal, Walt—and buttoned his pad and pencil securely into his breast pocket. "Dispersal?" he asked, looking back at the group.

It seemed like it. The six men were on their feet, began walking slowly toward the stable. The instructor, still on the terrace, called after them, "Leave nothing behind. Be ready to move—sixteen-thirty out front. Don't keep me waiting!" With that reminder, he went into the main house.

Moving out by bus at half past four? Renwick and Mac looked at their watches: three-quarters of an hour to go.

"Need we stay?" Mac asked.

Renwick didn't answer. A cook, a watchman with a couple of Dobermans, an instructor—all of them seemed to live in the main house. Was that all? Gunter might have taken someone with him to act as driver and bodyguard. Understaffed, and yet—come to think of it—these were no ordinary men. Carefully selected, politically reliable from Gunter's point of view. A larger number would have attracted attention from Sawyer Springs, where no help was kept. For a house the size of Rancho San Carlos? Perhaps a couple. The neighbors would accept that as a normal extravagance.

"Do we?" Mac insisted as the six men filed into their dormitory.

He was answered by the door of the main house opening to let the two dogs run free into the field. This time their handler didn't stop on the terrace but followed them as they dashed for the fence and stood there, heads turned to watch his deliberate progress, bodies taut as they waited for him to come unlock the gate and let them loose on the hillside.

"Let's get the hell out," said Renwick.

Once they were safely over the brow of the hill, they could straighten their spines and descend almost at a half-run. They reached Buena Vista with six minutes to spare before the bus would leave Rancho San Carlos. Sal had heard it coming up from the town ten minutes ago, watched it pass. Only a driver, no one else, he reported. Also, no message had arrived from Merriman & Co.; nothing from Frank Cooper, either; and food was ready and waiting anytime they wanted it.

"Later," Renwick said. First, he and Mac would toss to see who was first for a hot shower, the loser posting himself as near the road as was safely possible. He lost, and barely made it to a cluster of trees and bushes before he heard the bus traveling downhill. The six men were inside, work clothes discarded, dressed normally like their instructor who accompanied them. Was he responsible for seeing them each scatter in the cars that waited for them at Escondido? Responsible, too, for the new group arriving one by one—collecting them, escorting them safely here tomorrow night, keeping their arrival circumspect? Altogether a low-key operation, Renwick reflected as he made his way back to the house, but organized and deadly.

In the kitchen, he sat down heavily, still covered with dust, his shirt streaked with dried sweat, and began briefing Sal. "It's more than either Frank or any of us bargained for," he ended. "We can't handle a nest of conspirators being trained for terrorist operations in this country. It's the FBI who should be taking over—it's their job."

"The boss will pass the word to them. If he thinks there's enough evidence to bring them in."

"If?"

Sal looked curiously at Renwick's taut face. "What's the plan for tonight?"

"We'll gather that evidence."

"We are going in?"

"We'll make a try."

"We may find nothing. You are risking a lot."

"I'd just like to complete our report to Frank, make his warning to Washington as strong as possible."

"Two Dobermans?" Sal was reflective. "They'll be loose in the compound by night. Well, we can pacify them. I expected dogs. What about their handler?"

"He relies too much on them. They're highly trained." And

* * *

why patrol the compound for endless hours when you had two Dobermans on the loose? "At least," Renwick admitted with a wry smile, "I'm counting on that." The handler had been careless today, taken security for granted.

"Just the cook and the handler? That's all? You're sure?"

"It's a quiet Saturday night with Gunter absent. No sign of trouble in these last three weeks, none expected now." And I am not sure of anything. Deductions and hunches—that's all I've got.

"One lock. One padlock at the barn. That shouldn't be too difficult. But this alarm system..." Sal was frowning. "If it's what I think it is, we'll use wire and clamps. When do we go in?"

"Around nine o'clock. When prime-time television is on."

Sal smiled broadly. "The baseball season is just coming to the play-offs. Wanted to watch the Dodgers tonight, myself."

Mac came downstairs, his yellowed face restored to its usual pink health, his movements once more brisk. "I'm famished!" he warned Renwick.

"Won't be too long," Renwick promised him. He left Sal going over Mac's sketches and diagrams. Sal was efficient, knowledgeable, a welcome surprise. He's as good as either of us for this kind of work, Renwick thought as he slowly mounted the staircase. Perhaps better.

They ate at five o'clock, still talking over their plans. By half past eight, well prepared, they were on their way. The hillside and its easier routes to Rancho San Carlos were becoming familiar. The half-moon was strong enough, the stars brilliant. Once their eyes became accustomed to the eerie shadows that played over the rough ground whenever a white cloud drifted across the sky, they found it a simple matter of putting one foot in front of the other. Renwick and Mac led the way. Sal, pockets bulging with equipment, a spool of wire dangling from his belt, followed their footsteps precisely.

As they came over the brow of the hill, they crouched low, but—provided they didn't clatter or stumble—they could even speed up their approach to this morning's vantage point. At the path to the fence, they halted; now Sal could see the layout of the place for himself. No one spoke. Dark-blue sweaters, the color of night, were pulled over their dark shirts. Mac's reddish fair hair, brightly silvered in moonlight, was covered by a navy-blue wool cap. Faces and hands were made less noticeable by a deep nut-brown tan out of a bottle.

There were lights behind the curtains of two downstairs windows near the doors onto the terrace. Three more lights, isolated, shone bleakly over the entrance to the armory (some mess hall, Renwick thought with a smile at himself), the side of the barn door, the corner of the stable-dormitory. The fence was left unlit, attracting little attention, making the gate unnoticeable. Sal stared down at the compound, then nodded. He was ready.

Renwick waited. It was an innocent scene; a house half asleep, three buildings abandoned. But the dogs were there, a pair of dark shadows moving constantly and in unison, prowling slowly around the compound's perimeter, alert, silent, their path undeviating.

Watching the rate of their patrol, Renwick calculated quickly. A near approach to the gate should be made when the dogs had reached the barn. From there, they'd pass the

stable; then the main house; then the armory and the beginning of the fence; then the sweep of the fence itself. When
they reached the gate, that was the moment to face them. On
this round he let them continue on their appointed way. Just
making sure they followed their training to the last detail,
he told himself grimly. As they passed the gate for the second
time and headed toward the barn, he signaled and moved
forward. Mac and Sal followed, equally cautious in their
movements. They knelt down, stayed low, waited for the dogs'
long patrol around the compound to come their way again.

Sal was already prepared for work. Around his head he
had slipped a broad elastic band with its attached shaded
flashlight over his brow ready to be switched on. He had
uncoiled a length of insulated wire from the spool at his belt
and was now feeling the small, high-pressure spring clamps
at either end of the wire as if to make sure they were secure.
If he had misjudged Renwick's description of the alarm system in use, tonight's operation would end before it had even
begun. But Sal would have had a close look at the circuit
connection, would have seen how it could be put out of action.
After that, all that could be done was to retreat to Buena
Vista, prepare for another attempt next weekend when the
dormitory was empty again. In one breast pocket he carried
keys; in the other, delicate probes if the keys proved useless.
He had a small transmitter in his hip pocket, a sheathed
throwing knife down the back of his neck.

Renwick and Mac also had transmitters in their pockets.
In their hands were the pacifiers—dart pistols loaded with
just enough sleeping power to put the Dobermans out of commission for one hour. ("No longer than that," Renwick had
warned Sal as he prepared the dosage. "We want the dogs on
their feet again before anyone sees they are doped." And what
if the handler came out before the hour was over? Mac had
wanted to know. Sal had grunted and said he'd take care of
that.)

The dogs were nearing the gate, heads down as if they
were following some scent—and perhaps they were, thought
Renwick: was that the secret of their well-trained patrol? He
signaled; the three men rose, moved swiftly. Renwick was
praying he could rest the pacifier on the mesh of the fence
and have a steady shot at the dog on the left. Mac would take
the one on the right. "Chest," Sal had advised, and Mac had

said bitterly, "Yes, they jump and go for your throat." A Doberman wasn't his favorite animal.

Abruptly, the Dobermans halted, heads lifting to the gate at the first sign of danger, teeth showing, muscles tightening as they began an instinctive leap. Renwick and Mac pulled the triggers. The pistols were soundless. Renwick even wondered if his had misfired. But the dogs' leap ended in a weak fall back to the ground. "Quick-acting," Sal had said. And the drug was certainly that. Their weak struggles to rise were soon over, ended in complete collapse and sudden sleep.

Sal hadn't waited for the pistols to be fired. With his flashlight switched on, he was examining the alarm system. Yes, it was a single-wire circuit with a make-or-break connector of two contacts linking the current that ran through them when the gate stood shut. Break that circuit by opening the gate, and the alarm would sound.

Sal nodded to Renwick. This job was his: the tallest of the three, he had a better chance of reaching the connector at its seven-foot height from the ground. But it wouldn't be easy, reaching up, keeping arms steady, making sure that the teeth of the two clamps—sharp as razor blades—would bite into the wire on either side of the connector at the same split second. Timing was everything.

Renwick shoved the pistol into a pocket, grasped a clamp in each hand. Sal held the wire that joined them, kept its length from twisting into a tangle—he had allowed double what they'd need for entering a half-open gate, but he never could tell how far the gate might swing with its heavy weight. He angled his flashlight upward to let its small beam shine on the circuit connector.

Renwick braced himself, slowly lifted the clamps, kept them parallel as he forced the small jaws open against the pressure of their springs. Briefly he hesitated, made sure he was aiming the teeth of each of them to bite cleanly into the wires. He took a deep breath. Then—at the same exact moment—he released the clamps, let them grip. No alarm sounded.

He stood back, arms dropping to his sides, hands suddenly weak, and stared up at the clamps. The long loop of wire, through which the circuit now ran, curved out like a balloon.

Sal redirected his flashlight, began working on the lock. It gave him an unexpected problem: the first key, useless, almost stuck. Two minutes passed, with seconds ticking away on Renwick's watch. One hundred and twenty-four seconds now, and more to come. They could only sweat it out while Sal eased and coaxed the recalcitrant key. Suddenly, it came free. Sal tried another one; it wouldn't go into the keyhole. The third fitted and turned. Gently, Renwick pushed the gate inward while Mac and Sal eyed the circuit connectors. The clamps were working.

Sal was the first through, running toward the barn. Renwick drew the gate closed as they entered the compound. Then Mac and Renwick, one dog apiece, had the heavy task—a nerve-racking one, too—of dragging the animals as far from the gate as necessary. Almost at the gable end of the armory, they judged the jut of the building would block any view of this spot from the terrace, and dropped their burdens. For a brief moment, regaining their breath, they looked down at the slumped bodies. Mac still couldn't believe it: he had hauled a Doberman over a stretch of ground and hadn't been mauled. Then, with a grin, he was racing toward the barn.

Renwick let him reach it and began a full-speed run. Rubber soles were soundless on grass, thank God. And praise be that the barn door faced the hill and was out of sight from the main house. He reached its safety with his heart beating wildly. Sal's work was finished there. The padlock had been easy. He had the door open and waiting. Renwick and Mac, stepping over the threshold into darkness, brought out their penlights.

Sal closed the door. With equal care, he started making his way along the side of the barn; from there to the stable that served as a dormitory when school was in progress; and at last, to a chosen patch of ground near the right-hand side of the terrace. It was deep in shadow—the lighted windows lay to the left of the door—with a small tree and some shrubs to reassure him. He got rid of his equipment in pockets that he buttoned securely, pulled out his small transmitter and held it close to his ear. The barn was the objective, and the objective had been reached. Halfway home: he'd feel better when they were safely out of this damnable place. If lights had been strung along the top of its fence, it would have looked like a prisoner-of-war camp. His thoughts flickered back to one he had known. Along with Frank Cooper. A joint escape that made them friends for life.

He waited patiently, scanning each building in turn. "No need to waste time on the armory," Renwick had said. "We can guess what we'd find there. And we know what to expect in the stable. But in the barn? A classroom with maps—books left for the next batch of pupils? Thirty minutes, Sal. Just give us thirty minutes inside that barn. Perhaps less." Sal checked his watch once more: eleven still to go. They must have found something, or else they'd have left before this. It was a comforting thought to help him through the last minutes: they were always the worst.

The door onto the terrace opened. Sal drew himself against the tree's thin trunk, reached for the back of his neck to grip the handle of his knife. Then he stood motionless, eyeing the light that streamed over the central flasgstones, listening to the outpouring of sound from a distant TV set. A sports commentator's voice was raised, a roar from the crowd burst out.

At his left ear, he heard Renwick's quiet voice. "Leaving. Okay?"

He risked a whispered reply as the roar from thousands of throats rose to a crescendo. "No! Wait!"

The door closed as unexpectedly as it had opened: this was an inning not to be missed. "Okay now. Hurry!" he told Renwick as he left the shelter of the tree. How near was the inning to its end? After that would come commercials and time to have a beer and look outside. Sal sprinted for the barn.

Renwick had already snapped its padlock in place. At a wild run, he and Mac—with Sal at their heels—headed for the gate. They were through, out, safe. "Quick, quick!" Sal told them as he locked the gate while Renwick released the clamps simultaneously and withdrew them at exactly the same instant. Some muffled curses from Sal as the wire almost snarled when he was winding it around the spool. Then they were scrambling up the path, all caution abandoned for speed until they reached the fringe of bushes. There, in good cover, they dropped to the ground. Slowly, breath returned to normal.

Mac pointed to the empty compound. "Look!" Two dark shapes were coming slowly out of the armory's shadow, still unsteady, still unsure of what had happened to them. "My God, Sal, an hour you said. Like hell it was."

Sal raised a hand for silence, his eyes on the main house. "Don't move yet," he whispered.

Renwick and Mac exchanged a puzzled glance, but they stayed where they were. The door to the terrace opened, a path of bright light spread halfway toward the fence. The silhouette of a man stood at the threshold, took three-dimensional shape as he crossed the flagstones. He halted again, looked around the compound as if puzzled. Then his hands went to his lips. The whistle cut through the night. The Dobermans heard it. They came slowly around the armory's end wall, hesitated. A second whistle, and they were out of their dream world. Obediently, they began their patrol. "Don't play tricks with me," the man yelled at them. He turned to go inside, met the small fat cook. "Lazy sons of bitches," he was saying, "thought they'd take it easy for..." The voice dwindled to nothing as the door was shut behind the two men.

Who's the lazy son of a bitch? Renwick was thinking. He rose and led the way. Mac made an effort and smothered his fit of laughter. Sal was grinning widely. "Wonder who's winning that game," he said softly.

They were over the top of the hill. Their pace increased on the home slope, the lights of Buena Vista welcoming them from behind carefully drawn curtains. Just as we left it, thought Renwick as they reached the back porch and heard the radio playing. First, we'll unload our gear: next, food and drink; then questions and answers. He could sense Sal's impatience. "Yes," he said to hold him meanwhile, "we got something. Enough, I think, to make Washington's eyes pop."

"Then it was worth it?" Sal asked.

"It was worth it."

Mac had a sudden fit of laughter. "Those dogs—" His laughter choked his words. "Groggy. A couple of old soaks—" The laughter increased.

Sal looked at the usually solemn MacEwan in amazement.

"He has these attacks," Renwick said. "Just be thankful he didn't let one explode on the hillside. Come on, let's heat up that soup. I'm starved." Strange ways we all have, he thought. After tension and fear are over, I get hungry. Mac goes into uncontrollable laughter. And Sal? Renwick studied him as he got rid of his tools, placing them carefully in a neat group on a counter top. There was much more to Sal than he, or Mac, had ever surmised. Chauffeur, cook, guardian angel? Not on your life, Renwick told himself. Without him we'd not have accomplished little. He watched Sal unfasten the light harness that held the throwing knife between his shoulder blades. "Thank God you didn't have to use that," Renwick said.

Sal only smiled.

* * *

Supper was quickly eaten. The windows were firmly closed, the radio turned on once more. The three men still sat at the table, plates pushed aside.

"So here's what we learned from the barn," Renwick said. "It looks abandoned, shuttered tight. But it *is* a classroom, with desks and chairs and good lighting. Air conditioning, too. The blackboard behind a lectern had been rubbed clean—except for some faint chalk marks on one low corner. They didn't mean much at first, until we began examining the big maps fixed on the wall. I took photographs of them—directed the strong light on the lectern at them, hoped they'll be clear enough. Three maps. One of them covered the southeastern states with red circles near certain small towns, but not on highways or roads. The circles were on railway lines. That was Mac's discovery: freight routes for inflammable material, dangerous chemicals."

Mac turned modest. "I just noticed one of the circles was crossed off, and remembered the name of the town. A bad derailment near there three weeks ago: town evacuated; two deaths; everything blamed on faulty equipment."

Renwick went on. "The next map showed the United States—not the usual relief map. Just a large stretch of white paper with the states outlined, and across them a spider web of black lines: heavy for main highways, thinner for first-class roads. Only certain towns were named. Near them, or within reach by road, were small red squares. We recognized some of these locations—major storage facilities for oil. At first we wondered if the markings meant atomic energy plants, but these can be dealt with by someone on the inside who forgets to turn a little wheel, or turns the wrong one. You don't need a squad of trained terrorists for that job."

"The third map was a real puzzler," Mac said. "It was a city, streets and buildings clearly plotted but unnamed. However, the layout—if you knew Washington—became recognizable."

"Washington?" Sal asked. "And where were the red markings this time? The White House, the Cap—"

"No. Not the White House. Not the Capitol. Not the busy center of the city, either. They were—most of them—in a row along one street. Bob's guess was—foreign embassies."

"Embassies?" Sal was incredulous.

Renwick said, "Seize them, blackmail their governments,

prevent them from helping America when she's under attack."

Sal stared at them in open disbelief. "Listen you two—" he said, suddenly breaking into a broad smile—"railroads, oil and gas storage, embassies. And all that taken care of by six young bastards with a week's training behind them?"

"Six young bastards each week," Renwick reminded him. "Rancho San Carlos has already been in operation for three weeks at least. Give it free rein until the end of the year. How many trained terrorists by then? A hundred and fourteen. All ready to command their own groups of men."

"Could be even more," Mac said somberly. "Once Gunter establishes that Foundation for Ecological Studies, he'll extend the numbers. Demolition, of course, would have to stop—unless he adds field trips out into the desert areas."

"But how good is their training?" Sal persisted.

Renwick said, "It's a refresher course. These guys aren't novices. It's just possible they've been brought here to learn how to operate as a team. Perhaps," he added with a pointed look at Sal, "we won't have one hundred and fourteen expert terrorists on call by the end of the year. We'll have nineteen well-functioning squads, capable of instructing others in close teamwork."

"Not funny," Sal said slowly. His dark eyes narrowed as he stared at the fireplace and its dying embers. "Equipment—how do you rate it?"

"Simple but effective. It can be just as deadly as more sophisticated hardware. And it's easier to procure."

"What's their purpose? Complete anarchy?"

"It could end that way." And that was more than Theo and his friends had been aiming for. Break down a dam, release a flood of water that would serve their needs; but what if it reached the strength of a tidal wave? They'd be swept away along with the rest of us. Poor comfort, thought Renwick.

There was a brief silence. Renwick's quiet voice continued. "We didn't find much in the desks. Just some textbooks on explosives. Elementary stuff but good for hard basic training. Also several mimeographed sheets dealing with urban guerrillas, treatment for tanks and armored cars in city areas. I filched a specimen." He went into his hip pocket and produced a folded sheet, handed it over to Sal.

Mac said, "There was a communications setup in one corner of the barn. Nothing too elaborate, just enough to teach them some electronic facts."

"What about the chalk marks on the blackboard?" Sal handed back the mimeographed sheet to Renwick.

Mac pulled out his notebook, opened it to the page with his copy of the marks. "Juncture of railroad tracks. A neat place for dynamite, I presume."

For a long minute, Sal sat glaring down at the table. He pushed aside his coffee cup and rose. "Yes," he said to Renwick, "the sooner the FBI gets into this, the better. I'll contact the boss late tomorrow afternoon—Sunday. He should be back in New York by then. He leaves for London that night."

"I'll contact London, too. They'll get in touch with Washington." We need someone at the highest level to start pushing the right buttons, Renwick decided. "I don't want our report, with copies of our photographs and that mimeographed sheet, to be dropped into an in-tray and left lying on someone's desk while he makes up his blasted mind whether to risk his promotion. I don't want someone, either, who'll read it and go shrieking the news to the outer office. Or someone who likes to leak hints to reporters, just to show his importance. None of that. We need someone who can start the action, and keep his own lip buttoned as well as all his agents' lips. They'll want time to observe, to follow the terrorists when they scatter from Escondido. Not too much time, I hope. If it were left to me, I'd gut out that suppurating sore next week."

"But we don't," Mac said regretfully. "We discover the facts, make our report, and fade away." He pulled himself onto his feet. "I'm fading right now, upstairs, into a sweet, soft bed. Call it a day, Bob."

"Shortly." Renwick listened to their heavy footsteps slowly making their way to their rooms. We're all dropping with fatigue, he thought. But we did the job. We did it; and left no trace. What remains to be done? Tomorrow, an urgent message for Merriman & Co., full report to follow next week; and a look, if possible, at the busload of new arrivals. On Monday—Gunter. How do I manage to see him? He could identify me, too. If he is Maartens. Maartens and Amsterdam and a green camper changed to brown, and Theo behind it all.

He knew this stage of exhaustion well. The mind was lost in a maze of possibilities and every solution ended in blank depression. They should have been celebrating their small victory tonight. Instead, all three of them could only think of the grim threat they had uncovered. To America. To the rest of the free world, too. Why else the foreign embassies? Blackmailed by terror into inaction? Allies split apart?

He roused himself, rose and switched off the radio, the lights, opened the front door. He stood there breathing the clean cool air, looking at the darkened mass of endless hills and valleys, listening to the deep silence of a sleeping land. At last he turned back and locked the door. A sleeping land, but with hidden strength, too. Remembering that, he felt better. He went upstairs ready to face tomorrow.

CHAPTER

18

On Sunday morning, the message went out to Merriman's listening station in Grace Street. Renwick kept it brief: he'd take the full report to London himself and, with luck, that could be in a few days' time. It was enough now to give Gilman the essential facts about Rancho San Carlos and let him contact Washington for an immediate response—if not action, then certainly containment. Renwick also appended advice about Frank Cooper: on his arrival Monday, get him to postpone his visit to Grace Street—not only for its security but also for his own safety; tell him to stick to the law business until Theo's interest in him has cooled off. Frank wouldn't like the sugegestion, but he would listen.

The message was received and acknowledged. Two hours later, Gilman sent a terse answer: *Will co-operate fully*. Renwick relaxed and began planning some way of slowing up the minibus later that afternoon. Keep it simple, he warned himself: all you need are photographs, a head count, a check on the bald instructor. Was he a regular, a permanent part of the training program?

So just before noon Sal paid a visit to Sawyer Springs in search of a Sunday paper and stayed for a chat with a couple of old-timers who sat on a bench outside the General Store and watched the passing traffic. There were three cars in twenty minutes by Sal's count, one of them stopping for directions to Palomar. "They're always getting lost," he was told as the car left. "Should have kept on the highway instead of coming around here."

"This road rejoins the highway, doesn't it?"

"About seven miles past the last house. A bad stretch of road, too. They'll be turning back. Just wait and see."

"The last house? Where's that?"

"Eight miles up the road. Used to be a big ranch. Horses."

"Oh, the San Carlos place? Miss Gladstone was telling us about it. A lot of new money. That should be good for business."

"Haven't seen it." A look was cast in the direction of the gas station. "Stan was expecting some. Didn't get it."

"I'd have thought there would have been a lot of gas sold. It's a big establishment, Miss Gladstone said."

"They don't go driving around. Don't keep many cars anyway."

Only a jeep, Sal learned, and Mr. Gunter's Mercedes-Benz. A beauty. Silver gray and fast, held the road, didn't need to slow down for the turns. Serviced in Escondido. Understandable, it was admitted: no spare parts for it here. The workmen didn't bring their cars. A small bus was provided for them by the contractor. Saved energy, it might be said; this gas shortage and all; was there an oil shortage? Never knew what these big companies were up to.

Sal got the drifting talk back to its moorings. "A bus can use a lot of energy, too. That is, if it makes many trips back and forth."

It didn't do that; Saturdays to Escondido, Sundays back here. He could see for himself if he just waited around until four-thirty. He'd see the truck, too. Brought in supplies for the week. Nothing too good for these boys.

"A truck? They must eat a lot." And need constant supplies of ammunition and explosives. Sal, leaving a couple of laughs behind him, waved good day and went back to Buena Vista empty-handed. There had been no newspaper to buy: all copies spoken for.

By quarter past four, Mac was driving the Chevrolet into the service station at Sawyer Springs. "Can you spare a few gallons? My tank is half empty." The owner and sole attendant (Stan, if Sal was correct) was glad to oblige, glad to talk with someone new. "Pretty quiet around here," Mac said as he got out of the car. He didn't have to add anything more. Sure it was quiet: few Sunday drivers, scared they'd run out of gas, what did you expect with all the odd-and-even-day rules, and the rising prices and that OPEC and those oil companies? The surmises and opinions lasted a full ten minutes. Then water and oil were checked while Mac strolled around the car and listened sympathetically to Stan's woes as a small businessman.

Mac halted, turning his back to the road as he heard a heavy engine coming uphill into Main Street. He raised his hand to his lips, kept watching. Quietly, he spoke into the small transmitter hidden in his palm. "Small truck. Passing now."

"Who found the goddamned oil wells anyway?" Stan was asking as he polished the windshield. "If I had my way..." He broke off, stood hands on hips, looking at the bus now traveling into sight.

"Bus. About to pass," Mac told his transmitter. He shut it off as he slipped it back into his pocket, took out a cigarette. "Have one?" he asked Stan. Not one head in the bus was turned in their direction.

"Don't even give us a good-day," Stan said, staring after them. He noticed the offered cigarette, shook his head. "Gave up the habit when I bought this place, started working the pump."

"Who was Sawyer?" Mac asked, getting into the car.

"Who?"

"Sawyer."

"Oh, him. Been dead for ninety years."

"Where are the springs?"

"They dried up."

Like everything else around here, thought Mac. He reached for his wallet. "What's the damage?"

He paid, talked some more. There was no need to hurry. Up at Buena Vista, a traffic jam should be in progress.

Sal let the truck pass. Then, as he received Mac's message signaling the approach of the bus, he began backing the station wagon out of Buena Vista's driveway. He turned the wheel just enough to put the big Dodge at an angle athwart the road. There, he stalled the engine, kept trying to restart it. All he created was a series of rasping sounds and a strong smell of gasoline.

Perfect, thought Renwick. He was well hidden by bushes, his favorite camera ready. The bus ought to come around the curve of road below the driveway and stop. There would be plenty of curses and genuine confusion until Sal could get the ignition started again and angle the station wagon around to face downhill. Even that last maneuver would take time: the Dodge was long, the road narrow.

The bus came around the turn, groaned to a halt. Renwick was barely fifteen feet away from it. He didn't expect a clear view of faces through glass windows, but he did hope to get— if curiosity and surprise were strong enough—several heads stuck out of the windows to see what the hell was going on.

His hopes weren't disappointed. He began photographing. Six newcomers, he counted. And the baldheaded instructor.

They stayed inside the bus, let their driver get out to yell at Sal. "You're flooding it! Let your foot off the pedal. Stop pumping, goddamn it!" There were accompanying calls from the bus, far from complimentary. Sal pressed the pedal firmly to the floor, held it there, gauged when he could turn the ignition, and got the motor running. Now it was a matter of straightening the car. The bus driver shook his head, walked back, yelling now at his passengers to shut up. Renwick managed two pictures of him before he climbed into his seat. A good one, too, of old Baldy coming to the door to talk with him. And one, of course, of the rear registration plate of the bus as, at last, it started moving. Once past the station wagon, it picked up speed and soon was out of sight.

Mac returned from his visit to the gas station and found Renwick and Sal with broad smiles on their faces. "So it worked," he said with relief. He had had his doubts. They went indoors to have a quiet drink to celebrate.

Sal had one ludicrous note to impart. "The funny thing was the way that busload passed me: no more leaning out of windows; no more catcalls; all faces turned away from me." His amusement ended. "Foul-mouthed little bastards. There was a moment when I felt like getting out of the car and ramming those twelve-letter words right down their throats."

So Sunday's operation was over, thought Mac, and successfully. As a man who was devoted to the sophisticated device, he was still astonished by the simplicity of Renwick's approach. "What about tomorrow, Bob? Got another bright idea?"

"We'll think of something." A view of Gunter may not be so easy to arrange. We know he must either come through the town or make a detour by way of the Palomar highway. But there is a bad stretch of road linking up with that highway; that much we've learned. Can we take a chance Gunter won't risk his silver-gray Mercedes there? He'd have to slow down to a crawl, which would make it easier for me to see him—if there was any cover nearby. But we haven't enough men. If I'm stationed near the worst patch of road near the Palomar highway, will my transmitter carry all the way back to Buena Vista or Sawyer Springs, where Mac and Sal would be waiting? The distance could be beyond its range: we'd be left out of contact, floundering around; not know what was happening at the other end. "We'll take the chance that Gunter will choose the regular route. But we can't stage anything near our driveway again. We'll keep the action closer to Sawyer Springs." There was a long pause. Then suddenly Renwick was smiling. "How many bottles can you produce, Sal?"

On Monday their vigil began at daybreak. "We haven't a clue when he will arrive," Renwick had said as they finished a hasty cup of coffee in the kitchen. "So it's a fourteen-hour stint for us. Perhaps longer."

"And if he doesn't show?" Mac wanted to know.

"There's tomorrow. And tomorrow. And tomorrow."

"After four days—what? If he doesn't appear—"

"Then he risked using the other route, and we'll be facing another close-up view of Rancho San Carlos. How does that suit you, Mac?"

"Not much," Mac said and headed for the Chevrolet. He'd be stationed three miles below the start of Sawyer Springs' Main Street.

Sal and Renwick, carrying their load in two knapsacks, walked at an even pace down toward the town. On its outskirts, at a carefully chosen bend in the road after it had left Main Street, they halted and took shelter beside some trees with heavy undergrowth. They eased the packs off their backs, settled down to wait. It was now five o'clock. By ten o'clock, as the air warmed up, they had pulled off their sweaters. At eleven, they ate a chocolate bar, drank some water from Sal's flask. A garbage truck growled uphill. A bronze-colored, two-door Cadillac came down. An elderly man was at its wheel, a blue-haired lady sitting beside him: next-door neighbors going shopping in Escondido, or farther afield for a luncheon date. The garbage truck (unnamed, but Renwick had already caught its license number) returned, traveling at considerable speed. It made the curve safely. Well calculated, thought Renwick: the man knew this route, must be the regular driver for Rancho San Carlos. It was ten minutes to twelve.

September heat was rising. There was shelter in the shade of the bushes under which they lay, but the sun now beamed full strength at the road in front of them. On its other side, the far vista of open countryside lost its sharp outlines and lay peacefully drowsing in a warm haze.

At twenty minutes past twelve, Mac's signal came through.

"Silver-gray Mercedes now passing. Estimated speed seventy."

Renwick and Sal were on their feet and out of the bushes, knapsacks in hand. In haste, they unfastened the buckles, opened the sacks and spilled out the contents across the road. Jagged fragments of broken glass lay gleaming in the bright sun. They kicked a few pieces into a better position, didn't waste any of them near the road's left-hand ditch or the fall-away of land on its right side. Renwick stood back for a second, eyeing the bits and pieces of glass. They didn't look carefully placed or too purposely set. Well worth the sacrifice of all their soda water, which had been poured down the kitchen sink, of their beer, of the jam and pickles and olives now in bowls; and of two large vases which could never have been anyone's delight.

Sal was already across the ditch and onto the low bank where their section of trees and heavy bushes lay. He waved frantically, relaxed as Renwick followed at high speed. They dropped on their faces, rested elbows on knapsacks, risked less than three inches of viewing space between the leaves. They wouldn't have long to wait: seventy miles an hour must have slackened for the run through Main Street, and then back to seventy for the surge uphill, with another slowdown for the bend in the road. If the driver was paying any attention, he'd see the glint of broken glass. He'd have time to slam on the brakes, bring the car to a halt. Just in front of us, thought Renwick as he reached for the camera in his hip pocket.

His hand had scarcely grasped it when the car came swiftly around the corner. He heard it, couldn't see it, daren't risk lifting himself on his elbow and twisting his head to his right for a better view. The shriek of brakes told him enough. He could almost feel the jolt of the car as it stopped dead, its hood no more than twelve feet away from him. Sal's body had stiffened, too. They lay absolutely still, waiting for the curses to end and the driver to step onto the road.

He wore a thin blue suit and a chauffeur's cap well pulled down to cover his hair. His face was rigid with anger, his jaw clenched, his chin and nose prominent as they pointed at the spill of broken glass. He walked quickly toward it. Renwick, his eyes still on the car, could hear him kicking the larger fragments aside.

"Clear it all!" a voice shouted from the car, and a man

stepped out on its other side. He was tall enough for shoulders
and head to be visible; the rest of his body was hidden by the
Mercedes. His hair was fair and neatly cut, but that was all
Renwick could see; the man was facing out toward the fine
view of hills and valleys, but not in admiration. His head
turned slowly as he scanned the sloping fields below him,
looking for a movement, one sign of someone hiding down
there. Then he swung around to look at the opposite side of
the road with the same careful intensity. Renwick held his
breath, didn't even risk an arm upraised to get his camera
into position. There wasn't much need for it anyway. Gunter
was Maartens.

The chauffeur shouted, "Can't clear it all. Not the smaller
pieces. We need a broom."

"Use your cap and sweep them away," Maartens called
impatiently, and studied the view once more. Now Renwick
could angle his head, look up the road to catch a glimpse of
the chauffeur's back as he swept the last remnants of glass
aside. The man straightened up, turned toward the Mercedes,
dusting off his cap against his thigh. Gray hair, cut short.
Prematurely gray, for his face was that of a fairly young man
with a sharp jaw line and a beak of a nose.

It can't be, Renwick thought, it can't be.... For a moment
shock gripped him. Then as the man reached the car, saying,
"You might have given me a hand," Renwick took his photograph, with Maartens in the background.

"Now, Hans," Maartens said, his bad temper subsiding as
his worry and suspicion died away, "you've got your job, I
have mine." One last look around him, and he stepped into
the car.

Hans settled his cap firmly down over his gray hair, slid
into the driver's seat. The Mercedes gently passed over the
small glass particles still clinging to the road and gathered
speed.

Renwick got up. "We better waste no time. They could
send a couple of their yahoos down here to beat around these
bushes, see if any trace was left." It can't be, he was still
thinking, but it is. "We'll keep to the rough ground, circle to
the back of the house. Come on, Sal, come on."

Sal straightened a clump of grass, swept his knapsack
across the shorter blades where they had lain, adjusted a
branch. "No traces," he said. He looked curiously at Renwick,

but kept his silence until they were well away from the road. "Well?" he asked at last.

"That was Maartens. Now calling himself Gunter."

"And the other—you recognized him, too, didn't you?"

"He's a killer."

"The gray-haired fellow?" Sal shook his head. "You never can tell. He looked the spitting image of a math teacher I once had. What's his job at San Carlos—classes in assassination?" His amusement faded as he noticed Renwick's anger.

"How the hell," Renwick burst out, "did he escape custody? That's the guy who tried to kill me. How did he get loose, goddamn him?"

"Where was he being held?"

"Near Brussels."

In silence, they reached the house. Mac had just parked the Chevrolet in the garage. He looked at the two unsmiling faces. "Okay?" he asked anxiously.

"Okay. Very much okay," Renwick assured him.

Sal said, "I'll contact London. Gilman ought to know about this."

Renwick nodded. "I'll encode the message." And then he turned to Mac, clapped his shoulder. "Come on, I'll explain later. Now I need a drink." He led the way into the living room, still thinking about Hans, and found the one bottle of Scotch that hadn't been sacrificed. As he lifted it, he came out of his memory of a bad dream, his thoughts now on the scattered fragments of glass gleaming in sunlight. He began to laugh. "It worked. It actually worked."

"No suspicions?"

"At first, yes. Maartens lives on a diet of suspicions."

"He could have an attack of second doubts."

"We'll pack tonight, leave early tomorrow." Renwick frowned. "That real-estate girl—Gladstone?—yes, I think we owe her an explanation. Just can't walk out on her cold."

"We owe her," Mac agreed. "But what explanation?"

Renwick studied his drink. "Have you noticed many birds around here?"

Forest fire and blackened trees... "Not too many." Mac began to smile. "Most discouraging for a naturalist."

"I'll call her this evening," said Renwick. His spirits lifted: we are leaving; our job here is finished; and ten days ahead of time. Frank Cooper had allowed them two weeks. "I'll get that message off to London," he said, "and then I'll tell you about Hans."

Sal joined them, his eyes worried, his lips tight. "Got through to London and had an instant reply. Here!" He handed over Gilman's message to Renwick, who read it aloud. It consisted of three words: *Where is Frank?*

"He hasn't arrived?" Mac was unbelieving.

"Delayed," said Sal. "I'll contact his New York house." But he knew, as the others did, that Frank Cooper ought to have let Gilman know if there had been a delay.

There was no response from Cooper's place on East Sixty-first.

"What about his office?" Renwick asked. "Anyone there you know, Sal?"

"Wallace Rosen and Chet Danford."

"How many partners are there?"

"Forty-eight."

Two out of forty-eight... Possibly they were Frank's close friends. Renwick said, "You'd better drive down to Escondido, Sal. Telephone from there."

Sal nodded. "I'll try East Hampton first. If there's no answer, I'll try the office." He glanced at his watch. "One-thirty. Four-thirty New York." And it would take him half an hour or more to reach a telephone in Escondido. "I may just catch them," he said, already at the door.

"Let's hope Rosen and Danford are working late," Renwick said as he heard the Chevrolet being driven out of the garage.

"Are they part of Frank's brain trust?" Then as Mac watched Renwick, now walking restlessly around the room, he said, "Bob—stop that, will you? Frank's a wily old bird. He will outlast us both. Come on, lunch is on me: bread and cheese and a gallon of coffee. Then we can start packing some of Sal's gear. Three heavy suitcases, and a fourth for the clothes."

"How did he get that hardware through airport security?"

"He didn't. He borrowed most of it from a friend in San Diego." That, at least, got a laugh out of Renwick. Much better, thought Mac, as they went into the kitchen.

"Sal and his friends," Renwick was saying in wonder, and shook his head.

* * *

Sal was late. It was almost six o'clock before he returned. His face was set, his eyes expressionless.

"Didn't you reach them?" Mac asked.

Renwick said nothing, just kept watching Sal.

"I spoke with Rosen. Danford was down in East Hampton. Identifying the body. Frank is dead."

"What?" Mac burst out.

"He was found by the cleaning woman this morning. In his den. The police think it was suicide."

With a vehemence that startled even Mac, Renwick said, "No! Not Frank. No!"

"He has been depressed. Overworked. That's what the office is saying."

Renwick made an effort, controlled his emotion. "When?"

"Saturday." Sal's voice was unnaturally quiet.

"How?"

"A bullet through the head. With his .38. The pistol was beside him. The bullet was found."

Mac said, "I can't believe it. Frank?" The color had drained from his cheeks. "Any sign of intruders, Sal? Anything burglarized?"

"Rosen said nothing was disturbed. The back door was locked, the front door, all windows. The keys were on the hall table. He was sitting at his..." Sal couldn't finish, turned away, walked stiffly to his room.

There was a long silence. Then Renwick said, "I don't see Frank sitting at his desk with all the windows closed. In September?"

"You're telling me it was murder? Good God, Bob—the doors were secured. No forcible entry. He might have locked the windows to keep the sound of a bullet—"

"He would certainly have locked doors and windows if he were taking a walk. Frank wouldn't leave the house open—there were legal papers he was working on; his collection of guns and pistols was in his den." Renwick frowned, his eyes half closed as he tried to recall his memories of the cottage. "There's a lot of ground, left rough and natural, trees. No neighbors within sight. Yes, they could have jumped him on that driveway to the road."

"You're saying he might have been knocked unconscious and carried back into the house? You're supposing they'd find the door key in his pocket. Then they placed him at his desk, took the revolver from his collection, shot him in cold blood.

God in heaven, Bob—you can't believe that! And what about
the door? It was locked. The keys were on the table."

Renwick's eyes studied Mac. "I remember that door. It
shut me out one afternoon. It locks automatically." Frank
had thought it a very great joke: Bob Renwick forgetting to
push a button and keep a door from locking. No kind of joke,
any more...He looked up quickly as he heard a footstep behind him. How long had Sal been there? How much had he
heard? I hope nothing, Renwick thought. But Sal was in control again; almost too controlled, too emotionless. This wasn't
the Sal he had known. "We'd better send out word to London,"
Renwick said, rising to find paper and pencil.

He completed the message after several attempts. In the
end, he simply wrote: *Frank died Saturday. Will give details
Wednesday*. He signed it with his old code name, *Bush*. And
suddenly his thoughts flashed back to a message he had to
send almost two years ago; a message to Brussels with the
exact same wording, days and all. Except the name wasn't
Frank. It had been *Avril*. Oh, God, he thought, the more it
changes, the more it's the same bloody thing. In silence, he
handed the slip of paper to Sal.

"Uncoded?" Sal asked.

Mac had been watching Renwick. Old Bob has been worse
hit than I thought: first, Jake Crefeld; now, Frank Cooper.
"I'll do that, Sal. And then I'll call the airports at San Diego
and Los Angeles, book the first flights out of there for all of
us. We'll leave as soon as possible. The more distance we put
between us and Pretty Boy Maartens and Killer Hans, the
easier I'll be. Bob, you're heading for London. Right? Sal's for
New York, and I'm for Montreal."

Sal was suddenly himself again. "We could leave tonight,
stay in San Diego if necessary," he said to Mac. "We'll split
up, of course. Go as we came. I've got some things to leave
with a friend in San Diego; probably won't fly out until late
tomorrow. Okay?"

"Fine. Can you drop off the house keys at the real-estate
office? Make our excuses to Miss Gladstone—we won't have
time to phone her tonight. Come on, let's move it." At the
door to Sal's room, he halted to call back. "Did you hear what
we're planning? Any improvements to suggest?"

Renwick said, "Don't forget the outside antenna."

He has recovered, Mac thought with a surge of relief. As
he followed Sal into his room, he began explaining about

forest fires and lack of birds—something that wouldn't hurt Gladstone's feelings and would raise no wonder in Sawyer Springs.

Mac was right: keep busy. Renwick went upstairs, started emptying their rooms of small items and clothes, making sure that not even a matchbook was left behind. For a few last moments, he stood at the window, looked at the rise and fall of hills stretching far to the south. The sun had set; the light was fading. But another day would follow tonight, take him to London and reports from Claudel and his friend the rug buyer. Istanbul must have had some messages from them: by this time they'd be following the camper out of Turkey. If all went well, they'd be following.

He carried the two suitcases downstairs. "Ready when you are," he told Mac.

One hour later, they were leaving. For their final minute together in the darkened driveway, all talk ended. In silence, they shook hands. In silence, they got into their cars. Mac and Sal were the first to go. Ten minutes later, Renwick followed. Sawyer Springs seemed already asleep, didn't even notice their departure.

CHAPTER
19

They crossed the Turkish-Iranian frontier in late afternoon, a small cavalcade of four cars and one brown camper, all heading for the nearest town before dusk set in. Tony Shawfield was in a thoroughly bad mood, partly due to the long delay at the border when Turkish officials were intent on how much money was being taken out of their country and Iranian officials were scrutinizing passports with heavy frowns. One Englishman, three Americans, one Frenchwoman, one Dane, one Italian, one Dutchman, was a total that baffled them; or perhaps it was three young women traveling with five young men, and only one couple married. But at last, with no drugs found and the pills in Shawfield's medical kit—all bottles clearly marked as aspirin or malaria or dysentery or digestive—briefly inspected, the campers were free to leave. Selim, their Turkish guide, who was accompanying them as far as Tabriz—this district spoke a Turkish dialect—hadn't been much help. The Iranian border officials were not of this province, he was explaining now to Shawfield and Kiley; they came from Tehran. "Religious fascists," he ended. "But we'll—"

"Shut up," Shawfield said. Kiley laughed and the rest of the group joined in. Except Nina. There was nothing funny about Selim's perpetual excuses to cover his failures; nothing funny, either, about the way all the others would laugh so easily without even knowing why they were laughing. But, thought Nina, I'm beginning to guess why, and I hope I am wrong.

"Are you all right?" Kiley asked, coming to sit beside her.

"Just tired and hungry."

"Well, it won't take long now. Selim recommends a small hotel on the outskirts of Tabriz. I thought we could all use proper beds tonight."

Nina stared out at the rolling plain and hills, at the backdrop of mountains. "That's Russia over there—to our left?"

Kiley nodded. "And to our right, the Kurds. We're giving

them a wide berth—a lot of fighting, I hear." He spoke conversationally; he always did when politics came up. None of his business, there were other things in life, let's all be sane and sensible—and tolerant of people like Selim.

"What would Selim call them? Nationalist pigs?" That was a phrase he had used of the Armenians, of the government in Ankara, of both Turks and Greeks in Cyprus. "I wonder if he approves of anyone," Nina added with a smile. "His idea of politics seems to be hatred for everything: tear it all down, destroy, destroy. He belongs to Genghis Khan and a pyramid of skulls."

"He just likes to speak. Too much rhetoric. It's endemic in this part of the world." Kiley slipped an arm around her shoulder, drew her closer. The gesture, like his voice, was gentle, reassuring. Then he was talking about the field they were passing: a lot of cultivation around here, good grazing land, too; markets, plenty of markets in Tabriz—tomorrow she and Madge could go exploring them. "What are you going to buy?" he teased her. "Another skirt?"

"If I can get some money changed. Perhaps at this hotel—"

"I can get better rates for you tomorrow. I'll be going into town." He turned the conversation back to safer channels. "It was a good move to pack your jeans away. A pity, though. They suited you."

"If Madge and I had been wearing tight pants, I wonder how much longer we'd have been delayed at the frontier." She laughed. "We might even have been refused entry. Then Tony would really have had something to make him mad. Why does he get so uptight?"

"Selim gets on his nerves." And will I have a bad report to make on that loose-mouthed idiot, thought Kiley grimly: a playacting revolutionary who can't resist driving home the obvious. Not that the Dutchman Tromp or his good and dear friend Lambrese paid much attention to anything outside of archaeological remains, photography, and themselves. The French girl and her stolid Dane were lost in their world of music. Madge—a small problem at first—had stopped concentrating on him and now found some consolation in Tony Shawfield and his magic pills. If the Iranian border guards had taken five blood samples or listened to the confident voices and fits of laughter, they would have examined Tony's medicine chest with real interest. Nina was the holdout. ("I hate pills," she had said; "won't even take aspirin unless I have a hundred-and-three-degree fever.") And Nina was the one who noticed everything. But he could manage her. At this moment, he felt her body relax against him. "Also," he went on, "Tony hates driving with a pack of cars at his heel."

"He could slow up and let them pass."

"Tony?" That amused Kiley. "He wants to reach our sleeping place—I guess it's an Iranian version of a motel—before it's dark." And the four cars following might have the same idea, thought Kiley. Still, they had seemed fairly innocent. During the delay at the frontier he had drifted back, chatted with the drivers, made a genial exchange of small talk. The Mercedes immediately behind the camper had three Germans in the oil business. Next was the gray Fiat with a couple of Turkish carpet buyers. Then came a station wagon with a Swedish newspaperman, wife, and three children on their way to India. The last car was a rakish red Ferrari with two Australians bound for northern Pakistan. A race against weather, they had said; the newly completed highway over the top of the world, from Pakistan to China, could be closed by heavy snows in another six weeks. "In any case, no one passes Tony on the road. Or haven't you noticed?"

"Who are they—did you find out?"

Yes, Nina notices, Kiley thought. Not that it mattered in this instance. So he could give a humorous account of the people traveling behind them. "They'll never make it," he ended his description of the Australians. Brawn but no brain, he decided. Certainly not undercover men. No intelligence agent would travel in anything so noticeable as a red Ferrari.

But Nina's interest was caught by something else. "Carpets—Persian carpets? Oh, Jim, can you persuade Tony to take us to one of the towns where they are made? Not to the factories—to the places where families still spend years on one carpet. The designs—"

Kiley laughed, shook his head. "Oh, yes—designs again." Careful, he warned himself: don't imitate Selim and give a lecture on impoverished families being exploited by a few rich people who wanted an expensive rag to throw over a floor. "Why don't you ask Tony yourself? All right, all right—I'll do it," he agreed, watching the fleeting expression on her face. It seemed a good moment to probe. "What have you got against Tony anyway?" he joked.

Nina shrugged her shoulders.

"He isn't a tyrant, you know. He's easy to get along with."

"For you, yes. For the rest of us?"

"Madge seems to think he's okay. He talks a lot with her, doesn't he?" Kiley had made sure of that, even if Shawfield had at first resisted the idea: stupid little blonde, Shawfield had said. Kiley had insisted: Madge was Nina's confidante and a sure way at getting to Nina's private thoughts. She had them, thought Kiley as he looked at Nina, yet I never feel she tells me anything that really matters. Was that reserve part of her nature and nothing to worry about?

Yes, Nina was thinking, Tony talks and laughs with Madge now. Now. Not before our little trip through Greece, though. Only since Istanbul. It isn't the kind of thing I can even mention to Madge: she's convinced she has made a conquest. Perhaps she has. I'm only certain of one thing: Madge and I don't talk any more—not the way we did in London. What has happened to all of us? We've changed: Henryk and Guido, always sharing their own private jokes; Marie-Louise and her Sven, polite and amiable but remote somehow, impossible to talk with them except with pleasant little remarks that only skate over the surface. And everyone except me—and Jim and Tony—worrying about nothing, accepting everything, wild attacks of laughter and giggles followed by stranger fits of lethargy and vacant stares. They look but they don't see. They aren't on heroin—there are no punctures on their arms. What is it, then? This isn't just my imagination, she told herself. Or is it?

Kiley said, "And were all these thoughts for Tony? I'm envious."

She pointed to a background mountain. "What is it—a volcanic cone? We've seen so many of them all day."

Was this just a way of changing the subject away from Tony? But Nina did notice scenery. "You're a puzzle, Nina. What's in a view? Just another collection of hills."

"But not like those we saw in Greece, or in Yugoslavia, or in Switzerland or Austria. All those were different from each other, too. Just like the people who live among them."

"People are people. They're all the same. It's their economic environment that makes them seem different. And these are the differences that can be changed." Changed with a revolution that would end the differences, the inequalities, the barbarities of privilege.

"Changed by force? By proclamations and edicts? Social

engineering, my father would call it. He'd give you a good argument against that, Jim."

"I'd probably agree with him," he said lightly. "Who talked about force or edicts anyway?"

"Then how do you change people into all the same pattern? First, you'd have to destroy all their values, all their achievements, everything that didn't agree with your ideas of how people should live. Then you'd have to get them to accept all your laws and regulations, change them into—"

"My ideas? My laws? Oh, come on, Nina." He was laughing now.

"Not *yours,* Jim. You know what I mean. It's a manner of speech." Suddenly she smiled. "My father would agree with you there. He never uses 'you,' always 'one.' One does this, one doesn't do that."

"What is your father exactly?" Kiley knew quite well what Francis O'Connell's function was: he headed the Bureau of Political-Economic Affairs in Washington and was about to be given that peculiarly American position of ambassador-at-large. He would be jetting around the world mending political fences, shoring up breaks in economic dams, Mr. Almighty in International Affairs, Pinhead Supreme.

"Economics and politics, that's his thing," Nina said.

"You don't sound impressed."

"But I am. I just don't like impressing other people."

"Did he talk with you at all? Or was he too busy?"

Nina was angry. "We talked. We traveled together. At one time." Then she recovered, said, "He taught me a lot, actually. I'd put forward my ideas, and he'd argue them out. But patiently. I remember once—I was fifteen at the time—I wanted everything in the world to be equalized." Nina shook her head, laughing at herself.

"But he didn't believe in equality?"

"Before the law, yes. In civil rights, too. But how on earth, Jim, do you keep people equalized in what they do or what they want? I mean, you may force everyone—if you are ruthless enough—to be equal in earnings and in possessions, but how do you *keep* them equalized? I don't see how you can make a program of behavior for the whole world and expect it to stay the way you want it to be."

There was a brief silence. Thoroughly indoctrinated, Kiley thought, as he looked at the girl beside him. He raised a hand and pushed back a lock of her hair behind her ear. "There's

that 'you' problem again," he said, and won a smile. "You're
so beautiful, darling. Why do you bother your pretty little
head with all that political talk?"

Bother your pretty little head . . . "I wasn't talking politics.
I was talking about people."

"Of course," he said soothingly. "I think I'd better spell
Tony at the wheel. He's just about had it with Selim chat-
tering in his ear."

Whispering would be a better word for Selim, seated up
front with Shawfield. "He looks like a conspirator out of a
grade-B movie."

For a second, Kiley stared at her blankly.

"Selim," she explained. "Who else?"

Drawing his arm away from her shoulder, Kiley prepared
to rise. "We'll soon reach our stopping place. Selim says the
food is good there—plentiful, at least." With a brief touch of
his hand on her cheek, he went forward. Seemingly, however,
there was no need for him to take the wheel. He stayed beside
Shawfield after elbowing Selim aside, cutting him out of their
quiet conversation. Nina watched them for a few moments.
Now we've got two conspirators, she joked with herself. Then
her eyes turned to the gray landscape, a high plateau of dusty
green surrounded by hills. As fields gave way to trees shel-
tering small cubes of houses built of earth-toned brick, she
reached across the narrow aisle to shake Madge awake. "We
are here."

"Where?" Madge straightened up, looked out the window.

"At the oasis."

"Oasis?" Madge's wits were slow in gathering. "Oh, you
mean the town?"

"The outskirts." Always the outskirts, thought Nina. But
tomorrow, somehow, I'll get into the center of this city, find
the bazaar and a skirt to change with the one I'm wearing,
find a bookstore and look for a map, newspapers, and magazines (will there be any in English?), and get malaria pills
at a drugstore or chemist's or whatever it's called. "Madge,"
she said softly, "don't take any more pills from Tony. I think
they're some drug."

"What's wrong with them? They are harmless, make you
feel wonderful."

"They may not be harmless. They may lead—"

"It will soon be dark," Madge said curtly. The long road
ahead, tree-lined, was unlit and already slipping into night

shadows. To her relief, the camper slowed down before a flat-roofed building of virulent pink, one-storied, with a small gas station at one side. At the other side, where the camper was now following a rough driveway into a rear courtyard, was a café with its name in bold lettering of dashes, dots, and curlicues sprawled above a bleakly illuminated door.

They drew up in the courtyard, a large square of packed earth surrounded by trees on three sides. Other cars were following them, but there was room—and space to spare—for everyone. Shawfield still sat at the wheel as his crowd followed Selim out of the camper; he was ready to angle it into another corner of the yard if some cars were parked too near him. But they settled for the garage side of the inn. He noted them carefully: the Fiat with the Turks; the station wagon with the Swedes; even the red Ferrari and the Australians. Only the Germans in the Mercedes had preferred to go on their way with a more expensive lodging in mind. As his crowd straggled slowly across the yard to the entrance of the building, Kiley joined him. "We'll get them asleep by midnight," Kiley said. "Does that give you time?"

"That should do it. You'd better give O'Connell a pill tonight, make sure she's as stretched out as the rest of them."

"She's tired enough."

"Don't chance it," Shawfield warned him. "Hey, what is she doing now?"

Kiley looked across the yard to the small group halted outside the inn's central doorway. He swore, jumped out of the camper, then checked his pace to a saunter. Nina was talking with one of the Turks. The other was listening in rapt attention. So was Madge. And the Swedish couple. "Hello, hello," Kiley said genially as he reached them. "Quite a traffic block we've got here."

"I'm getting some names," Nina told him, excitement and success bringing her face to life. "Names of places where the best carpets are made." She turned back to the Turk, a handsome man with large dark eyes and a sweeping black mustache. "Would you repeat them again, please?" And then to Kiley, "Jim, can you note them down for me?"

"We may not be anywhere near these places," he warned her.

The Swedish newspaperman had his notebook out, ready for dictation.

"There are a few places in Tabriz," Nina was saying, "and some on the outskirts of Tehran."

"Ab 'Ali," prompted the Turkish carpet dealer. "Good as Isfahan. Ver' good at Shiraz. Also Kerman ver' good."

"I've got them," said the Swede, scribbling hard. "I'll give you a copy," he told Nina. "Tomorrow morning? I will draw you a little map, too."

"Wonderful."

"Very educational," he remarked to his wife as they left in search of the children.

"Thank you," Nina said to the carpet experts. They bowed gravely, spoke a phrase in Turkish as polite good-bye, and entered the inn.

"Their Turkish sounds better than their English," Kiley said, letting the Swedes pass inside. "Must be Eastern mind readers, too. How did they know you wanted to see carpets?"

"I asked them," Nina said. "It was simple."

Madge was laughing. "You know Nina. She just goes up to a stranger with her best smile and asks him if he speaks English. He looked a little astounded, I must say. Then he answered, 'Ver' good English.' But it did take him a few moments to understand her questions."

"Ver' simple," Nina said.

Kiley took her arm, led her indoors. "We'll have some music tonight. Marie-Louise tells me she has mastered two of the gypsy tunes that she heard in Istanbul. That was a good night, wasn't it?"

On the outskirts of Istanbul, Nina thought. But that had been a good night. In spite of her anger and almost-revolt on leaving the Hilton, she had enjoyed herself. Negative emotions had ebbed away, leaving only a touch of guilt: Jim was thoughtful, Jim was kind, and what was she? "Marie-Louise says one of these songs was brought from India by the gypsies. It's one of the ragas that are played there. She's hoping to trace it—"

"Ragas? We're getting fancy, aren't we?"

"Well, that's their name."

"How do you pick up all these little pieces of information?" He half turned to the entrance, where Shawfield and Madge had appeared. "I know—you go up to a stranger, stun him with a smile, and ask if he speaks English. That's how she does it, Tony. Got the names of carpet towns from our Turkish traders. Everything okay outside?"

"Locked up and secure." Shawfield looked around the small hall suffocated with large posters above its side counter, where Selim was superintending their registration. Ahead of him, through a wide doorway, he could see a dining room. Sparse lighting, but plenty of space. It looked clean even if it was overdressed with garlands of bright-colored paper flowers decorating cracks in newly plastered walls. Posters there, too: religious leaders in black turbans, the cult of personality, brooding over several large tables. At least, he thought, we won't be packed together with a mish-mash of strangers. "Could be worse," he said and relaxed.

Selim was triumphant. "We have three rooms. The Australians have one. The Turks have one. The Swedes have one. But I have obtained three."

"All together?" Shawfield asked.

"Impossible. Only three bedrooms on each side of this hall. The biggest one was required for the Swedish family. We have one on either side of them." He pointed to a corridor on his left.

"That will do." The three girls in one of them: Tromp, Lambrese, and Dissen in the second. "Kiley and I will take the room on the other side of the hall."

Selim's eyes were pleading. "And me?"

Nina said, "You could sleep in the camper. Couldn't he, Tony?"

Tony gave her a look that chilled her bones. "No one sleeps in the camper. It stays locked for the night."

Hastily, Selim said, "I'll sleep in the dining room. Okay? Now I need your passports."

"I'll collect them," Kiley said. Then to Nina, "Let's find your room and see if you'll be comfortable."

"Where are the bathrooms?" Madge wanted to know.

"One bathroom. Very nice," Selim assured her. "Next the kitchen." He pointed to his right. "Very new."

The kitchen would be easy to find: women's voices were loud and the smell of food was rich. Madge started in its direction.

"But much engaged," Selim called after her. "Everyone standing in good line."

Kiley led Nina along a narrow hall to its farthest room. "All right?" he asked anxiously.

"Fine." It was small, with three narrow cots, two wooden chairs, one window, and a row of pegs on one wall. "And we do have a bathroom even if we must stand in good line. Poor Selim—must he sleep in the dining room?"

"Do you think we want him bending our ear all through the night?" Kiley looked around the room again. The window, covered by a straight hanging curtain, was barred. "All right?" he asked again.

"Of course it is!" Nina handed him her passport. "I'll need that back by tomorrow morning. I'm going into town, and I'd better carry some identification, don't you think?"

"Why not wait until the next day? I'll take you into Tabriz then."

"Tomorrow you'll be busy?"

"Bank—a travel bureau to meet our new guide—a visit to the university to see a professor of English, an old friend from Chicago. Yes, I guess you could say I'll be busy. Everything takes time in this part of the world. I'll leave fairly early in the morning. Around eight. You just rest up or explore the food markets nearby. You'll see a lot of new types there." Again he looked anxiously at her. "All right?" he asked for the third time.

"Yes." Her voice softened, a smile came into her eyes. "I do notice the trouble you've taken. I'm not ungrateful, really I am not."

He caught her in his arms, kissed her long and hard, would have kissed her again but the door opened and Madge came in.

Almost three o'clock in the morning and wide awake. Nina turned over again on her cot. Its mattress was thin, with a middle depression. Silence everywhere outside, making Marie-Louise's snores seem louder than they were. Madge lay still, gently breathing. Both had fallen into deep sleep by midnight. I'm tired, yet I can't sleep, Nina thought: it's this small room and the window closed, securely locked. What are the owners of this inn afraid of? Prowlers or night air? I'm suffocating.

She rose, drew on her dark-blue robe—practical in weight and color for traveling—and found the pen flashlight in its pocket. She switched it on to search for her sandals, and then played its weak small beam across the floor to lead her safely to the door. Quietly, she turned the key. "Keep this door locked," Jim had said as he kissed her good night. So she drew the key out, closed the door and locked it, slipping the key deep into her pocket as she started along the corridor.

Dark and silent, with deep breathing from the Swedes' room, with steady snores from Sven, Guido, and Henryk next door. She switched off her flashlight before she reached the entrance hall, where one small bulb had been left burning. The counter that served as a reception desk was empty. The owner of the inn must be in bed and asleep, lucky man. But voices were coming from the dining room. One meager light there—such extravagance, she thought with a smile, recognizing Selim's voice. The other talker? It could be the owner's son, who had bustled around the dining tables, directing the waiters—four small boys, thirteen or fourteen years old, anxious and willing and overworked. She looked at the front door, wondering if Selim and his friend would hear the turning of its heavy key. It might be better if she told them that she was only wanting ten minutes of cool sweet air. But she knew what would happen: Selim would come with her, talk and talk. No, she decided; not that. She'd be driven inside within four minutes flat.

She reached the door. The key in its lock was massive. It wouldn't turn. Then she realized it wouldn't budge because it was already in the unlocked position. Some security, she thought: windows shut and covered with iron screens, and an entrance door left open for anyone to enter. She stepped out into the yard, pulling the door closed behind her to cut off the insistent murmur of voices from the dining room.

There was only a sliver of moon, but the stars were clear and beautiful. She drew long deep breaths, welcoming the cold air. Dawn was still some time away. No wind, not even a breeze to stir the surrounding trees. The parked cars, three neatly placed shadows, their color eaten up by the night, were at one side of the yard. The camper, curtains drawn, stood aloof like some proud beauty. And its lines were good, she admitted. Custom-built, outside as well as in. It must have cost Tony all of his savings; no wonder he guarded it so constantly. Then, as she studied it, she saw a faint almost imperceptible glow spreading into the darkness from the ventilation window on its roof. Careless of Tony, she thought at first: he left one of the small lights turned on. Or has someone broken into the camper?

She hesitated, looked at the door behind her. No, she had better make certain the camper really had been entered before she alerted Selim. A false alarm and she would be apologizing all tomorrow for waking up everyone: Selim wouldn't handle this quietly; of that she was sure.

Cautiously, she approached the camper. Its hood pointed toward a line of trees, its rear end—with its door—stretched into the center of the courtyard. If anyone is inside, she told herself, I'm not risking that back door: it could be opened at any moment. The side of the camper was safer; its curtained windows, slightly opened at the top to air it thoroughly, should let her hear the sounds of anyone moving around. She reached it and steadied herself against its smooth surface, her legs suddenly weak. She was more nervous than she had realized. Nervous? She was terrified.

She calmed down. There was no movement inside the camper. Tony had been careless about the light, that was all. With relief, she was about to turn away. And then she heard a voice raised in a sudden burst of anger. Jim's voice. Good old American swearwords, she thought, and smiled. And stopped smiling as he broke into German. Another voice answered him, speaking German, too. Tony's? The pitch was Tony's—that short bitter laugh was Tony's—but in German? Neither of them knew much German, had never been in Germany, had called on Sven Dissen for help in being understood when they were in Basel, in Innsbruck.

Disbelief and shock seemed to paralyze her body. Unable to move, she stood with her hand resting on the camper's side. She couldn't hear much, now that the voices had quietened. In any case, their fluent exchange was too quick for her, far beyond the German she had learned at school. Something about "a change," "arrangements canceled," "new arrangements made." The word "Afghanistan" was repeated twice. So was the phrase "absolutely necessary."

And then Tony's voice became clearer—he must have moved close to the window near where she stood. "They will call us again. At twelve noon. What is your message?"

Jim's reply was less audible, but it sounded authoritative. Tony said, "Okay. I will tell them."

There was a brief silence. Suddenly, she heard the rear door open. Nina took an uncertain step away, abandoned her hope of reaching the inn. Instinctively she edged toward the front of the camper, feeling some protection from its solid body. They were talking as they closed and locked the door, their voices sounding so near that she was unnerved. Quickly, she moved to the nearest tree, only six paces away. She drew behind its trunk, her heart beating wildly, her eyes on the two men as they started a slow walk to the inn. From behind her, an arm went around her waist, a hand went over her mouth.

"Don't scream," a voice whispered in her ear. "Please don't scream. And how could we explain this situation to Mr. James Kiley?" Her struggles ceased. The hand left her lips. "Sorry. There was no other way." The arm was still firm around her waist, supporting her now. She needed it. "I'm a friend," the whispering voice said. "Your Turkish adviser on Persian carpets."

Nina turned her head to look. It was too dark to see anything clearly beyond black hair, black mustache, and a wide smile. "Your English has improved."

"Sh!" he told her, his eyes on the courtyard. He drew his left arm away from her waist to let him raise the small object he had been gripping in that hand to his ear.

Nina heard a faint murmur of voices, stared at the small object. A radio? No—something else, picking up the sounds of talk in the courtyard. "You're eavesdropping!"

"Weren't you?" He pulled her closer, so that she could listen, too.

"They're speaking English now," she said in astonishment.

"Someone at a bedroom window might hear them. Wiser to get back into character, don't you think?"

She stared at him.

He remained silent, listening, until Kiley and Shawfield had entered the inn. Then he clicked off his receiver and slipped it into his pocket. "Did you get any of that?" he asked.

"Not much. I stopped listening," Nina said unhappily.

"It was of little importance." Nothing compared to what had been already discussed in the camper, Pierre Claudel thought. "Merely their projects for tomorrow. Shawfield will have extra work to do—he will study maps, plan a new route. Kiley leaves at four o'clock to meet his friends."

"At four? No, he said . . ." Eight o'clock, she remembered, and closed her eyes.

Claudel glanced at his watch. "Thirty-five minutes before he leaves. I think you had better remain here until then. He might be having breakfast in the dining room."

Nina nodded, bit her lip, fought back a sudden attack of tears.

"I'll stay with you. Bob Renwick would insist on that."

"Bob Renwick?"

"Yes," Claudel said mildly. "We are good friends. I saw him in Istanbul before I left. When he heard I was traveling this way, he asked me to keep an eye open—speak with you— find out if you were all right."

This is a trick, Nina thought. This pleasant, frank-spoken man could be lying—just as Jim Kiley has lied. She said, "I don't believe you."

"Bob thought you probably wouldn't. So he gave me this." Claudel reached for his wallet and handed her a card. Then he pulled out a thin pen, flashed on its small light, shielding it with his cupped hand as he turned his back to the yard.

Nina read: *J. P. Merriman & Co., Consultant Engineers. Advisers on Construction Abroad. Surveys made.*

"Look at the back," Claudel urged.

Courtyard of the Janissaries. Nina looked up in amazement, held Claudel's eyes with hers. Then her face hardened. "You could have been there—seen us together."

"Yes." He switched off his flashlight. "But I couldn't have heard how you pitied the tribute children." He heard her sharp intake of breath. She kept staring at him.

"Not even with that listening device?" she asked.

"By the time you were talking about janissaries, I was far away, too far for even the—that device to reach. It has its limits even with all its latest improvements." That reminded him of something. He said, "Wait here. I'll only take five minutes. I'll come back. I promise you. Will you wait?"

She looked toward the inn. Jim Kiley might be in his room; again, he might not. She nodded. "I'll stay."

Claudel took the card from her hand. "It's safer with me," he told her. It went back into his wallet. He touched her hand encouragingly. "My God, you're freezing!" So the wallet went into a trouser pocket as his jacket came off and was placed around her shoulders. "Five minutes," he said and left.

He didn't go directly to the camper, although it was only a short distance away. Instead, he used the trees on his left to circle partway around the yard until he found a spot where the camper's bulk would block his approach if anyone was looking out a bedroom window. Then, as he judged it safe enough, he darted forward. Nina could see him, barely twenty feet away from her, reach the side of the camper that was not visible from the inn. His hand was raised, touching something on one of the windows, pulling it away. Then his hand was lowered and he pocketed whatever he had removed, and he was retracing his steps exactly. She watched his dark shadow merge into the row of trees, lost him completely as he worked his way back to where she stood. What had he taken from the window? Another gadget, something to let him listen clearly to any sounds inside the camper? She could only guess. And guess at this man's interest. It wasn't with her—it was with Jim Kiley and Tony Shawfield. Why? But I'm interested in them, too, she thought bitterly. I've been used. All of us have been used, manipulated. The rest of our group still don't realize it, never will. And I never would have if Bob hadn't sent his friend—Where has he gone? She panicked for a moment, and then relaxed as he left the neighboring tree and stood beside her.

"Okay," he said softly. He fell silent, his eyes on the inn.

That was all he was going to say, Nina realized. But she had questions. "Who are you? You are not Turkish, are you?"

He dodged that neatly. "My mother was French. I went to school in England." Both statements were true.

So that explained his accent: idiomatic English with a hint, every now and again, of French. "What shall I call you?"

"My mother chose Pierre," he said briefly. Again, true.

She looked at the inn. "Are they German?"

"I don't know. They aren't strangers to the language, that's certain."

"Why use it?"

"They may have received a message in German, just continued talking in it."

"May have? Didn't you hear it?"

He hesitated. "It doesn't work that way. They received a message, yes. In code. They decoded it from German and continued talking in German."

"Received a message . . . But how? On our camper radio?"

He repressed a smile. "No. Something more sophisticated than that."

"Hidden. Where?"

He shrugged his shoulders. He had noted its antenna, the long wire that ran cleverly under the edge of the camper's roof. "It could be anywhere inside the camper."

"I'll find it."

"No," he said sharply. "What you have to concentrate on now is—escape. Leave tomorrow. With me. I'll see you onto a plane to Tehran. You'll fly to Rome. Renwick will meet you there. I'll let him know."

She said slowly, "So that's why Bob wanted you to meet me.... This was his idea, wasn't it?"

"Yes. But not exactly this kind of meeting, at this time, in this place. He wants you out. He's counting on that."

"What about Madge? We're together." More or less. Without Madge I'd never have joined the camper. I wanted the world trip, yes. It seemed a dream for the taking. But I'd never have come alone. "I can't walk out on her. I'd have to tell her."

Claudel shook his head to that idea. "Ask her—in a general way—if she's had enough. Suggest leaving, but give no details. Don't mention tonight, or this talk. If she's willing, bring her along. If she says no, then you'll feel free to leave. Would that work?"

"No. Madge would wonder, be alarmed. She'd talk. Shawfield has become her friend. It's too dangerous, Pierre. For you as well as for me. Shawfield would have you arrested at the Tehran airport for kidnapping."

Nothing quite so official as that, Claudel thought. Shawfield's type of friends in Tehran would do a little kidnapping of its own: two bodies found in some back alley. Silently, he cursed Madge and the problem she presented. "Leave," he urged. "Get out of this mess. Why do you think I told you so much, let you see so much? Goddamn it to bloody hell, I've—" He broke off in frustration.

"I know," she said. "You risked everything in order to shock me into leaving. You did shock me. But I can't leave. Not yet." She reached for his arm, pressed it reassuringly. "I won't go running to Shawfield. Or to James Kiley. Or anyone."

He stared at her in disbelief. "You really think you can go on, never let them know, never give your real feelings away? No, no. Now that you've learned so much, you're in double danger."

"On the contrary. Now that I know—and it isn't so much, either—I'm on guard."

"Not so much?" My God, he thought, when Renwick hears how I broke the rules tonight, he'll—no, perhaps Renwick wouldn't. He can guess what I'm dealing with here; he warned me about Nina. And I thought I could handle her.

"No," Nina was saying. "You didn't tell me who sent Kiley's instructions tonight."

His quick French wits failed him for a moment. He searched for an answer, found none.

"Are Kiley and Shawfield working for the Russians?" she asked.

"Indirectly," he hedged.

"What on earth does that mean? The Russians are in charge?"

"From a safe distance."

"Then who is—"

"Sh!" he said. Their voices had been kept to a murmur all through their talk, but now complete silence was needed. He pointed to the inn. Its door had opened. And simultaneously, from around the far corner of the inn where the gas station lay, a farm truck, small in size, loaded with baskets, drove quietly into the yard. It barely stopped at the inn's door—less than a minute to let Kiley emerge and climb on board. Then it left, easing its way into the rough driveway, and turned right as it reached the main road. It looked like any truck heading for one of the early markets in Tabriz. Claudel glanced at Nina. Yes, she had seen it all.

She slipped off his jacket, handed it to him. "It will soon be daylight. When do we meet again?"

"You won't leave with me tomorrow?"

"No. But couldn't we meet—"

"Not here. You'll be taking the southern highway out of Iran—into Baluchistan, then Pakistan."

"No Afghanistan. Why? There's been some trouble, I know, but we were to have an escort. Jim said it would be safe."

"No longer. Eight foreigners killed last week, one on a tourist bus. There's more than trouble there. It's war. Atrocities on both sides. Soviet troops, Soviet tanks are massing at the border, and Muslim rebels are massacring anyone who looks like a Russian."

"Then why did we ever plan to go through Afghanistan?"

"Because the planning must have been done months ago. You don't imagine, surely, that this trip was arranged in a few weeks? That camper you're traveling in—it wasn't custom-built in less than three or four months. History just caught up with them: their plans had to be changed. So, as there are only two decent roads leading east out of Iran, one through Afghanistan, one through Baluchistan, I know which one you'll be taking. I can't tail you. Too many bare stretches. But I'll meet you. Somewhere. Possibly near Kerman. Remember that name."

"The carpet place."

"Have you got a map?"

"No." She thought of the kindly Swede. "But I can get one. Safely."

He was beginning to see the expressions on her face. Daylight was coming up. "Back to the inn," he urged her. "They've left the door open. You may find a woman sweeping out the hall. They rise early here."

"I'll think of some excuse. And thank you. And don't worry. Tell Bob—" Her voice faltered. "Thank him." She slipped away, quickly reached the camper and then slowed her pace to a normal walk.

Claudel watched her enter the inn. So I failed, he thought, and the admission was bitter. But he'd have another try at Kerman. And this time he would have a plan prepared. Beyond Kerman, at Zahidan, not far from the Baluchistan frontier, there was a crossroads where the road to the east met the road coming down from the north. It had been built by the Soviets, in one of their agreements with the ex-Shah, to run south to the Persian Gulf. That could be our escape route, he thought. If she will come. What is holding her back? It's just possible she has done what Renwick didn't want to do: she has recruited herself. She doesn't know it yet, but that's what she has done.

The inn remained quiet, undisturbed. Nina must have made it safely to her room. With relief, he began making his way along the rows of trees that edged the yard, aiming to reach the inn from an angle that was the opposite of Nina's approach. And there *was* a woman, smothered in black, who was washing the floor of the dining room. Selim's voice, speaking in Turkish dialect, was listing his complaints about an uncomfortable night. The woman was dutifully silent, just moved on her knees to the next part of floor to be washed. Claudel slipped silently down the dark passage to his room.

Fahri was awake and waiting. "Well?" he demanded.

Claudel repressed his excitement. "We have big news to send out."

"Anything about Turkish terrorists?"

"Yes. They were discussed. They are not inclined for united action, insist on continuing assassination as their best means at present. But they took Kiley's money, listened to his proposals. If Shawfield can guarantee shipment of weapons—they gave him a list—they'll use them as he directs." Claudel took out his receiver. Nina, he thought, would have opened her blue eyes even wider if she had known it could record as well as listen. "The little miracles of modern technology," he said with a laugh. He kissed the receiver and set it gently on top of his suitcase. "It's all in there—discussions about Bursa and more. Much more. Okay, let's start it talking to us, and we'll condense its news." Tomorrow, somewhere on an empty stretch of road, they'd send the completed report to Kahraman in Istanbul. From there, it would be transmitted to London. Another report would go to London, too: for Renwick, about his Nina.

"Now?" Fahri asked. "Do you need no sleep?"

"I'll catnap while you drive."

"We are leaving? Is one day here enough?"

"Quite enough. Let's get to work."

Fahri was listening. The stillness outside was broken by a distant voice calling from the peak of a minaret, chanting its summons to the faithful. Fahri rose, unrolled his prayer rug.

So night is over, Claudel thought, and the new day begins. He stretched out on his cot, closed his eyes. He'd snatch twenty minutes of deep, delicious sleep.

CHAPTER
20

By the last week of September, they were on their way out of Iran. It had been a start at daybreak from Kerman. "Not much more than two hundred miles to the frontier," Kiley said as encouragement to his shivering flock as they sat in bleak silence, sweaters and jackets around hunched shoulders, and stared out at less and less foliage, more and more sand. "In another couple of hours you'll start complaining that you're being roasted." He's sharp-set this morning, Nina thought as she heard the edge in his voice: what is worrying him? It can't be our Iranian guide and interpreter—Ahmad isn't a continual talker like Selim.

Ahmad and Shawfield were tense, too, their eyes on the road ahead. It was empty enough: one car, occasionally visible when the road straightened and the small hills—sand dunes, actually—no longer interfered with the view. For once, Tony Shawfield wasn't trying to pass the car in front of them: he let it draw well away, eventually be lost from sight. Ahmad looked at his watch, spoke to Tony, who nodded and put on his usual speed, and began watching the wind-molded desert on the left-hand side of the road.

"There are cars behind us," Kiley warned. "I make out two."

"How far behind?"

"Difficult to judge. These damned sand hills—" He broke off, noticing Nina's strange mixture of interest and dejection. "You don't look too happy, Nina. Didn't you see enough carpets at Kerman?" he teased.

She nodded. But in our two days there, I saw no sign of my Turkish friend who had a French mother and an English education. Near Kerman, he had said. "It's all this emptiness," she told Kiley. "No one lives here. Not one real village."

"Only caravan routes. Actually, this road used to be one of them. We're in luck, the north wind—the Wind of a Hundred and Twenty Days, as Ahmad calls it—has blown

231

itself out." That diverted her attention, as he had guessed it would.

"Is it the wind that causes all this erosion?"

"Lifts sand out of one place, builds it up in another. It can be violent. So we're in luck," he repeated. Good management, he told himself, and waited for her to notice that. But the barren land had silenced her completely. A signal from Ahmad caught his attention. At last, he thought with a surge of relief: this shouldn't take long—not much talk to be exchanged, just a packet of money. He would be glad when he had got rid of the bulky envelope strapped to his waist. This country was too lonely for a feeling of safety.

"Look!" called out Guido Lambrese, and had Henryk Tromp reaching for his camera.

"What is it? A fort?" Sven Dissen suggested.

"It looks empty," Madge said. "Couldn't we stop?"

All of them were too startled by the sudden appearance of the solid, strong, unembellished building, rising squarely from a stretch of flat sand, to notice that Shawfield had already slackened speed. The camper came to a halt. There was a rush to get out. "Hold it!" Kiley warned them. "Let's make sure it's deserted. Safety first."

"Safety? What's dangerous in an old fort?" Madge asked.

"It may not be deserted," said Nina. There were fresh tire marks leading from the road toward the silent building. Cars might be parked out of sight behind the towering bulk of hewn stone. "What *is* it, Jim?"

Ahmad said, "A caravanserai. A place where caravans stopped for the night. Their camels and donkeys went inside also, and slept beside the women. The men protected them from any attack."

"How?" Madge asked. "Through those slits in the walls?" There were no windows.

Ahmad, as was his way, didn't answer the obvious. With his usual disdain for all foreigners' ignorance, he descended onto the road and waited impatiently.

Damn him for a know-it-all, thought Kiley: he has said the one thing that will make them determined to get inside the place. Its vast door, high enough for a fully loaded camel to enter, was wide open to show gaping darkness. An invitation to explore. He cursed under his breath. "It may not be empty. So we'd better find out who is inside before we walk into something we can't handle. Tony—you come with me.

And we'll need Ahmad to speak the language and get us out of there—if we meet any sign of trouble."

"Trouble?" Madge was excited.

"You want to lose that little Kodak of yours?" he joked, and dampened her enthusiasm. It also ended Tromp's. His Japanese camera had cost eight hundred American dollars. "Wait here," Kiley told them. "Guard the camper. Don't leave it, remember! We'll signal you if we find only a couple of camel drivers having a midmorning rest."

"Where are the camels?" Madge asked.

"Inside with the women and children," Nina said. "Watch out for those slits, Jim. There's a homemade rifle pointing at you right now."

He looked at her sharply, and then laughed.

"A funny sense of humor that girl has," Shawfield said sourly as he walked off with Kiley and Ahmad. The distance ahead of them was short, barely a hundred yards.

At the camper, the group gathered together. Lambrese studied the uncompromising shape of the caravanserai. "Pathetic," he said. His taste ran to the Parthenon, or at least Doric pillars.

Tromp said, "It was built for defense, Guido."

"Even so—just think what the Knights of Rhodes could have made of it."

"Grim," Dissen agreed. "What's that lying outside its threshold?"

"It doesn't move," Marie-Louise said. "Something dead?" She took a step forward. Then another. Her husband followed her, so did Lambrese and Tromp. All four were soon walking slowly toward the caravanserai. They halted as Kiley looked round, waved them back.

Nina watched them, Madge still indefinite about staying beside her or joining the others. We aren't meant to see inside that place, Nina thought. Jim and Tony and Ahmad were now skirting the motionless object to step into the yawning blackness beyond the entrance.

Curiosity drew the others another twenty yards nearer the caravanserai. Again they halted. "It's a dead donkey," Marie-Louise cried out. *"Affreux!"*

At that moment, a car from Kerman passed the camper, traveling rapidly. Behind it came another—a gray Fiat. It slowed down, stopped. "Have you trouble?" a man called in halting English. "We help, perhaps?" Pierre got out, raised his eyebrows. "Ah, the young lady who wish to see carpets. You like them?"

"Damn!" said Madge, looking at the rest of the group, who were now halfway to the caravanserai. Henryk was busy photographing. "We're missing all the fun."

"I'll guard everything here. Go ahead."

Madge needed no urging. Kodak in hand, she left at a run.

Quickly, Pierre came forward, took cover at the side of the camper, placing its body between him and the caravanserai, beckoning to Nina to follow. She watched in astonishment as he bent to feel something underneath its rear fender. Whatever he had checked there pleased him. He gave a broad smile and a forefinger salute to Fahri, who sat at the Fiat's wheel, then began speaking rapidly. "You'll stop at Zahidan for lunch. I'll be watching for you. Make some excuse; leave them, and follow me. To a car—not this Fiat; it goes on to Pakistan. We'll drive back into Iran and then head south for the Hormuz Strait. We'll get a boat easily and sail—"

"No." That whole terrain was a wasteland. The map the kindly Swedish couple had given her in Tabriz showed only hundreds of miles of nothingness. "I am not leaving. There's no need. I'm safe enough."

"Your friend? Is she still—"

"Still determined to stay. Besides, there's too much risk for you. You're putting yourself in danger."

He could agree with that, but it was worth a try. "Who, me?"

"You," she said firmly. "I can't leave. Later—"

"It would have to be much later. In Bombay." He shook his head.

"Another month. The last week in October—so Jim Kiley told me. I think it was the truth. This time."

The date agreed with the one he had overheard in the Tabriz courtyard. He stared at her. She was obdurate. "Do you know Bombay? Have you a map of it?" There was a quick shake of her head, a look of momentary fear in those blue eyes. "One of the big hotels—they're close together, central; you'll find them easily; any taxi driver can get you there—is the Malabar. You'll see its name—in big letters." He had taken out a small pad and pencil, was jotting down some figures. "Ask for Mr. Roy—A. K. Roy. Give your name: Nina. That will be enough." He tore off the sheet of paper and handed it to her. "That's his private number."

"Roy," she repeated. "The Malabar Hotel. Is he English?"

"Indian. Someone at that number will take your message and arrange a meeting at the hotel with me or with—" He stopped short of saying Bob Renwick. Why promise what might not be? "With someone you can trust. We'll get you safely out of Bombay. I can't risk meeting you before then, but don't be surprised if you see two Australians around. The red Ferrari—remember it?—well, it needs repairs. So if you've learned about any further stops on your journey, tell them. If you sense danger to yourself, tell them. They will improvise. And remember—" Fahri had a fit of coughing. Pierre moved toward the Fiat. "Destroy that number" were his parting words. He stepped into the car. It left.

For a moment, Nina wished she hadn't been so firm in her refusal. She slipped the piece of paper into the deep pocket of her wide skirt. Later, she'd memorize its numbers and then drop it, in a dozen small pieces, down the horrible hole in the floor of some abominable bathroom. Now, she must walk around the camper and face the caravanserai. Kiley and Shawfield were in view, their heads turned to watch the departing Fiat. Ahmad was shouting at the Dutchman, who had taken a photograph of the donkey just as the three men had emerged. The others were protesting: why couldn't they go inside—they wouldn't take long—just a quick look? But they listened to Kiley, as they always did, and he shepherded his flock of straggling sheep back to the road.

He repeated his explanation to Nina. "There are a couple of men inside there, ugly-looking types. Ahmad had to do a lot of fast talking to get us out. They looked as if they'd slit our throats for our shirts and shoes."

"Couldn't we risk a crowd of us going in?" she asked.

"They're armed. We are not."

"I wish I could have seen it." That seemed the expected remark.

"Not much to see. An empty space with a well in the center—silted up. It's dark—has a roof over it, probably to keep the sandstorms out."

"Was that all?"

"There's a stone staircase—no guard rail—leading to a small gallery around the walls. They must be four feet thick. Once that place was as strong as a fortress. Now—just piles of refuse. And the smell! The dead donkey was no help. Its belly was swollen, bloated—enormous. I thought it would explode any minute."

She looked at him in horror. "Just left to die... Oh, Jim, let's get away from here."

"I agree. Sorry to leave you by yourself. The others shouldn't have deserted you. You weren't feeling lonely, were you?"

"I was," she admitted. "Then a car stopped—they thought we might need help—had run out of gas or something."

"That was the gray Fiat?" he questioned.

He recognized the car, she realized: he knows who was inside it. She managed a smile. "Yes. Our ver' good Turkish friend—remember? At the inn near Tabriz? We talked carpets until his English ran out."

"Absorbing topic," Madge said as she brushed past Nina to climb into the camper. "Never mention 'carpet' to me again. I've had it."

So have I, thought Nina, aware of Shawfield's sharp glance, first at her, then at the camper's interior, as he held out a hand to pull her up its steep step. At this moment, she again wished she had listened to Pierre, gone with him, left Shawfield's constant scrutiny. He frightened her: there was something hard, unbending in his expression. He just didn't like people—he was too absorbed by mechanics and his own efficiency. See, Tony, she told him silently, nothing has been disturbed: I guarded the camper well. She mustered a steady hand as he helped her mount the step. Unusual gallantry: did he think he could feel her nervousness? "Lunch at Zahidan?" she asked, her voice as steady as her hand had been.

"No. We'll wait until we reach the Baluchistan frontier. There may be a wait for customs and inspection. The Pakistanis worry about arms; the Iranians worry about drugs. The Baluchis on both sides of the border live on smuggling."

"Drugs?" Lambrese asked, exchanging a covert glance with his friend Tromp.

"Sure. The stuff is manufactured in Pakistan—something halfway between opium and heroin." That should catch their attention, thought Shawfield.

"Morphine sulfate tablets," Sven Dissen informed them all. His friendship with Pakistani medical students in Paris made him an authority on the subject. He needed no urging to enlighten everyone. He did so at length as they settled in their seats and the camper started forward. The poppies grew in northern Pakistan, but the tablets were manufactured all over the place. Now, the old Turkish-Marseilles connection had become interested: they were organizing the drug trade from Pakistan to Amsterdam, Zurich, Copenhagen, Frankfurt.

"But never to Russia," Nina murmured.

Kiley heard that small remark. He said, "Perhaps your Turkish friends aren't so interested in carpets after all." As she stared blankly at him, he added with a smile, "If they meet us again, better keep clear of them. Which reminds me—" he raised his voice for all to hear—"no smuggling from Pakistan across the Indian frontier. Prisons in this part of the world are no health resorts. So don't try smuggling, anyone. Remember!"

Lambrese and Tromp exchanged a second glance. "No one is interested in smuggling, James," Lambrese assured him with perfect truth.

Just in pleasant dreams between frontiers, thought Shawfield. "Traffic is increasing," he called, and pointed to a slow file of five heavily laden camels, three overloaded donkeys, four men and two boys wrapped in odds and ends of old clothes. Bulky head scarves were wound loosely around their heads to form rakish turbans, then twisted around their necks to cover half of their faces. "Baluchis, I think."

"Stop!" Henryk Tromp called out. "Just five minutes for a photograph."

"No time," Shawfield told him. "You'll see plenty of caravans in the next three weeks. Caravanserai, too." Under his breath he said to Ahmad, "That bloody camera."

"Do not worry," Ahmad told him quietly. No one took photographs of Ahmad coming out of that caravanserai. His brows came down, his lips tightened, his heavy mustache bristled. He looked at the passing Baluchis with contempt.

Shawfield nodded. "You deal with it." He glanced over his shoulder. Kiley was talking with O'Connell, had started her laughing. Everything was under control. The gray Fiat was not even in sight on the longest stretch of this goddamned road.

"Well?" Fahri wanted to know as the Fiat picked up speed. "Will she go with you?"

Claudel shook his head.

"I am glad. A crazy idea."

"The only one possible at this time."

"No towns to hide in, no safe house to—"

"Okay, okay Slow up, Fahri. We're getting too far ahead of them."

Fahri slackened speed but not his criticism. "They saw the car. You took a risk."

"Less risk than we would have to take at Zahidan. Remember how she was guarded at Kerman." And how they slipped away, a day earlier than they had told their innkeeper. If it hadn't been for Fahri's early prayers, Claudel might not have seen the camper being readied for departure. (Now, apparently, the idea of sleeping bags in open country had been discarded for the overnight safety of a town and a small inn. The campers were finding out that what had been romantic fun in Europe was becoming increasingly difficult in stranger lands. Just wait, thought Claudel, until they start down through central India: leopards, a tiger perhaps, certainly packs of wild dogs.)

"They saw the car," Fahri repeated. "That was your second contact with the girl. We must not risk a third at Quetta or a fourth at Lahore."

"I'll wait until Bombay."

"That is good." Fahri relaxed, his teeth a brilliant white in contrast with his olive skin and black mustache. He glanced at the small speaker on the dashboard, its beeps now sounding steady and true. "We've got contact. They are catching up." He increased his speed.

"We can switch it off. We don't need to track them now."

"Just testing it. You are sure your Australian friends have the right receiving device?"

"I'm sure," Claudel said with a brief smile. "They are already outside Quetta, waiting for the camper to appear." There was only one road reliable enough for motor traffic coming down from the Baluchistan plateau. Shawfield wouldn't risk the weight and size of a camper on anything less than a solid surface. "They'll pick up its signal easily."

"A long wait for them. Seven, eight days."

"That's part of the job, isn't it? Waiting." Claudel thought of Nina. She would have the longest wait of all. "That girl has courage. Underneath, she is frightened. But what is courage without fear? Blind stupidity," he answered himself.

"Will she survive?" Fahri had his doubts. "One little innocent against a pack of wolves? No place for a woman. They should stay where they belong."

There was a moment's silence. "Tonight," Claudel said, "we'll send our report to London."

"We send a report to Istanbul, too?"

"Kahraman has no interest in the girl."

"Just ask if I may go south with you to Bombay." That was where the real action could be. Fahri's dark eyes gleamed at the prospect.

"You've got business in the north where carpets are made and refugees come over the mountains from Afghanistan," Claudel reminded him. It was better that Fahri should leave him once they reached India, let him travel alone. From now on, he thought, we are a marked pair.

CHAPTER

21

J. P. Merriman & Co. was becoming—to Ronald Gilman's surprise and Bob Renwick's amusement—a successful business. Its downstairs department found its advisers on construction abroad in demand and its surveyors actually at work: their services were seemingly what was needed by hotel chains with an eye on expansion into romanticized areas for well-heeled tourists, such as Tahiti, Bali, Fiji, Kashmir. "It was your idea," Renwick told Gilman, "so why be astonished? It will pay the rent, keep a roof over our heads."

"Your idea has been expanding, too," Gilman said, not to be outdone in generosity. "It's working."

"Slowly."

"That's always the way. Slow but sure. And then—the end is in sight. Suddenly, one more file can be closed."

"One way or the other," Renwick said. It may have been the cold October drizzle outside, or the lack of heat in Gilman's attic room—the small electric fire looked better than it felt—but Renwick's usual optimism was chilled. Too much inaction, too many reports analyzed and broken down and reassembled in different ways to give new leads and clearer assessments.

Gilman said, "Don't tell me you are depressed by the way Interintell is growing. It had to increase its scope, Bob. Couldn't be confined to NATO. Terrorism doesn't belong only to the North Atlantic areas. We've got three additional investigations running at this moment, and two countries outside NATO are concerned enough to ask for our help."

"I know, I know. Expansion is necessary, but it might just be happening too soon." With expansion, there would come—inevitably—publicity. And at this moment, any publicity might give Theo warning of a new force moving against him. "Theo—" began Renwick, and stopped. Theo had been his investigation from the beginning. "So much seems to be hanging fire. Perhaps it's time to give Theo a jolt, make him feel that the best-laid plans may need a change here or an alteration there, set him a little off balance. But let's avoid publicity—if we can. Keep Interintell's name out of it, Ron. For now."

"And take no credit for nailing Theo?"

"Whoever got credit for keeping the peace—except the politicians?" Renwick drew his chair closer to the fire.

Gilman smiled. "Just think of Bombay and temperatures around ninety degrees. Are you really leaving tomorrow? You'll be a week ahead of the camper's arrival."

"Its scheduled arrival," Renwick said pointedly.

"They've still more than seven hundred miles to travel, and none of them easy." The camper, on reaching Pakistan, had traveled south, still keeping in Pakistan, to reach Hyderabad and some students at its Sind University. From there, heading for India at last, it had been faced with the Great Desert. That had been skirted more or less, but even after that success the camper's direction was convoluted, turning north before it swept around to the south again. "One hell of a route they chose."

"Chosen for them," Renwick said. Then he actually laughed. "So Theo does make miscalculations. When he decided on that route, he must have been trying to have the camper avoid any heavy monsoon rains—these last from June until October, usually. But this year the monsoons have failed. There's drought instead of floods."

"That was his second miscalculation," Gilman observed. The Afghanistan scene hadn't seemed to need Soviet military intervention when the camper's route had been initially planned, but the invasion forces were already beginning to group along the frontier.

"Otherwise," Renwick reminded him, "he has done too damned well. He has now set up offices for West-East Travel in Honolulu and Hong Kong." The pattern established in Los Angeles and Istanbul had been repeated: Theo, with a supply of false passports and changes in his appearance to match their photographs and descriptions, had entered foreign countries with the greatest of ease. Once there, he had only needed a couple of hours to appear as Mr. Otto Remp from Düsseldorf in order to sign the final documents—and to keep his home office convinced that their Herr Remp was doing exactly what they had sent him traveling to do. "Two offices still to be arranged," said Renwick thoughtfully.

"Singapore. Bombay. Where will he appear first?"

"I'm betting on Bombay. James Kiley will need a hefty dollop of hard cash when he arrives there." The last place where he had picked up a quantity of money had been in Hyderabad—at a small private bank where an account had been established in Kiley's name. "Theo must have an army of agents scattered around."

"Well, he has pretty strong backing. We may not have their army of agents, but we're doing not so badly." At least Claudel and Fahri had delivered the camper over to Mahoney and Benson, the two Australians, who were old friends of Renwick's. They had managed to stage a breakdown of their Ferrari at Quetta, given themselves the excuse that their trip over the Himalayas to India was out of the question until next summer, and had succeeded—by an exchange of cars—in following the camper as far as Hyderabad. After that they had noted its direction for the Indian frontier, notified A. K. Roy in time for his two agents to pick up the trail. "Roy is a formidable type," Gilman said. They had been good friends since their Oxford days. "I've known him for twenty years, and one thing is certain: he is not going to let Mr. Otto Remp set up a front for espionage right in his own back yard. He comes from Maharashtra, you know, and that's the province where Bombay lies."

So that, thought Renwick, is why Gilman, who had several strong contacts in India, had chosen Roy for this operation. "I hope he has been investigating any recent foreign interest in Bombay real estate." For once we might learn in advance where Theo-in-disguise reverts to Otto Remp for the final transactions.

"Roy is doing that right now," Gilman said. "When do you want to meet him?"

"As soon as I arrive in Bombay." Renwick's depression had lifted. He was already seeing several possibilities of getting close to Theo at last. "Theo—" He smiled. "What about giving him a real shock in time for his Bombay appearance?"

"Shake him up," Gilman agreed. "But how?"

"Ilsa Schlott." Yesterday she had been arrested by New Scotland Yard's antiterrorist squad, but quietly: nothing had yet appeared in the newspapers. "Would your inspector friend consider a little publicity?"

"How much?"

"Nothing to damage any of his continuing investigations into her contacts here in London. The news of her arrest will

have to be made public, you know. Why not now? We'll use
the information that we got from Diehl last week to flesh out
the bald details that Scotland Yard will give to the press."
Richard Diehl, in West Germany, had done a mammoth job
at digging deep into the past history of the People's Revolutionary Force for Direct Action—enough to send Erik and
Marco, its founders, and Theo, their adopted counselor and
friend, into convulsions. "Your contact at Scotland Yard
wouldn't object to that, would he?"

Gilman took off his glasses, polished them thoughtfully.
"It might be a boost for his section. Only he'd have to see a
copy of Diehl's report—just in case the politicians came asking too many questions."

"We'll give him a copy of one part of Diehl's report—the
one that we are willing to have published. That should bolster
any answers he has to give."

"He'll give the minimum. What shall he call Diehl—a
reliable source of information?"

"Should be enough for the moment. Later your friend can
be more exact. He understands that, doesn't he?"

"He's more security-minded than even you are." Gilman
replaced his glasses and rose. "Eleven o'clock. I'll make us
a cup of tea. Gemma bought me this electrical gadget to boil
water. Let's see if it works. And you can get your thoughts
into shape for a press release."

"How much will be reported—before we add our contri-
bution?"

"Ilsa Schlott arrested in a Camberwell garage—charged
with recruitment of terrorists for a training period abroad.
Two terrorists returning to London last week, their training
complete, also arrested. So were the owner of the garage and
his chief mechanic; three employees detained for questioning—and two are talking—regarding cars altered to suit Miss
Schlott's specifications. Two of these cars have been identified: used for the transport of weapons. Miss Schlott, enrolled
at University College as a medical research student, has been
resident in London since September 1978. On a false passport.
Name and nationality are both invented."

"She was actually caught on a visit to that garage? That
was pretty neat timing by your friend," Renwick said ad-
miringly.

"It seemed a good opportunity to nab her. Flagrante de-
licto. Stands up nicely in court. You know—" Gilman broke

off in exasperation—"I don't think this bloody thing is going to work, dammit."

Renwick let him struggle with Gemma's brainchild, and concentrated on the garage in Camberwell. "No mention of a green camper?"

"Actually, yes. But I wasn't sure you'd want that publicized."

"When did the garage start working on that camper?"

"In early February. Finished the job by May. There was a good deal of work needed. Including the services of an electronics expert whose shop just happens to be next to the garage. He and his electrician are in custody, too. Altogether, a nice haul."

"No records kept, of course, on Schlott's special orders."

"None. But the two talking employees saw the camper, knew it was something special although they weren't allowed to work on it. One of them—he's an odd-job man—was in the garage when a thin dark stranger, young, six feet tall, took possession of the camper in June. Arrived with Ilsa Schlott, said nothing; just got into the camper and drove off. The quickest exit our odd-job man had ever seen." Gilman gave up his battle with tea-making. "I'll ring for Liz to bring us some of her brew."

"I'd rather talk." No interruptions wanted, thought Renwick. "Ron—why don't we use the camper? Or would your inspector be against that?"

"No. Because the green camper cost a lot of money. Because Ilsa Schlott pretends to be a student on scholarship. That would make the press and the public realize there is ample justification for these arrests."

"Then let's give Theo a real jolt."

"You think it out. And I'm having that cup of tea." Gilman pressed the button twice to warn Liz. "She'll be here in five minutes." He sat down behind his small desk in the little office he had walled off from the main floor of the communications section, reflecting how much of a contrast it was to his regular office a few streets away. Here, everything was scaled down, built in, made of metal and plastic: there, his panel room had a real desk, a fireplace, and armchairs that sagged in the right places. Renwick seemed oblivious to the discomforts of this hygienic setup. He had even lost his early-morning depression. "I see you've hit on something. Let's hear it."

"Let's wait for that blasted tea to arrive," Renwick said. "Would you rather have coffee?"

Renwick shook his head: Liz made coffee out of some concentrate in a bottle. She arrived within the next minute, bringing not only a tray with a brown teapot, two cups, milk and sugar, a plate of digestive biscuits, but also a folder tucked under one arm. "The latest reports, just arrived," she said in her high, fluting voice, and placed them in the last free foot of desk space. A pretty girl, thought Renwick, who plays beauty down: neatly competent in tweed suit and flat-heeled shoes. No frills about her manner, either. She left at once, with a friendly nod for Gilman's "Thank you, Liz," and a shy smile in Renwick's direction.

Gilman noted it and shook his head: I get the nods, Renwick gets the smiles. It never failed. He opened the folder, saw the message came from Richard Diehl, in West Berlin, glimpsed James Kiley's name. He said, "We'll deal with this later. First, let's finish that press release." He poured the strong black tea, adding milk and sugar generously. Renwick, who wanted neither, took his cup without comment. "Well?" Gilman asked.

"Just after the mention of the two cars that were used for the transport of weapons, we could insert a brief description of a camper, green in color, that was collected in June by a friend of Ilsa Schlott's." Renwick paused. "And then we insert more about Schlott, just after that bit about her residence in London since 1978."

"Such as?"

"Informed sources state that Ilsa Schlott had been known to the West German police as 'Greta,' a member of the People's Revolutionary Force for Direct Action, which, over the last five years, has claimed responsibility for bombings that resulted in deaths and many injuries. The two founders of this terrorist group are of the extreme left and are now being sought for their part in the attempted destruction of the Duisburg waterfront in June. Reliable sources have identified them as 'Erik' and 'Marco.' Although their joint manifesto for Direct Action preached the philosophy of nineteenth-century anarchism, it is now believed they are working for the more orthodox left-wing forces—temporarily, at least." Renwick smiled. "That should throw a few fits around Theo's circle."

"It's too long. The newspapers will print only half of it. A pity." Gilman poured himself another cup of tea.

"Well, even if there's only space for half of it, enough will get through. And I'm hoping some intelligent reporter will pick up on the anarchist angle. For that's the key to the extreme left of today, the red-hot activists. They want no bosses, no leaders, no organization in government, and down with all systems. Everything is to be done by committee, by joint consultation. All decisions unanimous—in the name of the people." They forgot, apparently, that even a large-size committee became a boss over those who obeyed it; that within a committee, a leader emerged when one of them produced better ideas, better plans. "In theory, it has a noble ring: pure equality for all in each and everything. In practice, it's either chaos or the bloodiest-minded approach to power."

"The new dark ages."

For a moment there was silence. Then Renwick returned to the business on hand. "Before we give out the names of Erik and Marco in that press release, we had better clear them with Diehl. The West Germans might not want them broadcast until they've—"

"They won't object." Gilman opened the folder, extracted a flimsy sheet of paper, gave it a quick scan. He handed over the message from Diehl. "West Germany is asking India for the extradition of Erik and Marco, now traveling under the names James Kiley and Antony Shawfield respectively. Wanted for arson, bombings, murders, in Berlin and Frankfurt."

So Kiley *is* Erik, thought Renwick, and read the details. Diehl had appended his own report, giving the facts uncovered. Erik and Marco attended Lumumba University in Moscow—met at North Korean training camp for urban guerrillas—Erik sent to the United States, Marco to England—met again in West Berlin and founded the People's Revolutionary Force for Direct Action. Three members of that group had defected, had been in hiding from reprisals for the last four years. Now, with the arrest of Erik and Marco a real possibility, they had given a full physical description of the two men. Additional help had come from the Rotterdam police— physical description of man who had evaded them at Schiphol Airport tallied with description of Erik previously obtained from three ex-terrorists: height, coloring, features. Also, description fitted young student from Mexico University (Ramón Olivar, born Venezuela of Swedish mother and exiled Spanish father) who traveled to Lumumba University, never returned under that name. Olivar had also been known as Jan Andersen, Henrique Mendes, Kurt Leitner, James Kiley. Former members of the terrorist group knew him only as Erik.

Renwick handed back the sheet of paper to Gilman. "It's worth reading—all of it."

"Later. You're the one, in any case, who wanted the evidence as clear as possible. Satisfied now?"

Renwick nodded. "Diehl did a first-rate job."

With you forever sending messages to suggest some new approach. Bob would drive us crazy, Gilman was thinking, except that his ideas pay off ninety percent of the time, and that's a better average than most. "What do you make of this? We've had three unsigned messages from America."

"Using what wavelength?" Renwick asked quickly.

"The one you had for your Sawyer Springs transmissions. But the messages come from New York, we think."

"Could be Salvatore Marini—Frank Cooper's man."

"You didn't recruit him?"

"He was an expert at his job. I liked Sal. But I didn't recruit him. He doesn't even know how to reach us here, except by that wavelength."

Gilman unlocked a file and removed a folder, studied three sheets of paper. "Two messages were brief. The first one states that Maartens and his friend Hans took a flight to New York from Los Angeles on Friday, September 7."

"That's all?"

"All."

Sal must have delayed his own departure from San Diego, checked both there and in Los Angeles while memories were fresh and records easily available. But why hide that from us? Renwick's face was grave. "And the next message?"

"It states that Maartens and Hans hired a small plane under the names Jones and Brown to travel on Saturday, September 8, to East Hampton. A car waited for them at the airfield. They returned to New York on another plane that night."

Sal, thought Renwick, is telling us that Maartens and Hans are guilty of Frank Cooper's death. "Has he gone to the FBI?"

"No mention of that in his third message. It came yesterday—four weeks later than the others. It is—apparently—a word-for-word transcription of a San Diego newspaper report. Have a look, Bob."

Renwick took the sheet of paper. The news date was of last Monday, October 15. The headline read: TRAGIC ACCIDENT AT SAWYER SPRINGS. Renwick looked up at Gilman, and then went on reading. "A fire occurred on Saturday night in the garage of Rancho San Carlos, the residence of Mr. Walter Gunter. The local volunteer fire fighters of Sawyer Springs responded as soon as they received a call for assistance. It appears that Mr. Gunter and his guest, Mr. Hans Smith, were preparing to drive out of the garage. The caretaker reports that he heard the car backfire. Then flames swept the garage, where several cans of gasoline were stored because of the present shortages. Mr. Gunter and Mr. Smith were trapped inside the car with fatal results. The firemen said there had been a delay in calling them, but they managed to save most of the house. Mr. Gunter's caretaker and cook were the only other occupants of the establishment at that time."

Saturday night, carefully chosen. Renwick shook his head. "For Gunter read Maartens," he reminded Gilman.

"Marini is a lunatic! It was he, wasn't it?"

"Yes."

"Thank God he isn't tied in with us. Just acted on his own. Like that. Avenging Frank—" Gilman broke off. "You're taking this pretty calmly, Bob. If Marini had been our man, we'd have had an agent out of control."

"But he wasn't our man. He was Frank's—to the end." Without knowing it, he had avenged Jake Crefeld, too.

"I am not shedding any tears over Maartens and that murderer of his, but an eye for an eye isn't the best intelligence work. Is it?"

"No. But it must have given Theo a bigger jolt than we've administered—so far. Why don't you try to get our press release timed for the end of next week?"

"Just as the camper is arriving in Bombay?" Gilman was thoughtful. Then he nodded his agreement.

"Well," Renwick said, rising from his tubular plastic chair, "time to push off. Not a bad morning's work. We've dealt with Schlott, and Kiley and Shawfield, too. When will the extradition process begin?"

"It usually takes a little time. But with some special effort, it could be in ten days or two weeks. In Bombay." He studied Renwick's face. "Bob," he said gently, "I know you want to get Nina O'Connell safely out. But you have to remember that our first priority is—"

"Theo," Renwick said. He hesitated, then added, "No extradition for Theo?"

"On what charges? The use of false passports, changes of identity?" Gilman shook his head. "He's deep into conspiracy, but he has covered his contacts. That house in Sawyer Springs wasn't bought in his name."

Renwick was frowning. "There's something he hasn't covered, and that's worrying him. A little. Not much. But enough to keep him from traveling openly as Otto Remp of Düsseldorf."

"He must have other business on this world trip—"

"I know, I know. Other business, other contacts, and none of them to be connected with Otto Remp's name." Then Renwick's impatience ended. "Essen! He set up an account in an Essen bank. And the only person who cashed checks on that account was Erik. There's your connection, Ron: Remp with Erik."

"The account was under a false name," Gilman reminded Renwick.

"Yes. But was Remp using a disguise, then? Banks take photographs nowadays—automatic surveillance—definite records."

"They could be destroyed by this time."

"We'll leave that for Diehl to find out. He knows the date of the last withdrawal of money from that Essen account. Twelve thousand dollars. Done in a great hurry—to pass some of it to Erik and Marco for their escape."

"And you think Theo used no disguise?" Gilman asked slowly.

"If he didn't bother to use one when he deposited the money originally—didn't see any need for it, no sense of danger, enough protection from a false name—then he had to look more or less like the same man when he withdrew such a large sum."

Gilman smoothed back a thinning strand of fair hair, adjusted his glasses more securely. "It's a long shot, but you've talked me into it. Poor old Diehl, you give him no rest."

"You'll contact him at once?"

"Right away."

With that reassurance, Renwick left. A long shot, he echoed Gilman's phrase, but worth a try: the one small mistake that Theo had made—if he had made it. Yet, last November, when he had opened an account for a substantial amount, there had been no alarms, no crises. Everything had been going very much in Theo's favor. A false name, false identity cards might have seemed ample protection.

But what, Renwick wondered as he reached the street, what if the Essen bank didn't have any system for filming its daily business? Then—a still longer shot—there might be a good memory of a client's face, height, weight. After all, small banks did note large deposits and speedy withdrawals. Particularly withdrawals of twelve thousand dollars that closed an account for good.

The drizzling rain had stopped, but there was a chill that struck upward from the damp pavement. A gray overcast saddened rooftops and lent a sameness to all these stone walls of tall houses converted into business establishments. It may have been the weather, it may have been a return of his depression, but when he thought of Theo being comfortably flown back for trial in West Germany, he could empathize with Sal.

CHAPTER
22

The room was dimly lit: not much sun came through the diamond pattern of the wooden trellis that covered its window and protected it from the street outside. It was airless, too, in spite of the door on the opposite wall that lay open onto a verandah, narrow and covered, that ran around all four sides of the building's inner courtyard.

A strange mixture, Nina decided, studying the carved wooden ceiling, a single bulb dangling from sagging wires that ran exposed to a plaster wall, the decorative tiles on the floor, the stone window seat, the low wooden platform—complete with thin mattress and bulky cushions—filling a large corner of the room.

Madge, seated on the bed with her back resting against the wall, glanced up from her diary. "Stop prowling around. You make me nervous."

"And you'll ruin your eyes."

"Well, I've got to start filling up the gaps." Madge picked up her pen. *Bombay,* she wrote. "What day did you say this was? Friday?"

Too many gaps; Madge had scarcely opened her diary in the last month. Even now it was only a half-hearted attempt. In another ten minutes she'd be asleep. Like Marie-Louise and Sven next door, like Guido and Henryk. The five now alternated between euphoria—excited talk, wild plans, high laughter—and complete lethargy. I don't know which scares me the more, thought Nina, and began emptying her bulging duffel bag onto the window seat. She picked out the Greek dress—she hadn't worn it since Istanbul. It was clean, but it could use some pressing. She shook it, hung it carefully on one of the wooden pegs driven into the once-white wall, and hoped that Bombay's humid air might work wonders. Then she found her two shirts.

Inside each neckband she had inked—as if it were a laundry mark—three numbers in sequence. The blue striped shirt, her favorite, had the first three numbers Pierre had given her five weeks ago for that telephone call to Mr. Roy. The green striped shirt had the next three. A simple idea, but it made sure she wouldn't mix up their order. Now, holding the shirts close to the light from a diamond-shaped space in the trellis, she went over the numbers again and again until she knew she wouldn't forget them.

Money... She searched in her wallet. She had only a few rupees as well as her two remaining traveler's checks. She would need to cash one of them. But where? Kneeling on the window seat, she looked through a space in the trellis. Two floors below her was a busy street with workaday traffic. No shops, no taxis, no tourists visible. This was no luxury quarter of the enormous city. It was somewhere near the harbor: beyond the flat roofs on the other side of the street, she could see a crane, the tip of a distant mast, and the smokestack of some ship, hear a tug's sharp blast. Not much encouragement: Bombay's waterfront must be vast, with busy quays and warehouses at one end and, at the other, a place where hotels could have pleasant views. She stared out at the block of apartments across the street, with the morning's wash hung out unevenly over every wooden balcony and window sill. It was a sad display: bits and pieces of clothing, not one recognizable as shirt or trousers, and all needing more hot water and soap than had been available.

She went back to unpacking: nothing inside her canvas bag that she needed except a thin scarf to cover the bare neckline of the low-cut dress. She began changing her clothes. It was almost two o'clock. Jim Kiley had already left. (He was collecting mail and money—he expected both at the American Express office. He was sorry, terribly sorry, but after that he had an important interview with a local politician—set up for him by Gopal, the guide who had met the camper at the Indian frontier and was still with them. But he would be back by late afternoon, and this evening they'd go out to dinner and see the town, and wouldn't Nina like that?) Tony Shawfield was absent, too; he was attending the camper at some garage over on the other side of the city. The camper was in bad shape, Jim had told her to excuse their strange arrival in Bombay. Tony would probably have to sell it—if he got a good price for it.

Strange arrival...Surely Madge must have noticed it. "Wasn't it odd this morning—" began Nina. "Madge, *please* don't fall asleep. I have to talk with you."

Madge roused herself. "It's so hot. Don't you feel it?"

"Yes. But I have to talk with you."

"About what?"

"About our arrival this morning."

"Well we got here, didn't we?"

"Four days late. And after spending one day in a village right outside Bombay. Why didn't we drive in yesterday? Why did we wait for this morning at six o'clock, and stop at a restaurant on the edge of the city for breakfast, and not have breakfast?" They had left the camper outside the small restaurant, with Tony staying inside it—well inside it; hadn't he wanted to be seen?—and then walked through a front room into a courtyard. Jim Kiley hadn't liked the look of either place, so he had led them through the courtyard's back gate, out into another street, where two Fiats were waiting. And that way they had driven southward to follow a wide curving bay and crossed handsome streets with skyscrapers and new buildings; and old buildings; and older buildings sardine-packed on narrowing and still more crowded thoroughfares.

"We got breakfast here," Madge reminded her. "Stop grumbling, Nina!" She went back to her travel diary.

"What about the camper? Tony is thinking of selling it. Madge—please listen. Tony is selling the camper. How do you travel then?"

"Tony is going to put the money he gets for it into our expenses. A plane across the Pacific makes more sense than a set of wheels." Madge giggled faintly at the idea of a camper with water wings.

"And before you reach the Pacific?"

"We'll go on a freighter and stop off at all kinds of interesting places." Madge's patience ended. "Ask Tony. He can tell you all about it."

"Where is he? Or is he spending all day at the garage?"

"Making travel arrangements. He will be here soon—no later than three o'clock. He's taking me up to Nehru Park. We passed it this morning, remember?" Madge giggled again. "Did you see that marina?"

Nina was wasting no more time. She pulled on her dress, combed her hair again, fastened her earrings in place, picked up her scarf and shoulder bag. Then she remembered her toothbrush, almost laughed as she found it and her precious cake of soap, and added them to her bag.

"The one that Tony pointed out to us? 'Swimming Baths

and Sailboat Club.'" Then Nina's change of clothes at last caught Madge's attention. She sat up on the bed, said slowly, "And where are you going, Nina O'Connell?"

"Away. Will you come with me? Last chance, Madge."

"Leaving—actually leaving? Where will you go?"

"I'll manage. I managed in Greece. And I have friends—" Nina halted. "Just get yourself together. And be quick! Leave everything except your shoulder bag. *And* your passport."

"Nina!"

"While you get ready, I'll have a word with Shahna—is that her name?" The girl, no more than twelve years old, was sitting on the verandah just outside their room door. "Our little watchdog," Nina added. "But she does speak English, and she can get us to a telephone. Madge—please hurry. I can't leave you alone here."

"I am not alone. And I'm not leaving." Madge's face was set. "Do you think I'd give up this trip? Easy for you—you'll just cash a few checks and travel where and when you like."

Nina reached the door, hesitated. "Madge—"

"No." The word was definite. Madge's head was bent over her diary.

Nina stepped outside. Shahna looked up at her with a shy smile, and rose to her feet, shaking her long cotton skirt free from the verandah's dust. She was slender-boned and fine-featured, a smooth little face with large dark eyes faintly shadowed. Her gleaming black hair was brushed tightly off her brow, caught into a heavy plait. Small gold studs of pinhead size decorated two pierced ears and one nostril. Nina said, "I don't see Gopal. Where is he?"

"He left. He will come later."

Good. "Has the Englishman arrived? Mr. Shawfield?"

Shahna shook her head.

Good again. "I need to telephone. Is there a place near here where I can find a phone?" If there was one in this house, which was doubtful, Nina had decided to avoid it. Gopal had recommended this place, and his relatives and friends were all around. Even now, eight men of various ages—some old, some mere boys—were sitting in the shaded side of the courtyard, talking, as they had done all morning. The women were out of sight, but audible even at this distance from the kitchen on the ground floor: voices drifted up along with the lingering smells of cooked spices. Not a word was understandable to Nina—among themselves, the clan of closely knit families who occupied this collection of rooms spoke Maharathi. English was kept, so Kiley had said, as a kind of lingua franca, useful for other Indians in Bombay who spoke quite different languages. Lucky for me, thought Nina as she waited patiently for Shahna's reply: lucky, too, that all the shops and street signs she had seen on the drive through the city this morning had been in English. She drew out her wallet, selected one rupee but held it in her hand.

Shahna began walking along the verandah, lithe and graceful. She kept close to the house wall, as far from the railing as possible. But with its overhanging laundry, it would be difficult for anyone in the courtyard—if he could spare a moment from talking—to see what was happening on the third-floor verandah. At the narrow staircase, Nina stopped, looked back. Madge had come to their room door. Nina beckoned. Madge shook her head. But she waved. Nina waved, too, and with a lighter heart she followed Shahna down the enclosed staircase. They reached the entrance to the courtyard and turned toward the street.

Hot, narrow, bustling with traffic, filled with people. Nina halted in dismay.

"This way. It is near," Shahna said. She looked at Nina's dress, touched it lightly with her thin fingers. "Pretty."

"Are there taxis?" Nina could see none. Plenty of cars, a bus, trucks, small carts. She began walking quickly.

Shahna shrugged. "Sometimes from the pier." She gestured vaguely along the street. "Ballard Pier. Very big. Very nice ships."

"How far is it to the waterfront where the big hotels are?"

"What hotel?" Shahna's eyes gleamed. "I'll come, too. I'll show you."

"In what direction are they?"

"Back there." Shahna pointed behind them.

"How far? One mile, two miles?"

"Two miles, maybe three." She was charmingly vague.

She's probabably never been there, thought Nina. So how do I calculate how long it takes to walk from here to the Malabar Hotel?

Shahna stopped, pointed to a wide doorway.

"A money exchange?" The room inside was cavernous, without windows, dependent on light from its wall opening onto the street. Nina hesitated.

"Much business. Sailors come here from the ships. It has a telephone."

I bet it has, thought Nina, which is more than can be said for that side street we have just passed: a local market of crowded stalls with strips of canvas overhead and a mass of people moving around. "Thank you, Shahna." Tactfully, she slipped the rupee into the delicate little hand. "Now you must go back." The girl looked at her reproachfully. "Thank you," Nina said again.

The decision was made for them both by the man standing at the side of the door. He was young, alert, and much on guard. He raised his voice to Shahna, lifted the back of his hand: clear out, he must have said; no beggars allowed here. Shahna was accustomed to this apparently, for she retreated quickly out of his reach, gave Nina a bright smile to retrieve her dignity, and walked away with her hips swinging and her head held high. The man nodded to Nina, stood politely out of her path.

Nina halted at the threshold. The place was bare and clean, its one counter securely caged, a man behind it, two customers with red perspiring faces, fair hair, and bright Hawaiian shirts. Three other men—one a venerable figure in white tunic and narrow trousers; two young and strong, dressed like the guard at the door in European clothes—sat along the opposite wall. And there was the telephone, strangely encased in a plexiglass stall—privacy?—only four paces away from the door. She looked at the old man, who scarcely seemed to have noticed her. "May I use your telephone?" Everyone lost interest in her, except the two sailors.

"How much?" Nina asked.

One of the younger men rose, came forward, saying in excellent English, "Twelve rupees. You pay me, and I shall dial your number."

"Five rupees. It is a local call. And short."

"Eight rupees." The tone of voice was polite; the smooth face—fine-boned, light-skinned—broke into a persuasive smile.

"Five rupees." Nina was definite. There was a slight pause. She shrugged, looked toward the street, seemed about to leave.

"Five," he agreed, and held out his hand. He had a handsome wristwatch, a heavy gold ring. Like the other young men, he wore a cream silk shirt and well-cut gabardine trousers. "The number?"

"I can manage." Nina gave him five rupees and stepped into the plexiglass enclosure—no door, just two transparent side walls. The telephone was a dial model, much the same as she had used in London. The young man stood close, perhaps curious to see the number or hear her conversation. There was nothing she could do about that, except turn her back to him, try to hide the dial from his interested eyes, and keep her voice low. For one blank moment she almost forgot the figures she had memorized; and then, her nervous fingers began turning them in careful sequence. A distant voice said, "Malabar Gift Shop."

I have the wrong number, she thought. "Mr. A. K. Roy?" she tried timidly. Oh, God, I've got the wrong number—what now?

"Who is speaking?" The voice was clearer. "Who is there?"

"Pierre?" In her overpowering relief, she was almost incoherent. "Nina. I'm near the Ballard Pier. I think. I'll need perhaps an hour to reach you."

"I'll come and get you."

"No. Not here. I can't wait here. It's a money-changing place. And the street outside—impossible."

"Then meet me in the hotel's bookstore. It is in the arcade—next to the gift shop."

"Yes. Yes."

"Are you all right?"

"I am now. I'll see you—" she consulted her watch—"at half past three. Perhaps later. I can't judge."

"Don't worry. I'll wait. Your old friend is in Bombay—the Courtyard of the Janissaries—remember? He'll be glad to see you again."

Bob Renwick? She said, her voice suddenly unsteady, "I'll be more than glad." She hung up the receiver.

The young man stopped lounging against the plexiglass partition, followed her to the door. "The streets are very crowded. It is very difficult to walk alone." He was summing up her dress, the silk scarf that covered her shoulders, her earrings. But most of all, it was her manner that impressed him: she did not belong in this quarter. "Too many beggars ready to follow you. They give no peace. Perhaps you should take a taxi."

"Is there one?" Nina glanced along the street.

"My cousin's car is there." He pointed to a vintage Chevrolet standing by the curb just ahead of them.

"How much?"

"To where?"

"Oh—" she floundered a little, recovered enough to say—"to the waterfront near the big hotels."

"Which hotel? There are several of them."

"How much?"

"Twenty rupees."

"What?" She was scandalized. "Impossible." She began walking.

He caught up with her. "Fifteen."

"Twelve."

"The price of petrol is high," he said sadly.

"Twelve," she repeated. "Not twenty, not fifteen. Twelve."

With his gentle smile, he led the way to the Chevrolet. His cousin could have been his twin, but he spoke little English. The two of them had a quick conversation, unintelligible to Nina.

It was a long long street lying ahead of her, and how many other long streets after that? "It's a short distance," she said, trying to appear as if she knew her way around Bombay.

"If you would pay me now," her mentor suggested.

First, she got into the car, making sure it wouldn't drive away without her. Then she counted out the last of her rupees. He accepted them gracefully, handed over three of them to his cousin, and bade her a polite good-day. Now I know, she thought as she nodded her thanks, why the cousin wears a cotton sports shirt and a cheap wristwatch. It was a wild ride, and speedy. She reached the approach to the Malabar International Hotel with fully thirty minutes to spare.

She entered the vast lobby and was greeted by ice-cold air. Shimmering lights cascaded from the vaulted ceiling, marble floors and walls gleamed, trees—twice her height—had ornamental shapes to match the flowers around their feet. People everywhere; and from everywhere: many well-fed and well-groomed Indians, Japanese, Singapore Chinese, all in well-tailored business suits. Europeans and Americans were noticeable by less expensive clothes—sports shirts and linen jackets. Their women in limp drip-dry dresses were quite silenced by the bright-colored saris that floated past them.

Nina recovered, looked around for the arcade. It must be at the other end of the lobby, perhaps at the back of this incredible palace. But she saw a large travel desk, a counter where Thomas Cook and American Express had staked their claims. She'd have time to cash one of her checks; then she'd stop being destitute. It had been a horrible feeling, all through the journey here, to realize she had nothing spendable in her wallet. At least I'll be able to visit the powder room, she thought as she took her place at the counter. And I'll find out where the arcade is, and I can buy a paper or a magazine in the bookstore if I have to wait for Pierre. Her fear and terrors were leaving her. She began to feel normal again.

She looked normal, too. Her eyes were bright with interest, lipstick and powder and freshly combed hair perfect, as she left the ladies' room. She passed a bank of elevators and the clearly printed English signs that directed people to the Coromandel Bar, the Victoria Grill, the Ajanta Room, the Gateway to India Restaurant. At last she found the arcade, open on one side to a lavish garden; on its other side, a series of elegant displays of gold and silver and ivory. She reached the gift shop, with a window of gossamer silks and rich brocades that would entice the last rupee out of a tourist's pocket. Next door was the bookstore.

She halted at the entrance, beside a tall rack of newspapers, both local and foreign, quickly scanning the people inside the shop. Tables with books piled on top, shelves packed ceiling-high with more books. Was Pierre there? Bob? A clerk was near her, looking at her intently, so she pretended interest in the newspapers, glancing at a headline just at her shoulder level, and stood transfixed. GREEN CAMPER MYSTERY—SPY ARRESTED. And the opening line of the newspaper report was: *Ilsa Schlott, a recruiter for terrorist*— That was all she could see. As her hand went out to pick up the paper, a man's grip, strong and painful, encircled her wrist. Tony Shawfield said quietly, "So you thought you would run off and leave us."

Nina tried to pull her wrist free. Gopal was behind Shawfield; another Indian, too.

Shawfield's voice hardened. "You came to meet someone. Who?" To Gopal's friend, he said, "Get the car. Side entrance." Then again to Nina, "Who? Who is meeting you here?"

"No one."

"You telephoned." Shawfield's grip tightened.

"Let go! I'm buying a paper and—" She caught sight of

Pierre stepping forward. No, she thought frantically: stay back, Pierre—you'll be recognized.

The clerk was approaching. Shawfield had doubled his hold on her: one hand on her wrist, the other on her elbow, forcing her into the arcade.

She went unresisting. Three of them, and Pierre alone— no, this wasn't the place for any confrontation. Her steps lagged, delaying as much as she could. Pierre would follow. She hoped. But I'm not endangering his real mission, whatever it is, and it's not me.

"Whom did you call?" Shawfield was insisting.

"The American Consul. That was all."

"The truth, Nina! I'm no fool. You were to meet someone at that bookstore. And he was late or you were early."

"No. There was no one." She sounded desolate, bewildered. And she was. They had reached a street, crowded with people. Shawfield was pulling her toward a car that was just drawing up in front of him. Pierre will never be able to follow, not here, she thought in sudden panic. She glanced back but could see only strange faces; she tried to break free, run. But Shawfield forced her through the car's open door, into its back seat, followed her. Gopal jumped in beside the driver, the doors were locked, the car moved. Only then, as it edged its way out of the jumble of traffic and tried to pick up speed, did Shawfield's grasp ease on Nina's wrist.

Gopal was worried. "That clerk followed us out. Another man, too, I think."

Shawfield's head jerked round to look back. Too many people, too many cars: impossible to see if anyone was attempting to tail them. He gave up and studied Nina instead. He had a feeling that Gopal's words had jarred her. Encouraged her? She needed discipline, this girl. Jim had been too easy with her. "We'll lose them," he told Gopal. And teach Milady a little lesson. "Falkland Road," he said.

The driver and Gopal exchanged a startled glance.

"Falkland Road," Shawfield repeated. To Nina he said, "So you thought you'd leave us. Why?"

"I was bored with sitting in that room."

"And you headed for the Malabar? Why?"

"It was some place I could change a traveler's check—buy a magazine, a guide to the city. I wanted to see Bombay."

"And so you shall." His voice had eased. He could relax a little: he had found her. A wild search, not a moment wasted after he had returned (and that was luck—arriving earlier than he had planned) to find Madge alone. "She has left," Madge told him, "left with Shahna." And Shahna had talked, of telephones and hotels; had even led him to the money exchange nearby. There, it took only five rupees to loosen a man's tongue: the blonde had hired a car; it had just returned from the Malabar Hotel. There, it hadn't been so easy: fifteen minutes of searching, of inquiries, of growing anger and desperation. Then quick-eyed Gopal had seen her, vanishing into the arcade. Did she think she could outwit me? Just wait until Jim gets back from his meeting with Theo and hears what could have happened. But it didn't. Who planned her moves anyway? Shawfield reached for her bag, pulled it out of her hands.

He found no slip of paper with a name or address or a telephone number. The wallet held a quantity of rupees: some large bills, some coins. They went into his trousers pocket along with her remaining traveler's check. "Much safer. You could have them stolen. I'll keep them for you."

Nina stared out at a broad square, an enormous stretch of ground where traffic circled around a statue of Queen Victoria on her lofty pedestal and streets branched off in every direction. This was far from the waterfront, from anything she knew. Her hopelessness increased with her sense of isolation. No one could follow this car, she thought as it entered a narrow thoroughfare; not Pierre, not even Bob. I know now what I should have done outside the bookstore: kicked and screamed and brought people running to help me. But would they have run? Any of them? Or would they have drawn back, avoided an unpleasant scene? Only Pierre would have come; and been recognized.... How did Shawfield find me anyway? Surely Madge hadn't... Yes, perhaps she had. Perhaps she led him to Shahna, and Shahna to the money exchange.... I don't want to believe that, Nina told herself, but despair seized her heart. "Where are you taking me?" she asked.

"Sightseeing."

In silence, the strange journey continued.

CHAPTER

23

That afternoon it had been Pierre Claudel's turn to wait near the telephone in A. K. Roy's most private office. It was a neat setup, spacious, comfortable, secluded, lying behind the accounting department of the Malabar Gift Shop, with a second door into the adjoining bookstore, and a third door into the arcade itself.

He was alone except for one of Roy's men, a silent restful type, in charge of Roy's communications. Roy and Bob Renwick had left only a few minutes ago, allowing themselves ample time to get into position. Soon, they would be searching the busy street where Mr. Otto Remp was scheduled to visit, at half past three, one of the small banking establishments that offered its expert and discreet services to substantial depositors. There, in a quiet room, the banker would welcome Mr. Remp, along with the senior partner of a real-estate firm *and* its legal representatives *and* the new manager of the equally new Bombay office of West-East Travel. The final transactions would be completed: signatures here, a large check there, witnesses recorded, all in order, polite bows, good-byes. And then— Claudel smiled, wished he could see that scene.

Roy was to be congratulated. Renwick, too. For the last week they had gone through the list of real-estate agents who dealt in expensive properties and foreign buyers. While Roy ran thorough checks on their finances, personnel, business records, Renwick visited their establishments as a likely prospect—he was interested in acquiring a branch office for his London firm, specializing in construction problems. Were they accustomed to handling requests from abroad? What caliber of sales to reputable clients? His firm insisted on dealing only with the best agents, they must understand; ones who had been successful in satisfying important customers. They understood and offered their most recent triumphs in the selling of real estate. "A highly respected firm from Düsseldorf" had been one testimonial.

Then Roy had zeroed in, concentrating on the small law firm that handled contracts for the real-estate agency with Düsseldorf connections, securing their co-operation and sworn silence. And so today, one of Roy's agents would be among the legal representatives attending the meeting in the bank. Two plain-clothes policemen would be posted at its side entrance. Two others would move forward toward its front door as soon as Otto Remp stepped inside. One of Roy's best agents would attend to the limousine that brought Remp there, making sure its driver sent no warning message. And Roy and Renwick would be waiting in a radio car a short distance away.

Roy was making sure this time, Claudel thought with wry amusement. The disappearance of Kiley's little band of travelers early this morning from some insignificant restaurant with a miserable courtyard had roused the equable A. K. Roy to fury. The camper itself had also evaded his two undercover agents: a well-planned maneuver that increased his rage. But at least he was now convinced he was dealing with a mastermind directing two very clever young men. Worthy opponents. That thought had calmed his anger, redoubled his efforts. The extradition of Otto Remp, Kiley, Shawfield, was no longer a politeness from one democracy to another: it was an imperative. As Roy said, once more bland in manner, "There is enough trouble in our countries without such men adding to it." It was particularly gratifying that Remp had been linked with Kiley through an Essen bank, drawing him into the extradition net, too.

Well, thought Claudel, we are almost sure of one of them: Remp would be caught in the bank. He would be out of disguise, of course, for that appearance, playing the authentic Düsseldorf businessman for the benefit of his firm back home. Renwick had made a bet before he left with Roy this afternoon: Theo will get into his car wearing a wig and other removable transformations, and, as he is driven to the bank, he'll take them off, change his jacket, march in as Otto Remp. On leaving he intends to put on the disguise again, reappear at the house or hotel where he's staying under his fancy new name. What d'you bet, Pierre? No takers, Claudel had said.

But what about the other two? Although Kiley and Shawfield and their wandered students had faded from sight, they were in Bombay. Somewhere. The two highways out of the city, as well as the main airport at Santa Cruz, the central railway station, even the docks where coastal freighters were loaded, were now on the watch for eight young Westerners loaded down with duffel bags. The sleeping bags had been found in the abandoned camper four hours after it had slipped away from the restaurant, so they must be staying in some small hotel, some lodging house. Somewhere, Claudel thought again.

He studied the large-scale map of Bombay that he had spread over Roy's six-by-four-foot desk, lightly tracing in pencil the streets he and two of Roy's agents had checked this morning. All these cruddy little hotels—have you seen, have you heard, do you know of anyone who has seen, heard? He began memorizing the streets of the next likely section. That would be tomorrow's task, and Renwick would have his turn sitting at this desk while he waited for any possible call from Nina. They had agreed that one of them must be ready to answer the telephone, reassure Nina that she wasn't among strangers in a strange city. A. K. Roy had merely raised a well-marked eyebrow at such concern; he was more perturbed by the fact that Claudel had given one of his private telephone numbers to a young girl. "It was the only Bombay number I had," Claudel had protested. "What else could I do? She's important. She could lead us to Kiley." That had clinched the argument. The difficult moment was over. In any case, thought Claudel now, Roy would have that number changed once Nina made contact.

Would she? Or—and this was Renwick's worry—could she?

An unpleasant question. If Nina didn't, couldn't, call, then they would have to find her by searching. Claudel concentrated on his map, memorizing the directions and names of the streets in the poorer sections of the city. It wasn't likely the campers, now looking like a troupe of gypsies, would be living in a luxury hotel, or in a skyscraper apartment in the business district, or in a mansion in the green hills overlooking Bombay.

The telephone rang. It was Nina.

The call ended. Roy's communications expert had been listening, too. "Got all that?" Claudel asked him. "Then make contact with Mr. Roy's car. Give the American all the details—every word. I am going to the bookstore. If there is any reply, any message, you'll find me there."

Half past three, she had said. But if she took a taxi she could be here much earlier. Would she enter by the main lobby of the hotel? Or, if the driver saw she had no luggage, he might give her the choice of lobby or arcade. It had its own entrance on a side street and was frequently used by shoppers from outside the hotel. Better to stay in the bookstore, Claudel decided, keep to the arrangement, and be available for any message from Renwick. Besides—if Nina couldn't find a cab—he might have to wait longer than half past three. The bookstore was the safest place: people loitered there quite naturally. But he still wished he could meet her as she got out of a taxi or came walking up the long approach to the hotel. And then? Renwick had arranged it with A. K. Roy: a pleasant room adjacent to Roy's own suite in this hotel; well guarded, discreet, servants all tested and true, not one whisper to give away Nina's presence. And it might be for only a day or two—until all danger was over. What could be a better hiding place than a large hotel with four hundred rooms?

Claudel had skimmed through two magazines, concentration broken continuously as he verified the time or glanced toward the door of the bookstore. There was only one of Roy's younger assistants on duty here—the Theo assignment had depleted the ranks—and Claudel had stationed him, as a clerk, in the front of the shop. Lavji was his name, and eagerness was his manner. Almost too quick: he had already signaled the entrance of three various blondes, none beautiful. Or perhaps in Lavji's eyes, all blondes looked the same.

The monotony and tension, strange mixture, were broken by a message from Renwick. Claudel took it on his transceiver, retreating to a rear table piled with books where its use wouldn't be noticeable and he could still see Lavji. "No go," Renwick said. "Illness prevented our boy's appearance. He has rescheduled the signing for Tuesday. By which time he will be out of Bombay."

"But why? Give up his West-East office?"

"Something has made him change his plans, and change them damn quick. Something more than the news from London about the camper—he got rid of it this morning. His apologies arrived at the bank only ten minutes ago—by telephone. Our legal representative was chatting with the receptionist when the call came through—swears it was from some phone with distant voices and recurrent chimes in the background."

"Recurrent chimes—used for paging people in a hotel lobby?"

"That's the system used at the Malabar. Of course, he could have been lunching there, or passing through. But we'll start checking on its recent arrivals. He might just possibly be staying there." Renwick didn't sound optimistic.

"And how is Roy taking that?" Staying at A. K. Roy's hotel? A bitter joke.

"Furious. As I am, damn it to hell. A week's work down the drain. We're on our way back to you now. Let us know—"

Claudel said quickly, "Signing off. Lavji has spotted a blonde." He switched off the transceiver, shoved it in his pocket as he started forward, hoping that Lavji—this time—was giving no false alarm. He wasn't. Nina was there. As yet, she hadn't entered the store, was standing at the door with three men grouped around her. Shawfield. Shawfield was one of them. He had a grip on her wrist. And suddenly, as she saw Claudel, she turned and left—Shawfield firmly holding one arm, leading her toward the side-street entrance of the arcade. Left willingly, it seemed. Claudel stared at the empty doorway, signaled Lavji to get on their tail as he pulled out his transceiver and sent the message to Renwick and Roy: "Nina intercepted by Shawfield. Am following. Will keep in touch." Then he, too, was heading toward the side street, a busy street, lined with cars, crowded with people. There was no sign of Nina.

"She's in that gray Fiat," Lavji said. "We'll take this car." He was already inside the dark-blue Citroën that was always parked there—on Roy's orders—for any emergency. "They haven't traveled far. We shall soon catch up."

"Not too closely," Claudel warned.

Lavji only smiled for such a naïve assumption. Wasn't he as expert as any Frenchman in following a car through heavy traffic?

Claudel flicked on his transceiver again, made contact with Renwick and Roy, began identifying streets and directions.

"We'll join up with you," Renwick said. "And Roy is calling in some backup. Keep sending."

Gradually, as Lavji kept the Fiat in sight, Claudel's emotions calmed. His thoughts, too. No, she hadn't left willingly or stupidly. She must have resisted walking quickly along that short stretch of arcade to the street, slowed their pace enough to let Lavji keep them in sight. So what did you think you were doing, Nina? Trying to protect me and my cover? He almost smiled, shook his head in wonder.

He kept sending directions to Roy's car, somewhere across the city in the big-business belt. Ahead of him, the gray Fiat left the Victorian Gothic buildings of red brick, chose a modest street of three-story houses and shops. No new skyscrapers here, but small businesses; men in shirt sleeves, with ever-present briefcases; women in saris of cotton instead of silk but still attractive and constantly smiling. Caste-conscious, too. They avoided a poorly dressed man and his young son, untouchables, who were sweeping a sidewalk with a straw broom near Gandhi's house.

Streets and more streets to be identified... Suddenly, the names and signs above the small shops changed, no longer in English but in Arabic. "Now reaching the Muslim quarter," he told Renwick. "Quiet here, shops closed, traffic light. Friday, of course—their Sabbath."

"We'll soon be with you." Renwick paused. "Are they skirting the Muslim quarter?" There was worry in his voice.

"No. Looks as if they're heading straight through. Odd direction. They'll run up against six square blocks of—" Claudel cut off the sentence. Tactless. Renwick knew what adjoined this Muslim section: he had studied the map of Bombay, too. "Turning left into a small lopsided square. Muslim quarter ending. They are slowing down—about to stop—yes, they've stopped. At the beginning of Falkland Road."

There was only silence from Renwick. Roy's voice took over. "Stay back! Don't intercept. Keep in your car. We'll soon be there. A backup car, too. Wait!"

Lavji eased the Citroën to a halt at one side of the little square, the Fiat nicely in sight. There was only very light traffic at this time of day. By dusk—that would be a different matter. Claudel mastered his flare of temper. "Wait?" he asked bitterly as he watched the Fiat's door open. Shawfield was stepping out, his hand grasping Nina's wrist, pulling her to stand beside him. "What in hell..." Claudel began, staring at Shawfield, who was now at the entrance to Falkland Road.

Nina wrenched her arm free, began running, taking the road that lay in front of her. Shawfield seemed unperturbed, let her run, followed at walking pace.

"The cages!" Claudel exclaimed, got out of the car. Roy's

Mercedes came into the square, stopped beside him. "He's heading her into the cages!"

Roy stared at him, said "Wait!" to Renwick. But Renwick was already out of the Mercedes and running. Roy shook his head. "Now we may lose Shawfield."

"I'll give Bob a hand," Claudel said, and started after him, leaving Roy to give brisk orders to his driver and Lavji— secure the Fiat, hold the two men inside it, let neither escape.

Nina had felt Shawfield's grip slacken on her wrist. She broke free, ran into the road that stretched in front of her. It was empty of traffic. People crowded one sidewalk to her left, the shadowed side of the narrow street: men, poorly dressed, lying asleep against a house wall, loitering aimlessly or squatting near small braziers where they were cooking food; a few gaping entrances of dark cavelike shops wide open onto the pavement—a carpenter in one of them stared out at her. The other sidewalk, in sunlight, was empty, quite empty. But its long line of three-story houses was crowded. Crowded with women, packed into every story, standing at the huge glassless windows that stretched from floor to ceiling. They were eyeing her, laughing, calling out in a babble of languages.

She halted in confusion, staring at the women behind the widely spaced wooden bars that decorated the open ground floors. Women of every age—from nine or ten to fifty, sixty. Slender and fat, fair and dark, samples of beauty from everywhere, all of them barely covered by transparent silks, all of them with heavy make-up carefully applied even to the exposed breasts.

She looked at the long stretch of houses, never-ending; across from them, the crowded sidewalk with men in ragged and stained clothes, thin dark faces with unreadable eyes. Those awake were watching her with a silence that terrified her. She hesitated, fighting back her panic. No escape, she thought in despair; not this way. Or could she force herself to run on—reach another street with luck, another street that was normal? Or would it be the same as this? She froze, paralyzed with fear. Shawfield's hand gripped her wrist. "We'll walk on," he said, and dragged her farther along the street.

He kept talking. "Educational. See what can happen to a girl who is stupid enough to run away from her friends in a strange city. Look!" He gestured to the windows, seemed a little nonplused by the inviting gestures and voices that now concentrated on him. "Some are sold by their families, some drift in, and some were like you today—they thought they could take care of themselves." He may have been too absorbed in his lecture or by the street scene around him, but he didn't notice the lightly running footsteps until they almost reached him. He swung around, dropping Nina's hand, and faced the stranger.

Renwick caught him by the collar of his shirt and smashed his left fist at the startled jaw. Shawfield staggered, regained his balance; his hand went to the cuff of his sleeve, pulled out his weapon. Renwick was ready, struck Shawfield's wrist a short and savage blow that gave no time for the trigger to be pressed; the cyanide pistol that looked like a fountain pen dropped onto the road.

Claudel reached them, in time to catch Shawfield's arm in a locking grip and twist it behind his back. "I'll take care of him," he said grimly, increased his pressure, and forced Shawfield toward the cars.

Renwick picked up the cyanide pistol, shoved it into his pocket out of harm's way: too many eyes from the sidewalk were fixed upon it. "Nina," he said, holding out his hand.

She had been standing motionless, her face rigid. She looked neither at him nor at the offered hand.

"Nina," he said softly.

She came to life, began walking slowly, averting her face, ignoring any help. He fell into step beside her, said nothing more. At this moment, Renwick thought, she is hating all men. He looked at the cages, at a slender child with kohl-darkened eyes and scarlet lips. At this moment, he could agree.

Roy was at his efficient best. The backup car—a Renault—had arrived, now giving him a total of five men available. The number was enough to quell any resistance from Gopal. His friend, the driver of the gray Fiat, had bolted—been allowed to run, more accurately, and had been picked up by the police car parked out of sight. Gopal was now sitting in the Renault, his show of righteous indignation to no avail, waiting for Shawfield to join him. Lavji and the Mercedes driver were guarding its doors, but Roy had briefed them quickly and they—like the other three—knew what was expected of them.

Then, as Claudel marched Shawfield back to the cars with a firm and painful grip on Shawfield's twisted arm, Roy motioned two of his men to take charge. Quickly they relieved Claudel, handcuffed Shawfield, brought him to face Roy.

Shawfield recovered his dignity, drew himself up to his full height. "What authority have you for this outrage?" he demanded.

Roy's heavy-lidded eyes studied the young man; then he flashed a smile along with an identification card. "The authority to take you to the police station and have you charged with attempted kidnapping. Put him with the other," he directed one of his men.

Shawfield stood his ground. "There was no kidnapping." He nodded in Nina's direction. "We are tourists. She wanted to see Falkland Road. So we came to see it." He looked at Renwick, who was leading Nina to the Mercedes. "I charge that man with assault. He struck me."

"Not hard enough," Renwick said.

Nina halted, aware of the puzzled glances in her direction from the Indians who stood near Shawfield. He was saying indignantly, "She asked me to bring her here. Is that kidnapping?"

Nina drew closer to Renwick. He said quickly, "No one believes that, Nina. No one."

She stood there, uncertainly. In a low voice she said, "He took all my money. It is in his pocket. I didn't ask him to bring me here, Bob, I didn't ask—" She broke down.

Renwick called out, "Have his pockets searched. He took her money." Then, with a hand on her elbow—no more resistance to his touch, thank God—he drew her to the car. Inside, away from the curious faces, she wept bitterly. This was a Nina he had never seen before, distraught, shaken. He put an arm gently around her, let her cry her anguish away. "Safe now, darling, you're safe," he said, smoothing her hair back from her brow. He fought the impulse to take her in his arms, hold her close, kiss the tears from her cheeks, kiss her eyes, kiss her lips. "Safe," he repeated. It seemed to be the magic word.

Outside, the scene had changed. A slight interruption to my plan, thought Roy, but a brief one. Shawfield's pockets had been searched. A wad of new rupee notes had been found, quite separate from the money in his own wallet. There was also a traveler's check in Nina O'Connell's name. "She gave them to me for safekeeping," protested Shawfield. "She was leaving her bag in the car, so she asked me to carry the money."

"But she left her passport in her bag," Roy said. "Is money more valuable than a passport?" Yes, he thought as he watched Shawfield: I won that round. "Get him into the Renault," he told his men. To Claudel, who had been standing apart, his back turned as he watched a small group of curious Muslims gathered on the far side of the square, he called, "Let us talk with the young lady. I am interested in her story." They fell into step. Very quietly, Roy asked, "Did he identify you?"

"I tried hard to avoid it," Claudel said. He was worried by the way the cars had been parked. The Renault was too far from the Mercedes and the Citroën, too near the empty Fiat. "The man held in the Renault—he isn't handcuffed."

"He heard me say I had only one pair. So I was reserving them for the one who needed them most."

Claudel looked sharply at Roy; then wisely said nothing. At the door to the Mercedes, he glanced back at the Renault. Shawfield was being forced inside. The door beside him was closed and locked. One man guarded it. Only one? On the other side of the car, Lavji should have been on guard, but he was now advancing on the crowd that had gathered, ordering it to stay back, keep away, go home. Roy seemed not in the least perturbed by this, or by his three remaining agents, who were walking slowly away from the Renault, their duty done, their prisoner secured. Wondering, Claudel followed Roy into the front seat of the Mercedes.

Nina's body tightened; she looked quickly at Renwick. "A friend," he assured her. "It's all right, it's all right, Nina."

Roy handed her the bag and scarf she had left in the Fiat. "Yes, everything is all right. Your money, too." He inclined his head. "My name is Roy."

Renwick said, "Did you mention extradition?"

"Not a word. A nice little surprise to come. But now—please!" Roy put a finger to his lips for silence, switched on the car's radio. The voices came in, quiet but clear. It was Shawfield speaking, Shawfield and Gopal.

Shawfield was asking, ". . . the car keys?"

"I have them. Did you think I'd leave them?"

"Where are we being taken?"

"The central office, I heard. They talked with themselves, not with me."

"Where's that?"

"I've never been there—how can I know? Police headquarters, perhaps. But what can they arrest me for? I told them I didn't know where we were going, I didn't—"

"Listen! Your hands and ankles are free. There is no guard outside your door. It isn't locked. Get to the Fiat—it's near—no one watching it. Drive straight ahead, down that street, lose yourself in the city. Then telephone. Call the Malabar Hotel. Ask for Suite 12A. Give this message and only this message. Don't add any words!"

"Suite 12A. Malabar Hotel. And the message?"

"Marco was arrested at four-forty-five on false charges of kidnapping. Will be taken to central office—perhaps police headquarters."

"That is all?"

"All. After the phone call, get back to your house. You'll find Kiley there. Tell him to get everyone out—all five. He knows where I planned to take them—he will instruct you—you'll be in charge of them. And above all—ditch that Fiat. It's hot."

"Money—I'll need money."

"He will give you plenty. Get going—quick—quick—now!"

There was silence, scarcely broken by the opening of a door. Gopal's movements weren't audible. But he must have stepped outside: quietly, the door clicked shut.

Roy switched off the radio, rolled down a window, listened. The view of Gopal's escape was blocked by the Citroën, but the Citroën would also block Shawfield's clear view of the Mercedes. Roy smiled. His favorite game was chess. "Gopal won't get far. There is a police car waiting out of sight—near the end of the street that Gopal must take, the street that faces the Fiat. The other exit from this place—" Roy's smile increased—"we are blocking it. Ah, there he goes now!"

There were shouts of general confusion as the Fiat shot recklessly into the narrow street straight ahead. Lavji was in his Citroën, trying to get it started. The Fiat was out of sight before he could begin to follow.

Roy watched the scene with a look of triumph on his usually placid face. He stepped outside the Mercedes to get a better view of his driver, posted near the Renault, who had now come out of his daydream and swung around—belat-edly—to face his prisoner. "Good show," Roy said approvingly. "Not one smile, not one laugh. Very good." He signaled to his driver to return as the other three agents reached Shawfield in the Renault. Within a minute, it was driving away, head-ing for the exit that had been barred to Gopal.

"Damned neat!" Renwick said. Claudel was laughing, shaking his head. And Roy, tactfully avoiding any near ap-proach to the white-faced girl who was still tense, still be-wildered, squeezed into the front seat beside the driver (now grinning widely) and Claudel. The Mercedes left, too, with a cluster of curious diehards, obvious Muslims with heads covered by turbans or caps, staring after it in wonder, or perhaps with the increasing conviction that all infidels, whether Hindu or Christian, were crazy. That opinion would have been reinforced if they could have seen Roy pick up a phone and reach his office, miles away behind the Malabar Gift Shop, to start inquiries about Suite 12A. He had dropped his Oxford-accented English to speak volubly in a language that was strange even to his driver. "We'll soon know," he told Renwick when the call was over. "Before we reach the hotel, we will know."

"I've one serious reservation," Renwick said. "In fact, it's more than that. Nina—well, I don't want her staying at that hotel." And, his tone of voice said, that was final.

"There's no time to make other arrangements," Roy ob-jected. "Your hotel, Robert, is neither so comfortable nor so well protected. She would be alone there: you have much business to finish."

Renwick needed no reminder of that. "I have two friends who are on call for any emergency. They'll guard Nina until Pierre or I can take over." He looked at Nina. We've frozen her out of this conversation, he thought as he noticed she was uncertain and troubled once more. He drew her into it, said, "Remember the two Australians in the red Ferrari?"

She nodded.

"They'll have you on a plane as soon as it's safe enough. But not alone," he added quickly. "There will be someone with you all the way home."

"You?"

"If that is possible," he could only say. If I'm still alive, he was thinking. He tightened his hand on hers, felt a small response. I'll damned well make it possible: I'm not going to lose her this time.

Suddenly she was relaxed. Her voice was almost normal as she said to Roy, "I'm sorry to be such a complication. I'll stay at Bob's hotel."

A most unnecessary complication, thought Roy, but at least she realizes that. It seemed a good moment to press an urgent question. "Before you reach there, would you help us? Can you describe the district where you stayed? The street—do you know its name? The house—had it a number?"

"I didn't notice—didn't see any names...." She shook her head, felt stupid.

"Somewhere near Ballard Pier," Claudel prompted her. "Wasn't that where you telephoned, Nina? From a money exchange in the harbor area?"

"Yes." She tried to focus her thoughts, bring back a memory she wanted to dismiss forever. She made an effort. "If I saw it again, I'd recognize it. The house—" so many of these houses looked alike—"wasn't far away. Quite near. Have you time to—"

"Time? You could save us hours of searching," Roy said, forgiving her completely for having upset his plans. "It will take only a few extra minutes," he told Renwick, countering any objection from him. "And," he clinched the matter, "we'll drive past the house; we won't stop."

Before they entered the harbor area, the return phone call from the Malabar came through. Roy had his information: Dr. Frederick Weber, an antique dealer from London, occupied Suite 12A. He had registered last Tuesday for a five-day visit, along with his secretary and his valet, who occupied the same accommodations. "All is well," Roy reported. "He travels in style." Later, his eyes told Renwick and Claudel, I'll give you the details later. He glanced at his watch. Almost five o'clock. Just over two hours ago there had been nothing but apparent failure. He beamed happily at Nina.

"Travels in style, does he?" Claudel murmured. "Some expense account!"

Yes, thought Renwick, that's Theo.

CHAPTER

24

Theo's instructions, sent in code to the camper before it had entered Bombay, were precise. Kiley was to meet him at two o'clock in the Malabar Hotel. Kiley was to be circumspectly dressed. Kiley was to avoid the four large elevators (attended) and make sure that one of the smaller elevators (self-service) was empty before he used it. Kiley was to get out at the twelfth floor. Kiley would be met by a red-haired man who would greet him in Italian: "This is warmer than Rome in August." Kiley would reply in Dutch: "And as hot as Jakarta." Kiley would then be conducted to Theo's rooms, pausing—if anyone should appear in the corridor—to chat with his guide until they judged it was safe to enter.

In spite of a sense of urgency—why else had such an unexpected meeting been arranged?—Kiley felt real amusement as he stepped into Suite 12A. Tony would blame that on Nina's bad influence, he thought; and perhaps it was. Back in Essen, he wouldn't have seen anything comic in the contrast between a secretive approach and an open rendezvous. For what else would you call a meeting in a luxury hotel? No shadowed Gothic pillars this time for Theo, no slipping into the aisles of the Minster.

His escort entered a room on the left, where Kiley glimpsed a blond, thin-shouldered man at a table with elaborate equipment. The door closed. Kiley waited, looking at the elegance around him. The last comfortable hotel room he had seen— the only one, in fact, he had ever occupied—had been at Russell Square in London, and it looked like a hen house compared to all this. Then his critical study of Theo's living quarters ended as the door to his right opened, and Theo appeared. The three minutes' delay had been calculated, thought Kiley. He overcame his surprise at Theo's appearance—apart from his height and weight, he was difficult to recognize. He was now a white-haired man without glasses, a white mustache on his short upper lip, slow in movement and dressed in a dark-gray silk suit.

But Theo's voice was as crisp as ever as he greeted Kiley in German. His gray eyes had the same strange alternation of bland innocence and calm scrutiny. "Four months since we met," he said, shaking hands briefly. "You look well, Erik. They have agreed with you. Not too unpleasant a journey? Sit down, sit down. We have much to discuss without wasting time. I must leave here no later than three o'clock—an important meeting at three-thirty." He pointed to a low chair on one side of a small gilded table, and selected the one (firmer, higher, more commanding) opposite.

"I sent regular reports—" Kiley began, slightly on the defensive.

"Read with much interest. A successful trip on the whole. You had a tendency, however, to give more importance to the revolutionaries of the extreme left than to members of the Communist groups. In Iran, for instance, you saw only two of the Tudeh—"

"I spoke with them."

"So the Soviet Embassy informed me."

It would, thought Kiley: it had agents and spies everywhere, the biggest intelligence network in all of Iran. "I found the Tudeh people waited too much for instructions. The militant revolutionaries may be more extreme, but they'll take action on their own whenever they see the chance."

"And that appeals to you." Theo shook his head. "Are you still unwilling to admit that anarchists won't succeed—in the long run? That is what counts, Erik. Not today's quick victories but tomorrow's permanent success." Theo smiled. "You'll come around to seeing it yet." He dismissed the topic with a wave of his hand. His mood turned solemn. "I have had some disquieting news. We have to alter our original plan."

"Which one?"

Theo's eyebrows were raised.

"We had three objectives, hadn't we?" As Theo kept a watchful silence, Kiley went on. "First: Marco and I were to drop out of sight completely, leave the West Germans baffled. Second: we were to recruit and encourage while we traveled, select the most promising material. Third: I was to gain acceptance into the O'Connell household, possibly as a future son-in-law."

There was a brief silence. The third objective had never

been detailed. Erik was smart, thought Theo, sometimes too smart. "Have you actually asked the girl to marry you?"

"Not exactly. Hinted at it. It seemed wiser to—"

"Are you lovers?"

"Not yet. I planned that for Bali." Kiley was embarrassed. "Just making sure of the last stages in our journey to Washington."

"Too bad that we must cancel your visit to Bali."

Incredulous, Kiley stared at him. "What? *Cancel?*"

"You will go directly from here to America—to a training camp I have established in Southern California. One of my best agents was in charge, but he died—along with his chief assistant. I need two capable men to replace him: you and Marco. It's an important assignment—the final training of students who have graduated from camps abroad, preparing them for specialized work in the United States."

Angrily, Kiley said, "What about the O'Connell project? You told me, back in Essen, that it was of top priority. You said it had approval and backing at the 'highest levels'— wasn't that what you said?"

How much does he need to know to be kept in line? Theo wondered. "Yes," he said smoothly, "my first suggestion was very well received at the highest levels. It was, quite simply, the idea that you would be a very useful son-in-law—for us— when Francis O'Connell becomes Secretary of State. He is in line for that; and, in fact, if his new wife has her way, he may even run for President."

"That's not my kind of future, and you know it, Theo."

"Yes, I know it. And so, once I was given a small department of my own—necessary to prevent any leaks, any information about such a project being whispered around—I emended that original idea, added more action for you and Marco."

"Such as?"

"A more explosive situation, shall we say?"

"And is it approved by the highest levels?"

Theo side-stepped that question. "I've been given full charge of this project."

"Of the original idea," Kiley corrected him, and then frowned. "Very clever of them. They thought they'd keep me hanging around Washignton for years. And who'd be leading Direct Action in Europe, then? One of their stooges, I bet." Or one of yours, he added silently.

"Relax, Erik. I changed all that."

"Do they know?"

"Time enough for them to know when my plan succeeds. It will be far more devastating than having access to a future Secretary of State."

"O'Connell might learn he's being used."

"What could he do? Let the world know that his daughter is married to a terrorist—of *your* reputation and importance, Erik?"

Kiley wasn't to be silenced by that compliment. "I don't see why you have to ditch me now. If there's some action ahead, I can handle it." The target must be big, bigger than O'Connell himself. In rising excitement, he added, "Don't cut me out, Theo. You owe me—"

"Arrangements have already been made," Theo said. That was final. "The O'Connell assignment has been given to another agent."

"Are you sure that agent knows enough about explosives? You did mention an explosive situation, didn't you?"

Theo regretted his joke. "The agent will not have to deal with explosives. We have found other specialists for that job. All my agent will have to do is—substitute. Scarcely an assignment worthy of your talents, Erik." And that should end his interest.

Kiley almost laughed. Even if Theo believed in simple means backed by elaborate stratagems, a substitution was too damned simple. No use arguing that. Theo would answer that simple means were the hardest to detect: anything normal aroused no suspicion.

"Yes?" Theo had noticed the fleeting amusement in Kiley's eyes.

Something normal, arousing no suspicion...Kiley's quick mind made a stab at several possibilities. "Just speculating on what you've chosen to hold your bomb. Something portable, I'd imagine—unless you intend to blow O'Connell's house to pieces. But that would be hardly worth the effort. Nothing of importance there."

"Really?" Theo was on guard. "And what would you use to conceal your explosives—something portable, you said?"

"Well—" Kiley hesitated, spoke half-jokingly—"something like a briefcase. It's just simple-minded enough to succeed—if the right man was carrying it into the right place."

"Amusing idea." Theo managed a thin smile. "But forget

it. A briefcase did not work with Hitler." And that, he thought, ends all discussion.

"I imagine—" Kiley ventured a touch of sarcasm—"there have been a few slight improvements in explosives since Hitler's day."

"So I've heard," Theo said coldly.

"I could rig a briefcase with enough power to blast not only a large room apart but also every adjacent room and corridor." Kiley's confidence was returning. Yes, he thought, I'll show him that Marco and I are as good a team as he could find for any O'Connell assignment. "How to set off the explosives? We could use a timer or remote control."

The best way to stop all speculation, thought Theo, may be to give him full rein, and then pull him up to a sudden and sharp halt. "Which would you choose? Supposing, that is, you were planning to use this hypothetical briefcase?"

"Not a timer," Kiley decided. "A meeting in a conference room could be delayed, or ended sooner than expected. Remote control is surer—with someone in a corridor nearby to see when everyone has entered the room. We'd need advance information, of course, to make certain the meeting was important and would be well attended."

"Of course," Theo echoed, all innocence. "You'd have your sources for that information, I presume."

"Right. And that makes it a sure thing. Give the room twenty minutes or more—perhaps half an hour—to settle down. Then press the button."

"The man—or woman—in the corridor would be killed, too."

"He—or she—wouldn't know that."

Theo studied his hands. "A well-trained intelligence officer might have a better solution."

Kiley's lips tightened.

"Your hypothetical briefcase could be installed with a miniature transmitter—give notice to someone a safe distance away to press the button." Judging from the chagrin on Kiley's face, Theo had pulled him up to a very sharp halt. "But your idea is interesting. You might even use it someday. With your ingenuity, it's a pity I had to take you off the O'Connell assignment."

"But why? Why change—"

"Because James Kiley can no longer exist. Nor can Tony Shawfield."

"What?" Kiley's stare passed from amazement to incredulity. *"What?"*

"Tonight you will leave for the United States, using new names, new identities, and Canadian passports. You will travel separately, of course, taking different directions. You will meet at Rancho San Carlos in Sawyer Springs, California. It is easily reached from either Los Angeles or San Diego. Marco already has these orders. I saw him an hour ago."

He actually met Theo? Actually saw him? That was a first. And he heard the orders before I did? I am being disciplined, Kiley realized. He said nothing.

"It was a brief meeting," Theo said, as if he had guessed Kiley's thoughts. "Minimal but necessary information, along with his instructions for tonight. He is to take his five charges to the cargo area of the airport—there is a plane arriving at nine, unloading some pilgrims returning from Mecca while others continue their flight home to Indonesia. He will dangle the prospect of Bali before their eyes, get them on board, and once he loses them in Indonesia—and I mean *lose* them—he can leave for America. You'll see him later this afternoon and give him the money for all these expenses along with his Canadian passport. Quite clear?"

I'm still in command, Kiley thought. Five of the group to be bundled off, abandoned, lost for good...."What about Nina?"

"Your problem. A major one." Theo was suddenly angry. He hadn't liked the use of "Nina" in just that tone of voice: O'Connell was enough. "Do you think these changes in plans are a whim on my part?" He rose, crossed over to a bureau, removed several items from a drawer—a thin folder, a thick envelope, traveler's checks, and a newspaper. "Today's," he said curtly, thrusting it into Kiley's hand. "I had the information last Monday. Why do you think I ordered you to make a complicated arrival in Bombay, ditch the camper, lose any possible tail on you? Oh, yes, there was one." He dropped the envelope packed with dollars and the traveler's checks at Kiley's elbow. "Read, read! The headlines are big enough."

Kiley read. About Ilsa Schlott—"Greta"—the green camper—recruitment of terrorists for South Yemen training camps—her past association with the People's Revolutionary Force for Direct Action...

He said, "She won't talk. She'll never mention Erik or

Marco." So why all this uproar? This news report was bad, but it could have been worse. Theo was losing his grip.

"She won't need to talk. Read column two on page nine."

Kiley found it. It was a close analysis of the "philosophy behind terrorism." Some historical patterns were given, brief excerpts from the anarchist writings of the nineteenth century—Bakunin, Kropotkin, Malatesta—leading into the People's Revolutionary Force for Direct Action, founded by two militant terrorists known as Erik and Marco. Past activities were listed: bombings, robberies, kidnapping, and murders. The column ended with Essen, the attempt on Duisburg—discovered in time to prevent half the town from being wiped out in a fire storm generated by the huge propane tanks on the docks—and the expert disappearance of Erik and Marco.

Kiley reread the column, paid little attention to the red-haired man who had moved quietly in from the room next door and handed Theo two slips of paper. "That one," the man said, "was in code. This one is a report we picked up from United Press only a minute ago."

Kiley looked up as Theo waved the man back to his room. "Who is responsible—" Kiley began. But Theo was engrossed by the two small sheets of paper.

Suddenly, Theo's smooth white face went rigid, carved out of marble. For a full minute he stood motionless. Then he shouted, "Klaus!" and the red-haired man reappeared.

Theo glanced at his watch: five past three. "Telephone the bank," he told Klaus. "Say I am ill, unable to attend the meeting. We will rearrange it for—" he paused—"for Tuesday. My sincere regrets." As Klaus started toward the telephone on the desk at the window, Theo yelled, "Not there! Downstairs! A public phone in the lobby. And waste no time!" He stood glaring after Klaus. Then he dropped into his chair, glaring now at Kiley, yet not seeing him, not seeing anything.

At last Theo said, his voice almost normal, his face unreadable, "The press report comes from California—from Sawyer Springs. There was an explosion at Rancho San Carlos—one building totally destroyed. The FBI were immediately on the scene. Several men, asleep in a dormitory at the time of the explosion, have been arrested. A barn was searched; its contents removed. The main house was partly destroyed. Three men living there were injured; one seriously. All three are arrested, too."

"Who did it?" Kiley was aghast. "Were there no guards posted?" Damn those Americans, always asleep on the job.

"The fence alarm was bypassed. Two guard dogs were drugged. The body of an unknown man was found near the explosion. Unidentifiable."

"One man alone?"

We may never know, thought Theo. One thing we do know: the FBI had San Carlos under observation. How else could they arrive so quickly unless they were stationed in the village? "We will have to find you and Marco a safer house. In New York. We need you in America. No delay in leaving here tonight. No delay, you understand?" He glanced at the decoded message: *Reliable source identifies new arrivals at West German Embassy New Delhi as security police preparing to escort terrorists back to Essen. Extradition.* That information stays with me, Theo decided. Mention extradition and those two might not even wait for tonight—they could leave immediately. Stop to dispose of O'Connell and get rid of those five young fools? No, I don't think Erik or Marco would waste any time on that. Extradition was a powerful word. He struck a match, pulled a large jade ashtray in front of him, and set the slips of paper burning over it.

Kiley folded the newspaper, laid it on the table. "Who informed?" he asked bitterly. "Greta?"

"It took more than informers to piece all that material together."

"CIA—MI6—NATO?"

"It could be a new intelligence unit. I've had two reports based on rumors, nothing substantive as yet. But I think I know one man who may be connected with it." And I wrote him off: his resignation from NATO seemed entirely probable—it had been rumored for weeks, and its timing fitted in with that death scare and the stupid affair in Brussels which could have ended his career anyway. "He never seemed to be too important. He just happened to be on the scene of any action." Such as in Vienna, over two years ago. "Always with a reasonable excuse for being there." Such as in Essen, which he visited on his way back from observing NATO maneuvers in West Germany.

"What makes you suspect him now?"

"His friends—who have been interested in your recent movements. Two carpet dealers—"

"I reported on them," Kiley said quickly.

"And we investigated. One works for Turkish Intelligence. The other is French, once connected with NATO, a friend of—"

"We dealt with these two," Kiley interjected. "They are out of the picture."

"Indeed? The Turk is now in Srinigar on his carpet business. The Frenchman was reported to be traveling south from Delhi. To Bombay?"

"But we had hashish planted in their car at Quetta. Well hidden. And we warned the Indian customs—"

"By the time they reached the frontier, no hashish was found. So no arrest, no prison sentence. With whom did you think you were dealing? Amateurs?"

Kiley bridled, decided to make little of that jibe. It wasn't the first time that Theo had emphasized the differences between the training of a terrorist and that of an intelligence agent. "Why Bombay?" he asked. "India is a continent in itself. South of New Delhi there are hundreds of towns, thousands of villages—"

"You and Marco are in Bombay. Nina O'Connell is in Bombay."

Kiley stared at the placid face, had the wisdom to keep silent.

Theo said, "The Frenchman is following the girl. She leads him to you. That is his plan. Obviously."

If he *is* in Bombay, thought Kiley. He could not resist saying, "And I lead him to you, Theo?"

"I do not think that will be likely."

"You certainly risked a lot in bringing me—and Marco—to this room."

"I've had many visitors—some quite legitimate," Theo said sharply. "What is better cover than a large hotel with a busy lobby and five entrances? Four hundred double rooms—with seven hundred guests at least? How many outside visitors to the restaurants, grill, bar? To the arcade for its shops and bargains? To the barbershop and the massage room, and the travel bureaus? A hotel such as this is safer than any private house, provided—" he added with amusement— "you have a man permanently in your rooms who will watch the hotel maid or service waiter."

Kiley seemed convinced. But one thing puzzled him. If Theo felt so secure, why had he not kept his appointment for half past three?

"Yes?" asked Theo, quick to notice.

Kiley shrugged.

"Yes?" Theo's voice had sharpened. "You have something to add?"

"Why cancel your business at the bank? It wasn't connected with me, or with Nina."

"Too many storm signals," Theo said abruptly. Until I find out what they mean, I do not risk a public appearance as Otto Remp from Düsseldorf. Could Renwick have traced any connection between Remp and Essen? I was careful there; used a false name and address for that bank account from which Erik drew his monthly allotments. And there was no other obvious connection with Erik: our meetings were rare and well disguised.

"The Frenchman won't be in Bombay alone," Kiley said thoughtfully. "I could recognize him—if I had a close look." Unless he's wearing a white wig and mustache. "What is his name?"

"Claudel. Major Claudel." Theo opened the folder. It contained a page of information, very little by Theo's usual standards. There was also an envelope marked "Negatives" with a small photograph clipped to it. Theo removed the photograph, passed it to Kiley. "Have you seen that man anywhere on your travels?"

The snapshot was of two people: a man, young-looking, handsome, laughing; a brunette beauty, with a smile on her face. Judging from the background, the bedroom belonged to a woman with taste and money. "No. Never. Who is he?"

"Claudel's friend. If my informant is correct, he could be the originator of that intelligence unit I mentioned. It is called Interintell, according to Johan Vroom, the new chief of one intelligence section at The Hague."

"He's your man?" Kiley was impressed.

"No. He is just too eager to silence his colleagues—he is younger than they are, so he asserts his importance by parading his knowledge. You can keep that photograph. I have the negative."

"Interintell . . . What the hell does that mean?"

"International Intelligence. To be used against international terrorism. A good idea—from Renwick's point of view."

"Renwick." Kiley looked at the photograph again, memorizing features and the build of the shoulders.

"About your height. Your color of hair. Gray eyes. Age—late thirties. Keeps himself in good shape."

"I can see that. Also his good taste in women. Who is she? Someone who installed a camera in her bedroom?"

"We had it installed. With her knowledge, of course."

"A little more action here—" Kiley tapped the photograph—"and you could have blackmailed him nicely."

"I have other negatives," Theo said with a small smile. "But blackmail? And risk exposure for our agent? Destroy her future value?" Theo was thoughtful. "And I don't know if blackmail would work with Lieutenant Colonel Renwick. But someday we might try."

"Lieutenant Colonel?"

"Ex-Lieutenant Colonel, I should have said. He resigned from military intelligence. Actually, I think—" Theo looked sharply at the door to his suite as a gentle knock, repeated twice, sounded on its panel. It opened, and Klaus returned, pocketing his key. "You are late!"

"I walked around some streets after I telephoned. I thought that was better than returning here direct."

"We have been waiting for these passports! And the histories to go with them? Are they complete?"

"Almost ready. A few minutes." Klaus hurried into the room he shared with the radio-transmitter expert.

Theo was impatient, Theo was glancing at his watch again, Theo was restless. He rose, went to the room where Klaus was typing a last line on a sheet of paper. "That will do, that will do," Theo said and dropped his voice as he gave further instructions. Then he came back with two passports and two sheets of paper. "Here you are. Brief histories. They will carry you and Marco safely enough to New York. There you will receive other passports and much more detailed legends. Call the Soviet Consulate as soon as you arrive. Now I think that's about all. Safe journey, Erik."

Kiley glanced at the sheets of paper. "Shouldn't I memorize them here—they're short—destroy them before I leave? I'd rather not carry them around."

"Of course, of course," Theo agreed, but not too willingly. "Would you excuse me? I have much to do. Let me know when you leave." He picked up the folder from the table, pointed to the envelope and bundle of traveler's checks, and went into his room. The door closed.

He is packing up, thought Kiley, clearing out. Movements

from the room next door were careful, subdued, but that sound might be said to belong to a drawer creaking open. Certainly, from the other bedroom, the activity wasn't disguised. But why conceal his departure from me? Kiley wondered. It could be that Theo's "storm signals" were of hurricane strength; perhaps he hid the worst from me in case Marco and I cleared out, too, and the hell with Bali and our five idiots. But what about Nina? Your problem, Theo had said. Not enough; he'd better be more precise than that. Quickly, Kiley began memorizing the two new histories. Graduate students returning from a year's study abroad; Marco came from Quebec, Kiley from Toronto, et cetera, et cetera...

In ten minutes, he was sure of place names and dates. Brief legends, compared to others he had learned in the past, but enough to skate through an entry into New York. It would have been a different matter if Marco and he had to face Quebec or Toronto. Changes, changes, he thought as he set the pages alight over the ashtray and watched them turn to black quivering leaves.

Yet change was the essence of his beliefs: spontaneity in action, flexibility in thought—he had praised them in his manifesto, had attacked stability and the status quo as enemies of true progress. As they were. So welcome change, he told himself, and stilled a qualm of regret for the end of four months that had been a pleasant interlude, could have been more.... But there had been successes in recruitment: that was one achievement that couldn't be halted—the tide was running his way. And Nina? He could have won her, but he had followed Theo's plan—no personal involvement for him—and whatever he had hoped for the future, in his return to America with Nina, was now ended.

He pocketed the checks and the money and knocked on Theo's door. "I'm leaving. Everything taken care of. Except..." He waited until the door opened.

"Except what?" Theo's tone was sharp. He was in shirt sleeves. The white wig and mustache were gone. Suitcases were on the bed. "What?"

"Marco takes five of them to Bali. Where do I take Nina?"

"Nowhere. She can identify every stop you made on your journey. Get rid of her."

"Kill her?" Kiley asked. His face was tense.

"What else?" Theo stared at him unbelievingly. "Do I need to tell *you* how to make it look natural? No gun. Use your cyanide pistol. Or an overdose. She isn't one of your addicts, but who is to know that?"

Abruptly, Kiley turned to leave.

"It is possible," Theo said, "she has duped you completely. She may be one of Renwick's agents. As you said, he has good taste in women. He knew O'Connell—very well indeed, I heard."

Kiley left. In the corridor, he paused. A lie, he thought, a lie to make sure I'd deal with Nina. Because if she's one of Renwick's agents, then the stupidity in sending her on the world trip belongs to Theo. He selected her; I didn't. And before he ever chose her to accompany me, he had checked her background: no intelligence training of any kind. It was a lie. Nina and Renwick? Ludicrous. He pulled out Renwick's photograph, tore it into shreds, thrust them deep into the sand of a giant ashtray.

He walked on, almost forgot to take one of the small self-service elevators, found himself still arguing with Theo. Then, about to pass through the lobby to its huge front door, he came to his cool calm senses again and switched directions. Five entrances, Theo had said. Kiley chose one that led out of the bar onto a side street. He'd take the usual evasionary tactics, allow himself a spell of wandering around, catching a taxi here, another taxi there, before he headed for the house near the docks. He had told Nina he'd return by four o'clock. His watch said it was now past that hour. For a second he was tempted to go back directly, but habit and training prevailed. He began his tortuous, seemingly purposeless journey. No one followed.

CHAPTER
25

Kiley's roundabout route was long enough to bring him back to normal, to a sense of reality. No matter how he felt about Nina, she was a danger. The sooner he dealt with that problem, the safer for him, for Marco. His pace increased as the houses on the harbor road came in sight. Joined together to form a continuous line, they seemed so similar that he might have passed Gopal's place had he not spied Madge—Madge and the little Indian girl—loitering in front of its entrance. What the devil were they doing there? he wondered, his mood changing into sharp annoyance.

Madge saw him. Like the idiot she was, she came running to greet him right there in the open street. "I'm worried about Tony," she began. "Have you seen him?"

"Let's get inside." He pulled her into the cover of the entrance almost as far as the foot of the verandah stairs but out of sight from the courtyard. A murmur of distant voices told him that the men still sat there.

The Indian girl followed them, saying, "She is gone, she is gone. The Englishman went looking. Gopal, too. And Gopal's friend who drives the car." Her words, spilling out in her excitement, were scarcely understandable.

Kiley stared at her. "What the hell is she talking about? Nina?" Nina gone? Gone? He mastered his rage.

Madge, almost as incoherent, tried to explain. It was Tony's absence that worried her. Two, almost three hours since he went searching for Nina. Yes, Nina had left. That's the way she wanted it, so let her go. But Tony—

"Yes. You need Tony," Kiley interrupted harshly. Tony and some more hashish to meet the evening ahead. He looked at Madge with contempt: gaunt face, vacant eyes, drooping lips; she had become a caricature of herself. In anger, he turned on the little Indian, who was still babbling away about a phone call and the American in her pretty dress and a taxi ride. "Shut up and listen! Is Gopal's cousin here—the man with the scar on his cheek? Bring him to me. At once!"

288

Storm signals, Theo had said. Kiley was sensing them now, and taking their warning. "Madge, you'll all have to leave. This place will be raided for drugs. You've got to get out, all of you. Get the others together. Tell them to pack. Gopal's cousin will take you to a plane. It leaves tonight. For Bali."

"Bali?" Her sudden smile of delight faded. "But what about Tony?"

"He will join you at the airport. He's making the arrangements now. And if he is delayed—don't worry. Gopal's cousin will travel all the way to Bali with you, keep you safe. Tony will join you there. Now hurry—don't waste a moment! Get the others down here in ten minutes—five, if you can manage it."

Madge started toward the staircase. "How long did Tony search for Nina? Really, she caused so much trouble. But he shouldn't have worried. No need."

Something is behind these words, Kiley thought. Carefully, he said, "Tony had travel arrangements to make. He has more on his mind than Nina."

"Just as well. She met her friends. I saw them. They drove past here."

"When?"

"Oh, just before you came back. Shahna and I had gone walking to the market. I was—I was restless after Nina left. Trust Nina to travel in style—a Mercedes!" She giggled nervously. "And with Robert Renwick. Did she ever tell you about him?"

"Often." He even smiled. "Now, get the others. Quick! Make them understand you could all be arrested."

"I haven't any drugs." But she was climbing the staircase.

Gopal's cousin was interested in the fee for his services—half paid now, the rest in Bali. Certainly he could find the runway where the cargo planes loaded. Certainly he could arrange for transport among the returning Muslims. Certainly he would see everyone safe—as far as Bali. His sharp brown eyes glistened at the prospect. They were a little dashed when Kiley handed over the money, for fares and food and his fee's second installment, to the tall Dane, who came downstairs with his French wife and her guitar, followed by the Dutchman and the Italian and the American girl.

"What about transportation to the airfield?" Sven Dissen

wanted to know, stowing the wad of notes inside Marie-Louise's handbag, which he'd carry under his arm.

"The cars that brought us here this morning," Kiley answered. Yes, he had been right to make Dissen the treasurer.

"There's only one left," Gopal's cousin said. "The Englishman took the other along with—"

"Then get the one that is left," Kiley said sharply. "It's parked in the courtyard next door."

"There will be a payment necessary."

"Yes, yes," Kiley said, and handed out more money. "Now get to it!"

There was a short wait. To Kiley it seemed interminable. No one around him had much to say: they were all a little dazed, but no objections were voiced. There was the usual lament from Henryk Tromp about his stolen camera—and now he was going to Bali, where he'd need it more than ever. "I'll lend you my Kodak," Madge told him. "Just don't talk about your camera any more. Or the film that disappeared with it." She looked around her, said, "This place is really crummy. I'll be glad to leave." She led the way to the street, where the Fiat had drawn up at the curb. Then she noticed Kiley wasn't following. She turned and waved, "See you in Bali, too?"

He nodded.

They settled into the Fiat with squeals and laughs at the tight pack, everything forgotten except the excitement of the journey ahead. The car moved off. Twenty minutes to six, he saw by his watch. Time to start leaving.

Ignoring the men sitting in the courtyard, he ran up the stairs to the room he was to have shared with Shawfield. Both their duffel bags were padlocked. He opened his own, extracted the cyanide pistol and some extra pellets. The knife he strapped above his ankle. His .32 was anchored in his belt. His movements were brisk, precise. Soon he was ready.

In haste, he checked the rooms to make sure those clowns hadn't left any identifications behind. Strange how quickly they had moved at the threat of a narcotics raid, although they pretended they never took drugs, never began squirreling them away as soon as they were safely across a frontier. Hooked on hashish—and heroin, too: Lambrese and Tromp had graduated to that along with the gold chains around their necks. Well, they could sell these for food when the money ran out in Bali. And after that? If they had any will power left, and that was improbable, they might find a way to leave. Perhaps Sven Dissen could manage that, unless he was kept paralyzed by his Marie-Louise. As for Madge—he could see nothing for her. But no one had forced hashish or morphine sulphate tablets down their throats. It had been their own free choice, and their stupidity.

In Nina's room he halted. Her canvas bag lay on the window seat: two shirts unfolded and abandoned. The blue one matched her eyes, he remembered, and then choked off that treacherous thought. A movement from the entrance to the room caught his ear: the little Indian girl was there, looking at the shirts and the open bag.

"Take them," he told her. "But don't let the police see them."

She shook her head. She ran forward, swept up the bag and shirts in her thin arms, hurried to the door. "Wait!" he called, stopping her at the threshold. She looked at him fearfully, brown eyes pleading, while she clutched her new possessions more tightly to her chest. "Take this, too." He tossed over Shawfield's bag, watched her drag it away with her other arm still full of Nina's clothes. Like a little pack rat, he thought. "Remember," he called to her, "tell the police nothing. Nothing! Or you'll get arrested for stealing."

Out of fright, she almost dropped her load, but gripped it again, and vanished from sight. The last of Antony Shawfield...The last of James Kiley, too, as soon as a brazier or a kitchen oven could be found on the ground floor, and a passport could be destroyed.

He gave a final glance at the window seat where the blue striped shirt had lain, his lips tight, his jaw clenched. Suddenly, he felt a surge of relief: he didn't have to face Nina, deciding—even as he smiled and talked—how she would die. She'd stay alive. And Theo couldn't blame him.

And that reminded him: he must find the nearest telephone, call Theo, tell him what had happened. The news about Renwick would send him flying out of Bombay. That should be easy for Theo: he was already preparing to leave.

He hoisted his duffel bag over his shoulder, stepped out onto the verandah. And where do I go? he wondered. To New York? Hide there, inactive, waiting for Theo's orders while someone else takes over my Washington assignment? But damned if I know why Theo canceled me because of Greta and a onetime green camper and a column on Erik. There was no identification of Erik with Kiley or of Marco with Shawfield. So why was I ordered to drop out after all the work I've put into this mission? To hell with New York: I'm not a puppet, jerking at the end of a string.

He heard a movement from the room just ahead of him, its door flung wide open for air. He halted, waited until the footsteps had ceased, made sure that no one would emerge. Marco, he was thinking, Marco wouldn't be in New York, either. Once he gets back here—what the hell has detained him?—and finds we have all cleared out, he will get the message. He will head for Germany and our friends there. That's where our connections are. Ours. Not Theo's.

The movements in the room ceased. Carefully, he slipped past the open door. Yes, he decided, we'll reactivate Direct Action. We'll move; in our way, not in Theo's. We'll scare him witless, him and his Leninist friends. We'll show them what revolution really means. And if his plan in Washington succeeds—all the better for us. Devastating, he had said. America to be paralyzed, unable to act—even temporarily? For that, Theo, thank you.

Kiley reached the end of the verandah. Suddenly, the courtyard erupted in noise: protests, shrill cries, authoritative voices. He halted, took one look over the balustrade, drew back. Police. Three in uniform, two in plain clothes.

Beside him was the last room on the verandah, its door gaping wide. He threw his duffel bag across its threshold and started down the narrow staircase. His .32 was in his right hand, held close to his thigh, unnoticeable. His left hand concealed the bogus fountain pen. As yet he hadn't been seen from the courtyard. Walk normally, he told himself; don't hurry, don't rush, don't look as if you were escaping. Keep cool, Erik. This isn't the first time you have strolled out of a tight spot.

He reached the last flight of stairs. One man had been posted at the foot of the steps and was watching the courtyard scene with amusement. "They've all left, they've all left," the little Indian girl was screaming, "all left in a car." Forever the center of attention, Kiley thought. She throve on drama, that girl; and on a gift of clothes.

He continued down the stairs. The guard turned his head to look up at him. Kiley smiled easily, said, "What's happening out there? A family fight or something?"

The policeman studied him. "Stay there, please!"

"Of course," Kiley said pleasantly. He took three more casual steps and halted only a few feet away from the upturned face. He took a long deep breath and held it. He raised his left arm.

"What's that in your—" The man's question was never completed. Kiley pressed the release on the cyanide pistol, aiming it directly at the opened mouth. The man groped for support, began sliding to the ground.

Kiley stepped around the crumpled body, kept on walking, released his breath. The man would be dead before Kiley reached the street. But even policemen could have heart attacks, he thought as he slipped the pen into one pocket of his jacket, the .32 into the other. He kept firm hold of it, straightened his tie with his free hand, and ignored three cars drawn up in a phalanx before the entrance to the house.

Automatically, he turned to his left—away from the city's center and toward the docks—and mingled with the crowd.

"Stop!" came a yell behind him.

He walked calmly on, people around him on every side. Then as another "Stop!" was yelled, his pace increased. He was ready to break into a run, but he reached a side street, jammed with people and stalls and happy disorder. Well into this excellent cover, he slipped off his jacket, removed his tie as he stopped at a cart where morsels of food were being cooked. He chose two of the small brown objects, highly spiced, and enjoyed them while he sat on a narrow sidewalk beside a group of men and listened to the fading sounds of alarm from the main street.

He sat there amid dirt and debris taking stock of his resources. Money, yes. Three passports: two Canadian, one of them now unnecessary; one American, now dangerous. Three weapons.

At last, he felt he could risk walking slowly out of the market with his tie out of sight and the jacket tucked under his arm. The approach of early night was a help, too. So was the closing of the stalls: under a load of curling green vegetables, he slipped the French-Canadian passport. It would lead the police nowhere. The Kiley passport, however, would have to be destroyed, not abandoned. As soon as he reached the docks he would tear up its inside pages, drop the whole thing into the filthy waters. A sad ending for James Kiley.

And a new beginning for Louis Krimmon, graduate student traveling abroad, Toronto-born and raised, now in need of a berth on a freighter, any honest job to help him work his passage home. No luggage? Stolen. Everything lost except what he carried. Innocent Canadian deceived... Yes, that was the angle.

He had gone barely fifty yards along a street seething with people when he reached the lights of a money exchange still open for business. He saw a telephone just inside its wide door. Call Theo? Warn him of Renwick? Hell no; Theo was saving his own hide, right this minute. More important now was the group of seamen at the exchange entrance. Foreigners, all of them. This was his chance: choose an American, if possible—someone who'd be free with advice, if not help. His eyes were so busy searching out a likely soft mark that he didn't notice a slight small figure tugging at a man's sleeve.

Shahna said to Roy's man, Lavji, "That's him."

Lavji signed to the two men who had been waiting behind him for almost an hour. All three reached Kiley, took firm hold. They disarmed him there and then: a .32 in his jacket pocket, a knife strapped above his ankle, a thick fountain pen and pellets. Their car was waiting, drove off before a curious crowd could start gathering.

As Roy had said when he had learned of the escape, of the death of a policeman, "He will telephone a warning. As soon as it grows dark, he will come out of his hiding place—it can't be far from that house—he disappeared too quickly. So where is the nearest public telephone? Where?"

And Shahna had obliged.

CHAPTER

26

"Seven o'clock and all's well," Claudel said.

"So far," Renwick added to that. Nina was safely asleep nowhere near the Malabar; his friends Mahoney and Benson, the Australians whose room was opposite Renwick's, were taking turns at guard duty.

Roy, relaxing at his desk in the office behind the gift shop, was entitled to some self-congratulation: the report from Lavji had just come through; Kiley had been taken, too surprised to offer much resistance. "Two down," he told Renwick.

"And the biggest one to go."

"Well, he's still in his suite. When Lavji and the others return, we'll pay 12A a little visit. Meanwhile..." Roy shrugged and smiled. He had installed a floor waiter to keep watch and a chambermaid who had even entered the suite ten minutes ago with a batch of fresh towels. True, she hadn't got beyond the central living room, been dismissed by the red-haired valet; but she had glimpsed suitcases packed, ready and waiting.

"And when Theo leaves," Renwick said, "he won't be Dr. Frederick Weber with white hair, white mustache, and slow movements." That was all the information on Weber that the hotel desk could provide; that, and the fact that he had been a normal guest—sometimes visiting the bar, sometimes eating in the grill, and sometimes taxiing out for dinner. His announced visitors had been businessmen—antique dealers—which was to be expected.

"We know his height, his approximate weight," Roy said. "That won't be altered."

Probably not, thought Renwick: this climate made added girth unpleasant; heavy padding around Theo's waist would have him sweating like a pig. "I think I'll take a walk around the elevators," he said.

"Again?" Roy was amused, slightly annoyed, too. "I have men posted there: one on each elevator along with its operator. Anyone descending from the twelfth floor whom the operators haven't seen before will be detained. We'll hear about it as soon as it happens. Time enough then to have our confrontation. The elevators are only a minute away—less—from the accountants' room next door to us. And don't worry about the self-service elevators. They are out of commission."

Renwick stayed where he was, even if unwillingly: Roy was in charge; he had co-operated fully and well. That's the hell of it, Renwick was thinking: you take assistance, and you're in a subsidiary role. No matter that all Roy's information about Theo had come from Claudel or himself: Roy was in control at this moment and, with two successes already claimed, he was in no mood to have his excellent arrangements questioned.

Claudel said tactfully, "Extraordinary news we received from London, Bob." Gilman had given it when Renwick had contacted him about Marco's arrest and Nina's safety. "Have any idea who blew up that San Carlos ammunition dump? He did more than that: he has the FBI swarming all over the place."

And died, too. It could only have been Sal. He knew the way to enter that compound, silence the dogs, approach the armory. "I didn't arrange it—wish I had," said Renwick.

"He was working alone?"

"Must have been."

"Someone with a grudge?"

"Or his own sense of justice."

"That can be dangerous."

"It was—for him." But Sal would have thought the price well worth it.

"How important was Rancho San—?"

Roy's telephone rang. It was a message from the hotel desk. "Did you announce him? He was expected? I see. What's his description?" The call ended and Roy could turn to Renwick and Claudel. "A visitor for Dr. Frederick Weber. Introduced himself as Schmidt, an antique dealer. Said he had an appointment for quarter past seven. The desk cleared that with Weber's suite. Schmidt is now on his way up to 12A."

"Inconvenient timing," Claudel said. "Unless Dr. Weber isn't planning to leave tonight." That had been Renwick's hunch: Theo would clear out of Bombay as soon as possible; Theo was running scared—why else cancel that vital meeting in the bank, and at such short notice? "Oh, I know," Claudel went on, catching a sharp glance from Renwick, "his suitcases are ready to go. But some people do pack on the night before an early-morning start."

Renwick said, "What description did you get, Roy?"

"Cream-colored suit. About fifty years old, wears heavy glasses, has dark-brown hair—worn long but well brushed, carries a Panama hat. Very presentable." Roy frowned. "Sounds possible. All open and above board, wouldn't you say?"

"Height? Weight?" Renwick asked quietly.

Roy stared at Renwick, but he picked up the receiver again and—after some delay—got the information. "Medium height and weight and a deeply tanned face. Anything more, Robert?" he asked with a touch of sarcasm.

"Check with the twelfth floor. When did Schmidt enter the suite?"

"The floor waiter will report when there is anything to report," Roy said. "See!" he added, pointing to his expert over by a proud battery of radios and powerful transmitters who was receiving a message by means of a humble transceiver. It came from the twelfth floor. A visitor in a cream-colored suit, dark-haired, had been admitted to 12A eight minutes ago. He was just leaving now.

"The old shell game," Renwick said softly.

Claudel and Roy exchanged puzzled glances.

"He stayed just long enough for an exchange of suit and tie, an adjustment in make-up if needed." Renwick was on his feet, halfway to the door. "Let's move! Come on, you two, come on!" He left.

Claudel recovered, followed quickly.

"I'll warn the elevators," Roy said and began trying to contact their operators.

Renwick's run through a startled accounting department brought him into a short stretch of narrow hall. He checked his pace to a brisk walk as he entered the hotel lobby. A bank of four elevators faced him: two doors open, waiting for customers; one door closed, its indicator showing an ascent; the last door, also closed, its indicator beginning its descent from the upper floors.

Renwick nodded to Claudel, who had joined him, looked around for one of Roy's agents. Yes, there was the Mercedes' driver, trying to appear inconspicuous.

Claudel said, "I see Lavji arriving—he looks a very happy man. Promotion assured."

"Does he see us?"

"Yes."

"Good." So had Roy's driver. He folded his newspaper and walked slowly forward. "Keep your eyes on that elevator," Renwick told him. "Look for a cream-colored suit." And then Renwick stared at the indicator. "It has stopped." Stopped at the second floor.

"Not for long," Claudel said as the elevator started down again.

It reached the lobby. Its doors slid open. Several people emerged. Nine altogether. And not one light-colored suit among them.

"Goddamn it—" began Renwick. Then to Roy's agent, "Where's the staircase?"

"The main staircase or the fire staircase?"

"Where are they?" Renwick's voice was urgent.

"There—near the hotel desk—that's the main staircase. The fire exit..." He was pointing now to the rear of the lobby, close to the arcade, where a handsome door had a small orange light glowing overhead. "There are other fire exits, too," he said helpfully. "In all quarters of this building..."

"Any of them near these elevators?" Renwick cut in.

"That one!" He pointed again to the orange light.

Quickly, Renwick said to Claudel, "Take the front entrance. Lavji, too. I'll watch the arcade with helpful Harry. Keep in touch, Pierre." He had pulled out his mini-transceiver, small enough to be concealed in his hand: not much range but good enough for the lobby's long stretch. Pierre nodded, moved off with his transceiver ready.

Renwick signed to Roy's driver to follow, left for the lobby's exit to the arcade. The bar and restaurants lay that way, each with an entrance from the lobby, each with its door onto the arcade's covered walk. Theo would have plenty of choices for an escape if he used the fire stairs. Renwick kept his eyes on that door with the subdued orange light, expecting it to open any moment. Wish to God I had my Biretta, he thought: a courtesy to Roy, who had forbidden the carrying of any gun in crowded places; Renwick's role was to identify Theo and leave Roy's men to deal with him.

Renwick glanced around for his backup; but the man wasn't following. He was explaining everything to Roy, who had just appeared. For God's sake, thought Renwick—and then froze. Beyond where Roy was standing, the main staircase swept down into the lobby, its balustrades banked by flowers. A man in an ice-cream suit was descending at a leisurely pace, his shoulders visible, his Panama hat being donned over his dark hair as he prepared to step down into the lobby and join the flow of people.

Renwick swung around, retraced his steps, resisted breaking into a run: haste would attract Theo's attention—he had been studying the lobby, gauging its safety in his measured progress downstairs. You blasted fool, you damned idiot, Renwick told himself: you were wrong, you were wrong—he's going to stroll out by the front entrance into a nice dark night. But why? Not just because of a grand exit—not Theo: he'd take the surest way to certain escape. Through a crowded lobby where he couldn't hurry? Then Renwick guessed the answer. As he reached Roy, saying quickly, "He is in the lobby, just passing the hotel desk," he raised his transceiver and pressed its signal for Claudel's attention. "Pierre—he is taking the main entrance. Schmidt's car and driver—they could be waiting at the front steps. Best get him there—away from the lobby. Check outside. Take Lavji and whoever is with him."

"Will do. He's now in view—partially. Just glimpsed him—walking slowly—using a cane. We'll move out ahead of him."

A cane... "Look out, Pierre! Warn Lavji! That cane could be dangerous."

Slight pause. *"That* kind of walking stick?" Pierre asked with an attempt at nonchalance.

"We'll be close on his heels." Renwick signed off, looked at Roy. "We can risk hurrying. Theo will be keeping his eyes on the entrance."

Roy, without a sign that he objected to having his men ordered around by anyone but himself, fell into quick step with Renwick, his driver following closely.

"A cane?" Roy asked, his eyes searching past the islands of ornamental trees and clusters of people. "Lavji is trained to deal with that. No, I don't think it's too dangerous a weapon. Look—there he is!" Roy had caught sight of the cream-colored suit and the Panama hat. Theo had joined a small group of people: two more light suits beside him—almost indistinguishable from Theo's. There was also another Panama hat visible, but below it was a gray suit. "He merges well. A clever man," Roy said.

"And cautious." Renwick's hand grasped Roy's arm, slow-

ing their rapid pace. Theo's group had drifted away from him
to the porter's desk, and so now he had drawn close to a
decorative tree, appeared to be studying the flowers around
its base as he looked back along the lobby. Renwick's face
was averted. He seemed to be deep in conversation with Roy,
who kept a smile on his lips and his eyes now entirely on
Renwick.

Renwick was asking, "How many men with Lavji?"

"Two." Roy's smile widened. "Enough to take care of that
very dangerous cane."

"It's lethal. As lethal as that fountain pen James Kiley
used."

The smile was gone. "You are sure?"

"Why is he carrying it? Schmidt didn't."

"He has started moving again," Roy said.

They quickened their pace, pressed through the last fringe
of people standing just inside the entrance. Theo was already
outside.

He was waiting on the steps, looking for his car, speaking
angrily to the puzzled doorman. "It should have been here.
Where is it? A black Lancia—"

"There it is now, sir!" It came slowly out of the darkness,
reached the brilliant lights of the hotel's entrance.

Theo brushed the doorman aside and went ahead of him
down the steps, quickly reached the car. The driver was not
in uniform. Two men were in the rear seat, opening the door,
coming out at him. He backed two steps, turned as he heard
footsteps behind him, gripped his cane. He saw an Indian,
tall, immaculately dressed, and with him a younger man,
European or American, of medium height, watchful, alert.
Theo stared.

"Yes, Theo," the American said, "I am Renwick."

Theo's cane was raised. His eyes flickered toward the trees
and flower beds on his right, gently illuminated, partly shadowed.

Roy said, "Otto Remp, I am placing you under arrest for
extradition to—"

Theo moved, a sudden dash toward the trees, lunging at
Renwick as he passed. Renwick caught the cane, deflecting
its aim, wrenched it free from Theo's grip. Theo tried to run
on, but Claudel and Lavji had closed in, grasped his arms
and forced them behind his back. Deftly, Lavji handcuffed
his wrist to Theo's.

Roy, his Oxford English still more noticeable, said, "Otto Remp, I am placing you under arrest for extradition to West Germany. You will now be taken to police headquarters, where you will be questioned. That may delay your extradition for a few days." His voice became cold, his eyes hard. "But we, too, as well as West Germany, have questions to ask you about certain projects you are planning." Roy nodded to Lavji, and Theo was led to the car. His face was composed. Not one protest, not one comment. An old hand, thought Renwick, a real professional.

Claudel said, "Here, Bob, let me hold that piece of evidence." He tried to take the walking stick from Renwick's fingers, found it was too tightly gripped. Renwick relaxed, attempted a laugh, slowly released his grasp. Damn me, he thought, noticing a tremble in his hand, and stuck it deep into his pocket.

Roy eyed the cane with distaste. "Leave it in my office— you will have a report to send to London. I shall join you there. At nine o'clock." He looked toward the Lancia. "I am taking that one in myself. A tricky customer." Roy shook his head. "Canes and fountain pens that can kill and—"

"I forgot," Renwick said. "This belonged to Shawfield. He had it with him today—at Falkland Road."

Roy took the small cyanide pistol. It was similar to the empty one that had been found on James Kiley. It could be a useful piece of evidence—destroy Kiley's protest that it was only a fountain pen. "Is this one loaded?"

"Yes. He didn't manage a shot."

Roy pocketed the imitation pen gingerly. "And you've been carrying it around?" he asked with marked disapproval.

"I forgot," Renwick said again, and smiled.

Roy studied him, decided to forget this lapse of memory. "We talk too long. I must leave—"

"The longer we talk," Renwick suggested, "the more Theo will worry. And there is a little information you could use. He has many names. But you could shake him by dropping his real one—Herman Kroll, of East Germany."

"Herman Kroll," repeated Roy. "An East German?"

"KGB-trained. He arranged his own accidental death, came back into the world as a new man. He thinks Herman Kroll's file is closed, if not forgotten."

"A little name-dropping? Yes, that is always useful."

"Also a little word dropped into Theo's ear—about the kind of questions he will be facing."

"Concerning his future projects here in India? Yes, he has several—why else did Kiley and Shawfield have secret meetings with certain Communist students?"

"Mention Washington, too. I have a strong feeling that's a major project. Oh, just a feeling—but he was sending James Kiley there on a special mission."

"What mission?"

"That is what we would like to uncover."

Roy was thoughtful. "He will not talk, that man."

"No. But if he believes we know about this project—he will send out word from prison by way of his lawyer. Perhaps the project would be postponed—until we are all assuming it has been canceled. Theo's people don't act unless they have a good chance of success."

"If this project were postponed, then you might uncover it?" Roy asked slowly.

"We'd make a pretty good try. But we need time."

"You don't think the project could be canceled altogether?"

Renwick shook his head. "There's been too much preparation, too much careful planning."

Roy nodded. Thoughtfully, he turned away.

As the car moved off, Claudel asked, "Will it work? Will Theo believe that his Washington project is blown?"

"A few of his other plans have disintegrated recently. He's shaken." The attempted flight from Bombay was proof of that. "Let's walk a little—ten minutes of fresh air to clear our minds." Renwick chose the path that led into the garden. Soft perfumes stirred by the night, soft lights bringing out the bright pinks and purples of the flowers. The spaced trees were smooth-barked, as light and graceful as ballet dancers with the lift and droop of their arms.

Claudel was thinking of Theo. "You were expecting him to bolt."

"I was watching his eyes." Renwick tried to make a joke of that. "Always notice the front wheels of an approaching car, then you'll know when to dodge."

"A clever effort. He couldn't escape. He knew it, but he made it look like a real attempt. When he pointed that cane, it seemed as if he was just fending you off—a natural movement." And who would have known what caused Bob's death if he hadn't warned us the cane was a weapon? "How long does this take to kill?" Claudel held up the walking stick.

"Depends what is used. The Bulgarian method was a matter of four days and a raging fever. The one used against Jake Crefeld—" Renwick paused, said abruptly, "Paralysis. Death in thirty minutes. And for God's sake, Pierre, stop brandishing that damned thing around."

"Sorry, sorry."

Renwick calmed his voice. "Let's see if it was loaded." He took the cane, advanced near a floodlight. Then he examined the handle and found a small button that could be released sideways. He took aim at the tree beside him, pressed the button. There was no sound. Only an indent so small that Claudel had to use his cigarette lighter, holding it close to the smooth bark before they could see a pinhead hole. "I guess it was," said Renwick.

"Roy won't like missing the demonstration."

"Better that than having Roy play around with it and shooting himself in the foot."

"Risky business we're in," Claudel said with a wide grin. *And I might have shot myself in the foot,* he was thinking as he remembered the casual way he had handled that cane. "Time you got out of it, Bob—out of field work at least. Why not? You're a split personality. You've got ideas and you put them to work: that's one part of you. The other is that you hate being stuck in an office: you want to see what the big bad world is doing."

"And it's doing plenty."

"Well, fight it with ideas. You've got them, Bob."

"And sit at a desk, signing memos?"

"You don't have to sit at a desk. Sit in an armchair with a telephone on the floor beside you, prop your feet up, take a clipboard with paper and pencil, and let the little secretaries sign the memos. Ideas and plans come just as easily that way. You'll have to rise now and again, of course, to study maps, or go into the hush-hush room to see how your boys in the field are coming along." *At least,* Claudel thought, *I've got him laughing. But his luck can't run forever, and he knows it. It must have been hell for him tonight, waiting for that bloody cane to come within a few inches of his body, a replay of what nearly happened before.*

"I'm trying to imagine an antiseptic office in Merriman's with a chaise longue for the weary brain," Renwick said. "You forgot the pink and purple velvet cushions, Pierre."

"I'm serious. I'm also serious about something else. Why
don't you marry the girl? You would if you'd stay in your
think tank in London. People who work there don't leave
young widows behind."

Renwick said nothing.

"If you don't marry her, I will."

Renwick halted, looked at Claudel.

"I mean that. I've meant everything I've said." Claudel's
usual bright smile returned. "Now, come on—let's make Gilman happy."

Their report to London was barely ended when the telephone rang in Roy's office. Renwick answered it. It was Roy
himself. "Get the scrambler working," he said.

The untalkative communications expert obliged. "Something important," Renwick told Claudel and brought him over
to the desk to listen, too. "Ready," he said to Roy.

"He killed himself."

"What?"

"He killed himself."

"How? Where?"

"In the car. He had one hand free. He was fingering his
tie, pulled off one of his shirt buttons, bit into it. One minute—
less—that was all."

"Why?" asked Renwick.

"Difficult to say. He was silent, didn't seem worried when
I mentioned he would have to answer many questions. Just
sat with a small smile on his lips. And so I dropped the name
Herman Kroll, and he stopped smiling. But he was still silent—even when I mentioned his Washington project and
said he would have to answer more questions about that. And
then—suddenly—as quick as a snap of the fingers—he bit
into the poison. Cyanide." Roy paused. "There will be inquiries about this. My critics will be delighted."

"I don't think so," Renwick said quickly. "Not when they
hear you saved Bombay from a new tourist agency that was
geared to make travel arrangements for your terrorists—and
supply them with expense money under the counter. That
should shut up any of your critics. Besides, what have they
done for Bombay?"

Roy's gloom gave way to laughter. "You have a point there,
Robert. I'll see you tomorrow before you leave—won't manage

an office visit tonight." He paused, added, "Too bad about Theo: he told us nothing. Not that I expected it. Ah, well— good night. It has been quite a day, wouldn't you say?"

Renwick replaced the receiver. Theo, he was thinking, told us a great deal. Something was most definitely planned against Washington. Something so big, so important that he wouldn't risk being questioned. Surely he didn't expect Roy's people to use the brutal methods that he knew from his early KGB days—God knows, Theo had enough practice. But he did know what clever interrogation can do with hypnosis or truth serum or the new wonder drugs that can drag the facts out of any man. Questions about this Washington project? He made sure they'd have no answers. Not from him.

Claudel asked, "Are you thinking what I'm thinking, Bob?"

"Probably. Let's discuss it on our way home." A strange slip: home? A small hotel run by a retired British sergeant and his Pondicherry wife? But Nina was there. Safe in his room. That was home enough for him.

CHAPTER
27

The guard was still posted at the end of Renwick's corridor, and he was staying there—that was obvious by the way he smiled politely, vaguely, when Renwick suggested the alert was over—until Roy himself countermanded the order. The Australians' room had its door wide open: Mahoney sat just inside, with a clear view of Renwick's room opposite, while Benson had been doing his stint of watching down in the Back Bay Hotel's lobby among its wicker chairs and potted palms.

Mahoney rose briskly. He looked at Renwick and said, "So it's going well?"

"Two arrested. One dead: Herr Otto Remp—Theo, no less."

"Who got him?" Mahoney lowered his voice to a whisper as Renwick had done.

"Himself."

"Well, I'll be—"

"How's everything here?" Renwick glanced over at his room. The door was slightly ajar.

"She wanted it that way," Mahoney said quickly, "so that I could hear her. She slept. Then she woke, and I had Madame smuggle up a tray of food. She didn't eat much, but she's recovering rapidly. What happened?"

"Claudel will brief you. He's in the dining room. Benson is joining him. Why don't you?"

"You don't expect trouble?"

"Not here. The Bombay assignment is over."

"So we push off—"

"Claudel will brief you," Renwick repeated. "See you later. And thanks, Mahoney."

"Anytime." Mahoney pulled his room door shut. "It was a pleasure," he said and left for one of Madame's hot curries.

Renwick hesitated. Then he knocked lightly to warn Nina if she were awake. There was no answer. He pushed the door quietly open, closed and locked it behind him. She was asleep.

He went over to the bed, looked down at her. She had been

306

reading a newspaper, its pages slipping over the sheet that barely covered her. Her hair lay loose and tangled on the pillow, her cheeks were flushed like a child's, her arms stretched out for coolness. Smooth firm arms, smooth and firm as her shoulders and breasts.

He folded the pages of newspaper, placed them on the table beside her. Carefully, he drew up the sheet, left her shoulders bare for the breath of air that came through the heavily screened window. He didn't switch off the light—let her see him when she opened her eyes and not have a wild moment of panic in a strange dark room. Then he dropped into the high-backed wicker chair facing the bed, pulled off his tie, pulled off his jacket, and let them fall beside him. He listened to the soft whirring of the fan overhead, to the gentle play of water from the small fountain in the courtyard below. Peace. Peace and thankfulness.

He opened his eyes. Nina was propped up in bed, watching him with a smile. "How long have I been asleep?" Incredulous, he looked at his watch. Almost eleven o'clock.

"I wouldn't know—I only woke up five minutes ago."

"Why didn't you wake me, too?"

"I hadn't the heart to do that. You were so completely out of this world."

With one hand she pushed back the sweep of hair that had fallen over her brow; with the other, she clasped the bed sheet over her breast. Above the white linen, her sun-tanned skin was the color of golden honey. Renwick steadied his voice. "I was," he admitted. "Just slipped away without knowing it." And that's a first, he thought: I've never fallen asleep in a chair with someone else in the room; my guard was really down. "Fine watchdog I make," he added with a smile. "Just as well the door was locked."

"I know." She was laughing now. "I went to look—make sure we were safe." Then the laughter vanished. Blue eyes were anxious, questioning. "Are we?"

"Yes." He was still watching her.

"Then you—your business is all over?"

"In Bombay, yes." He rose, took the few steps that separated them; then he halted, unsure, uncertain, as she looked abruptly away.

"I have so many things to ask." About Madge and the others, and Jim Kiley. And Tony Shawfield...Her voice became low, strained. "I thought he was going to leave me there.

In that street. He nearly did. As a lesson. Educational, he said."

"Don't, Nina. That's all over." All over, Renwick told himself, too. He crushed down the memory: his hand outstretched, Nina turning away.

"But it *was* educational. In this room when I was awake, I lay and thought and—" She broke off. Then her voice strengthened. "I know more about myself than I ever did. I know that I—" She raised her head, let her eyes meet his. I know that I love you, she ended silently. "Oh, Bob—" She held out her hand.

He grasped it, took both her hands, held them tightly, felt her draw him nearer. His arms went around her, and he kissed her mouth, her eyes, her cheeks, her slender neck, her mouth again—long deep kisses lingering on yielding lips. Her arms encircled him, pressed him closer.

Nothing else matters, he thought, nothing else in this whole wide world.

He had showered and shaved, pulled on trousers and shirt to let him bring in the two breakfast trays he had ordered before he woke Nina with gentle kisses to draw her slowly out of sleep. "Yes, it's early, I know," he told her, "but there's some business to be finished before we leave." Pleasant business: thanks and good-bye to Roy; last messages from Merriman's to be collected; warm clothes to be bought for Nina to let her face an October arrival in London. "Now come and have breakfast. It's waiting and ready."

"When do we leave?" She slipped out of bed, headed for the little bathroom, as lithe and graceful and unconcerned as a nymph on a Greek frieze.

"Today if possible." There was an Air India direct flight at nine o'clock this evening. Before, he hoped, any of Theo's agents in Bombay came out of shock, tried to put things together. "We'll go to London first. I have some things to clear up at the office." Mostly a matter of sending inquiries to Washington, of trying to find any possible clues to the question that kept nagging him: why was Francis O'Connell so important to Theo's plan? O'Connell's job was not so sensitive as all that. If he had been in defense or intelligence, that would have made sense. But for Theo—and Kiley—to have taken such infinite trouble to reach O'Connell, that was a real puzzler. Or was Kiley to have been a long-term infiltrator, a mole burrowing his way into O'Connell's circle? That didn't feel right to Renwick: Theo's sudden suicide didn't match with something that could wait for a year, two years, before it was put into effect. No, thought Renwick, that doesn't feel right: there's a reason beyond anything I can latch onto. I'm just stuck with this goddamned hunch—no more than that, but it's biting deep.

Nina had washed the sleep out of her eyes and was now combing her hair as she came back into the bedroom. She watched him curiously. So serious now—how many men is he? It would take a lifetime with him to find out. A long long life, she prayed, and then laughed with the joy of it. But did Bob feel that way? The thought ended her laughter.

He noticed her change of mood. "What is it, honey?"

"I hate leaving so soon." She looked around the little room. "I wish we could stay here forever."

"Leaving it won't end what we've begun," he said softly, and kissed her. "I'm not going to let you get away from me, ever. Ever," he repeated, and kissed her again. "So don't try."

The laughter was back in her eyes. "Or else you'll put all of Merriman's bloodhounds on my trail?"

For a moment he was startled, and then amused. "That's one job I'll do entirely by myself. And I'd find you," he warned her. "More easily than I found you this time." He kissed her again, ruffled her newly combed hair. "Now come and have breakfast before the omelette turns to cotton wool."

"Omelette?" Nina picked up a sheet from the bed to wrap around her, sarong style. "However did you manage that?"

"Madame did. She's Pondicherry French."

Nina went over to the table at the window and looked at the heaped little dishes that almost overflowed two trays.

"Parathas," Renwick identified the whole-wheat bread. "And these are *jalebis*—doughnuts to you." The omelettes, flecked with parsley, had been well covered and still looked edible. "I don't know what the rest of this stuff is. But we'll soon find out."

"Actually," Nina said, "I'm famished. I could even eat cotton wool—if I had some of that jam over it. What is it? Marmalade, for heaven's sake!"

"That's the ex-sergeant's touch of home."

"I really didn't eat much yesterday. Did you?"

"Not much." Nothing since yesterday's breakfast, in fact. Quite a day, as Roy had said. Quite a day.

"Now tell me about Madge," Nina reminded him as the last plate was emptied. "Where is she? And the others? Did Mr. Roy get them out of that place, put them up at his hotel? He owns one, doesn't he?"

"I shouldn't be surprised." Renwick poured the last of the coffee into Nina's cup.

"Not fair," she said, and emptied half of the coffee back into his cup. "Madge must have been terribly upset when she heard about Tony Shawfield's arrest."

"She hasn't heard. None of them have. They left before the police arrived at the house. That was just about the time I was bringing you here."

"But where—" Nina began in horror.

"We don't know. All that Roy could learn was that the five of them drove away in a Fiat—one of the two cars that brought you into Bombay yesterday. The police are searching. Perhaps we'll hear something this afternoon."

"And if we don't, Bob? If they have left Bombay?"

"They'd need money for that. Have they any?"

She shook her head. "I think they've spent most of what they had." Drugs, those damnable drugs, she thought. "Shawfield was going to buy their fares." No, Shawfield had never returned. "Jim Kiley always had a lot of extra money after we arrived at certain places. That's the first thing he did: cash checks or something. Was Jim at the house? He might have sent them all away. But why?"

Because of orders, Renwick thought: new orders, obviously. "He could have. He was there." Renwick hesitated, then said, "The police came to arrest him. He escaped, left a dead policeman behind him, and was caught later. He may face a murder charge here—if the weapon he used can be proven to have killed—but in any case, after that, he will be extradited to West Germany. Like Shawfield." Renwick caught her hand. "I'm sorry, Nina. But you'd learn the truth sometime."

"Extradited—for what? For spying? Was that what they were—agents?" She remembered a courtyard near Tabriz, the voices in German, and Pierre listening. . . . "Against whom?" Her hand had tightened under his. Her voice had risen.

"Against most of the world," Renwick said very quietly. "They are terrorists. They are being extradited for bombings, arson, murders, and a brutal kidnapping." There it's out, he thought unhappily. He raised her hand to his lips.

For a long moment she stared at him. "I could believe that of Tony," she said slowly. "But Jim?...Oh, I knew he could lie—he had an explanation for everything. Yet, I had to like him. He was kind. He looked after me—he really did. He was thoughtful. Bob—he was *gentle*." Except once, she remembered. But that was my fault perhaps—I was uncertain, indefinite. "Oh, I don't know," she said helplessly. "It's just hard to believe."

"Have you ever heard of the People's Revolutionary Force for Direct Action?"

"But of course! It was in all the newspapers last winter. They kidnapped and killed—"

"Kiley is Erik. Shawfield is Marco. Erik was the leader. Marco was second-in-command."

"Oh, no!" She turned to point at the bedside table where yesterday's folded newspaper still lay: Ilsa Schlott, known as Greta; once a member of Direct Action; connected with Erik and Marco—terrorists; a green camper delivered in a Camberwell garage. "Ilsa Schlott invited Madge and me to a concert," Nina began. Then Ilsa had backed out at the last moment. And her seat was taken by James Kiley. "That's how we met," she said. "At that concert." Her eyes met his, her lips trembled. "Oh, God!" she said. "What an idiot! What a complete and total idiot I was."

He caught her around her waist, pulled her onto his lap, held her close. "We have all been idiots at one time or other. It's the human condition, my love." He smoothed back her hair.

"Not you, Bob. Never you."

"Oh, yes, me, too." He kissed her ear.

"When?"

He hesitated. "For months on end, my sweet. Not just for a few weeks."

"Was she beautiful?" Nina tried to laugh.

Well, he was into it now, right up to his neck. "Yes." When Nina said nothing more, he went on. "She was a widow, lived in Brussels, ran an interior decorating business."

"She sounds entrancing," Nina said with a most definite lack of enthusiasm.

Renwick threw back his head and laughed.

In spite of herself, Nina joined in.

"As entrancing, it turned out, as a black widow spider," he said and drew Nina closer. My God, I'm actually laughing about Thérèse Colbert, he thought; talking about her and laughing. "You're good for me, darling—good in every way." His hand slid over her thigh, gently caressed her. "Nina— will you marry me?"

Her face turned toward him. Her eyes searched his.

"Will you?" His voice had tightened.

"Yes and yes." She threw her arms around him. "And yes."

"Look, darling," Renwick said, "it's almost ten. We'd better get organized around her." Quickly he began dressing again.

"Oh, Bob—"

"I mean it, love. There are a few things I *must* do before we leave. I want you to stay here—"

"But why?"

"Because you'll be safe. There's a plain-clothes policeman still on duty at the end of the corridor. I don't want you to be seen walking through Bombay."

"I thought the danger was over," she said slowly. "I mean, Tony Shawfield isn't around any more. Or Jim Kiley."

"I'm just making sure there's no more danger. I'm taking no chances with you. Trust me, honey."

She nodded. "I'll shower and wash my hair and wait for you." Then she remembered her muslin dress, hanging on the back of the bathroom door, and thought of London in late October. "And you know what? I haven't a thing to wear." That sent her into a fit of giggles. I'm already sounding like a married woman, she thought.

"You'd be a smashing success at Heathrow. But I'll get something for you—a skirt, shirt, sweater, coat? In shades of blue, if possible. It won't take long." Roy's gift shop had a variety of departments and helpful assistants.

"But the fit—" she began doubtfully.

"I've got your sizes—approximately." He grinned and added, "Don't worry about the styles. Claudel has a sharp eye for women's fashions."

"Claudel?"

"Pierre."

"Then he *is* French?"

"As Parisian as they come."

"Is he an engineer, too?"

"Sure."

"And these nice Australians? Or are they Australians?"

He evaded the last question by answering the first. "They are pretty good engineers." Mahoney knew a lot about planes; Benson had once helped design submarines.

"Are they all flying back to London with us?"

"Claudel will be there. But separate. So don't speak to him, or even look at him."

"Not the tiniest smile?" she teased. "Oh, Bob—before you go—would you help me put a call through to Father? I really should let him know."

"Yes, I suppose so." Not through Merriman's—Gilman wouldn't want the firm to be connected openly with Francis O'Connell. Not through A. K. Roy's gift shop, either: the Washington problem wasn't in Roy's field of inquiry; there had been no need to spread Renwick's interest—the less known about it, the better.

She noted his hesitation. "Would it be so difficult?"

"We may have to place a call, wait a little. And there's the time element, too. A rough guess—" He calculated quickly, checked his watch again. "I'd say it is now half past eleven yesterday in Washington." Phone from this room? Well, we should be out of here before any interested party starts trying to trace any calls. "Where would we find your father near midnight? I've got his new number somewhere." Renwick went over to the chair that held his jacket, found his small book of innocuous addresses. "They've just moved into a house in Georgetown."

A new house? What was wrong with the old one? And how does Bob know its number—has he been in touch with Father? Yes, it was Father who sent him chasing after me. Her eyes lost their smile, her lips were strained. "He may be at home, perhaps even gone to bed. Oh, it doesn't matter. And you haven't got the time to waste on a call. Let's forget it."

Watching her, Renwick made up his mind. He hadn't the time, but he couldn't leave her looking dejected like this. "We can try," he said, picking up the phone, enlisting the help of the ex-sergeant. No problem at all, he was firmly assured: he'd have a Washington line in a matter of minutes. "Now we wait," he told Nina as he replaced the receiver. He looked at it thoughtfully. "Dammit, my brains are really scrambled this morning. Look, honey—if your father wants to know how you found his new number, just tell him you had telephone-operator assistance."

"Didn't he give you that number?"

"No." Renwick looked at her in surprise.

"He didn't send you?"

"He doesn't even know I am here. No one sent me looking for you. No one." My God, he thought, if she only knew how everyone kept prodding me to think of that damned camper first and put her second. He lightened his voice. "There wasn't any camper in Lesbos, was there? Or in Istanbul when we met?"

"You arranged all that?" Her eyes brightened.

"You bet I did. All I wanted was to get you out—away from Kiley and Shawfield."

"And I wouldn't listen."

"You've got a pretty strong mind of your own."

"I'm sorry—"

"No, no. I love it. It may be hell at times—have you any idea what you put me through?—but you've got spirit, darling. Did you think I just adored you for the way you look? Oh, there's that, too." He thought of last night, this morning. "Very much so," he said, and watched a blush spread delicately over her cheeks. "God, you are the most beautiful girl. How many men have wanted to marry you, Nina?"

"I never said yes to any of them. And I never—" She halted in embarrassment. "You're the first man I've ever been—who's ever made real love to me."

"And you're the first woman I've ever asked to marry me."

"The very first?" Her heart lifted.

"The first. And the last."

"Oh, darling—"

The telephone rang. "We've got through." He handed her the receiver. "Keep me out of it."

Of course, she thought, no one knows he is here. With a smile in her voice, she began speaking. "Daddy? Yes, it's me. In Bombay . . . Why yes, I'm fine—wonderful, in fact. . . . Look, I can't talk long—this call is costing the earth. But I'll be home soon. Next week probably. I'll phone you from London, let you know." Then she looked over at Renwick, gestured helplessly as the phone call went on and on. "Please, Beryl—don't worry about my new room. . . . Yes, I'll be home next week, but don't worry. . . . I'm sure it will be beautiful. . . . Yes, yes . . . My love to both of you." With a decided bang, Nina put down the receiver.

Renwick tightened the knot on his tie, reached for his jacket.

"She means well. But it's really comic. Father doesn't know a thing about anything: he is so glad I had such a splendid time, but wishes I had sent more than one postcard. I sent four, actually; and two letters. Then Beryl cut in. All she's worried about is that my new room isn't ready, but Madame Colbert will have the painters start on it at once."

Renwick had been drawing on his jacket. He stopped for a moment, then jammed his arm into one sleeve. "Colbert?"

"Some interior decorator—French or Belgian, Beryl said, with marvelous taste. A pink-and-blue bedroom for me. That's where I ended the phone call."

So James Kiley hadn't won entry to the O'Connell household, but Thérèse Colbert had. Renwick settled his jacket comfortably on his shoulders, eased his shirt collar slightly. "I'll be back by one o'clock. No—" he looked at his watch— "make that one-thirty." I'll have to warn Gilman to get in touch with Washington immediately and prepare the way for some FBI collaboration: Colbert to be put under discreet but complete surveillance. And what is security like at O'Connell's home? Check workmen, all visitors. Any bugs installed? Any phone taps? Gilman can make a start on that before I reach Washington—without delay, critical. Yes, he thought, critical. "No good-bye kiss, Miss O'Connell?"

She came running over to him. He caught her, kissed her, said, "We'll have lunch here in the room." And four hours at least to wait before leaving for the airport. "Lock the door behind me. Don't let anyone enter."

"I'll be safe. Don't worry about me."

"I always will," he said softly. "My pleasure."

"Bob—" She looked around the edge of the door as he stepped into the corridor, keeping her body out of sight from the rooms opposite. "About Madge—"

"I'll find out what I can." He looked at her anxious face, kissed the tip of her nose, started her smiling as he pulled the door shut, waited until he heard the lock turn. Then briskly he took the stairs—quicker than the elevator—and ran lightly down. For a man who had had less than a couple of hours' sleep, he felt wonderful.

CHAPTER
28

It was the last day of October. Nina and Renwick had spent the four nights since their arrival from Bombay in the Gilmans' London flat. By day, Nina—with Gemma Gilman's help—had rescued her trunk from storage and selected some suitable clothes for November in Washington. The rest went back into the trunk for further storage until she and Bob returned to live in London. When that would be, she didn't know: Bob had said simply, "It depends." Depends on what? She didn't ask: she was learning quickly.

Gemma was a help there, too. "Why ask questions if they can't be answered?" she said in her quiet, competent way. A pretty woman of forty—even that age didn't disturb her—with dark hair and eyes, and almost as tall as her husband's six feet.

"Doesn't Ron tell you anything about his work?"

"Whatever can be told, sweetie." Gemma smiled encouragingly at Nina's thoughtful face.

"You must trust him a lot."

"Why not? He trusts me."

"I know. He must," Nina said quickly. The Gilmans were happy; and close friends, too. That was evident as soon as you saw them together. "It's just that truth is part of trust, isn't it? I mean—" She halted, sighed helplessly.

"Bob will give you the truth if it can be given. If not—then he won't answer you at all. That's your signal to ask no more questions. Inquisitive people aren't really very attractive, are they?"

"No," Nina agreed with a smile.

"Truth and confidences," Gemma mused. "Oh, you'll have plenty of them, don't worry. Provided you don't gossip. And you don't. It's a very private kind of life, actually. Rather nice, too: it draws you closely together. It has to. Or else it would all fly apart."

A very private kind of life... "A lot must depend on the woman, doesn't it?" Nina asked hesitantly.

"Of course. And very flattering it is," Gemma said cheerfully. "Now, what about that call to your father to let him know you'll be home tomorrow? It's eight in the morning, Washington time. You'll catch him just before he leaves for the office."

"Yes. I'd better tell him. But this has to be a collect call, Gemma. Really, it must! If Beryl comes on the phone, she'll talk and talk."

"No telephone sense at all?"

"Not much. She's never had to worry about money. Oh, well—" Nina's smile was real—"Beryl keeps Father happy— he doesn't even have time to worry much about me any more. And that, frankly, is a relief. I'm free and can choose my own life." And have Bob to worry about me, she thought. "A very private kind of life," she added softly, and went into the hall to telephone.

Renwick and Gilman spent a long day at J. P. Merriman & Co. collecting last reports and pieces of information about Francis O'Connell's house, habits, and job in Washington. There wasn't much to establish any kind of purpose behind Thérèse Colbert's interest in O'Connell.

"Let's see what we've got," Renwick said at last. They were seated, facing each other, at Gilman's desk. Renwick's office would be ready for his return to London, with the antiseptic furnishings removed: all he wanted was one large table with one telephone, some maps on the wall, good lighting, a small safe, a radio for some music, and a leather armchair with a leg rest. (The file room was next door, the typist pool was at the end of the hall, the communications setup was within easy reach. What more did he need?) "Take it from the beginning, Ron."

"Washington listened to us and was receptive. They are studying Colbert carefully; she is now under close surveillance. So far, they've found nothing derogatory in her past. She arrived from Switzerland in July, had some helpful friends to establish her in Washington, where she has been a success—both socially and as an interior decorator."

"Nothing derogatory." Renwick shook his head. "Didn't Belgian security spread the word?"

"Seemingly not. Perhaps they couldn't find much against her. You didn't spread the word, either," Gilman reminded him.

"And let Theo know I was still functioning?" If I had been the one to pass the word to Belgian security, Theo's listening post would have picked that up. I'd have had more to worry about than getting Interintell working, Renwick thought. Still, that had been a door left unlocked—my fault, even with good reasons—and Thérèse Colbert had slipped through.

"You hadn't much choice," Gilman agreed. "Anyway, Colbert is moving around the best circles quite easily. They like her charm and her French accent. She has become Beryl O'Connell's friend as well as her adviser on colors and wallpapers. So far, her telephone conversations have been blameless. She doesn't take circuitous routes to appointments. She has had no meetings with anyone outside her own circle of acquaintances."

"During the last five days." Before then? When she wasn't under surveillance? Perhaps, thought Renwick, the warning about Colbert has gone out too late. "So she seems totally harmless. Yet we know she was working for the late Mr. Maartens, who worked for Theo. We know Kiley worked for Theo, and Kiley was heading for the O'Connell house. She headed for the O'Connell house, too. Were they to work together? Is she now adding his assignment to hers?"

"Is she capable of that? Could she carry out this assignment by herself?"

"If it's intricate, no. She'd need outside help. What's the security like at O'Connell's place?"

"He's against it. The Secret Service insisted on the usual two guards, but all he wants them to do is to drive him around. He can't conceive of anything happening to him right in his own home."

"Frankly, I don't think anyone will take a pot shot at him even in the streets or at his office. Kidnapping? I'd rule against it. It's not money that Theo was after. Top-secret papers to be stolen or photographed?"

"The FBI says he keeps them in the safe at his office. He's not known for breaking the rules. He brings no highly classified material home."

"And the FBI reports they found no bugs," Renwick said, frowning. They had sent in two men to check the telephones on Monday. Yesterday, they had had an agent appear as an inspector of all the new electrical wiring. "Nothing."

"A lot of workmen have been in and out of that house in the last six weeks. But no doubt they are being checked right now. I must say, Bob, Washington did take our warning seriously. I just hope..." Gilman sighed. "Well, it would be rather a sour joke on us, wouldn't it, if no warning was needed?"

"But it is."

Gilman said nothing.

"Kiley used Nina to be accepted by O'Connell." Renwick ran his hands through his hair, rose, walked over to the electric fire, stood staring down at it. "What if—" he paused— "what if Kiley was then going to use O'Connell?"

"Use him?" Gilman was suddenly interested. "For an introduction higher up? Could be, could very well be."

"Except," Renwick said, "that would have to be a long-term project. Kiley gets the entrance into high circles of government, but he'd need time to insinuate himself even with all his powers of persuasion. Theo didn't die to protect some project in the distant future. What's more, Kiley was trained as a terrorist, not as a diplomat."

"He could have been aiming at assassination."

Renwick nodded. "Use O'Connell to get him into some place where Kiley could get off one shot—" He stopped, reconsidered. "That could mean Kiley's death, too. I don't think he would be in favor of that," Renwick said with a brief smile. "He's a man with a mission: Direct Action. He was following Theo's plan because it would help the cause—his cause. His death wouldn't help it one bit. In fact, as its leader, he'd intend to stay alive."

"Hold it, hold it!" Gilman exclaimed. "You've got something there, Bob! He was following Theo's plan because it would help his cause—Direct Action. And what is that but anarchy?"

"Theo would have got more than he bargained for."

"Always the danger when you play along with terrorists."

"But," said Renwick, beginning to walk slowly around the room, his head bent, his hands in his pockets, "Theo might have been aiming at a temporary anarchy—just enough confusion and disaster to throw America into panic. The Western world, too. Make them helpless, unable to move if aggression took place—" He halted his pacing, stared at Gilman. There were three danger spots in this world right now, ripe for aggression. Last night, he and Gilman had discussed them at length and ruined a perfectly good chess game. First, turmoil; and then aggression; and propaganda to wrap it all up.

"Throw us into confusion and panic," Gilman repeated. "An attack on your White House—kill the President? Kiley was to use O'Connell in order to reach the President?"

Renwick thought quickly over the report they had received on O'Connell's duties beyond his daily office routine. Special advisory sessions at the White House—but others were present, too. Breakfast last week at the White House—but with others there, too. A National Security meeting last month—full attendance. "He never sees the President alone."

"Then," Gilman said, "Theo may have planned something bigger than we thought. What was he aiming for—the National Security Council?" It was intended as a joke.

"A full house," Renwick said slowly.

"Look—we might just be allowing ourselves to get carried away." That was always the danger with thinking out loud. But he still brooded over Renwick's wild and outrageous idea. "They couldn't possibly turn poor old O'Connell into some bomb. Wire him for an explosion?" He began to laugh, choked off his amusement. "Would it really be possible to have some explosive device on O'Connell without him knowing it? In his watch—in the heels of his shoes?"

"Nothing that would be powerful enough except to blow him to pieces. If he carried some reference book to back up any statement he wanted to make—"

"It would be examined by security, before he ever reached the council table."

"Yes. Any briefcase, too. He does carry a briefcase, doesn't he? Now that could pack a real blast."

"As you said, it would be opened and examined, wouldn't it?"

"I hope to God it would be." Dead end, thought Renwick. He stopped pacing around, dropped back into his chair. "Theo's target," he said softly. "Hidden. With extreme care and cunning."

"And how the devil do you hit a hidden target?"

"You can damn well think your way toward it. And then be ready—for one small glimpse. Just one quick sight, that's all we'll need."

"Perhaps a little pressure on Madame Colbert?" Gilman suggested.

"Yes. I think that's what we'll try. Shock tactics. They worked on Theo. Damn it all, Ron, we keep talking of that man as if he were still alive. Who's in charge of Colbert now,

I wonder? It could be Boris or Kolman or—what the hell. Let's call them the opposition."

"What kind of shock tactics on dear Thérèse?"

"Sudden confrontation. Inform her that I know she's one of their agents. That might shake her. But then, the opposition might try shaking me."

"How?"

"Blackmail. They must have taken photographs in her Brussels apartment. How else did Maartens' killer recognize me so quickly when he came at me with that damned walking stick?"

"Blackmail." Yes, that was always a possibility, thought Gilman. "What would be your reaction?"

"Publish and be damned."

"But now there's Nina."

Renwick said nothing.

"Would she stand by you?"

Still Renwick was silent.

Gilman studied his friend. "I'm sure she will, Bob." Then he rose quickly. "I think I'll get in touch with my friend A. K. Roy. We had a long chat yesterday. But there's something I'd like to ask him. Shan't be long."

"It's probably early in the morning Bombay time," Renwick reminded him.

"Then I'll be certain of reaching him at his home," Gilman said briskly and left Renwick to his own thoughts.

They weren't pleasant.

But I'll be damned if I'm taking myself off this case now. I've been with it since Vienna—uncovered that terrorist bank account—found it in Geneva, one and a half million dollars already paid out. And I traced them, even if they had been carefully laundered, to Düsseldorf and Herr Otto Remp. Then there was Essen, and Erik and Marco bowing in. And Otto Remp, once Herman Kroll—nicely dead in some helicopter accident, now Theo again. We got him; we got Erik and Marco. I'll be damned if I take myself off this case.

And Nina? I've told her about Brussels, thank God for that.... At least, the shock won't be so vicious if she finds photographs with an anonymous letter in the mail some morning. That's how Theo would have worked it: no press release, just a quiet threat using Nina.

Who is succeeding him? More important, who is in Washington directing Colbert? She has a control, possibly a resident well disguised in their embassy: the harmless chauffeur, the quiet press attaché. Well, if we move quickly enough, I'll nail Colbert and get her out of the picture. Who takes over for her, then? That could delay Theo's plan, set it back some weeks, some months, before a new operative could insinuate himself into O'Connell's household.

And whatever that plan is—Renwick began from the beginning again. Kiley, Nina, O'Connell. And from there? Renwick ended with the same deductions: O'Connell's importance was only as an intermediary, leading to—leading to what? "Just can't get my mind to take any other direction," he told Gilman when he returned. "About O'Connell," he added. Not about Nina. That was a torment that no thought could resolve. He loved her, would always love her. Nina? He could only hope and trust. "Did you have to haul friend Roy out of bed?"

"He didn't object. He's on top of the world. That was a big haul he pulled in—at Theo's suite. Theo was traveling light, remember? He, himself, was carrying only a new passport, an automatic, and a wad of money. All his baggage was to be taken out by his two men and that joker wearing Theo's white wig and mustache. Yes, quite a haul for Roy, a lot of valuable stuff there." Gilman paused, then added in his most offhand manner. "I'll leave for Bombay tomorrow morning."

Renwick said, "That's a quick decision, isn't it?"

"I'd like to see what Theo left behind—before it all gets listed and dispersed."

"Roy has no objections?"

"None whatsoever." In fact, the visit to Bombay had been Roy's suggestion. "Shan't stay around too long. Quick in, quick out. I'll be back here in three days—let's say by Sunday, November the fourth. Claudel will take any messages you send from Washington."

"I'd have liked to have had him with me."

"Better keep separate. You were in Bombay together."

"Who'll be my backup then?"

"Why not Tim MacEwan?"

"Mac?"

"He's in Ottawa at the moment. But he does know his way around Washington."

"He's good. But does he have any helpful contacts in Washington?"

"He has been working with the FBI. Gave them as much

as possible on the layout of Rancho San Carlos, the weapons, the drill, the faces and builds of the men. Neat sketches. He has the sharp eye for that kind of detail."

"That he has." Renwick grinned. "You should have seen him crawling on his belly, his face covered with antisun lotion, having his first close-up view of terrorists in training. Later that night..." Renwick's smile faded as he remembered Sal. "Well, we'll keep Dobermans out of Mac's way in Washington. Now what about getting back to your flat? I'll take a bus and walk the rest."

"It would be safe enough to give you a lift if you'll join me on the side street."

"No, thanks, Ron. I'd like to walk." He left first.

Gilman waited to make arrangements for his three-day absence. He, too, was thinking about Nina.

It was almost nine when Gilman reached home. "Bob is taking a walk," he told Nina, and kissed his wife. "Anything to eat, Gemma?"

"You haven't had dinner?"

"Not so far. A busy day. By the way, I'll have to leave tomorrow morning. I'll be home by Sunday."

"Did Bob have dinner?"

"No. Better make a double helping of sandwiches."

Nothing can be wrong, Nina thought: Ron isn't worried; his voice and smile are easy, natural. "I'll help," she offered.

"No need," Gemma told her. "Ronnie and I have a system. And no more than two people can crowd into our kitchen anyway. Open the door for Bob when he rings, won't you?"

The ring came soon. Renwick entered to be met with Nina's arms around him and a happy laugh. The best welcome a man could get, he thought as he tightened his grip around her waist and kissed her upturned face. They stood there in the small dark hall holding each other.

At last Gemma's voice from the sitting room called them back to reality. "The sandwiches are getting cold, Bob." She shook her head at her husband, who'd have left them alone for another ten minutes. "They can't stand there forever," she murmured.

"Didn't we?" he asked.

Gemma smiled. Two thin shirts and a lightweight suit, he had told her in the kitchen. For some place hot and humid, she guessed. She'd hear about it when Ronnie got back. Perhaps. Certainly this trip must be important, highly important. He was giving up *Così fan Tutte* tomorrow night, and he had been looking forward to it for weeks. "When do you leave?"

"Just after breakfast." He rose to his feet as Nina and Renwick came to join the picnic at the coffee table. He glanced at Renwick. All's well, he thought with relief: whatever he decided on that walk, all is well. Then they sat down and relaxed. It was a very merry party.

Gemma was talking about her morning with Nina—a visit to Harrods nearby for some last-minute shopping. "And when we got back, Nina called home."

"Collect," Nina said.

"Now I understand why. How long did that call last? Must have been ten, fifteen minutes." Gemma poured more beer for the men, another cup of tea for Nina and herself. "Beryl must be so accustomed to money that she never asks the cost of anything."

"Beryl," said Nina, "is filthy rich. But that isn't the reason Father married her. It isn't, Bob!"

"Okay, okay, honey. I didn't say a thing."

Gilman looked over at his wife. "Now wouldn't it be nice if you were filthy rich, darling?"

"Indeed it would be. I could have breakfast in bed—like Beryl. Was that why she talked endlessly? All cozily wrapped in a satin quilt?"

"Was your father there?" Renwick asked Nina.

"For two minutes. He was dashing out—a breakfast meeting. Yes, one of those. He was a little on edge, in fact definitely cross, until he realized it was me on the phone. Then he became normal, started arranging my arrival. But I told him not to worry: I was taking the same flight as a friend, so I would have company all the way."

Renwick looked at her, a smile spreading over his face.

Taking the same flight as a friend, Gilman noted. "Not bad, not bad at all," he said, exchanging a glance with Renwick.

"Then Beryl came on from the phone in their room." Nina was amused. "She seems to listen in, doesn't she?" It had happened in Bombay, too.

"What did she have to say?" Renwick asked. "Is your new bedroom ready? I hope it isn't."

"I'm afraid it is." And we'll be separated, Nina thought

"But Beryl hardly mentioned it. She was too busy persuading me that Father's bad temper had nothing to do with her."

"Probably couldn't find a cuff link, or his shoelace had snapped and there wasn't a spare one around. Nice picture: economics expert entering the White House tied together with string."

"Oh, Bob!" She laughed and shook her head. "It was his attaché case that spoiled his morning. It's his favorite, uses it all the time. I gave it to him for Christmas two years— Something wrong?"

"Not at all," Gilman said quickly. "Unless he had important papers in it. When was it stolen?"

"It wasn't. And his papers weren't in it—they were in his safe. It just got ruined."

"Ruined?" Renwick asked, avoiding Gilman's eyes.

"Well, not ruined exactly. That was Beryl's word. It was badly stained—acid got spilled on it—some kind of paint remover that was being used in Father's study. You see, the painter almost dropped the can and some of the remover splashed on one side of the desk and on the attaché case. The whole house was thrown into an uproar. Madame Colbert was furious—Beryl said it really was appalling how she screamed at the poor painter. But in a way, it was her fault for hurrying everyone with their jobs. Father wasn't there at the time. Didn't know his attaché case was missing until this morning."

"Missing?" Gilman asked.

"Oh, he will get it back in a day or two. Madame Colbert took it to one of her 'little men' to have the stains removed and the leather restored. There's a furniture polisher working on the desk now. And Father went off to breakfast with an old leather envelope holding his papers. Much ado about nothing."

"Much ado, certainly." Gilman took off his glasses, polished them, looked at Renwick, who was equally thoughtful.

Renwick said, "Stains removed in a day or two? From leather? Not likely. Nina, I'm afraid your father is going to have a well-marked attaché case to carry around. Hasn't he others?"

"Bulky briefcases, which he hates."

"Spoils the silhouette," Renwick agreed. O'Connell was a careful dresser, neat and dapper. "He will just have to buy a new attaché case; that's simple enough."

"Beryl wanted to do that, but Madame Colbert wouldn't hear of it. Said it was quite an unnecessary expense."

"I like that," Renwick said, suddenly smiling, "considering the thousands of dollars she's charging for color schemes and wallpapers." Yes, he thought, I like that last touch: unnecessary expense—any quick excuse to keep Beryl from buying a new attaché case; a different-looking case. Why was dear Thérèse so intent on keeping the old one in use?

"Why don't I buy Father an attaché case?" Nina asked. "His birthday is next month. Bob—wouldn't that be a good idea? Sort of a peace offering for all the postcards he didn't receive?"

Renwick's smile broadened. "A peace offering for bringing me into the family?"

"Bob! He likes you—he told me in Geneva you were the brightest young man he knew."

"Except?" he teased.

"Except that you were a soldier," Nina admitted. "But you aren't a soldier now, are you?"

"Would it matter?"

She shook her head. "I thought you looked *wonderful*, but wonderful, in uniform."

"And when was all this?" Gemma asked. She had never seen Renwick in anything but civilian clothes.

"In Geneva. Six years ago," Nina said.

Gemma looked slightly bewildered. "When you were fifteen?"

"Yes," Nina said.

"Oh," said Gemma.

Renwick rose, catching Nina's hand. "We'd better finish packing." He pulled Nina to her feet. "An early start tomorrow."

"Not so early," Gemma suggested. She was enjoying herself. "Tomorrow, if you leave here by half past nine, you'll be in plenty of time—" Ronnie, she suddenly noticed, was giving her that fixed look, one of his specialties. "I've really got to do some packing myself. Ronnie, will two shirts be enough?" She let herself glance after Renwick and Nina as they entered the corridor to the guest room. "Fifteen," she asked in a hushed voice. "Do you think he—"

"No, I don't think," Gilman said. "You're an incorrigible romantic, my love."

"After all," Gemma said as she gathered plates and teacups, "Juliet was only fourteen. Would you bring those glasses, darling?"

They were about to leave. Renwick made a last quick check of the guest room. "All clear, I think." He looked at Nina, radiant and ready for travel. She was wearing the coat he had bought for her in Bombay, and that pleased him. "One moment, Nina." He caught her hands. "I've been thinking about this—a matter of security. We can't talk about it in the taxi or on the plane. But listen, darling, will you? I'll leave you at your father's house, see you safely inside. But don't mention—not for a few days—anything about our marriage. Don't mention we are in love. Please, Nina. Just keep those pretty lips closed." He kissed them lightly. "Also, honey, don't talk about Bombay—about Erik or Marco. Never mention these names in your house: Kiley and Shawfield will be enough. For a few days, anyway. I'll explain everything, then."

She was startled, puzzled, too, but she nodded.

"And don't tell anyone that we met in Istanbul. Or that you ever saw Pierre. Or how we met in Bombay."

"Nothing about you at all? Not even that we met in Amsterdam?"

"Nothing. Not yet. I'll telephone you night and morning; and then, in a few days, I'll call at your house—a friendly visit. That's all. And after that..." He didn't finish.

"It will be difficult to hide what I feel," she said unhappily. "Bob—must it be this way?"

"It has to be this way. But it won't last long." *I hope to God it won't.*

"Am I endangering you? Is that why—?"

"No, darling. You've got it the wrong way around. I could endanger you."

"But how?"

He hesitated. One last warning was needed. "Keep Thérèse Colbert at a distance. Be careful. Very careful. Remember the interior decorator in Brussels? I told you about her and—"

"The black widow spider? Yes, I remember." Then she caught her breath. "Thérèse Colbert?"

"Yes. She's an enemy agent."

She stared at him. "In Father's house?"

"In your father's house. He knows nothing. Nor does Beryl.

Just you—and I. Will you keep that secret, honey? Be on guard?" He caught her in his arms, held her close. "I've told you more than I should have. But I couldn't leave you in that house without—"

"I'll take care," she said. Her hand touched his cheek. She had never seen him so serious, not even in Istanbul when he had listened to her with eyes grave and worried. "Darling, I'll take every care." She kissed him. "I needed to know. It will keep me safe." And you, too, she thought. I could stamp on that black widow, stamp her to death.

He picked up the suitcases, and they entered the corridor. "One thing I know, Bob Renwick," Nina said. "Life isn't going to be dull with you."

Nor with you, he thought, nor with you.

CHAPTER
29

A cool afternoon made pleasant walking around the sweep of Potomac waters called the Tidal Basin. Unpoetic name, thought Renwick, for a romantic spot. The encircling cherry trees, even when touched by early November, had delicacy and grace. Yellowed leaves loosened their hold on black branches, drifted gently to the grass below. Soon, bare slender arms would stretch to a winter sky, wait patiently for spring to come and cover them in sleeves of white-petaled silk. Lincoln had his Reflecting Pool, Washington his Mall, why not give Jefferson a lake? Tidal Basin...Was that the best we could do for a man who named his home Monticello?

Renwick glanced at his watch: three-forty-five. Tim MacEwan should be coming into sight any moment now. Midway between Lincoln and Jefferson, Renwick had suggested yesterday evening when they had arranged today's encounter. He wondered now if Mac had had time enough to find the answers to all his questions. "I'll keep out of the picture, let you meet with your federal friends," Renwick had said. "But these questions are vital, Mac."

Mac had nodded his agreement, and in his own Scots way qualified his chances of success. "Not much time to find the right answers." Renwick had reminded him grimly, "Not much time for anything, Mac."

There he was now, reviewing the cherry trees at a brisk march, high color in his cheeks, red hair mostly covered by his tweed hat. "Hello, how are you?" Mac said, stopping to shake hands with a friend met by chance. A few sentences, and Renwick seemed persuaded to change his direction to walk alongside. There were several couples as well as singles taking an afternoon stroll. Renwick and MacEwan looked completely in place as they walked and talked. Nothing—apparently—serious; just a pleasant chat.

"Did you get the answers?" Renwick asked.

"Yes. First, that type of stain on leather is not easily or

quickly removed. Wood can be scraped and refinished, but leather is a problem—usually permanently blemished."

"Okay."

"Next: there was no complaint made by Madame Colbert to the firm that employs the painter."

A show of temper, of real anger over a careless job, and no follow-up? "I see," said Renwick.

"He came to work for the firm last week. He left of his own accord yesterday. No explanation. My friends at the Bureau are having him traced, if possible."

"Good."

"Colbert was followed to the shop of that 'little man' who does special leather repairs for her. But when we went in to see him this morning with a suitcase that needed attention, we were told he did no work on damaged leather, just stitching or reinforcing corners."

"So he is now being watched, too."

"Yes. My friends—Joe and Bill—" Mac smiled. "Simpler to keep it Joe, Bill, and Mac. Anyway, their interest is now aroused. At first, they were just politely helpful—they owed me that from the case we had in Canada last winter: two Berlin activists using Toronto to slip over the border into the States."

"How far does their interest reach?"

"Far enough to have a couple of workmen in O'Connell's house adjusting the burglar-alarm system, checking all the wiring. One window's circuit was somehow broken yesterday—" Mac smiled again—"so the whole system went out. Work is going on there today—and tomorrow."

"Tomorrow's Saturday," Renwick reminded him.

"They'll work time and a half. O'Connell agreed. Burglar alarms have got to be in order."

So there would be two FBI agents in the house through Saturday. "Who is covering Sunday?"

"Joe and Bill are planning that now. Might even tip off the two Secret Service agents to loiter around. By the way, Bill has a question for you. That briefcase was bought here in Washington, wasn't it?"

"Yes. At Burke and Evans. Just before Christmas, 1977."

"Burke and Evans carry the same basic line, don't they? There are some suit and attaché cases that are always in stock."

"Yes. Nina is probably shopping there right now—she

wants to give her father a birthday present of an attaché case."

"Similar to the damaged one?"

"As close as possible. He liked it a lot."

"Then Bill's question makes sense: if a duplicate could be bought at Burke and Evans, wouldn't it be used for the substitution?"

"That worried me, too. But it could mean too difficult a job to line a case with some explosive device and have it absolutely perfect with no sign of any tampering. And—" Renwick paused for emphasis—"with no alteration of the inside space for O'Connell's papers. So my guess is that the substituted case will be custom-made."

"You mean," Mac said thoughtfully, "the outside dimensions might have to be increased a little to hold the explosives? So that the inside measurements would stay the same?"

Renwick nodded. "Who notices if his attaché case is a bit longer or deeper? But he damn well notices if he finds his papers curled up at the edges instead of lying smoothly in place. Does that answer Bill's question?"

"I guess it does. Theo really thought of every detail, didn't he?"

"Right to the end."

"Well, that's about all. Have you met Colbert yet?"

"I decided to keep our little confrontation for the right moment. I'm depending on Bill and Joe for that."

"Oh, they'll know when Colbert carries a case back into the O'Connell house. She is being tailed."

"And they'll send me the message? No delay."

"You'll receive it on that communicator Bill supplied." It was a small beeper, the type that gave the warning to call headquarters at once. In Renwick's case, he wouldn't need to telephone. One small signal, and he'd know what that meant and he'd be on his way. Since his arrival with Nina yesterday afternoon, he had never traveled far from the area. This meeting place today was within direct reach, and his hotel on Wisconsin was only a few blocks from O'Connell's house on Dumbarton Road. "I think it's all pretty well arranged," Mac went on. "How long do you think we'll have to wait?"

"I don't know. But I think that accident to O'Connell's case could have been the beginning of the action."

"There could be a delay in returning it—with the excuse it needed a lot of repairing."

"Yes. But too much delay and O'Connell will get impatient. He will buy himself a new one. Wouldn't you?"

And Mac, who was neither extravagant nor impatient, agreed completely. "How's Miss O'Connell holding up?"

Renwick smiled. "Pretty good, I think." He had called her this morning—as old friend Jack. Tonight he'd phone again, as Tommy. Tomorrow it would be Ed and Steve. Nina and he had agreed on this idea on the flight across the Atlantic. And if she managed to find the right attaché case, she'd just say, "Sorry I couldn't meet you for lunch. I had a birthday present to buy." Any mention of the present, and Renwick would know it was now wrapped up as a gift and waiting in her closet.

"She doesn't know we expect an attaché case to be substituted?" Mac asked.

"No. Nor what it could contain. Nor how it might be used. I just told her to be careful answering questions about her trip; and extra careful with Thérèse Colbert."

"I suppose you had to warn her about all that," Mac said.

"You're damn right."

"A tricky situation. What if she panics, thinks she is in some danger?"

Renwick's face tightened. "I gave her a number to telephone." And I'll be at Dumbarton Road within six minutes.

"Not *your* number?" Mac was horrified.

Renwick didn't answer that. "By the way, who has Colbert been calling? Any particular friends?"

My God, thought Mac, still staring at Renwick. Renwick was taking too many chances, and all for Nina's sake. Gallantry and security didn't mix, that was for damned sure. "She has two. One is State Department. The other is a French journalist."

"Any contact with the Soviet Embassy?"

"Apparently not."

"Doesn't the journalist have meetings with any press attaché there?"

"He is covering the White House at present, concentrates on that. Joe says he is young and pleasant and well liked. He is constantly around—attends briefing seesions. He's accepted."

"Qualifications?"

"The best. He is deputizing for *Le Temps*'s correspondent, who is back in Paris for a couple of weeks."

"Bill and Joe—"

"Are checking him out," Mac answered Renwick's question efore it was asked. "Also Colbert's friend at State. He has een introducing her around. That's how she met Beryl 'Connell—at one of his parties."

"I don't like that particularly."

"Too many bloody moles everywhere," Mac agreed. "But ou know what's worrying Bill, Joe, and me? You, Bob. Colert hasn't seen you yet, but she probably heard you brought ina home. Who was there when you both arrived?"

"Beryl O'Connell."

"See what I mean?" Taking chances again. Like staying t a hotel instead of a safe address, just to be close to 'Connell's place.

"I didn't even enter the house. She didn't remember who was." An old friend of Father's, Nina had explained briefly. ll very casual."

"Even so," Mac began doubtfully. "The fact that you're ere in Washington could send Colbert running to the phone."

"In that case, the Bill-Joe team certainly overheard that nessage."

"Not if she telephoned from a drugstore."

"Well, whom did she meet after that call?"

He's got a point there, thought Mac: a possible lead to her ontrol, who might in turn lead to the resident agent who is n over-all command? But I'm still worried about Bob. "You re the one guy who can name her for what she is," Mac nsisted.

"She may think I'm just an easy mark." She must have een testing that out in New York last August when she rrived with her State Department friend at Frank Cooper's ocktail party and hoped to find me there. "Or," Renwick vent on calmly, "she may think she can have me blackmailed nd made impotent." Then he laughed. "I don't turn impotent o easily."

No, he wouldn't, thought Mac. He said, "I'll be moving into our hotel tonight."

"Oh, who set you up as my baby-sitter? Billy-Joe?"

Mac extended his hand, said, "Good-bye, old scout. Be eeing you in the distance. I'm your backup, goddamn it."

"Good-bye. Nice meeting you." And Renwick meant that. hey separated with a casual wave, MacEwan to pay a short but elusive visit to the Smithsonian, Renwick making for a taxi and—eventually—Wisconsin Avenue.

There was no signal from the alarm in his pocket.

Before six-thirty, when Beryl O'Connell might be in her predinner bathtub and safely out of the way, Renwick called Nina. No, she couldn't really make any appointment for tomorrow, and she was sorry she hadn't been able to lunch with him today: she had been shopping for a birthday present and hadn't found what she wanted until two o'clock. Next week, she would have much more free time—the first days home were really hectic. "Next week," he said, "we'll take in a movie and have late supper. I'll call you on Monday. Okay, Nina?"

He would have something to eat himself. Then he'd read. Then a long lonely night. But at least she sounded fine—a laugh in her voice that reassured him. So far, she was safe.

He decided on one of the nearby restaurants—there was a string of them along this busy part of Wisconsin—and chose one where he could have a rare steak and a real Idaho potato. That was one thing about European cooking, even in the best of places: no idea of how a baked potato should look or taste. With a tankard of nicely chilled beer, he had a pleasant meal. Quick service, too. He had little time to read the newspaper he had brought with him as insurance against a long wait. But the front page had two items of interest.

One dismayed him: the ex-Shah of Iran was in New York Hospital, and the loud demonstrations had begun in front of it. But what did politicians and diplomats expect? God in heaven, Renwick thought, don't they see more than six inches in front of their noses? And why the hell couldn't the Shah have had treatment in Mexico? The doctors there were good. If American doctors had to butt in, why hadn't they flown down there? They had traveled to plenty of places all over the world—Saudi Arabia, the Dominican Republic, among others—in order to advise or operate. These thoughts nearly ruined his appetite, but the second news item restored it: Erik and Marco, leaders of the Direct Action gang (the newspaper's word, not Renwick's) which had terrorized West Germany for the last five years, had been held in Bombay for extradition. Marco was already on his way; Erik was now under indictment for the murder of a Bombay security officer.

That charge may not stick, Renwick thought: what court

had ever dealt with a cyanide pen as a murder weapon even if refills for the little pistol had been in Kiley's pocket? But Roy's anger demanded justice: a long sentence in an Indian prison; and then extradition. Kiley's record as Erik would weigh heavily against him. Too bad for him now that the People's Revolutionary Force for Direct Action had always been so quick to claim proud responsibility for all their deeds. Out of their own mouths they had condemned Erik.

Was Thérèse Colbert reading that paragraph, too? She possibly didn't understand its significance—Kiley was Kiley to her—but the agent who was in control might. And if he, too, were ignorant about James Kiley's true identity, then the resident—the central spider in the web of espionage agents woven around Washington—should know.

Unless, Renwick thought as he finished his coffee, Theo had kept his agents entirely under his complete management, had not put them under any usual control or resident, had instituted his own branch of espionage for his own purpose. With approval of one or two at the highest level, of course. He would never have had so much power, so many resources, if they hadn't given assent to his plan. Indeed, they could very well have let him avoid the usual chain of command, bend the rules, in order to serve their own purpose: if he succeeded, excellent; if he failed, they had nothing to do with it.

In which case, Renwick decided as he paid the check, there could be one very ignorant resident in the Washignton area tonight. Ignorant... How much was known even by those who directed the KGB? Known of Theo's actual plan? He was inviting World War III, and why should the Soviets risk that—at a time when everything was going their way? He had been given immense power, certainly, and complete backing, but he could have added Theo's own touch to his initial assignment. It couldn't be that Theo had gone out of control, taking his own section or department with him?

The question halted Renwick abruptly at the restaurant's door. Now you're really going off half-cocked, he told himself. The KGB wouldn't let any agent, far less the head of a department, get out of control without pretty heavy retribution to be paid. Yet, if Theo's purpose was achieved, if he really produced a result that would send the world reeling, that would win World War III before it even began—well, the Soviets would live with that situation quite comfortably.

Renwick came out into the bright lights of Wisconsin Avenue. There was only one thing he could be sure of: Theo's death must have shaken those who did know about his Washington project. Would they back out? Or push forward their timetable?

Suddenly, he was aware he was being followed. Two men in loose overcoats, bareheaded, had left the restaurant almost on his heels. Presentable types, young, keeping a respectful distance. Too obvious. Was this Mac's idea, or his friends at the Bureau? *Worried about you*, Mac had said. Hell, I don't need baby-sitters, Renwick thought angrily.

He paused on the sidewalk opposite his hotel, glanced over his shoulder as he lit a cigarette. The men were no longer behind him—not in clear view, at least. They might have dodged into one of those doorways. Renwick's eyes narrowed, but he fought down the impulse to walk back and confront them. If they were Bill-and-Joe's agents, they'd have a cold wait out there. He was going straight to the warmth of his room. And if they weren't Bill-and-Joe's agents? So Beryl had talked about Bob Renwick to her dear Thérèse, and Thérèse had gone running for advice, and her adviser had decided on action.

Well, he thought as he waited to cross the avenue, I may not carry cyanide or a knife or a walking stick, but I'm damned glad to feel the weight of my little Biretta right here in my pocket. Then, glancing over at the hotel, he saw that the window of his room on the second floor was lit. The curtains were drawn, but they were not heavy enough to darken the light completely. It hadn't been burning there when he left.

He crossed the busy thoroughfare, entered the lobby, and took the stairs to his floor—a more silent approach than the elevator allowed. The maid had turned the sofa into a bed just before he had telephoned Nina. Fresh towels, too, had been placed in the bathroom. His room required no more attention tonight, but someone thought it needed company. Hadn't the intruder expected him back so early? Watched him leave for dinner, calculated on his absence for an hour and a half at least? If so, the man was wrong by thirty-five minutes.

About to enter his corridor, Renwick drew back. A woman was standing at the door to his room, watching the elevator. She was dressed in black as if she were one of the maids, but

no apron, no sensible shoes. All this floor had been serviced—
there were no maids around. No one in the pantry, either—
everyone was out to dinner.

He slipped off his coat, dropped it on the stairs' bannister,
walked into the corridor, his right hand in his jacket pocket.
The woman turned her head to look at him, stared, rattled
the door handle as she brushed past it on her way to the
elevator. Neat, thought Renwick: a complete picture of innocence; but I'll know you again, Milady.

He reached the door. The woman was waiting impatiently
for an elevator that was slow to respond. No weapon there,
he decided: a warning and a quick retreat were her tactics.
But why the delay from inside the room? What's waiting
inside? He drew the Biretta, threw the door open, side-stepped
quickly as he entered.

Two men faced him. Young. One tall and fair, one short
and dark. Both powerful. They had been preparing for him—
room in disorder, apparently burglarized—the tall man had
a silencer already fitted into place on his revolver.

There was a brief second of no movement, no sound. Then
a knife flashed across the room, missing Renwick by inches
as he swerved his body. He dropped to one knee, his eye on
the man with the revolver, and fired first. He caught the
man's right shoulder, deflecting the aim of the bullet, which
plunged into the wall behind him. The small man leaped
forward, a straight-legged kick aimed at Renwick's chin, and
ran.

"Far enough," said Mac's voice. He had a firm half nelson
on the struggling man. "All yours," he told one of the two
agents who were just behind him, and relinquished his hold.
The baby-sitters. Renwick would have laughed if his damned
jaw hadn't hurt: he had jerked back instinctively from that
lethal karate kick, but some of it had grazed him. Nothing
much, he told himself, considering what it could have been.

The tall man was no problem: a shoulder wound was painful and discouraged further action.

"Saw the light in your window," one of the agents said.
"Just wondered."

"Thank you," said Renwick and rose to his feet.

The other agent looked around. "A setup."

"I guess."

"Don't touch anything; we'll want—"

"I know." The bullet embedded in the wall; the knife there,

too, deep and holding. Mac was looking at them, his lips pursed.

As the prisoners were handcuffed, Mac said, "I'll help see them safely housed. Be with you later, Bob. You okay? Need anything?"

"Ice. A bucketful if ice."

Mac repressed a smile. "Will do." He followed the hand-cuffed prisoners into the corridor and closed the door, partly blotting out the rising voices now gathered outside. An agent was speaking with complete reassurance: nothing to worry about, everything was all right. The voices diminished. Soon there was silence complete.

One thing is definite, Renwick decided as he wrapped a towel around a handful of ice cubes, I cannot have it both ways. Either I take Claudel's advice entirely—no excuses, no halfway dodges to get into the field again—and stay in my nice new office with its inspirational armchair, or I don't marry Nina. I can't put her through this kind of thing.

Sure, a man can die crossing a road, a man can break his neck in his bathtub, a man can fall from his roof fixing a chimney. A coward dies a hundred deaths before he meets the real one. So what?

I'm not giving up Nina.

And what am I giving up, anyway? It isn't as if I were action-crazy. I like problems, bits and pieces of information to fit into something understandable. I like outthinking the opposition. When they challenge us, I damn well enjoy doing the greatest harm where it will do the most good. Fight their ideas with better ideas—or, at least, try. And all of that, I don't give up.

I won't stop traveling, either. There will be visits to various places abroad, exchanges of information. Interintell is growing—at last count we had twelve of the NATO countries and two other democracies, all interested and co-operating. Yes, there will be travel and old friends to meet. And Nina with me. In the field—impossible; not just for security's sake, not just for rules and regulations, but for her safety, too.

He studied his jaw in the mirror. It could have been worse. That kick could have snapped his neck.

Just remember, Renwick, you may have swerved from a knife, avoided a bullet, but you almost didn't dodge a kick. One hell of a way to learn that Pierre Claudel had been right:

move over and let the men in their twenties do their stint. He took another handful of ice, wrapped it in the towel, felt his jaw go numb with its chill. If it took another five hours, he'd have this damned face back to normal.

He settled down to wait for Mac's return with any news he had gathered about the two thugs. Bought with money? Or trained in another Rancho San Carlos? One thing he did know: whoever was now in charge of Theo's plan was pushing forward the timetable—hard.

CHAPTER
30

Saturday morning, except for Renwick's phone call to Nina, was uneventful—just a part of the waiting game.

"Ed here. Thought you might like to drive out to Mount Vernon. Would you come?"

"Oh, Ed, I'm sorry. I really am. But this afternoon, Beryl's interior decorator wants me to choose the curtains for my room. She is bringing samples of material, and I've got to look through them."

"Couldn't she postpone that until Monday?"

"I tried. But she's borrowing the samples from some wholesale house, and she has got to return them by Monday morning."

"Samples—you mean small scraps of cloth? That shouldn't take you too long. Just flip through them."

"No, no. Large samples—enough to show the repeat in the pattern." Nina was laughing. "It's a very serious business, Ed. There will be an hour of argument, I know."

"When do you expect her?"

"Sometime this afternoon—that's all she said."

"Well, why don't you give me a ring as soon as she arrives—would you, Nina?"

"Why, yes," Nina said slowly.

"We might make something yet of the afternoon. Just call me. Will you? And I'll drop in unannounced and hurry the argument along."

"I won't forget."

"See you then."

Renwick put down the receiver, looked at the blue-and-white roses climbing over the long yellow curtains at his bedroom window.

"Well?" asked MacEwan. He was lounging on the sofa bed, now back into early American shape, surrounded by sections of the *New York Times* and the *Washington Post*.

"What's a repeat in the pattern?"

Mac shrugged, and had his own question. "Do you remember the days when a newspaper came in one piece and could be carried in your coat pocket?" He watched Renwick in amazement. "What the hell are you doing with that curtain?"

"Got it!" Renwick said. "Yes, these samples could be quite large. Enough to hide an attaché case being carried into the house."

"Any case carried by Colbert will be spotted before she reaches the house."

."That's what she feared, perhaps."

"When is she expected?"

"Sometime this afternoon."

Mac pushed aside the newspapers. "Trouble brewing in Iran. I can smell it." He rose and picked up his leather jacket. "I'll contact Bill, make sure his alarm-signal boys will keep working through the afternoon."

"Tell them to stay near O'Connell's study. I'll give them the high sign when it's time to make their move. They know what to do."

"As planned. Shouldn't be difficult. You've got the tough part." Renwick had to keep Colbert in the house, prevent her from leaving or telephoning. "How will you do it?"

"Play it by ear."

"She may not bring the case back today," Mac reminded him as he opened the door.

"Then we wait for tomorrow. Or the next day. Or the next."

Mac made no comment, just nodded and left.

After lunch, Nina went upstairs to her room and chose a book and a chair at the window. From there she could see part of Dumbarton Road, and certainly any approach to the house. There was, she noticed, a heavy-looking van parked on the opposite side of the street. Probably it belonged to the workmen now tracking the burglar-alarm failure in the living room.

She couldn't concentrate on reading. Even the silence of the house seemed to increase her nervousness. Her father was at his office today, a sign of disturbing news if he stayed there on a Saturday. Beryl was in her room on the floor below. Mattie, the cook, was in her far-off quarters where no one could hear her television. Saturday afternoon—a strange time to select curtain material. Nor could Nina understand why the walls had been painted blue and the strawberry-pink carpet had been laid before the curtains had been chosen. A roundabout way of decorating, she thought. And if the Colbert woman saddled me with blue and pink, why didn't she complete the choice by herself? I'll never like this room; never. But I won't be here much longer. Whatever colors I choose in London for our flat, there certainly won't be a blue wall. Or a pink carpet.

She couldn't concentrate on a book; she couldn't concentrate on music from her record player. But at half past three, her impatience was rewarded. Madame Colbert arrived in her black Thunderbird, driven by the young man who worked in her showroom. Nina was already on the phone when two large books of samples were being hauled by him out of the car while Madame Colbert carried a lighter load of chintz and satin draped over one arm.

"Ed?" Nina asked as her call was immediately answered. "She's here."

"See you, darling." The call was over.

Darling . . . He forgot to be careful. Smiling, she combed her hair, put on fresh lipstick, took a last look in the long mirror, and ran downstairs. On the second floor she slowed her steps and arrived, sedate and decorous, she hoped, in the hall. It wasn't large: it still amazed her how expensive houses in Georgetown could be so crumpled up inside. But it ran through to a garden at the back, where Beryl had chosen to place a conservatory. Poor Father, Nina thought now, this house will never be finished. At least he had his study almost complete. Beryl and the Colbert woman were there, while across the hall the two repairmen hadn't yet tracked down their problem.

Nina avoided the samples deposited near the foot of the staircase, and hesitated. She could hear the Thunderbird being driven away. The Colbert woman must be planning a long visit. Nina overcame her aversion, and entered the study.

"Nina, come and see what Thérèse has managed," Beryl said. "Isn't she wonderful? The stains have all gone, and it's just the same old case as before. Thérèse, couldn't your little man have removed the scratch on the side and that bruised look at the corner, too?"

"I thought Mr. O'Connell wanted things just as he remembers them," Thérèse Colbert remarked. However much I dislike her, thought Nina, I've got to admit she's attractive: blue eyes and dark smooth hair and a ready smile. Her taste in clothes was elegant. And expensive. Today she had chosen a white wool dress to emphasize an excellent figure, half covered it with a mink coat draped over her shoulders. She pulled it off, dropped it on a chair.

Nina came forward slowly. The attaché case had been laid with pride on the center of the desk. "It looks very nice." And what do I do with another case, all ready to give as a birthday present?

Beryl stared at her stepdaughter. "Is that all you have to say? Nice? It's a *marvelous* job. Your father will be delighted." For a moment her hazel eyes looked reprovingly at Nina. She shook her head, auburn hair falling loosely, and exchanged a tolerant smile with Madame Colbert.

Nina recovered herself, said, "I know he will be. He hates that leather envelope he has been carrying around. But how did you manage to have the stains removed? I thought that would have been impossible." That is what Bob had believed, and Ron Gilman had agreed.

"Just a little trade secret," Madame Colbert said with a light laugh. "Now, shall we go upstairs and choose your curtains? I have brought a divine toile which I know you'll adore. It's one of the loose pieces of material in the hall, so that's easy to carry. But, Beryl, we'll need help with the sample books. Do you think your workmen would oblige? Who recommended them to Mr. O'Connell?"

"It's a firm we have always used."

"You must give me its address. I don't have any adequate people to install alarm systems."

"Of course. But before we go upstairs—" Beryl walked over to the paneling that covered low cabinets under the bookshelves—"do look at this. Awful, isn't it? Francis absolutely refuses to have any more paint stripped off. No more accidents, he says. We were lucky his books weren't splashed, too. So what would you suggest, Thérèse? Dark green enamel to continue the color of the carpet?"

The doorbell rang. "I'll get it," Nina said, halfway toward the hall.

Thérèse Colbert's smiling scrutiny of Nina ended. "Very shy, isn't she?"

"Oh, don't worry about her. This house is so very new to her. She must feel a stranger, but she'll soon become accustomed to us all."

"She talks little about her world trip."

"It couldn't have been comfortable. Francis is amazed that she endured it for so long. Now, about this woodwork, Thérèse—"

* * *

Nina opened the door, stood looking at him.

"Hello, darling," Renwick said softly, and stepped inside. A repairman gave a brief glance out from the living room— one of last night's baby-sitters, Renwick saw—and withdrew with a nod. Women's voices came from another room a short distance along the hall. "Beryl and Colbert?"

"In the study. Oh, Bob—"

"What's wrong?" He took her hands, resisted putting his arms around her.

"The attaché case—it's back. Stain-free."

"Where is it?"

"On Father's desk. And what will I do now for his birthday?" My last traveler's check went on it, she thought in dismay; I even had his initials, small and neat, printed under the handle exactly as before.

"Give him the one you bought. He'd like that."

"*Two* attaché cases?"

"Always useful." He drew her close, risked a kiss. "Where's the present—in your room?"

"No. Madame Colbert has been in and out of there every afternoon. She was upstairs when I brought the attaché case home yesterday, so—it's in the coat closet." Nina nodded to a narrow door in the wall under the staircase.

Renwick let go her hands to pull off his Burberry. He hung it in the closet, looked puzzled as he saw only hats on the shelf above the rod. Quickly, he held aside the coats and glimpsed a package propped against the wall, hidden by their skirts. "Pretty good," he said with a sudden smile, and shut the closet door. Pretty damn good, in fact. The smile vanished as he glanced toward the study: the voices were drifting nearer. "Get them upstairs, out of the hall. And after that— I've got to see her, Nina. Alone." There was a moment of fear in the blue eyes that met his. He said nothing more.

Nina's face was tense, but she nodded and moved away from him as the voices grew clearer. Renwick braced himself.

Beryl was saying, "Then you think we should keep the original brown? I did want something brighter. Oh—Mr. Renwick! But how nice!" They shook hands politely. "Did you come to see Nina?"

"To see your husband, actually." His voice was easy, completely natural.

"He ought to be home soon. At least I hope it will be soon. Oh, Madame Colbert—may I present Mr. Robert Renwick?"

Always correct, thought Nina: Beryl really reads her Amy
nderbilt. But, for once, Madame Colbert had lost her man-
rs. She was standing as if transfixed, the usual smile quite
ped off her face.

"We have met," Renwick said.

Thérèse Colbert's composure returned. "Really?" she asked
litely. "I'm afraid I—oh, yes, I remember now. Paris, wasn't
"

"Brussels."

"You meet too many attractive men, Thérèse," Beryl said
th a laugh. And to Renwick, very sweetly, "You can't expect
adame Colbert to remember all of you."

Quickly, Nina said, "I asked Bob to stay for tea—wait for
ther."

"Of course." Beryl recovered from her surprise. "That would
delightful. And you'll stay, too, Thérèse. Once we choose the
rtains, I'm sure you'd enjoy talking with—"

"I'm afraid I must leave before tea time. Another appoint-
nt."

"But I thought—" began Beryl. Then she stopped thinking
d could only feel a drop in the hall's temperature. In her
st tradition, she covered Thérèse's refusal with a spate of
rds. The curtains had better be chosen right now. What
out those heavy sample books, so cumbersome? Mr. Ren-
ck, would he be so kind?

Nina interrupted. "Carry those things up, and then carry
em down? No need. I think I see something I like here."
e lifted three loose pieces of material at random and started
ward the staircase. "Coming?" she asked Beryl. "Or do you
ust my taste?"

That decided it. "We'd better go," Beryl told Thérèse Col-
rt, who gave up her momentary hesitation with a show of
od grace. "Do excuse us, Mr. Renwick. You'll find maga-
nes in the living room."

"I'll be all right," he assured her. He waited until Beryl's
exhaustible talk dwindled into a far-off murmur. Then he
oved quickly.

Inside the living room, the men had packed their gear.
esk in the study," he told them, and left for the coat closet
one of them made his way across the hall. The other opened
e front door, signaled the van standing opposite to start
lling out of its parking space. Renwick had already torn

off the birthday wrappings, jamming them into the closet
farthest corner.

Altogether, two minutes. He gave one last glance at Nina
present, centered on the desk as the other attaché case ha
been, and left the study. The outside door was closing. A bri
silence. Then he heard the van pull away from the front step
traveling at slow speed, as he entered the living room. Now
it was a matter of waiting.

Not easy for him, but worse for the experts who wer
examining the attaché case, preparing to dissect it. He didn
envy them that job: finding the detonator, disarming the e:
plosive device—but what if they found nothing, just an empt
case with no deadly lining? Then Colbert could walk out tha
front door. She would be kept under surveillance, of course—
until she vanished one fine morning, heading for Lausann
again. And I would be the prize fool, the intelligence office
whose credibility lay in a thousand pieces. Interintell, to
It would suffer.

No, he told himself, there *has* to be something in tha
damned attaché case: stains aren't so easily and perfectl
removed. It's a substitution, it has to be. A clever piece (
work, prepared well in advance, with details and measure
ments and photographs to make sure it was an exact repr
duction. It has to be. . . . He turned away from the window a
he heard a light footstep in the hall, moved quickly.

He was just in time to stop Thérèse Colbert from reachin
the study.

"My coat," she explained. "I left my notebook in its pocke
I need it to mark down measurements and—"

"Of course. In here?" He entered the study before she di
picked up her mink coat while she hesitated at the door. Sh
glanced at the desk, seemed relieved. She was quite conten
to leave the study with Renwick.

"Thank you," she said with one of her old smiles. "Yo
know, Bob, I did give you—what d'you call it?"

"An out."

"That's it. Why didn't you take it? Why mention Brussels?

"Because," he said, grasping her wrist and urging her to
ward the living room, "I want to talk about Brussels."

"Have the workmen gone?"

"Yes. We won't be disturbed." *She knows they've gone*
She heard the van drive away. That's why she came dow

here, to check on the attaché case. I should have expected that, he thought. His wariness increased.

"I really ought to go upstairs—"

"They'll manage without you for a few minutes."

"And I have to telephone—my next appointment—I'll be late."

"We'll talk first." He released his hold on her wrist as he got her inside the living room. He took her coat and handbag, dropped them on a settee, and closed the door. "Sit over there." He pointed to a chair, well away from the window.

Startled, she looked at him; but she crossed the room and sat down. He chose a chair close to the door, and faced her.

"This," she said with a light laugh, "is hardly the way for old friends to talk. It isn't exactly tête-à-tête. You used to do better, Bob. Let's sit on the couch and be comfortable." She made as if to rise.

"No. Stay there! I'm perfectly comfortable."

She changed her tactics. "Oh, Bob—I'm really sorry. About Brussels. Leaving you so quickly. But my mother was ill, very ill."

"Is she still in Lausanne?"

Thérèse Colbert looked at him. "Yes," she said, trying to guess how much he knew about Lausanne.

"A useful place to drop out of sight."

"Really, Bob—"

"You heard Maartens was dead, of course."

That silenced her.

"And his gray-haired friend, too," Renwick said. "And talking of death, weren't you surprised to find me alive this afternoon?"

"I had nothing—" It was a mistake. She bit her lip.

"Nothing to do with that? Just a warning call to your control here in Washington? Who is he, Thérèse?"

"You are mad, completely mad." She rose.

"You aren't leaving," he told her. "I locked the door. The key is in my pocket."

"I only wanted my cigarettes. In my bag."

He reached for her handbag, saying, "I'll get them." He found the cigarette case and a small Derringer tucked into a side pocket. "Neat little toy," he said. "I hope you don't play with it often." He examined the cigarette case—this alarmed her—so he slipped it back into her handbag. The lighter was also dubious: a concealed camera, probably. He left it where it was in its own small pocket. He held up the Derringer. "Would you really have shot me with this?"

"If necessary. It's for my protection." Her eyes were hard and cool.

So she would have fired it, he realized. And pleaded? God only knew what story she would concoct: an accident, probably. He replaced the Derringer, snapped the bag shut, and dropped the bundle of evidence beside his chair. Sadly, he thought, she's well trained: not just the pretty woman being caught by money, being blackmailed one step at a time into a deeper and deeper morass. Right from the beginning, she knew what she was doing. "Sit down," he told her, "and let's talk about Theo."

Slowly, she sat down, even forgot to cross her legs and show a nicely molded thigh at the split of her tight skirt.

"You've never seen him, of course. And now you never will. He died in Bombay. Or didn't your control tell you? Probably not. Too many deaths are disturbing."

She stared at him.

"You really ought to tell us all you know about Theo's conspiracy. That might help you."

"Conspiracy?" She made an effort and smiled. "Ridiculous—"

"Tell us how James Kiley was to join you here, and Tony Shawfield." Keep out all mention of the attaché case, he reminded himself: that would come later, and not from him. "You'd have enjoyed working with them. Too bad they've been arrested and sent back to West Germany." He paused, noted her astonishment. "Or perhaps you didn't know their real names: Erik and Marco. You read the newspapers, don't you?"

"Terrorists—anarchists. I have never had any connection with them!" she burst out angrily.

"Indeed you have. You're up to your pretty little neck in a terrorist conspiracy. So tell me about it."

"Why? To help you give evidence against me? But I don't think you will. If you do, there will be nothing left of your career—or of your life. Renwick the laughingstock! No, I don't think a man with your reputation could face that." Her voice had risen, her face was triumphant.

"Oh, those photographs," he said. "I wondered when you'd get around to trying some blackmail."

"You're a fool. They will be used."

"Well, if my stock goes down in some quarters," he said with a good show of amusement, "it will go up in others."

"I've warned you. They will be used."

"And let yourself be exposed? In every sense," he added, smiling.

She looked at him in frustration, not knowing whether to believe him or not. "If it has to be," she said slowly, "it has to be."

"All for the good of the cause? Well, well—you really are a dedicated woman. Perhaps it might be better—for you as well as me—if you burned the negatives."

"You know I don't have them."

He knew that quite well. But who did have the negatives now that Theo had abdicated?

"I don't," she protested. "Theo—everything was sent to Theo. It was his idea, his orders. I never—"

"Of course not," Renwick said wearily. "You were just the little innocent trapped by the big bad men."

"But I *am* innocent, Bob." She had turned to pleading again, her eyes soft, her lips tender. "I loved you. I thought you loved me. Didn't you? And I still love you."

"In God's name," he said, his anger suddenly breaking through. He rose, went to the window.

"Expecting someone?" She looked at the door. Had there been a key in that lock? Even if he had it now, her bag was there—easily reached, easily opened.

"Yes." He turned to face her. "And don't try it!" he warned her as she took a few steps toward her handbag. He had his Biretta in his hand. "My own small piece of protection," he said as he pocketed it again. "Sit down, Thérèse. You may as well wait in comfort. But don't make up stories. Tell the truth. It will be easier for you in the end." He went back to his own chair.

"Would you have used that—on me?" she asked.

"Not to kill. Just to delay you a little." Would Mac and his friends never arrive? Or, he thought again, nothing has been found in the attaché case. I'll get a phone call telling me to let her go. And for me—hell to pay.

In silence, he waited six agonizing minutes. Then a car drew up at the front of the house. Could be anyone, he told himself: a delivery of flowers, liquor, even O'Connell. He kept his hopes down and his eyes on Thérèse Colbert.

The door to the living room opened. Two strangers, serious-eyed, entered with Mac. Mac was grinning all over his wind-beaten face.

They've found it, thought Renwick as he got to his feet and handed over Colbert's bag. "One weapon at least," he said quietly. He wasn't going to stay and hear her rights being read, or to see her being taken out handcuffed. Nodding to Mac, he turned away from the front door and walked slowly down the hall toward the back of the house.

He reached a white conservatory, barely completed, with decorative trees in giant pots, flowers in rustic boxes, all clustered in the center of the tiled floor to leave space for work-in-progress around the curving windows. Outside, the light was fading, the small remainder of a garden bleak with falling leaves. Well, he thought, that is one file we can close. Our part is done. The FBI and other security agencies can dig hard and come up with more. But for J. P. Merriman & Co., Theo's file is closed—ended along with his Washington project.

He heard a movement behind him. "Nina?" He turned quickly. But it was Mac.

"I asked her to give me two minutes with you," Mac said. "It's news from Claudel. He had a call from Bombay, just before Gilman caught his flight back to London. It's about that baggage Theo left in his suite—for his three men to bring out safely. Some safety!"

"Do we never get rid of Theo?"

"Gilman and friend A. K. Roy got rid of his negatives. Burned them. That's the message: all negatives burned. Does it make any sense to you?"

Renwick drew a long deep breath. "They found negatives?"

"Among a few special files. Theo's own small traveling office, I gather. We'll hear more from Gilman when we all get back to London. Clever bastard."

"Gilman?" A slow smile spread over Renwick's face. "Yes," he said gratefully.

"No. Theo." Mac shook his head. "You're right. He still keeps cropping up. For a man who'll never make the headlines, he's quite a personality. Which reminds me—my federal friends would like to have a little talk—just a general wrap-up, more background information."

"You could handle it."

"Sure. But don't you want some credit—share the congratulations?"

Renwick laughed. "Come on, Mac. Everything is okay. Leave it at that."

"It will be played down, of course. The newspapers will never hear of that damned attaché case. Do we tell O'Connell about it?"

Renwick shook his head. He would tell Nina. But O'Connell? Definitely no. "Not our job, Mac. We'll leave it to your friends Bill and Joe." They'd decide what should be told—or not told.

"Wonder what they'll come up with?"

"Oh—that the attaché case was damaged inside. Beyond repair."

"And that's a pretty fair description." Mac smiled at some memory. "But they'll certainly have to warn O'Connell about an enemy agent making free with his home."

"That could be enough."

"A shocker," Mac predicted. "At least he won't be carrying any high explosives into the White House. I wouldn't be surprised if there's an emergency meeting this week. Tomorrow, perhaps—when more news comes in. Iran of course. Sunday morning over there, now. Well, I'll see you in London. We'll have a celebration party. When?"

"In about ten days. I'm due some leave." Geneva, he thought: that's where we'll go.

Mac studied Renwick's face. "So you're getting married?"

"Yes."

"Saw it coming. Couldn't be any other explanation for—"

"And your two minutes are up, old boy." Renwick disengaged his hand from Mac's enthusiastic handshake, clapped his shoulder, gave him an encouraging push toward the hall.

"Best idea you ever had," Mac said over his shoulder. He half stumbled over some potted plants, swore, added, "You need some light in here." He shook his head, gave a mock salute, and was on his way.

Renwick waited. Yes, he decided, we'll fly to Zurich, drive from there to Geneva. But I'll surprise her: she'll think it's London, will never know until we are picking up our tickets at the airport.

And then he saw Nina walking down the hall toward him, walking slowly, almost hesitantly. "Nina," he called out, went forward to meet her. Suddenly she was running, joining in his laughter as his arms caught hold of her. He drew her away from the lighted doorway, into the island of trees and flowers.